D0343678

993471786 7

WAYFARING STRANGER

By the same author

Dave Robicheaux Novels

Light of the World
Creole Belle
The Glass Rainbow
Swan Peak
The Tin Roof Blowdown
Pegasus Descending
Crusader's Cross
Last Car to Elysian Fields
Jolie Blon's Bounce
Purple Cane Road
Sunset Limited
Cadillac Jukebox
Burning Angel
Dixie City Jam
In the Electric Mist with Confederate Dead
A Stained White Radiance
A Morning for Flamingos
Black Cherry Blues
Heaven's Prisoners
The Neon Rain

Hackberry Holland Novels

Feast Day of Fools
Rain Gods
Lay Down My Sword and Shield

Billy Bob Holland Novels

In the Moon of Red Ponies
Bitterroot
Heartwood
Cimarron Rose

Other Fiction

Jesus Out to Sea
White Doves at Morning
The Lost Get-Back Boogie
The Convict and Other Stories
Two for Texas
To the Bright and Shining Sun
Half of Paradise

WAYFARING STRANGER

James Lee Burke

First published in Great Britain in 2014 by Orion Books,
an imprint of The Orion Publishing Group Ltd
Orion House, 5 Upper Saint Martin's Lane
London WC2H 9EA

An Hachette UK Company

1 3 5 7 9 10 8 6 4 2

A CIP catalogue record for this book is
available from the British Library.

ISBN (Hardback) 978 1 4091 2858 8
ISBN (Export Trade Paperback) 978 1 4091 2881 6
ISBN (Ebook) 978 1 4091 2882 3

Printed and bound by CPI Group (UK) Ltd, Croydon, CR0 4YY

www.orionbooks.co.uk

In memory of my beloved first cousin,
Weldon Benbow "Buddy" Mallette, among the stars forever

Chapter 1

It was the year none of the seasons followed their own dictates. The days were warm and the air hard to breathe without a kerchief, and the nights cold and damp, the wet burlap we nailed over the windows stiff with grit that blew in clouds out of the west amid sounds like a train grinding across the prairie. The moon was orange, or sometimes brown, as big as a planet, the way it is at harvest time, and the sun never more than a smudge, like a lightbulb flickering in the socket or a lucifer match burning inside its own smoke. In better times, our family would have been sitting together on the porch, in wicker chairs or on the glider, with glasses of lemonade and bowls of peach ice cream.

My father was looking for work on a pipeline in East Texas. Maybe he would come back one day. Or maybe not. Back then, people had a way of walking down a tar road and crossing through a pool of heat and disappearing forever. I ascribed the signs of my mother's mental deterioration to my father's absence and his difficulties with alcohol. She wore out the rug in her bedroom walking in circles, squeezing her nails into the heels of her hands, talking to herself, her eyes watery with levels of fear and confusion that nobody could dispel. Ordinary people no longer visited our home.

As a lawman, Grandfather had gone up against the likes of Bill Dalton and John Wesley Hardin, and in 1916, with a group of rogue

Texas Rangers, he had helped ambush a train loaded with Pancho Villa's soldiers. The point is, he wasn't given to studying on the complexities of mental illness. That didn't mean he was an ill-natured or entirely uncharitable man, just one who seemed to have a hole in his thinking. He had not been a good father to his children. Through either selfishness or ineptitude, he often left them to their own devices, even when they foundered on the wayside. I had never understood this obvious character defect in him. I sometimes wondered if the blood he had shed had made him incapable of love.

He hid behind flippancy and cynicism. He rated all politicians "somewhere between mediocre and piss-poor." His first wife had "a face that could make a freight train turn on a dirt road." WPA stood for We Piddle Around. If he hadn't been a Christian, he would have fired the hired help (we no longer had any) and "replaced them with sloths." The local banker had a big nose because the air was free. Who was my grandfather in actuality? I didn't have a clue.

It was right at sunset when I looked through the back screen and saw a black automobile, coated with dust and shaped like a shoe box, detour off the road and drive into the woods behind our house. A man wearing a fedora and a white shirt without a tie got out and urinated in front of the headlights. I thought I could hear laughter inside the car. While he relieved himself, he removed his fedora and combed his hair. It was wavy and thick and brown and shiny as polished walnut. His trousers were notched tightly into his ribs, and his cheeks looked like they had been rubbed with soot. These were not uncommon characteristics in the men who drifted here and yon through the American West during the first administration of President Roosevelt.

"Some people must have wandered off the highway onto our road," I said. "The driver is taking a leak in front of his headlights. His passengers seem to be enjoying themselves."

Grandfather was sitting at the kitchen table, an encyclopedia open in front of him, his reading glasses on his nose. "He deliberately stood in front of his headlights to make water, so others could watch?"

"I can't speak with authority about his thought process, since I'm not inside the man's head," I replied. I picked up the German binoculars my uncle had brought back from the trenches and focused them on the car. “There’s a woman in the front seat. A second man and another woman are in back. They’re passing a bottle around.”

“Are they wets?”

I removed the binoculars from my eyes. “If wets drive four-door cars.”

“My first wife had a sense of humor like yours. The only time I ever saw her laugh was when she realized I’d developed shingles.”

I focused the binoculars back on the driver. I thought I had seen his face before. I heard Grandfather get up heavily from his chair. He was over six and a half feet tall, and his ankles were swollen from hypertension and caused him to sway back and forth, as though he were on board a ship. Sometimes he used a walking cane, sometimes not. One day he seemed to teeter on the edge of eternity; the next day he was ready to resume his old habits down at the saloon. He had gin roses in his cheeks and skin like a baby’s and narrow eyes that were the palest blue I had ever seen. Sometimes his eyes did not go with his face or his voice; the intense light in them could make other men glance away. “Let’s take a walk, Satchel Ass,” he said.

“I wish you wouldn’t call me that name.”

“You’ve got a butt on you like a washtub.”

“There’s a bullet hole in the rear window of the car,” I said, looking through the binoculars again. “My butt doesn’t resemble a washtub. I don’t like you talking to me like that, Grandfather.”

“Wide butts and big hips run in the Holland family. That’s just something to keep in mind as you get older. It’s a family trait, not an insult. Would you marry a woman who looks like a sack of Irish potatoes?”

He pulled open a kitchen drawer and removed a holstered revolver that was wrapped with the belt, the loops stuffed with brass shells. The revolver was the dull color of an old Buffalo nickel. It had been converted long ago for cartridges, but the black-powder tamping rod was still in place, fitted with a working hinge under the barrel. The top of the holster had been worn smooth and yellow along the edges of the leather. Six tiny notches had been filed along the base of the revolver’s grips. Grandfather hung the belt from his shoulder and put on his Stetson. The brim was wilted, the crown sweat-stained a dark gray above the brim. He went out the screen door into the waning twilight.

The windmill was ginning furiously, the stanchions trembling with energy, a thread of water coming from the spout, the tank crusted with dirt and dead insects and animal hair along the rims. "The moon looks like it was dipped in a teacup. I cain't believe how we used to take the rain for granted," he said. "I think this land must be cursed."

The air smelled of ash and dust and creosote and horse and cow manure that feathered in your hand if you picked it up. Dry lightning leaped through the heavens and died, like somebody removing an oil lamp from the window of a darkened house. I thought I felt thunder course through the ground under my shoes. "Feel that?" I said, hoping to change Grandfather's mood and my own.

"Don't get your hopes up. That's the Katy blowing down the line," he replied. "I'm sorry I made fun of your butt, Satch. I won't do it no more. Walk behind me till we know who's in that car."

As we approached the tree line, the driver of the car walked out of the headlights and stood silhouetted against the glare, then got back in his car and started the engine and clanked the transmission into gear. The trees were so dry they made a sound like paper rustling when the wind blew through the canopy.

"Hold up there," Grandfather said to the man.

I thought the driver would simply motor away. But he didn't. He stuck his elbow out the window and stared straight into our faces, his expression curious rather than alarmed. "You talking to us?" he asked.

"You're on my property," Grandfather said.

"I thought this was public woods," the driver said. "If there's a posted sign that says otherwise, I didn't see it."

The woman next to him was pretty and had strawberry-blond hair and a beret tilted over one eye. She looked like a happy country girl, the kind who works in a dime store or in a café where the truckers come in to make innocent talk. She leaned forward and grinned up into Grandfather's face. She silently mouthed the words "We're sorry."

"Did you know you have mud on your license tag?" Grandfather asked the driver.

"I'll get right on that," the driver said.

"You also have what appears to be a bullet hole in your back window."

The driver removed a marble from the ashtray in the dashboard and held it against the light. "I found this on the backseat. It was probably a kid with a slingshot," he said. "I saw a kid up on the train trestle with one. You a lawman?"

"I'm a rancher. The name is Hackberry Holland. You didn't give me yours."

"Smith," the driver said.

"If you'll tell me your destination, Mr. Smith, maybe I can he'p you find your way."

"Lubbock. Or anyplace there's work. I work on automotives, mostly. Is that an antique firearm?"

"A forty-four Army Colt. Most of the time I use it for a paperweight. You know automobiles, do you?"

"Yes, sir, you could say that. I see automobiles as the future of the country. Henry Ford and me."

"Turn left at the paved road and stay due west," Grandfather said. "If you see the Pacific Ocean, that means you passed Lubbock."

The man in the backseat rolled down the glass. He was short and not over 120 pounds and wore a suit and tie and a short-brim hat cocked on his brow the way a dandy might. He had a long face, like a horse's hanging out of a stall. He also had the kind of lopsided grin you see on stupid people who think they're smarter than you. His breath was as rank as a barrel of spoiled fruit. "My name is Raymond. This here is my girlfriend, Miss Mary," he said. "We're pleased to make y'all's acquaintance."

The woman sitting next to him had a cleft chin and a broad forehead and a small mean-spirited Irish mouth; her face was sunken in the middle, like soft wax. She was smoking a cigarette, gazing into the smoke.

"There's a busted spar in my cattle guard," Grandfather said.

"Don't pop a tire going out. I'd appreciate you not throwing that whiskey bottle in my trees, either."

"Tidy is as tidy does," Raymond said.

Grandfather rested one hand on the bottom of the window. He let his eyes roam over Raymond's face before he spoke. "The man who kills you will rip out your throat before you ever know what hit you," he said. "I'm not talking about myself, just somebody you might meet up the road, the kind of fellow who turns out to be the worst misjudgment you ever made."

"We apologize, sir," said the woman in front, leaning across the driver so Grandfather could see her expression more clearly. Her smile made me think of somebody opening a music box. "We didn't mean to bother y'all. You have a mighty nice spot here. Thank you for being so gracious and kind."

"No harm done," Grandfather said.

I wanted her to say something to me, but her gaze stayed fixed on Grandfather.

The driver slowly accelerated the car, a nimbus of brown dust rising from the wax job, our visitors' silhouettes framed against the headlights. There was a long bright-silver scratch on the left fender. After they were gone, I could feel Grandfather's eyes on me, like he was about to give me a quiz to see how dumb I was at that particular moment. "What are you studying on, Satch?" he said.

"The car and the way they treat it don't fit. You think they're bank robbers?"

"If you haven't heard, there's no money in the bank to rob. Or in the general store. Or in the bubblegum machine at the filling station. Where in the name of suffering Jesus have you been, boy?"

I picked up a rock and threw it in a high arc and heard it clatter through the trees. "Why do you have to make light of everything I say?"

"Because you take the world too seriously. Let's go see what your mother is doing. I bought some peach ice cream this afternoon. That's always her favorite."

"I heard you talking on the phone to the doctor," I said. Suddenly you could hear the crickets in the dark, the whistle of the Katy beyond the horizon. The dust clogged my nostrils and throat. "You're fixing to send her for electroshock treatments, aren't you."

"The doctor raised that possibility."

"They use electroshock when they don't know what else to do. I think the doctor is an ignorant man. In addition, he's stupid and thinks meanness and intelligence are the same thing."

"He says electroshock is the most modern treatment for what ails her. It's done in a hospital. She'll have the best of care there. It could be worse. Sometimes they push a steel probe into the brain."

"On the subject of care, I wonder why nobody gave her any when she was a little girl and had to fend for herself."

"You're developing a hard edge, Weldon. It's not in your nature. It'll eat up your youth and rob you of the wisdom that should come with manhood."

I hate you, I thought.

"Tell me something," he said.

"What?" I said.

"Do you ever think about forgiveness?"

"For you, Grandfather? No, I don't. If you've ever sought forgiveness for anything, I've yet to see the instance."

"I'm talking about forgiveness for all of us."

"Are you going to call the sheriff about the people in the car?"

"They're not our business. If they come back, that's another matter."

"The woman in the front seat caught your eye," I said.

"All women do. That's the way things work. That's why preachers are always railing about sex. It's here for the long haul."

I could not take my grandfather's proselytizing. "A stranger with a sweet smile is the light of the world, but your own daughter doesn't mean diddly squat on a rock."

I instantly regretted the harshness of my words. He walked ahead of me, the holstered revolver swinging back and forth under his arm, the windmill blades rattling in the wind. When we entered the house, my mother was eating from the carton of ice cream Grandfather had bought, and cleaning the spoon with her hair.

WHEN MY MOTHER'S spells first began, she told us she had dreams she could not remember, but she was convinced they contained information of vast importance. Behind her eyes, you could see her drawing a rake through her thoughts, as though on the verge of discovering the source of all her unhappiness. Her early hours seemed to be neither good nor bad; she said morning was a yellow room that sometimes had a sunny window in it. But after three P.M., when the sun began to move irrevocably toward the horizon, a chemical transformation seemed to take place inside her head. Her eyes would become haunted, darting at the row of poplars on the side lawn, as though a specter were beckoning to her from the shade.

"What's wrong, Emma Jean?" my father said the first time it happened.

"You don't hear them?" she replied.

"Hear who?"

"The whisperers. They're over there, by the garden wall."

"Look at me. I'm your husband, the man who loves you. There is no one else in the yard except you and me and Weldon."

My mother went silent, seeming to believe now more than ever that we were her enemies, and she could not understand the poisonous vapor that awaited her every afternoon when the sun became a red wafer inside the dust clouds rising in the west.

After Grandfather and I returned to the house, I washed my mother's hair in the upstairs bathroom and dried it with the electric fan, lifting it off her neck and eyes. When I finished, she got up from the chair and dropped her bathrobe to the floor in front of the closet mirror, staring at the flatness of her hips against her slip. She began tying a string around her waist, the way colored women do to keep their slip from hanging below the hem of their dress.

"Mother, I'm in the room," I said.

My words didn't seem to register. "I've lost so much weight," she said. "Do you think I look all right? Did those people in the automobile come here in regard to your father?"

"Why would they be here about him?"

"He might have found work and sent word."

"I think they were drunk and got lost."

I went downstairs and set up our checkerboard on a folding bridge table we kept behind the couch. My mother loved to play checkers, and while she played, she smiled as though allowing herself a brief vacation from the emotional depression that consumed her life. Her hair had been dark blond when she was younger; it had turned brown with streaks of gray. She still bathed every day but no longer wore makeup or cut her fingernails. I believed that if I did not take my mother away from this house, away from the doctors who planned to kill thousands of her brain cells, she would end up a vegetable in the state asylum outside Wichita Falls.

"Mother, what if you and I left here and went out on our own?" I said.

"Where would we go?" she said, staring down at the red and black squares on the checkerboard.

"Maybe Galveston or Brownsville, where the air is fresh and full of salt from the waves crashing on the beach. There's no dust there'bouts. I could get a job."

"People are coming to take me away, aren't they."

Through the kitchen door, I could see Grandfather reading his encyclopedia, which he did every day, one volume after the next. Behind him, out in the darkness, fireflies were lighting in the trees like sparks rising off a stump fire. I tried to think but couldn't. "We have to fight them, Mother," I said. "The doctors are not our friends. I wish they had rubber gags put in their mouths and their own machines were turned against them."

She stared at her hands. The heels were half-mooned with fresh nail marks. "I don't know why I hurt myself this way or why I have the thoughts I do. I feel I'm unclean in the sight of my Creator. Something is about to happen. It has to do with the people in the car. They were here before. I saw them from the upstairs window. They took off their clothes out there in the trees."

I knew then that my mother was absolutely mad. But her mention of our visitors made me think once again of the driver and his rugged good looks and thick walnut-colored hair and toughness of attitude toward Grandfather. He was no shade-tree mechanic, no matter what he claimed. "I'll be right back," I said.

I began hunting through a sheaf of old magazines stuck in a wood rack by the end of the couch. I flipped through the pages of a 1933 issue of *True Detective* until I came to a photo of a handsome man wearing a fedora whose expression had the intransigence of boilerplate. I took the magazine to Grandfather. "Does this fellow look familiar?" I said.

"No."

"You didn't even look. It's the man you had words with."

"I think I'd know if I was talking to Pretty Boy Floyd."

"Same eyes, same chin, same mouth, same expression," I said. "A real hard case."

"There's only one problem. Floyd was killed last year on a farm in Ohio. Before the feds finished him off, he said, 'Have at it, boys. It's been that kind of day.'"

Grandfather had one-upped me again. He closed his encyclopedia and removed his glasses. "I heard y'all talking in there," he said. "She'll be better off under the care of the state. Don't encourage her to think otherwise. You're not doing her a service."

"It's you they ought to take away," I said.

I had never spoken to my grandfather like that. As I walked back into the living room, the back of my neck was flaming, my eyes filming, my mother's image as distorted as a hank of hair and skin floating in a jar of chemicals. In my absence, she had illegitimately crowned two kings for herself and was obviously pleased with what she had done.

THE WEATHER TURNED hot unexpectedly. The power went out during the night, shutting down our two electric fans, and within an hour the house was creaking with heat. The sun came up red and angry and veiled with dust at six A.M. The notion of cooking breakfast on a woodstove inside a superheated frame house was enough to make anyone lose his appetite, and the thought of cooking it for my cranky grandfather was even more irksome. But duty before druthers, I told myself, and poked kindling and newspaper through the hob into the firebox and set it aflame, then put the coffeepot on the lid and walked outside, hoping against hope there would be a cloud in the sky that had water and not half of West Texas in it.

I followed the serpentine tracks of the four-door automobile through the trees and over a knoll and down a gulley humped with dead leaves. For me, it was like following the trail of a mastodon or a creature from ancient mythology. I didn't care if the people in the car were outlaws or not. The driver and the woman who had a smile like a music box represented not only the outside world but defiance of convention. Rather than accept their fate, they had decided to change it. The two-story gabled home in which I had been born no longer seemed a symbol of genteel poverty but an institutionalization of retrograde thought and cruelty that disguised itself as love, a place where surrender to a merciless sun and silo owners who stole people's land for fifty cents an acre at tax sales was a way of life.

Grandfather said the notorious outlaws of our times were disenfranchised farm people, hardly more than petty thieves lionized by J. Edgar Hoover to promote his newly organized Bureau. I wondered if Grandfather would call Baby Face Nelson a lionized farm boy.

Then I saw the whiskey bottle Raymond drank from, busted in shards on a rock. Grandfather had asked him not to throw the bottle out of the automobile. But if you tell a man like Raymond not to stick his tongue on an ice tray or to avoid lighting a cigarette while fueling his automobile, you can be guaranteed he'll soon be talking with a speech impediment or walking around with singed hair and a complexion like a scorched weiner.

The whiskey bottle wasn't all I saw. On the other side of the knoll, down by the river bottom, was a camp complete with a lean-to, a stone-ringed fire pit, and some sharpened sticks that somebody had roasted meat on. Tire tracks led in and out of the trees. Our visitors had not only spent considerable time here but had probably buried their waste in our earth and had sex in the lean-to and shaved and brushed their teeth with water from a canteen and poured the water on the ground, conflating their lives with ours, without our consent.

Who were they? In particular, who was the woman in the front seat? I sat down on the knoll and stared through the trees at our house. The wind had piled dust on the west wall to almost the window level of our dining room. Up in the Panhandle, the dust was stacked in mounds that reached the bottom of a windmill's blades. Would that be our fate, too? Would my mother be taken away and returned to us with the lifeless expression of a cloth doll?

I couldn't bear the thoughts I was having.

I lay down on the riverbank in the midst of our visitors' camp and closed my eyes. I think I fell asleep and dreamed of the strawberry-blond girl with the beret cocked on her brow. I saw her smile at me, her mouth as soft and moist as a rose opening at sunrise. I swore I could hear wind chimes tinkling in the trees. I wondered what her name was and what it would be like to run away with her. Even more, I wondered what it would be like to place my mouth on hers. For just a moment the world felt blown by cool breezes and was green and young again; I would have sworn the willow branches were strung with leaves that lifted and fell like a woman's hair, and there was a smell in the air like distant rain and freshly cut watermelon.

Six days later, a physician and a nurse with a scowl like a prison matron's came to the house in a white ambulance. They went inside and, with hardly a word, sedated my mother and took her away to the psychiatric unit at Jeff Davis Hospital in Houston. I suspected my mother's next stop was Wichita Falls, where they'd blow out her light proper.

I STOPPED SPEAKING TO Grandfather unless the situation gave me no alternative. I went to school and did my homework and chores but avoided physical proximity to him. I could not even bring myself to look into his face, out of both resentment and shame at what he had done. Unfortunately for me, Christian charity required that I do things for him that he could not do for himself. His ankles and the tops of his feet were a reddish-purple color, the skin stretched so tight it looked like it was about to pop. I suspected he had diabetes and had decided to let it take its course, regardless if that meant blindness or amputation or the grave, which was the kind of self-destructive irrationality that characterized most of his time on earth.

In my mind, he had become a traitor, or at best he had revealed the person he had always been—a self-centered, unfeeling, and brutal man who made use of his badge to indulge all his base appetites. The stories about his womanizing and drunkenness and gambling were legendary; so were the accounts of the men who had died in front of his revolvers. He joined the Hebron Baptist Church only after the coals of his lust had crumbled into ash.

Ten days had passed since my mother was taken away in the ambulance. "The doctor told me she would probably kill herself if she didn't get treatment," Grandfather said, watching me from the kitchen table while I put away our dishes. "That's why I finally gave in. I didn't see another door out, Satch."

"Don't call me that name anymore. Not now, not ever."

"All right, Weldon."

"The doctor is a goddamn liar."

"You're acquiring a personality that's not your own," he said. "That might be understandable, considering what's happened in your family, but it will cause you a shitload of grief down the road. Be your own man, even if you don't add up to much."

How could anyone pack so many insults into so few words? I worked the iron handle on the sink; the trickle that came out of it was rust-colored and smelled of mud. Leaves were spinning in the yard, clicking against the walls and screens like the husks of grasshoppers. I could almost feel the barometer dropping, as though another great storm was at hand, perhaps one filled with rain and thunder and electricity forking across the heavens. "I think I might go away," I said.

There was a pause.

"They say the people who went to California to pick fruit have come back home. Maybe it's better to starve among your own people than in a Hooverville. We have a nice house. A lot of people don't."

I turned from the sink. His pale blue eyes were fixed on mine. I saw no recrimination in them, no desire to control or belittle. It was an uncommon moment, one that made me question whether I'd been fair to him.

"I don't think I belong here anymore," I said.

"When you woke up this morning, your name was still Holland, wasn't it? If people stick together, they can always make do."

"It's not the same now, Grandfather."

His eyes went away from mine. "I sold off thirty acres this afternoon. That's part of your inheritance, so I thought you had a right to know."

"Who did you sell it to?"

"A man from Dallas. He tried to get it for five dollars an acre. I got him up to six-fifty."

I already knew the mathematics of predatory land acquisition, and I was aware that my grandfather was notorious for his poor handling of money and lack of judgment when it came to bargaining. I also knew he wasn't telling me the whole story. "You gave him the mineral rights, didn't you."

"There's nothing down there except more dirt."

"Then why does a man from Dallas want it?"

"Maybe he's going to build a golf course. How would I know? He'p me up."

I lifted him by one arm and fitted the handle of his walking cane into his right hand. He hadn't bathed that day, and a smell like sour milk rose from his shirt. "I'll walk you upstairs," I said.

"Get me my revolver."

"What for?"

"Somebody tried to rob the bank in San Angelo today. There was at least one woman in the getaway car. Maybe our visitors didn't head for Lubbock after all."

"Maybe it was Ma Barker," I said.

"I think that gal with the beret woke up the man in you," he said. "I don't blame you. If there's any greater gift than a beautiful woman in the morning, I'll be damned if I know what it is."

THAT NIGHT I heard an automobile in the woods. I went downstairs and unlocked the back door and went out on the porch. The air was cold, the moon showing behind the edge of a cloud, the sky free of dust. Through the tree trunks, I could see a white glow, but it disappeared as quickly as someone blowing out a candle. At daybreak I started a fire in the woodstove and set a pot of water on the lid, then removed Grandfather's double-barrel shotgun from the closet and walked through the woods to the riverbank. The river was almost dry, the bank dropping six feet straight down, the sandy bottom stenciled with the tracks of small animals and threaded with rivulets of water that were red in the sunrise. I must have walked a half mile before I saw a four-door Chevrolet parked under a live oak. It was a 1932 model, one called a Confederate, with wire-spoked whitewall tires and a maroon paint job and a black top and black fenders and red leather upholstery. The spare tire was mounted on the running board. It was the most elegant car I had ever seen.

The backseat had been torn out and propped against the trunk of the tree. A man with his arm in a sling was leaning against the seat, while another man worked under the car, banging on something metal, his legs sticking out in the leaves.

The woman with the strawberry-blond hair was tending to the injured man, but she wasn't wearing her beret. The second woman was eating a Vienna sausage sandwich. "Raymond, we've got a boy with a gun," she said.

The injured man, the one I'd thought might be Pretty Boy Floyd, winked at me. "He's all right," he said, looking at me but talking to Raymond, who was crawling out from under the car. "He's just protecting his property. Where's your grandfather, kid?"

"How do you know he's my grandfather?"

"Because you look just like him." He pointed at the collapsed wire fence behind me. "Is that y'all's boundary?"

"It was. We just sold off some of our acreage. Is that a Browning automatic rifle by your leg?"

"Is that what it's called? I found it in an empty house," he said. "Tell me, y'all have a phone?"

"No, sir," I said.

"Because we had an accident, and I might need to call a doctor. I thought I saw a line going into your house. That's your house with the gables, isn't it?"

"We couldn't afford the phone bill anymore."

Raymond was standing by the car now, brushing off his clothes with one hand. In the other, he held a ball-peen hammer. "I straightened out the steering rod, but it's gonna shimmy. What are you fixing to do with that shotgun, boy?"

"Shoot skunks that come around the house," I said. "I'm right good at it."

"You know who we are?" the injured man said.

"Folks who drive fine cars but who'd rather sleep in the woods than a motor court?"

Raymond was grinning. He walked close to me, his shoes crunching in the leaves. He had taken off his dress shirt and hung it on the door mirror and was wearing a strap undershirt outside his trousers. His shoulders were bony and white and stippled with pimples. I could smell the pomade in his hair. "You heard of people shooting their way out of prison, haven't you?"

"Yes, sir."

"Ever hear of anybody shooting their way *into* prison?"

"That's a new one," I said.

"Like you know all about it?" Raymond said.

"You asked me a question."

"You're looking at people who made history," he said. He lifted up his chin, a glint in his eye.

"Raymond is a kidder," the injured man said. "We're just reg'lar working folks. I've been fixing this car for a man. Like to give it a spin? I bet you would."

"Y'all broke into a prison?" I asked.

"I was pulling your leg," Raymond said.

"I read about it in the newspaper," I said. "It was at Eastham Pen. A guard was killed."

"Maybe you should mind your own business," said the woman eating the sandwich.

The only sound was the wind blowing in the trees. I felt like I was in the middle of a black-and-white photograph whose content could change for the worse in a second. I couldn't have cared less. "Could y'all bust into an asylum?" I asked.

"Why would we want to do that?" Raymond said.

"To get somebody out. Somebody who doesn't belong there."

The woman with the strawberry-blond hair took a brush from her purse and stroked the back of her head. "Somebody in your family?"

"My mother."

"She was committed?"

"I don't know the term for it. They took her away."

She began brushing her hair, her head tilted sideways. "You shouldn't fret about things you cain't change. Maybe your mama will come home just fine. Don't be toting a gun around, either, not unless you're willing to use it."

"I'd use it to get my mother back. I wouldn't give it a second thought."

The injured man laughed. "Keep talking like that, you'll end up picking state cotton. Can you forget what you saw here? I mean, if I asked you real nice?"

"They're going to give her electroshock. Maybe they already have," I said. "You think that's fair? She's an innocent person, and she's getting treated worse than criminals who deserve everything that happens to them."

Leaves were dropping from the oak tree, spinning like disembodied wings to the ground. They were yellow and spotted with blight, and they made me think of beetles sinking in dark water.

The woman eating the sandwich turned her back and said something to the injured man. It took me a moment to sort out the words, but there was no mistaking what she said: *Don't let him leave here.*

"Mary, can you get me a cold drink from the ice chest?" said the woman with the strawberry-blond hair. "I want to talk to our young friend here."

"I say what's on my mind, Bonnie," Mary said. "You like to be sweet at other people's expense."

"Maybe there's an ice-cold Coca-Cola down in the bottom," Bonnie said. "I don't remember when I've been so thirsty. I'd be indebted if you'd be so kind."

She took my arm and began walking with me along the riverbank, back toward the house, never glancing over her shoulder, not waiting for Mary's response, as though the final word on the subject had been said. She was wearing a white cotton dress with pink and gray flowers printed on it and lace at the hem that swished on her calves. "I want you to listen to me real good," she said close to my ear. "Pretend we came with the dust and went with the wind. Tomorrow when you get up, you'll still be you and we'll be us, and it will be like we never met. Your mama is gonna be all right. I know that because she reared a good son."

"Who killed the guard, Miss Bonnie? It wasn't you, was it?"

"Go home, boy. Don't come back, either," she replied.

I RETURNED TO THE house and replaced Grandfather's shotgun in the kitchen closet. A few minutes later he came downstairs, walking on his cane. I fixed oatmeal and browned four pieces of bread in the skillet and put a jar of preserves on the table. I filled his oatmeal bowl and set it in front of him, and set his bread next to the bowl. All the while, I could feel him watching me. "Where have you been?" he said.

"I took a walk down by the river."

"Counting mud turtles?"

"There's worse company," I replied.

"I guess it's to your credit, but you're the poorest excuse for a liar I've ever known. I heard a car out in the woods last night. Did that same bunch come back here after I told them not to?"

"They're not on our property. The driver was hurt. The fellow named Raymond was fixing a tie rod."

"Did the driver have a gunshot wound?"

"No, they were in a car accident."

He had tied a napkin like a bib around his neck; he wiped his mouth with it and set down his oatmeal spoon. "Did those people threaten you?"

"The lady with strawberry-blond hair said my mother was going to come home and be okay. I think she's a good person. Maybe they've already took off. They're not out to cause us trouble."

He got up from the table and went to the phone. It was made out of wood and attached to the wall and had a crank on the side of the box. He picked up the earpiece and turned the crank. Then he turned it again. "It's dead," he said.

"Maybe a tree fell on the line."

"I think there's something you're not telling me."

"The driver asked if we had a phone. I told him we didn't. He said he saw a line going into the house. I told him we couldn't afford the service anymore."

"So you knew?"

"Knew what?"

"That these people are dangerous. But you chose to pretend otherwise," he replied.

My face was burning with shame. "What are you aiming to do?" I asked.

"Let's clear up something else first. Why were you talking about your mother to a bunch of outlaws?"

"I wondered if they could help me get her out of the asylum."

I saw a strange phenomenon occur in my grandfather's face. For the first time in my life, I saw the lights of pity and love in his eyes. "I called the doctor yesterday, Satch," he said. "I told him not to put your mother through electroshock. I told him I'd made a mistake and I was coming down to Houston to get her."

I stared at him, dumbfounded. "Why didn't you tell me?"

"I was waiting on him to call me back, to see if everything was ready to go."

I got up and went to the sink and looked at the woods. I felt like a Judas, although I didn't know exactly whom I had betrayed,

Grandfather or our visitors down by the river. "The woman's name is Bonnie. The driver had a Browning. I think he might be Clyde Barrow."

"Are you trying to give me a heart attack?" he said.

HE TOLD ME to take our Model A down to the store at the crossroads and call Sheriff Benbow.

"Go with me," I said.

"While they burglarize our house?"

"We don't have anything they want."

"It must have been the tramp in the woodpile. That's the only explanation I have for it," he said. "Were you hiding behind a cloud when God passed out the brains?"

I drove away and left him standing in front of the porch, his khaki trousers stuffed into the tops of his stovepipe boots, the wilted brim of his Stetson low on his brow, his thoughts known only to him. I turned onto the dirt road that led past the woods where our visitors had camped. Our telephone wire was hanging straight down on the pole. There was no tree limb on the ground. A dust devil spun out of a field and broke apart on the Model A's radiator, powdering the windshield, almost like an omen. The crossroads store was still two miles away. I did a U-turn and headed back home.

Grandfather owned two horses. The Shetland was named Shorty and was blind in one eye. When Grandfather rode Shorty through a field of tall grass, all you could see were his shoulders and head, as though he had been sawed in half and his upper body mounted on wheels. His other horse was a four-year-old white gelding named Blue who was part Arabian and hot-wired to the eyes. All you had to do was lean forward in the saddle and Blue would be halfway to El Paso. A man Grandfather's age had no business on that horse. But try to tell him that.

I parked by the barn. Shorty was in the corral. Blue was nowhere in sight. I looked in the kitchen closet, where I had replaced Grandfather's double-barrel shotgun. It was gone.

I took the holstered Colt from the drawer and walked into the woods and followed Blue's hoofprints along the riverbank to the end of our property. Through the trees I could see the Chevrolet and four people standing beside it, all of them looking up at Grandfather, who sat atop Blue like a wood clothespin. They were all grinning, and not in a respectful way. None of them looked in my direction, not even Bonnie.

Grandfather had bridled Blue but hadn't saddled him. Blue was sixteen hands and had the big-footed, barrel-chested conformation of an Arabian, and he rippled with nervous power when he walked. If a blowfly settled on his rump, his skin twitched from his withers to his croup. I could hear Grandfather talking: "Times are bad. But that doesn't mean you're going to use my place for a hideout or be a bad influence on my grandson. I know who y'all are. I also know it was y'all cut my phone line."

"We're plain country people, not no different from y'all," Raymond said. "We're not on your damn property, either."

"No, there's nothing ordinary about you, son. You're a smart-ass. And there's no cure for your kind," Grandfather said. "You're going to end up facedown on a sidewalk or fried by Old Sparky. I'd say good riddance, but somewhere you've probably got a mother who cares about you. Why don't you try to change your life while you got a chance?"

"We're leaving," Bonnie said. "But don't be talking down to us anymore. Your grandson told us what you let happen to your daughter."

"Enough of this. Let's go," the injured man said.

"You're Clyde Barrow, aren't you?" Grandfather said.

"I told you, the name is Smith."

"You were born in Telico. You tortured animals when you were a child. You got your brother killed up in Missouri. You're a certified mess, boy."

"Yeah, and you're a nasty old man who's going to have tumbleweed bouncing across his grave directly," said the man who called himself Smith.

They all got in the Chevrolet, slamming the doors. That was when

Blue went straight up in the air, his front hooves higher than the Chevrolet's top. Grandfather crashed to the ground, the shotgun flying from his hands, his face white with shock, his breath wheezing from his throat. I thought I heard bones snap in his back.

Bonnie and her friends drove away with Raymond behind the wheel. One of them spat on Grandfather. In the shadows I couldn't tell who it was, but I saw the spittle come out of the window like wet string and stick on Grandfather's shirt. In seconds the Chevrolet was going up a dusty rise between the trees, the sunlight spangling on the windows.

I let the holster and belt slide free of the revolver and pulled back the hammer and aimed with both hands at the back of the automobile.

"Don't do it, Weldon," Grandfather said.

I didn't aim at the gas tank or a tire or the trunk. I aimed ten inches below the roof and squeezed the trigger and felt the heaviness of the frame buck in my palms and heard the .44 round hit home, whanging off metal, breaking glass, maybe striking the dashboard or the headliner. Inside the report, I thought I heard someone scream.

The car wobbled but kept going forward and was soon gone. I shut my eyes and opened them again, unsure of what I had done, my ears ringing.

"Why didn't you listen to me?" Grandfather asked.

My right ear felt like someone had slapped it with the flat of his hand. I opened and closed my mouth to get my hearing back. "I didn't think. Was that a woman who screamed?"

"No, it was not. You heard an owl screech. Do you understand me?"

"I heard a woman scream, Grandfather."

"The mind plays tricks on you in a situation like that. That was a screech owl. They're blind in the daytime and frighten easy. Get me up."

"Yes, sir."

"Tell me what you heard."

"An owl. I heard an owl."

"From this time on, you don't look back on what happened here today. It doesn't mean a hill of beans. Don't you ever stop being the fine young man that you are."

THE FOLLOWING WEEK, three of Grandfather's old friends came to our house. They were stolid, thick-bodied men who wore suits and Stetsons and polished boots and had broad, calloused hands. One of them rolled his own cigarettes. One of them was a former Texas Ranger who supposedly killed fifty men. They sat in the kitchen and drank coffee while Grandfather told them everything he knew about our visitors. He made no mention of me. I was in the living room and heard the former Texas Ranger say, "Hack, I'd hate to bust a cap on a woman." But he smiled when he said it.

Grandfather glanced up and saw me looking through the doorway. Something happened in that moment that I will never forget. Grandfather's eyes once again were filled with a warmth that few associated with the man who locked John Wesley Hardin in jail. The lawmen at his table were killers. Grandfather was not. "Go upstairs and check on your mother, will you, Weldon?" he said.

I read later about the ambush in Louisiana. Bonnie Parker and Clyde Barrow were blown apart with automatic weapons fire. Later, their friend Raymond would die with courage and dignity in the electric chair at Huntsville. His girlfriend, Mary, would go to prison. None of them was struck by the bullet I fired into their automobile.

It rained that summer, and I caught a catfish in the river that was as reddish-brown as the water I took it from. I slipped the hook out of its mouth and replaced it in the current and watched it drop away, out of sight, an event that was probably of little importance to anyone except the catfish and me.

Chapter 2

WHEN I WAS a newly commissioned second lieutenant in the United States Army, about to embark for England in the spring of 1944, I purchased a leather-bound notebook in a stationery store not far from the campus of Columbia University. I suspect I thought I might take on the role of a modern Ishmael, and my notebook would become the keyhole through which others would witness the greatest event in human history.

I was vain, certainly, and like most young men of that era, at least those from the heartland, unable to reconcile my vanity and eagerness with my shyness around girls and my discomfort among people who were educated at eastern universities. Maybe my notebook would give me an understanding of myself, I thought, opening the door of the stationery store, within sight of the plazas and green lawns and monarchical buildings of the university where I hoped one day to attend graduate school. Maybe writing in a notebook about things most people could not imagine would make me captain of my soul. I saw myself in a trench, my back against the dirt wall, writing in my notebook while artillery shells whistled out of the heavens and exploded in no-man's-land. All my fantasy lacked was a recording of "Little Bessie" playing in the background.

Like all young men about to go to war, I did not want to hear talk about the grand illusion. If war was so bad, why did those who served in one never indicate that they regretted having done so? Think of the images conjured up by mention of the horns blowing along the road to Roncevaux. Which lays greater claim on the human heart, *The Song of Roland* or cloistering oneself inside inertia and ennui while the world is being set alight?

My generational vanity was not of an arrogant kind. I didn't mean that at all. Our vanity had its origins not only in our youth but in our collective innocence. We told ourselves we had prevailed during the Great Depression because we had kept faith with Jeffersonian democracy and had not given ourselves over to the Reds or the American equivalent of fascism. The truth about us was a little more humble in nature: We were born and raised in a transitional era; we were the last Americans who would remember a nation that was more agrarian than industrial, with more dirt roads than paved highways. We would also be the last generation to believe in the moral solvency of the Republic.

This is not meant to be a dour evaluation of what we were or the era when we lived. In many ways, it was a grand time to be around. The cultural anchors of the continent were Hollywood on one end and Ebbets Field on the other. The literary staple of almost every middle-income American home was *The Saturday Evening Post*, which contained the short stories of F. Scott Fitzgerald and William Faulkner and John O'Hara. A cherry Coke at the drugstore cost a dime, the music was a nickel, and the dance floor was free. For most of us, each sunrise was like a pink rose opening on the earth's rim. Perhaps we created a myth and became acolytes in the service of our own creation; but if that was the case, the entire world was envious of us all the same.

Little of what I recorded in my notebook could be considered memorable or historically insightful, even after Normandy, where we waded ashore in the second wave, the surf a frothy red from the initial assault. War is always a dirty and unglamorous business. Most of it has to do with head colds and body odor and crab lice and trench foot and sleeping in the rain and sometimes throwing your own feces out of a foxhole with your e-tool. But I never hated the army or dwelled on the unnecessary cruelties of my fellow man (Sherman tank crews knocking down farmhouses just for fun). Many of the Southerners in my regiment could hardly read and write. The Northerners believed a factory job in a unionized plant was the fulfillment of the American dream. I admired them and thought most of them were far braver and more resourceful than I. If I had to go off to war with anyone, I could not have picked a better bunch. They were always better than they thought they were, no matter how bad it got, and never realized how extraordinarily courageous and resilient they were.

I settled in for the duration and wrote in my notebook more as a reminder of the city where I had bought it than as a process of self-discovery. I'd return to New York, I told myself. I'd have lunch with a beautiful girl in an outdoor café, under an awning, on a cool afternoon in spring, perhaps by a park blooming with flowers. I'd take her dancing, maybe in a ballroom where Tommy Dorsey and his orchestra were playing. And in the morning, I would attend classes at Columbia University, armed with the confidence that I, like Stephen Crane, had faced the Great Death and hence never had to speak of it again. Little did I know that the next few decades of my life would be altered as a result of events that began in an innocuous fashion at the bottom of a hill in the Ardennes Forest, at a time when we believed the Third Reich was done and the lights were about to go on again all over the world.

IN THE FADING grayness of the day, at the bottom of my foxhole, I opened my notebook on my knee and began writing. My field jacket felt as stiff and cold as canvas in subfreezing weather. I heard a pistol flare pop overhead, but inside the gloom it seemed to give off neither heat nor light and, like most day-to-day events in the army, seemed to signify absolutely nothing.

The fog in the trees is ghostly, I wrote, *so dense and smokelike and pervasive I cannot see more than thirty yards into the forest. The majority of trees are fir and larch and spruce. In the soil, where there are no snowdrifts, I can see stones that are smooth and elongated like loaves of bread, the kind used to make Roman roads or build a peasant's cottage. Around me are apple and pear and plum and nut trees that are not indigenous to this forest, and I wonder if an early-medieval farmer and his wife and children swinked in the fields close by, living out their lives to ensure the well-being of the man who lived in a castle atop a hill not far away.*

The evening is so quiet I can hear a bough bend and the snow sifting through the branches to the ground. There are rumors that Waffen SS made a probe on our perimeter, within one thousand yards of us. I don't believe the rumor. SS initiatives are usually accompanied by a large panzer presence. Major Fincher agrees with me. Unfortunately, Major Fincher is widely regarded as a dangerous idiot. At Kasserine Pass he ordered an entire regiment to dig slit trenches instead of foxholes. Tiger tanks overran their position and turned in half circles on top of the trenches and ground sixty men into pulp with their tracks.

Our regiment is made up of National Guardsmen, draftees, and regular army. The officers and enlisted men get along fine. It's a good outfit. Except for Major Fincher. Someone said the German army has been trying to find him for years in order to award him the Iron Cross. When the joke was reported to Fincher, a corporal had to explain its meaning.

I didn't get to complete my entry. Sergeant Hershel Pine stuck his head over the pile of frozen snow and dirt by the edge of my foxhole and stared down at me. His narrow face was red with windburn, his whiskers reddish-blond on his cheeks, his helmet fitted down tightly on the scarf tied over his ears. "We got a problem, Lieutenant," he said.

"What is it?" I replied, placing my pencil between the pages of my notebook, closing the cover.

He slid down into the hole. His breath was fogging, his field jacket flecked with ice crystals. He was carrying a Thompson, three magazines taped together, one of them inserted in the frame. Before he spoke, he rubbed his nose with his mitten to clear the mucus frozen in his nostrils. His mitten was cut away from his trigger finger. "Steinberg is coming unglued," he said.

"About what?"

"Waffen SS don't take Jewish or wounded prisoners."

"Send him to me."

"I say use him on point or get him out of here, sir."

"On point?" I said.

"If somebody's got to step on an antipersonnel mine, I say better deadweight than a good soldier, sir."

"Steinberg *is* a good soldier, Sergeant."

He was crouched down on one knee. He dropped his eyes. I knew what was coming. I didn't hold it against him, but I didn't want to hear it, either. It was the curse of his kind, in this case a man who was raised on a cotton farm in one of the Red River parishes of central Louisiana, an area notable only for the fact that a mass execution of Negro soldiers by the White League took place there during Reconstruction. "I say better one of them than one of us, Lieutenant," he said.

"Who are 'them'?"

"I don't think you want to hear what I have to say."

"I'm very interested in what you have to say. Take the crackers out of your mouth, Sergeant."

"They own the banks. They're the ones who lent Hitler the money to finance his war machine, sir. Actually, the Krupp family are Jews, aren't they?"

"Lose the rhetoric, and lose it now. Are we clear about that?"

"Yes, sir," he replied. He didn't look up. His eyelashes were as long as a girl's, his cheeks as bright as apples under his whiskers. I could hear him breathing, trying to hide his anger and distrust of those he would call people of privilege.

"What do your folks do on Christmas Day, Pine?"

His eyes met mine, uncertain. "Pick pecans out on the gallery."

"What else?"

"My mother usually bakes a fruitcake, and my daddy fixes a big bowl of eggnog and puts red whiskey in it, not moonshine. Me and my little brother and a colored man who works for us go squirrel hunting. The weather is almost always mild on Christmas."

"That sounds like a fine way to spend the occasion," I said.

"I need to tell you something, sir."

"Go ahead."

"Last night on patrol, Steinberg got the heebie-jeebies when we ran into a listening post. He could have got us knocked off. It's the second time it's happened."

"I'll talk to him."

"Sir, there's something else I need to say."

I waited.

"I can smell money. That's the honest-to-God truth, sir. I can smell old coins buried in the ground. I can smell oil and gas before the drill punches into a pay sand. You ever see a well come in? The pipes sweat all over just before the drilling floor starts to vibrate."

"I'm not sure what you're telling me."

"I got a second gift, Lieutenant. I sweat when a situation is about to hit the fan. Maybe Steinberg has a right to be worried. I think the Krauts might try to bust through right where we're at. I've been sweating inside my shirt for two days, sir."

His eyes were red along the rims, the bone structure of his face as lean and pointed as an ax. He was breathing through his nose, his nostrils white with cold, waiting for me to speak, clearly wondering if he had said too much. "Sir, I'm not crazy. I don't go to fortune-tellers or anything like that. I just know things. A nigra midwife delivered me. She was a voodoo woman from New Orleans. She said I was touched. She meant I had a gift. Nigras got a sense sometimes."

"Maybe you're right and we're going to have Krauts in our lap before dawn," I said. "Whatever happens, we'll do our job. I don't want to hear any more about Steinberg or clairvoyance or somebody sweating inside his clothes. Now get back to your position."

A HALF HOUR LATER, as the last gaseous, silvery remnant of sun died on the horizon, I heard the sound of small arms popping on our flank. From a great distance, the sound was like fat raindrops dropping on lily pads. It grew in intensity until the sporadic popping became an uninterrupted, self-sustaining roar, followed by the coughing of a fifty-caliber machine gun down the line, the tracers streaking like bits of neon into the winter darkness.

I climbed out of my foxhole just as I heard the creaking of tank treads, then tree trunks snapping, their snow-laden boughs slapping against the forest floor. The visual and auditory effect of a King Tiger tank's intrusion into an area defended by light infantry is difficult to describe. Its weight was almost seventy tons. Its Porsche engine could generate speeds of over thirty miles an hour. Its 88mm cannon could hit and destroy a Sherman tank at twelve hundred yards. Bazooka rounds and even the French 75mm often ricocheted off its sloped sides. Forty yards out, beyond a knoll, I saw giant trees crashing to the ground. Then the King Tiger topped the knoll, its front end jutting into the air, not unlike a horse rearing in a corral. I could feel the earth shake under my feet when the full weight of the tank slammed down on the incline, grinding boulders into gravel. For a moment I saw the head and shoulders of the tank commander sticking out of the cupola, its sides painted with the Iron Cross. He was wearing a black cap and a black jacket and had a face that was as one-dimensional and expressionless as bread dough in a pie pan. He sank down into the turret and pulled the hatch shut as the two MG-34 machine guns mounted beneath the cupola began firing.

The Tiger in front of me was one of many. The forest was being denuded. The trees were dropping so fast they didn't have adequate space to fall, colliding perpendicularly like kitchen matches tumbling out of a spilled box. I saw our BAR man firing at the viewing slit on a Tiger, then a spray of 7.92 rounds danced across his field jacket. He dropped his weapon and began walking into the trees, one hand pressed to his chest, as though he had heartburn. He fell to his hands and knees, his back shaking each time he coughed, chaining the snow with red flowers.

I cannot say with any degree of accuracy what occurred in the next few minutes. Someone was yelling for a medic. I saw Private First Class Jason Steinberg and three other men get hit by automatic weapons fire and run over by a Tiger. I remember picking up the BAR man and trying to pull him into a hole. I also remember shooting two Waffen SS at close range with my .45. I saw German infantry coming out of the fog behind the tanks, some of them wearing belted leather overcoats, small lightning bolts painted on the sides of their helmets. Then I was on one knee behind a boulder, firing a carbine that had a splintered stock and wasn't mine. Half my face was printed with wood splinters, one ear wet with blood, though I had no memory of a bullet striking the stock.

The Tigers smashed over our foxholes, their cannon firing into a snowfield behind us, one as white and smooth and glazed under the moon as the top of a wedding cake. The eruption of flame and sound from the barrels of the 88s was surreal, so loud and powerful that I couldn't hear the creaking of the treads eating up anything in their path, the explosions literally shaking the senses, as though my eyes, my brain, my organs were being emptied one by one on the snow. Out in the field, I could see two Sherman tanks burning. Three of the crew members were trying to run across the field to a distant woods, their legs locked knee-deep in the snow, their shadows as liquid and dark as India ink, their arms flailing under the stars as rounds from a machine gun danced toward them.

Behind me I heard a fir tree that must have been sixty feet tall topple through the canopy. I stared at it, stupefied, perhaps a bit like a condemned wretch watching the blade of a guillotine fall on his neck. The fog inside the forest and the screams of the wounded being executed and the guttural commands of the SS noncommissioned officers all melded into the creaking sounds of the Tigers, clanking like a junkyard across the snowfield. The tree crashed with the weight of an anvil on my helmet, razoring the rim down on my nose, mashing me into the earth.

Hours later, I woke at the bottom of a shell hole, my body covered by the branches of the fir. The canopy of the forest was gone, and the sky was clear and black and patterned with constellations, the temperature close to zero. I thought I could hear a mewling sound, like a baby's, coming from under the snow, not five feet away.

Chapter 3

I FOUND AN E-TOOL and started digging. The snow had been as tightly compacted as wet sand by tank treads. One foot down, the blade of the collapsible shovel struck a log, then another one, and I realized I was digging into someone's reinforced foxhole. The opening had been squeezed shut, as though someone had drawn the string on a leather bag, sealing a trapped infantryman inside a frozen cocoon that was hardly bigger than an obese woman's womb. I folded the shovel into the position of a garden hoe and began chopping at the rocks and snow and dirt and broken timber until I had created a hole large enough to stick my hand inside. My fingers touched an unshaved face that was as cold and rough as stone.

The trapped man's knees had been pushed almost to his chin. He was trying to speak, but his teeth were chattering so violently he could not form individual words. I grabbed him by the wrists and dragged him over the cusp of the foxhole and wiped his face. Tears had frozen in his eyelashes. He raised his right hand and placed it against my chest, as though reassuring himself that I was real. His mitten was cut away from his trigger finger.

"Are you hit?" I asked.

"Dunno, sir," he replied.

"Where's your Thompson?" I said.

"Dunno." He looked around and shook his head. "Where's everybody?"

"Dead," I said. "They shot the wounded. Can you walk?"

He had lost his steel pot, and his hair was studded with chips of ice that resembled rock salt. He stared at the splintered trees on the ground and at the blackened areas where German infantry had thrown potato-mashers over the tops of their tanks into our midst. He looked at the Tiger tracks leading right across the hole I had pulled him from.

"Did you hear me, Sergeant? We're behind enemy lines."

He seemed unable to fathom my words. I pointed toward the west and the lights flickering at the bottom of the sky. The intermittent flashes looked like heat lightning, or electricity bursting silently inside a bank of thunderheads. "That's our artillery. Neither of us is in good repair. We don't want to be captured."

He lifted his eyes to mine, as though remembering a dream. "What happened to Steinberg?"

"He got it."

"How?"

"Under a King Tiger."

"He was alive?"

"I don't know," I lied.

He tried to get to his feet, one knee giving out, then the other. He began swinging his arms. "The bastards left us?"

"No, they all died. They died right here." I found a knit cap and beat the snow crystals off it and fitted it on his head. "Pull yourself together. This will probably become a staging area. We don't want to be here when that happens. Are you hearing me, Sergeant?"

"I cain't walk, Lieutenant. My legs are dead."

"You will walk whether you want to or not. Place your arm over my shoulder and put one foot after another. It's just like Arthur Murray dance steps."

He tripped, then held on to my shoulder as tightly as he could. "There you go," I said. "We're the boogie-woogie boys from Company B. Am I right?"

"Yes, sir."

"We have to find a safe place before daylight. One way or another we'll find our lines. Do you believe me when I say that?"

"Yes, sir," he said, limping along next to me, through the shattered trees and the detritus of battle. "Lieutenant, I got to explain why I was crying when you pulled me out. It wasn't because of the tank."

"It doesn't matter."

"Yes, sir, it does. A Kraut is just a man, nothing more, nothing less. When I was a baby, I got wrapped up in a rubber sheet. A nigra woman hanging wash looked through the window and rushed inside and saved my life. My face was already blue. I've had nightmares about it ever since. I'm in a tunnel, and my arms are pinned at my sides, and I'm hollering for my mother. It's the worst thing ever happened to me, sir. Being down in that hole was like living it all over again."

"I understand, Sergeant."

"No, sir, you don't. Nobody does. I've been afraid of closed-in places all my life. I wanted to die in that hole and have it over with. If I'd had a weapon, I would have punched my ticket."

His breath was labored, his hip knocking against mine. I held him around the waist and used my other hand to keep his arm tight across my shoulders. I could see the eastern edge of the woods and a snowfield blazing as brightly as a flame under the moon. I had no idea where we were. The war had not only moved on, it seemed to have lost interest in us. In the distance, I could see a serpentine river shining like black oil, and beyond the opposite shore, a railroad embankment and a water tower. If the sky remained clear, our planes would be in the air at dawn, blowing up fuel depots and nailing every armored unit they could spot. But where were we going to hide when the starlight faded from the heavens and the sun broke on the horizon, and what would we eat?

We trudged across the snowfield, clinging to each other, our eyes tearing, our ears like lumps of cauliflower, the wind as sharp as a barber's razor when I turned my face into it.

WE STAYED IN the woods the entire day. A flight of bombers with a fighter escort passed high overhead, vapor trails barely discernable.

Later we could hear the explosions of bombs through the earth, probably blockbusters designed to blow gas and water mains before the incendiaries were dropped in strings that looked like cords of firewood. The forest contained no signs of either human or animal life. I could only assume the animals had been killed and eaten. That there were no human footprints except our own was more than disconcerting. As the sun descended, shadows formed in the sculpted, funnel-shaped tracks we had left in the snow, creating a trail not unlike ink dots leading to our hiding place.

Just before sunset, a lone Messerschmitt painted with zebra stripes came in low across the field, close enough for me to see the pilot's goggled face as he swooped past us. The area around his wing guns was black with burnt gunpowder. It seemed grandiose to believe that the pilot of a Luftwaffe fighter plane would have interest in two escapees from a one-sided slaughter, weak with hunger and in the first stages of frostbite. Less than one minute later, I heard his guns rattling as he strafed a target by the river, and I realized that others had probably survived the massacre. For a committed hunter, no target was too small or insignificant.

As soon as night fell, Sergeant Pine and I made our way down to the river and pushed a rowboat free of the ice and frozen reeds along the bank and rowed to the far side. We huddled at the base of the train tracks. I was exhausted and colder and hungrier than I had ever been, the kind of hunger that is like a rat eating a hole through the bottom of your stomach. To the east was another wooded area, and beyond it lighted buildings of some kind, perhaps factories manned by slave labor, operating twenty-four hours a day. I climbed up the embankment and placed my ear to one of the rails. For me, at that moment, the sound inside the steel could only be compared to the warm and steady humming of a woman's circulatory system when you rest your head against her breast.

The headlight on the locomotive wobbled past us. Most of the cars looked empty, rocking on their undercarriages as we ran alongside the tracks, gravel skidding under our feet. I jumped aboard a boxcar whose interior was blowing with chaff and smelled of grain and livestock, then I reached down and grabbed the sergeant by the wrist and pulled him through the door, the riparian, marshlike countryside dropping behind us. I prayed that we were headed north, into Belgium. I prayed that a great deliverance was at hand.

The train gained speed and began to bend around a long curve that took us due east. Far up the line, I could see the glow of the firebox in the cab and sparks fanning from the smokestack. I lay down in the back of the boxcar and covered myself with a pile of burlap bags, too tired to care where the train took us. As I closed my eyes, I heard the sergeant push the sliding door shut. Soon I was fast asleep, the boxcar's wheels clicking on the tracks, the floor rocking like a cradle.

I woke at sunrise with a start, the way you do when you realize that the problems surrounding you are real and that your sleep has only placed them in abeyance. The train had picked up considerable speed; the boxcar was one that Depression-era hoboes called a flatwheeler because it had no springs and bounced a passenger all over the floor. "Where are we?" I said.

Sergeant Pine had slid back the door three inches from the jamb. "It sure ain't Kansas, sir," he replied. "I'd say we're in the outhouse."

I crawled to the door and looked out. The countryside was shrouded with fog that resembled and smelled like industrial smoke, rather than vapor from rivers and lakes, the sun a lemon-colored piece of shaved ice on the horizon. There were bomb craters, rows of them, in fields that could have contained no military importance. "Sometimes the flyboys pickle the load before they get to the Channel," Pine said.

"We need to get off the train," I said.

"Sir, I found something at the other end of the car. There wasn't just livestock in here. There's human feces stacked in the corner. It's frozen. That's why there wasn't any stink," he said. "You think there were POWs in this car?"

"GIs or Brits would have marked up the walls," I said.

"You're saying maybe this train carries Jews, sir?"

"Who else would it be?"

"I'm not sure, Lieutenant. I don't know if I believe those stories."

"You saw the SS at work."

"That doesn't make the stories true."

"Maybe not." The train was going faster and faster, the boxcar shaking, the lines of chaff on the floor eddying back and forth like seawater sliding across sand.

"I've never been this hungry. I'd eat the splinters out of the wall. You reckon we're going to get out of this, sir?"

"If not, it won't be for lack of trying."

"Can I ask what you did in civilian life, Lieutenant? The reason I ask is you were having a dream. You said something about Bonnie Parker and Clyde Barrow, the outlaws. Dreaming about those two has got to be a new one."

"I knew them. Friends of my grandfather killed them. My grandfather was a Texas Ranger who put John Wesley Hardin in jail. I went to school in Texas and Louisiana and have a degree in history from Texas A&M and plan to go to graduate school and become an anthropologist. Does that help you out?"

"Jesus Christ, sir."

"What is it now?" I said, my attempt at affability starting to slip.

"Look yonder," he replied. He pointed through the crack in the door.

Two fighters made a wide turn in the sky and came in low, right down on the deck, directly out of the sun, the muzzles of their fifty-caliber machine guns winking. A white star inside a blue red-rimmed disk was painted on their wings. I saw dirt spout in a straight line across a cultivated field just before I heard the rounds smack like a bucket of marbles into the sides of the boxcars. It was thrilling to see my countrymen appear almost miraculously in the sky, their wings emblazoned with an insignia we associated with the light of civilization. Unfortunately, our countrymen were shooting at us as well as at the enemy.

The planes roared overhead and made another turn and came in for a second pass, this time with rockets mounted under their wings. The rockets caught the locomotive dead-on, blowing the cab and the boiler apart, the coal car jackknifing and taking half a dozen boxcars down the embankment with it.

Our boxcar rolled to a slow halt and was stock-still on the tracks.

The sergeant and I pushed open the sliding door and began running down a ditch that led to a canal overgrown on both banks with scrub brush and gnarled trees, so grotesque in their disfiguration that I wondered if they had been sprayed with herbicide. The current in the canal was brown and sluggish, more like sewage than creek water, the air as thick and gray as the inside of a damp cotton glove. Above the canal was a narrow, rutted road, bone-white in color, a viscous green rivulet running down its center. I thought I heard a sound like a metal sign clanging in the wind. I climbed up the embankment to see farther down the road, with no success. The wind changed direction, and the sergeant cupped his hand over his nose and mouth, trying not to gag. "God, what's that smell?" he said.

It wasn't a smell; it was an acrid stench, one whose density made the eyes water. Automatically, I tried to associate it with images out of my past: smoke from a chimney behind a rendering plant on a wintry day; the liquescence of unburied offal; cattle dead of anthrax sliding off the beds of dump trucks into a chemical soup. I thought of rats trapped in compacted garbage that had been sprinkled with kerosene and set aflame. The stench was all of these things but worse. In my mind's eye, I saw thick curds of yellow and gray smoke rising from human hair and skin stretched on bone. I saw fingernails curl and snap, and the eyes of the dead pop open in the heat. I saw lesions and blisters spread across the faces of children and mothers and fathers and grandparents, as though their expressions were being reconfigured long after they were dead.

I realized the sergeant and I had stepped through a door in the dimension and were about to enter a place that had no equivalent except perhaps in photos from the devil's scrapbook.

Chapter 4

TEN MINUTES LATER, we climbed up an eroded embankment on the creek and rested on our stomachs among the trees, staring out at an iron arch and a set of gates that formed the entrance to a fenced camp where there were at least four barracks-like tarpaper buildings and a gingerbread house.

Spirals of rusted barbed wire were strung along the top of the fence; poplars had been planted along it. The rusted arch and its stanchions were scrolled with English ivy that had turned to black string and bits of red leaves. The only sounds I could hear were a tin door banging incessantly on a tarpaper building, and the muttering of birds and a combative fluttering of wings.

Evidently, the camp had not included a crematorium when it was built, and the SS had made do with the materials they had on hand. Segments of train rails had been laid across bricks stacked four feet high, then piled with felled trees. Buckets of pitch that had been used for an accelerant lay empty on the ground. From the amount of ash under the rails, I estimated the fires had been burning for at least a day. Some of the bodies had been reduced to bones and leathery scraps hanging from the rails; others were smoldering, only partially consumed by the flames. Not far away, on a railroad spur, was a giant pit where other bodies had been thrown naked, one on top of another, and doused with lime.

Directly behind the improvised crematorium was a gallows, a single noose made of steel cable hanging from the crosspiece.

"What is this place, Lieutenant?" the sergeant said.

"Probably a supply depot for forced labor," I said.

"Where are the guards?"

"The guys who work in these places don't do well against armed troops. They probably got rid of their uniforms and hauled freight."

The sergeant wiped his nose on his sleeve. "Maybe there's grub in that gingerbread house," he said.

We had one weapon between us, my 1911-model army .45 automatic. I got to my feet and pulled it from the holster. It felt cold and heavy in my hand. "Let's take a walk," I said.

The gates were unlocked, the smoke flattening in the wind, the smell of charred flesh unbearable. I cleared my mouth and spat, then pulled my sweater over my nose. The sergeant kept looking sideways at the crematorium, his eyelids stitched to his brows, his cheeks sunken. "Lieutenant, there's a little-bitty child in that pit," he said. "Right yonder. Oh, man."

"We'll talk about it later, Sergeant. Concentrate on what's in front of us."

"Yes, sir. If this is a camp for slave labor, why is a child here?"

"Don't try to make sense out of a place like this," I said. "There are more of us than there are of them. That's what we have to keep remembering."

"Sir, maybe we should forget the house. I think there's poultry in that tarpaper building. Maybe turkeys. Maybe we should wring the necks of a couple and get out of here. Sir, pardon the expression, we're standing out here like shit in an ice cream parlor. Sir, I want to get out of here."

"You've got a point," I replied.

A gust of wind slammed the tin door shut on the tarpaper building. The sergeant grabbed it by the handle and jerked it open. Carrion birds clattered into the air, their wings beating against the walls and roof, their beaks red from their work. The building was not a barracks but a charnel house. The only difference between the bodies in the pit and those in the building was some of them were wearing clothes, if rags could be considered clothes. The bodies at the bottom were festooned with pustules, the skin waxy, almost luminous. Who were these poor creatures? Did they once have families and homes like the rest of us? Did they die from typhus or diphtheria, pneumonia or cholera? Or bullets? No one would ever know. From what I saw, I would say they died a little bit from all those things, and for most of them death came as a blessing.

"Did you hear that, Lieutenant?"

"Hear what?"

"A woman's voice," the sergeant said. "I heard it."

"I think you heard the hinges on the door."

"Listen. That's not the wind. Somebody's alive back there."

My hand was tight on the grips of the .45, my eyes trying to adjust to the weak light.

"There it is again," Pine said. "It's a woman. Who are you, lady? Tell us where you are."

"It's too late to do anything for these people, Sergeant."

"We cain't just walk out of here, sir." He was trembling from the cold, moisture running from his nose. "Right, sir? We cain't pretend we didn't hear what we heard. Look at this goddamn place. Oh, Jesus, sir, I cain't forget the way I talked to Steinberg."

I walked deeper into the building and saw her lying on the floor in a filthy gray dress pooled with blood that appeared to have come from the bodies around her. Her face was turned toward me, her eyes too big for her face, her hair thick and dark brown with streaks of black, cropped on the neck, probably with a knife or a very dull pair of shears. A number was tattooed in blue ink on the inside of her left forearm. I knelt beside her and looked into her face. "I'm Lieutenant Weldon Avery Holland, United States Army," I said. "Who are you?"

I thought she was trying to speak, but I couldn't be certain. I cupped my hand to her forehead. It felt as cool and smooth and bloodless as marble. "Can you tell me your name? Are others alive, too?"

She tilted her head slightly; her lips moved without sound. I leaned down with my ear to her mouth. Her breath smelled like shaved ice.

"I'm sorry, I can't understand you," I said.

"I never went to the whorehouse," she said. "My name is Rosita Lowenstein. *Viva la República. No pasarán.*"

I would have sworn she winked at me.

WE FOUND AN overcoat and a scarf and a pair of shoes in the house and put them on her. She told us that the camp staff had become frightened three days earlier, when British planes bombed a German convoy one mile away. The staff had also heard rumors that Americans were executing SS in retaliation for a massacre in Belgium. She said she was twenty-three years old, had grown up in Madrid, and spoke Spanish, German, English, and French. We found a jar of preserves and a half loaf of bread and part of a smoked ham in the larder. We fed her and ourselves, all the while eyeing the road.

"What was that you said to us back there in the building?" the sergeant asked.

"I told them if they put me in the whorehouse, I would kill the first officer I could. Then I would open my veins and tell the other women to do the same."

"What was the other thing you said?" the sergeant asked.

"'Long live the Republic' and 'They shall not pass.' I was talking about the Spanish Republic and Franco's Falangists."

The sergeant looked at me for clarification. "She's talking about the Spanish Civil War," I said. " 'They shall not pass' is a famous statement made by a woman called La Pasionaria. She was a speaker for the Popular Front. She lives in the Soviet Union now."

"You're a Communist?" the sergeant said.

"No. I was for the Republic," Rosita replied. "But they blighted themselves with the murder of the clergy. I am not political, except for my hatred of the fascists."

"Do you know if others are alive?" I asked.

She shook her head.

"You mean no?" I said.

"The difference between life and death is not measurable here," she replied.

Even after eating, she could not walk, and the sergeant and I had to take turns carrying her. Her body had no odor, as though her glands had dried up and her pores were no longer able to secrete moisture. We carried her through a network of irrigation ditches and hid in a culvert under a road that had been bombed and rendered impassable. We also hid under a train trestle and slept in a forest where we kept warm by heaping leaves and dirt on ourselves. My feet were blocks of wood. I unlaced my boots but did not remove them, for fear I would not be able to fit them on again. When I woke in the morning, three inches of snow had accumulated on top of me without my being aware of it.

The weather continued to worsen. The grayness of the day and the snow swirling out of the fields allowed us to keep walking; otherwise, we would have had to stay hidden in the woods until dark. We saw dead cattle in a field and a farmhouse pocked with holes, including the roof, probably made by aerial gunfire. We also saw a convoy of trucks filled with German infantry going up a dirt road toward the front, followed by three armored personnel carriers and two ambulances and a motorcycle with a sidecar on it. The motorcycle sputtered to a stop, and the driver and the officer in the sidecar climbed into one of the trucks. Later we saw a train carrying rail cannon and panzers boomed down on flatcars. Late in the afternoon the sergeant worked his way under the back wall of a farmer's barn and returned with five potatoes stuffed in his pockets, his face as red as sunburn from the wind, snow speckling on it like bits of glass.

We kept traveling into the night and stopped only out of sheer exhaustion. The moon was up, the countryside bright and cold and empty of sound or movement. Just before going to sleep, I wrote these lines in my notebook: *The woman is carrying lice. If she has typhus, Pine and I will soon have it, too. She sleeps with her head against my chest while I walk. My lower back is on fire and I have trouble straightening it. Pine is a yeoman and a solid fellow, with far more humanity in him than he is aware of. I hope he gets through this all right. Good night, Grandfather. Good night, Mother. Good night, Lord. See you all in the morning.*

Just before dawn, Pine shook me awake. We were at the bottom of a gulley, sheltered by spruce and fir trees that were white with fresh snow. "It's crawling with Krauts out there, Lieutenant," he whispered. "Mechanized infantry, lots of it."

"Going which way?"

"East. I think they're running out of gas. They parked a light panzer in the field. Three guys got out and left it."

"Where's Rosita?" I said.

"Still asleep."

"If they set up a perimeter in the woods, we're in trouble."

"Sir, when I went after food last night, I saw another farmhouse. It's just north of here. It looked deserted. I saw a cellar door in back."

I couldn't think. Those given to asceticism might disagree, but I never found hunger a friend when it came to imposing order on one's thoughts. "How far is the house from the trees?"

"A hundred yards, maybe. The woman was coughing, sir. She needs to be in a warm place. She needs a lot more food, too. We could use some of the same, Lieutenant."

"You regret taking her along?"

"I don't know how I feel, sir. I'm supposed to be a Christian. I got a wife back home. We'd only been married four months when I enlisted. I'd like to see her again."

"Spit it out."

"I don't regret taking the Jewish woman with us. I won't ever get rid of what we saw back there in that camp. If I get the chance, I'm going to write Steinberg's folks."

I heard the rushing sound of a 105 round arcing out of its trajectory, then a dull, earth-shuddering thump behind us, one that shook snow out of the trees. A second round landed out in a field, close to the road where Pine had seen mechanized infantry. The explosion blew a fountain of dirt and snow and ice into the air. Pine and I stared at each other. "We're registered," I said. "Get Rosita."

She was already up, standing on her own in the bottom of the gulch. Her scarf was tied tightly under her chin, her overcoat powdered with snow, her feet lost inside the big shoes owned by an officer who probably ordered her death and her fellow prisoners'. The cold flush in her cheeks, the hunger in her eyes, the tangled brownish-black thickness of her hair bunched inside her scarf, sent a pang through me that I could not quite explain. "Why are you staring at me?" she asked.

"You remind me of someone I met when I was sixteen. Her name was Bonnie Parker."

"Sir, they're going to throw a marching barrage in here," Pine said.

"You're a strange man," Rosita said to me.

"You want me to he'p you, ma'am?" Pine said.

"Who is Bonnie Parker?" she said.

"A beautiful outlaw woman," I said. "She was my first love. I ended up shooting a bullet through the back of her automobile while she was in it."

For the first time I saw Rosita smile.

I suspect it was foolish to be musing upon the allure of a young woman when there was a possibility that we might be blown into bits in a snowy, tree-lined gulch in the heart of a medieval forest. But the prospect of death sometimes creates an interlude when time stops and you see a portrait of what existence should be like rather than what it is. The artillery crews began firing for effect, the 105 rounds arcing into the fields, blowing craters in the earth that boiled and hissed on the rims and rained dirt clods on the snow. Pine and I each grabbed Rosita by an arm and labored up the gulch, the 105s marching through the forest, smacking down like Neptune's net on all of us, Jew and Gentile, German and American. Inside the roar of the explosions, I think I shouted out my mother's name.

WHEN IT STOPPED, the entire countryside was totally silent, as though we had been struck deaf. We were on the northern tip of the woods and could not see any German troops or hear any vehicles. The sky was pink and blue, the clouds puffy and white. The farmhouse Pine had seen the previous night was built of fieldstones and squared timbers that were notched and pegged and stained almost black by age and smoke from stubble fires. There were no animals in sight; sunlight was shining through the barn walls. The windows of the house were dark, the chimney powdered with frost, a snowdrift piled against the front door.

"What do you want to do, Lieutenant?" Pine asked.

The wind was blowing hard, enough to cover our footprints. I went first, my .45 drawn. I pulled open the cellar door and went down the steps into the darkness. When I lit a match, I saw a wooden icebox against one wall, the kind many people owned when I was growing up in Depression-era Texas. Inside the box were salted fish wrapped in newspaper, a big round of cheese, and two smoked sausages that must have weighed five pounds apiece. Pine and Rosita came down the stone steps and pulled the door shut behind them. "Welcome to the Lone Star Café," I said.

We ate until we thought we'd pass out.

ROSITA TOLD US her father had been a linguist and professor of classical studies at the University of Madrid. He had also been a member of the Popular Front, and after the fall of Madrid, he and his wife and Rosita and her little brother walked across the Pyrenees into France with members of the Abraham Lincoln Brigade. In late 1943 the family was arrested by the Gestapo. The father's name was on a list of suspected Communists, and he either died in a jail cell or was tortured to death; the mother and the boy were packed into a freight car bound for Buchenwald and never seen again. Rosita was selected for duty in a camp whorehouse.

"Maybe your mother and the boy made it through," Pine said. He was sitting against a wood post, his stomach full, his eyes sleepy. "It's not going to be long before the Russians are in Berlin. You can pert' near count on it."

"My brother was killed the second day after his arrival. My mother died three weeks later."

"How could you know that?" he asked.

"An SS colonel checked. He wanted to impress me with his honesty and his access to information. He had me play piano at a dinner he gave. He wanted me to be his mistress. He poured me a glass of wine when he told me what he had learned of my family."

"What did you do?" Pine said.

"I spat the wine in his face," she replied.

We heard heavy footsteps on the wood floor immediately above our heads. We sat frozen in the dark, breathing through our mouths, looking up the stairs. Then the door opened. A tall man stood on the landing, a lantern in his left hand, its oily yellow glow bouncing on our faces. A Schmeisser submachine gun hung on a strap from his right shoulder; his thick fingers, half-mooned with dirt, were clutched on the pistol grip. Rosita stood up, her hands in the air, and spoke to him in German. He walked halfway down the wood steps, lifting the lantern higher. He was wearing snow-caked boots and corduroy trousers and a leather coat seamed with cracks and lined with sheep's wool. His beard and hair were as wild as a lion's mane. He said something in reply, his eyes blazing.

"How about a translation?" I said.

"I told him who we were and that we were sorry for entering his house without permission," Rosita said. "I told him that Americans in large numbers would be here soon and they would reward anyone who helped us."

"What did he say?" I asked.

"That we shouldn't have stolen from him," she replied.

Chapter 5

OUR GLOWERING HOST turned out to be a Jehovah's Witness named Armin Bauer. He had been jailed as a pacifist and his Mongoloid son had been gassed during Hitler's racial purification program. Two days before our arrival, he and his wife, Charlotte, hid in a cave while the SS were in the area; they had returned home just after we took refuge in their cellar. For eight days they let us stay in their cellar and fed us and washed our clothes and heated water in pots on a woodstove so we could bathe. They gave us bottles of home-made beer and a plate of bread slices slathered with jam, treats I suspected they rarely allowed themselves. I tried to ask Armin where he had gotten the Schmeisser, but he refused to say.

Charlotte was a jolly, bovine person with upper arms as big as hams and blond braids she tied on top of her head. In view of the hardship and loss that had been imposed on her family, I was amazed at her good nature; finally, I asked her, through Rosita, about its source. She held up seven fingers and pointed at the back-yard. Then she drew a finger across her throat. She looked at me and said something in German and laughed.

"She says she gave the Wehrmacht soldiers some bread and jam. With poison in it," Rosita explained. "Seven of them are buried by the barn. She wanted to know if you'd like some more bread and jam."

At night we heard bombers flying overhead, and sometimes we saw flashes of light on the horizon and seconds later heard a soft rumbling sound, more like distant thunder than bombs exploding. I couldn't tell if the planes were American or British. We'd heard that the Army Air Corps had stopped conducting only daylight raids, which cost them terrible losses; like the RAF, they had commenced flying at night, lighting the target area with incendiaries.

It felt unnatural to be a spectator in the war and not a participant. We were being sheltered and cared for by people who would be summarily executed if we were discovered in their cellar. We were eating their food, burning their fuel, sleeping on the blankets and quilts they gave us, and in Rosita's case, wearing their clothes (the wife had given her a pair of trousers, a warm jacket, kneesocks, and a cute fur hat). The cellar was warm and dry, and we could sleep as much as we wanted, or stay up late at night and talk, the way people talk around campfires when their newfound companionship allows them to put aside pretense about their lives. It was a respite that I didn't feel I deserved. West of us, my countrymen were still dying. Sometimes when I fell asleep on my pallet with a quilt pulled over my head, the preserve jars on the cellar shelves would begin rattling, and I knew that someone who had taken my place was huddling at the bottom of a foxhole, knees pulled up in the embryonic position, trying to control his sphincter while German 88s were demonstrating what a firestorm was all about.

On the eighth night, the reverberations of the artillery shells were stronger, the clouds on the eastern horizon flickering with light from the ground. Pine was sound asleep at the back of the cellar, behind the stairs. Rosita was sitting on her pallet, her back to the wall, glancing up each time the house trembled.

"You never hear the one that gets you," I said. "At least that's what survivors say."

"Is it true?"

"I don't think it is. An eighty-eight-millimeter comes in like a train. You can hear it powering out of the sky. One of ours, a 105, sounds like automobile tires coming toward you at high speed on a wet highway. The sound can come right into your foxhole with the shell attached."

"Are you going back to the war?"

"I don't have a lot of say about that. I'd like to finish it, though."

"Why do you always address me as Miss Rosita?"

"Because in the American South, you don't call a lady by her first name without expressing a form of deference. You're obviously a lady. Actually, you're a little more than that. You don't belong in a category."

"You should go back home if you have the opportunity. You would be a very good university teacher." Then she seemed to revisit my last remark. "I am not categorical? That is an unbelievable thing to say to a woman."

She had gained weight, and the shadows had gone out of her cheeks. The cast in her eyes was unchanged, however. It was different from what survivors of the Great War called the thousand-yard stare. I had seen that. The eyes were unseeing, as though someone had clicked off a switch inside the person's head, shutting down his faculties. The expression was glazed, the facial muscles dead. None of these applied to Rosita. The look in her eyes was acceptance; she had seen the evil her fellow humans were capable of, and she did not try to find explanations for it. She also knew that few would want to believe the events she had witnessed, and her attempts to describe them would only make her a pariah. The truth would not make her free; it would become her prison.

"Lieutenant, you make me uncomfortable when you look at me like that."

"I'm sorry."

"Do I still remind you of a woman outlaw?"

"We grow them tough in Texas."

"I don't know what that means."

I got up from my pallet and sat next to her. My proximity seemed to make her flinch inside, though I had carried her in my arms for days. Her face was inches from mine. "The woman outlaw represented something greater than herself. When people's homes in Kansas and

West Texas and Oklahoma were being tractored out, a few outlaws fought back. In reality, Bonnie Parker was a murderer and treated my grandfather with disrespect, and that's why I shot at her."

"I'm a symbol of other people? How degrading."

"No, not a symbol. You have a huge soul. It dwarfs the souls of others. It certainly dwarfs mine. I've never seen eyes like yours. They're the color of sherry with light shining through it. You're the kind of woman who's beautiful inside a camera's lens no matter what pose she takes."

I hadn't meant to say the things I did. My cheeks were hot, my throat dry.

"You're a romantic," she said. "I think you see things in others that don't exist. You might be a famous writer one day."

"You winked at me, didn't you?"

"I did *what*?"

"When you said *Viva la República* and *No pasarán*."

"Like this?" she said.

I felt chills all over.

EARLY THE NEXT day Charlotte ran down the cellar steps, waving her arms. Before Rosita could translate, Charlotte threw open the cellar door and pointed joyously at the bluest, most beautiful sky I had ever seen.

"Better come look at this," I said to the sergeant, who was shaving with Armin's straight razor in a pan of water.

He walked up behind me into the sunlight shining through the door. "Great God in the morning!" he said.

The sky was filled with khaki-colored C-47s, more than I had ever seen, hundreds if not thousands of parachutes blooming one after another from one horizon to another. Three American paratroopers came down right behind the barn, rolling with the impact, then collapsing and gathering up their chutes. Pine and Rosita and I and our hosts went into the yard, the grass green and soggy, snow melting and sliding down the barn roof. A paratrooper came down forty feet from us and began pulling his chute from a mud puddle.

"Where the hell have you guys been?" Pine said.

"You know how it is, Mack. The traffic can be a bitch," he said.

FOR SOME REASON the German army was always praised for its efficiency and its practicality and even, by some, its ruthlessness. Their occupation of an area left no one in doubt about who was in charge. Their methodology was as subtle as a hobnailed boot stepping on an anthill. Unfortunately, unlike Roman imperialists, they didn't have a culture that transferred readily to the subjects of the countries they conquered.

The cultural and social changes caused by the United States Army's occupation of an area, for good or bad, were immediate, overwhelming, and almost cartoonish. The cultural assimilation that usually took place was mind-numbing. Fully equipped field hospitals were in business in hours, showers and sit-down latrines were built, water tankers and ambulances and long convoys of deuce-and-a-half trucks showed up out of nowhere. GIs played touch football in a pasture pockmarked by shell fire; they jitterbugged in a café with local girls who, days earlier, were thought to be the enemy, a Benny Goodman record playing on a hand-crank Victrola.

I should have been overjoyed to be back among my own. At first I was. Then I felt my initial happiness begin to fade, as though I were about to step aboard a passenger train that would take me away from home. The following day I couldn't find Rosita. I asked Pine where she was.

"Some guys from G-2 were talking to her," he said.

"What does G-2 want with Rosita?"

"Search me, sir," he said. "They caught some SS in Wehrmacht uniforms. Some of the women guards in those camps have posed as inmates."

"G-2 thinks she's an imposter?"

"She's probably okay, Loot."

"When did you last see her?"

"An hour ago. They put her on a truck with some other women."

"Why didn't you tell me?"

"Sir, the doc says I'm going to lose a couple of toes. I probably won't be seeing you for a while."

We were standing in the sunshine outside a mess tent, the wind ballooning the canvas top. I looked at the lean cut of his jaw and the moral clarity in his eyes and regretted my anger. I couldn't quite accept the fact that we were parting.

"You'll be headed back to Louisiana."

"Yes, sir, I will. I owe you, Lieutenant."

"It doesn't work that way. We do our job and go home, and then we eventually forget about all this."

He was shaking his head before I finished speaking. "We're going to be rich men, sir. I know everything there is to know about pipelining. I was hustling skids on the pipeline when I was thirteen years old. It'll take some capital, but we'll pull it off."

"I'm afraid I'm not connecting here."

"Know the secret to the Tiger tank's structural success? It's the rolled-steel and electro-welding process. When the war is done, the big peacetime score will be in oil and natural gas. That means pipelines, thousands and thousands of miles of them, all over the country. Oil might as well stay in the ground if you cain't get it to the refinery."

"I'm sure you're correct," I said.

"You all right, sir?"

"Never better," I said, looking at a deuce-and-half driving down the road, the back loaded with prisoners who may have been SS in civilian clothes.

I RECEIVED TREATMENT FOR frostbite but nothing else. I rejoined the regiment and stayed with it all the way to the Elbe River, where we met the Russians on April 25, 1945. We got wonderfully drunk with them. We punched holes in canned beer with our bayonets, and the Russians drained the fuel from the rockets at a nearby V-2 base. In the morning we woke up with hangovers and the Russians woke up dead.

I thought my hangover would fade as the day warmed and the

flowers opened along the banks of the Elbe and the hilarity of the previous night slipped into memory, left behind with all the other departures from sanity that wars allow us to justify. I had never been much of a drinker and thought the weakness in my joints and the spots that swam before my eyes were the result of exposing an inexperienced metabolism to too much alcohol. By evening I began to sweat, and my hair was sopping wet and cold as ice in the wind, and I entered the first stages of a hacking cough that I believed was either bronchitis or walking pneumonia.

There was no transition in the progression of my illness. By nightfall I was burning up and doubling over each time I coughed. I wrote in my notebook, *I feel like there's a chunk of angle iron in my chest. Maybe I'll be better in the morning. No word about Rosita. A captain in G-2 said many Jewish survivors were being placed in displaced persons camps, but he could find no record of her. I think of her constantly. I see her eyes in my sleep. The coloration and the inner light that shows through them are like none I have ever seen. I don't think I will be able to rest until I find her.*

I just coughed blood on my hand.

A medic came into my tent in the morning and took my temperature and placed a stethoscope on my chest. He was a tall, bony kid from Alabama and said he had worked in an X-ray unit in a Mobile hospital before he enlisted. He hung the earpieces to the stethoscope on his neck. "Is there a history of respiratory problems in your family, Lieutenant?" he asked.

"As a matter of fact, there is."

"You smoke a lot?"

"Never took it up. What are we talking about, Doc?"

"You're wheezing like a busted hose in there, sir."

"We're not talking about pneumonia, are we?"

"No, sir, we're not." He lifted his eyes into mine. "There's a new drug available that's supposed to work miracles."

Chapter 6

THE TUBERCULAR UNIT was in a converted eighteenth-century French mansion in vineyard country, one with a wide stone porch that allowed a wonderful view of the gardens and poplar trees and the low green hills in the distance and a meandering river and the white stucco farmhouses with red Spanish tile where the owners of the vineyards lived. The miracle drug I was given was called streptomycin. I took other forms of medication, too, but I do not remember their names. In the drowsy warmth of the breeze on an August afternoon, I would sleep the sleep of the dead, with no desire to wake up.

I had no dreams of the war, as though it had been airbrushed from my memory. I wrote in my notebook, *If I allow myself to feel, I will drop through a hole in the bottom of my stomach and begin to fall into a place from which I will not return.* If I dreamed at all, it was of my boyhood home, where I had lived with my mother and grandfather. Sometimes I dreamed of the pets we had owned, and the windmill creaking in the breeze at night, and the way the rains had returned in the form of gulley washers, our pastures blooming with bluebonnets and Indian paintbrush after years of drought.

But I did not dream of the war or hear the sounds that always accompany dreams about war. Perhaps this was due to the narcotics humming in my bloodstream along with the streptomycin, although I never asked what was being put into my system. The wooden wheelchair in which I sat, with its woven bamboo backrest, had become my friend. The countryside was a re-creation of medieval Europe, snipped out of time, the valleys cultivated, the grass on the hilltops golden in the sun, more like southern Spain than France. On a mountain not far away were the softly molded biscuit-colored ruins of a castle. A nurse told me it had been built by Crusader knights, and according to legend, a great treasure was hidden in its stone walls. *The Song of Roland* had found me of its own accord.

On a singularly hot day, I took my medication and fell asleep on the porch. I could feel raindrops striking my skin like confetti, but I didn't wake up. I felt a nurse wheel me to a dry place under the overhang, though I never raised my head. I was inside a chemical environment that was warm and cool at the same time; the air smelled of flowers and rain spotting on warm stone. When I woke, the sky had turned to orange sherbet, and I thought I could see Knights Templar wending their way on horseback up the hill to the castle, the sunlight melting on their armor. Perhaps I was becoming the prisoner of a pernicious drug. The truth was, I didn't care.

Mail was delivered early each morning. Somehow I felt one of my many attempts to find Rosita Lowenstein would be rewarded. I received APO letters from friends and my mother and other relatives. I also heard from Hershel Pine, who was back in the States. But there was no word from anyone about Rosita.

After breakfast I read the newspapers in the hospital dayroom and played checkers with a man whose left lung had been removed, which caused him to sit sideways in his chair as though his spine were broken. In a side room I could see a man inside an iron lung, a nurse placing a teaspoon of ice in his mouth. I went back to my bed and put the pillow over my face, trying not to think about the type of surgery that might be awaiting me. I thought I could smell an odor like wild poppies on the wind. Soon I drifted off to sleep and dreamed of a boxlike automobile that contained four individuals who had just robbed a bank and were heavily armed and dangerous. I opened my eyes and looked at the silhouette of a tall American officer dressed in suntans.

He was wearing aviator glasses. His hair had a metallic tone and was cut short and wet-combed, his skin sun-browned. He removed his glasses and placed them in a case. He snapped the case shut and slipped it into his shirt pocket, before letting his eyes settle on me. Major Lloyd Fincher was an officer who thought in terms of first things first. "Getting a little extra shut-eye?" he said.

"How you doin', sir?" I said.

"I'm back at Division now. Pretty nice deal, actually." He nodded and looked around as though agreeing with himself or indicating approval of the surroundings. "The nurses treating you okay?"

"They're fine."

"I'm quartered right outside Paris. It's quite the place in peacetime. Paris, I mean. French ladies love a liberator. You have to fly the flag, though."

"I'm hoping I won't be here much longer."

"I just approved your nomination for the Silver Star. We were a little slow on the paperwork. That'll give you three Hearts and the Bronze and Silver Star."

"Silver Star for what?"

"Gallantry in action at the Ardennes. You might think about going into politics when you get home. Or insurance. You know I run an agency in San Antonio, don't you?"

"I don't remember a lot of what happened at the Ardennes."

"Others do. That's what counts. For a promising young fellow like yourself, it won't hurt to have the right cachet."

I couldn't track what he was saying. Maybe that was because his gaze never really focused on me. While he talked, his eyes were constantly roaming around the room. He dragged up a chair and sat down. "Are you listening?"

"I was never keen on politics," I said.

"That's because you're a warrior." He was holding a manila folder on his thigh. His gaze followed a nurse. "We had some times, didn't we? You should come to Paris and enjoy the fruits of victory."

"It's a long drive down here, Major. I appreciate your coming."

"I thought we'd be in the Pacific now. Frankly, I was looking forward to it. You know Japs can't pronounce the 'l' sound, right? One of them starts hollering out in the dark, 'Hey, Joe, I'm hit! Help me!'

Then one of our guys hollers 'lollapalooza' or 'Little Lulu.' If the Jap doesn't yell 'Lily lollipop,' he gets hosed with a flamethrower. The marines are still burning them out of caves on Iwo." His eyes steadied and looked into mine. "You knew a camp survivor named Rosita Lowenstein?"

"I was in hiding with her."

"Hold on a minute. You were not in 'hiding' with her. You saved her life."

"Sergeant Hershel Pine and I saved her life. She helped us save ours, too, at least when she could. The people who hid us didn't speak English. Rosita did all the talking for us."

"Yeah, that's all in the file. But you know her, right? We're talking about the same person? Rosita Lowenstein? A Spanish Jewess?"

I didn't answer him. He opened the manila folder and removed several sheets of paper and read the top one to himself. "You don't need this kind of trouble, partner."

"Where is she?"

"That's not important. Some people think our next war is going to be with the Russkies. Some people think we'd have been better off allying with the Germans in 1940 and attacking Russia. Not everybody in the camps was there because they were Jews."

"I'm not following you," I said.

"Did she indicate to you that she might be a Communist?"

"She said she didn't have any use for Communists."

"According to both British and American intelligence, her father was a Communist representative in the Spanish parliament."

"So what?"

"She's related to Rosa Luxemburg."

I looked at him, my face empty, my eyes flat.

"You don't know who that is?"

"Not offhand," I lied.

"She was a German Communist known as Red Rosa. A bunch of brownshirts beat her to death and threw her body in a river. Red Rosa's mother was named Löwenstein. That girl you toted for miles probably gave you TB. Don't let her mess you up twice, son."

"Do you know where she is?"

"At a displaced persons camp not far from Nancy. She's probably trying to get to Palestine. That's how the Brits became interested in her."

"How can I contact her?"

The major replaced the sheaf of papers in the manila folder and rolled the folder into a cone. He tapped me on the chest with it. "They'll make mincemeat of you, boy. There's justification for their actions, too. We didn't fight a war in two theaters so Red spies could infest our system and use our constitutional guarantees to destroy us. These people are vermin."

"Say that again?"

His eyes went away from mine, his cheeks pooling with color. He got up to go. "I've got to run," he said. He picked up my hand from the bed and shook it. "I get hot-blooded sometimes. I suspect you had sexual congress with the Lowenstein woman and feel you owe her. Do the smart thing. Go back home and be a war hero. Smile a lot. Be humble. People will love you for it. Don't get them mad at you."

"You called her vermin? Or did I misunderstand?"

He put his aviator glasses back on. "I hope she's worth it. Come see me in San Antone if you want to learn the insurance business."

IN OCTOBER, UPON my discharge from the hospital, I went to the displaced persons camp east of Nancy, close to the German border. I had written perhaps ten requests for information about Rosita Lowenstein to the camp's administration, but I had never received a reply. When I arrived, I understood why. Many of the people housed there looked like shells of people. Many had numbers tattooed on their left forearm. Some stared through the wire fence with the vacant expressions of schizophrenics. Their common denominator seemed to be a pathological form of detachment; they seemed to have no continuity as a group, as though they didn't know one another and didn't care to. I saw none who appeared to be mothers with children, or children with mothers, or husbands with wives. I suspected that many of them were ridden with guilt because they had survived and their loved ones had not; I suspected that many of them would never tell anyone of the deeds they had witnessed in the camps or the deeds they themselves had committed when they were forced to choose between survival and perishing.

I saw a man wearing a white shirt with blown sleeves. His arms were spread on the fence wire as he stared into my face. His eyes were as white and shiny as the skin of a peeled hard-boiled egg, the pupils like distorted ink drops, his hair black and curly and uncut, his skin leathery, his teeth showing in either defiance or fear. He reminded me of the Christlike figure in the Goya painting titled *The Third of May 1808: The Execution of the Defenders of Madrid.* As a matter of politeness, I said hello. He made no reply. His chin was tilted upward, a question mark in the middle of his face, as though he were daring me to explain what had happened to him. I tried to hold his gaze but couldn't. I walked away, his recrimination hanging on me like sackcloth.

Rosita was nowhere to be seen. "Where is she?" I asked the clerk in the administration building.

"She left last week," he said.

"Where to?"

The clerk was sitting behind a vintage typewriter, his desk piled with paper. He was an international relief worker and spoke English with a British accent. "Are you a family member?"

"No. I pulled her out of a stack of dead bodies and carried her through an artillery barrage. I hid in a cellar with her for eight days."

"Ah, you're the one. She told me about you," he said. "She's in Marseilles."

"Do you have an address?"

"She's in a pension. It's run by a Jewish relocation group." He wrote an address on a piece of paper and handed it to me. "They have no telephone there. Do you plan to go to Marseilles?"

"Yes."

"If I remember correctly, she leaves today or tomorrow on a freighter. It's headed for Haifa," he said. "Good luck. I'm sorry we were not able to help you earlier."

"Was she sick?"

"No worse than anyone else here."

I CAUGHT A TRAIN that night to Marseilles. There was rain all the way to the coast. The chair car was crowded and overheated from a coal-burning stove and smelled of unwashed bodies and damp wool. The dawn was bleak when we pulled into the station, the sun little more than a pewterlike glow on the horizon, the railroad ties and rails in the yards shiny with waste that had been dumped from the passenger toilets onto the tracks. I brushed my teeth and shaved with cold water in the station and hired a cab to take me to the address of the pension given me by the clerk in the displaced persons camp.

It was located four blocks from the harbor on a decrepit cobbled street where most of the buildings had been pocked by small-arms fire. I could see two large rusting freighters lying on their sides by the entrance to the harbor, their screws in the air. The pension was three stories high and made of stucco and had a dirt courtyard in back and two balconies strung with wash. I could hear children playing beyond the courtyard wall. A solitary palm tree extended above the wall, its fronds yellow and serrated by the wind.

I gave the concierge Rosita's name and waited, my heart thudding, as though I had labored up a hillside only to discover that the air was too thin to breathe. The concierge's body was swollen with fat, her black dress almost ripping on her hips. Her eyes were as cautious and intense as a hawk's. "*Je suis un ami,*" I said.

"What do you want with her?" she replied in English.

"To see her."

Her eyes dropped to my lieutenant's bars. "The Americans machine-gunned my building. There were no Germans here. They robbed and destroyed the houses down the street."

"I'm sorry," I said.

"*Boche, les Américains, ils sont la même chose.*"

She gave me a dirty look before walking heavily up the stairs, her back bent, her hand clenching tightly on the banister. A moment later, Rosita came down the stairs. She was wearing a white skirt that went to her calves, with a frill on the hem, and a lavender peasant blouse. Her hair was thick and full of lights and cut short on her neck. She looked absolutely radiant. "Hey, kid," I said.

"Hello, Weldon," she said. "How did you know where I was? I've tried since March to find you."

"A major in my outfit told me you were in Nancy. I went there yesterday and took the train here last night."

"Your commanding officer knew where I was?"

"Don't worry about the major. Let's go to breakfast," I said.

"I leave for Palestine by boat tomorrow."

Outside, the sun had broken through a cloud and was shining on the cobblestones, slick with rain. "We can talk about that."

"Talk about it?" she said, looking up into my face.

"There are lots of options in this world. You have to open up your parameters. Why limit yourself to one or two choices?"

She started to speak, but I didn't let her. I put my arm around her shoulders and walked her with me out the door and down to a café whose windows were steamed with heat.

WE HAD YOGURT and smoked fish and freshly baked bread and marmalade and rolled butter, and coffee and sugar and hot milk, all the things you didn't believe you'd ever be able to buy again in a European café. Rosita's skin seemed to glow in the warmth of the café. Her hair had lightened during the summer months, and the streaks of brown in it had a gold cast that made me want to reach out and touch them. "Come to Paris with me," I said.

"I have to be on the freighter by nine A.M."

"I don't think that's a good idea."

She looked away from me and smiled. "Do you know how difficult it was to get passage on that ship?"

"What's in Haifa?"

"A new life. Maybe a new nation in the making."

"I want you to meet someone. We'll leave for Paris in two hours."

"Meet whom?"

"You'll find out when we get there."

"Do you realize how presumptuous you're being?"

"You're going, Rosita."

"It's been very good of you to come here. You're a fine man. We'll always be friends. But you should not be a romantic about these things. You shouldn't dictate to others, either."

"There are other boats to Haifa. We're going to Paris. We'll go back to the pension and pack your things. Then we'll go to the train station." I didn't know how long I could brass it out. My heart felt like a lump of lead. "Rosita?"

"What?" she said irritably.

I took her hand and held it on top of the table and did not let go of it. "You're the one," I said.

"One what?"

"You know what I mean. If things don't work out, I'll take you to Haifa myself. I give you my word of honor."

I GOT US A compartment for the trip to Paris. We pulled out of the station at 10:46 A.M. and were within sight of the Eiffel Tower at twilight.

"Where is this person I'm supposed to meet?" she asked.

"At the Jardin des Tuileries. Come on, he's quite a fellow."

"Where are we supposed to stay?"

"At a hotel on the Left Bank."

"How do you know Paris?"

"I was here the day we liberated it. I met Ernest Hemingway here. He bought me a drink in the bar at the Ritz. I'll take you there."

"I can't believe I've done this."

"You're going to love this friend of mine."

I hailed a cab in front of the train station. We got in the backseat, and she felt my forehead, then her own.

"Why did you do that?" I asked.

"I wondered if you might have a form of brain fever. Or if perhaps I do."

At the Tuileries I paid the driver and took our suitcases out of the cab and set them down on the walkway that led into the gardens.

The air was damp and cold and smelled of the sewers by the Seine and the sodden leaves of the chestnut and maple trees that stained the fountains and stone benches. The light had gone out of the sky, and I could feel the temperature dropping. The autumnal odor on the wind seemed to presage more than a change in the season; it spoke of a winter that had no April on the other side of it; it spoke of the way the world had been since September 1, 1939.

"Where is your friend?" she asked.

"He's coming."

She had tied a scarf on her head. She looked up and down the walkway. "I think we should go. I think perhaps both of us have acted foolishly."

"Look yonder," I said, pointing. "He's a little eccentric, but he's a man of his word."

The figure approaching us wore a cowl and had a face that was a cross between a Canterbury pilgrim's and a goat's. He walked with a thin cane and wore oversize shoes and baggy pants and probably could have been called Chaplinesque. His teeth were purple with wine. He smiled broadly at Rosita and bowed.

"This is Father Sasoon. He's not formally a 'father' any longer, but he's still called one out of respect," I said.

"Bonsoir, mademoiselle," Father Sasoon said.

"He's a defrocked priest?" she said.

"I think that's the term normally used."

"Defrocked for what?" she said.

"I've always been afraid to ask," I said. "Father, let me have a word or two with Rosita, then we'll take the next step."

"As you wish, my friend," he said.

I reached into my coat pocket and took out a small felt-covered box. "This belonged to my grandmother. My mother gave it to me just before I shipped out. She said, 'If you meet the right girl, give her this.'"

"You're asking me to marry you?"

"That's one way of looking at it. I actually think it's already a done deal."

"A *what*?"

"You're the most magnificent woman I've ever known. I've never seen eyes like yours. I've never known anyone as brave. Since last March, I've had you in my mind every minute of every day. You think I'm just going to walk away? That's a ridiculous idea."

"You know almost nothing about me."

"I know everything about you. You radiate light. You're unafraid. You probably have an IQ of over 160." I took the ring out of the box. It was set with two diamonds and two sapphires. "How about it, Rosita? You could get stuck with worse than me. You'll love Texas. I was thinking about getting us a place down on the Gulf. It's like the Riviera without the riffraff."

And that's where and how we got married, between the Louvre and the Place de la Concorde, not far from the tomb of Napoleon and the bells Quasimodo swung on, in the last week of October 1945, in a European city where the ashes from chimney pots rose into the sky, perhaps as a reminder of the past or as a harbinger of the future.

Chapter 7

By Christmas Eve of the same year I had been processed out of the army and we had taken up residence at Grandfather's ranch. At sunrise the fields and the barn and trees had been limed with frost, the stock tank by the windmill glazed with ice. As the sun rose higher into a flawless blue sky, the day warmed and the trees began ticking with water; steam rose from the tank and squirrels began racing about in the pecan orchard. It was another fine winter day in a land where all four seasons could visit us within a week's duration. From the front porch I watched a Western Union messenger come up the dirt road on a service cycle. He dismounted and pulled his goggles up on his face with his thumb, the skin white around his eyes. "Beautiful day, huh, Mr. Holland?" he said.

"None better," I said.

I tipped him and sat down on the steps and opened the telegram and read it. There are moments when you make decisions that seem inconsequential. Later you discover that your life has been changed in an inalterable way by a choice as arbitrary as not dropping a message in a drawer and forgetting about it. I reread the telegram, then folded it and stuck it in my shirt pocket. Let go of the past, I told myself.

Unfortunately, upon my return to civilian life, I had entered a troubling period marked by indecision and depression. At my age, the idea of sitting in a classroom and listening to a professor lecture on books I had probably already read did not seem very appealing. Also, I had begun to dream every third or fourth night about the war. I didn't tell Rosita about my dreams, nor did I mention them to my mother or to Grandfather. One night I sleepwalked into the kitchen and woke up only when Rosita turned on the light. I was at the breakfast table, my ears roaring with the sound of tank treads, Grandfather's ancient pistol in my hand.

Now Rosita was sitting behind me in a rocker. She was wearing jeans and half-top suede boots I had bought her, a magazine on her lap.

"Want to take a ride to Kerrville?" I said.

"What for?" she asked.

"Hershel Pine is coming in on the bus and wants to get together," I replied.

"Is he all right?"

It wasn't an unreasonable question, considering the times. The revisionists had not had adequate time to rewrite our recent history, and for many of us who had been participants, who knew war for the dirty business it was, resuming old relationships was sometimes another way of keeping the wounds green.

I took the telegram from my pocket and unfolded it and looked again at the words pasted in strips across the pale yellow paper. "He says, 'Told you I would pay you back.' "

IT TOOK AN hour and a half on the old road, most of it unpaved, to reach the café in Kerrville that served as the bus stop for our intrastate line. When Hershel stepped down from the bus, he was wearing an ill-fitting suit, the kind you could buy off a Robert Hall rack for twelve dollars, and a clip-on bow tie and brown shoes that didn't go with the suit. The backs of his hands were tanned and freckled, the top of his forehead pale from wearing a hat in the sun.

He carried a cardboard tube and a suitcase held together with a belt. "Y'all are a sight for sore eyes," he said. "The docs took off three of my toes. I could go the rest of my life without seeing snow again. How you like Texas, Miss Rosita?"

"Just call me Rosita, Hershel. It's very nice to see you again," she said. "We've thought of you often."

"That's kind of you," he said. He hadn't shaken hands and clearly felt awkward. He set down his suitcase and stuck out his hand to Rosita, then to me, his face coloring.

I patted him on the shoulder. "What do you have there in the tube?"

"Designs," he replied.

"Why do you keep looking at the bus?" I asked.

"A peculiar fellow was sitting in the back," he replied. "Maybe I've got a permanent case of the heebie-jeebies. That's what my wife says."

"Let me help you with your bag," I said.

"That's him now, that tall unshaved guy going into the café. I'd swear his eyes were burning holes in the back of my neck."

"He looks like a regular guy to me, Hershel."

"Maybe so. Linda Gail, that's my wife, she says I'm a worrywart."

"What are the designs?" I asked.

"I'll show them to you when we can relax. Boy, the sky out here is sure big."

I wondered how long it would take for the subject of money to come up.

BUT I WAS unfair to Hershel. He was obviously happy to see us, and filled with childlike curiosity about everything he saw on the drive to the ranch. I suspected the paintless Victorian home and six hundred acres I associated with "genteel poverty" was the equivalent of a kingdom to him. As soon as he set down his suitcase in the hallway, he went into the dining room and asked permission to spread the rolls from his tube on the table, as though he had to justify his presence in our home.

"What you're looking at is the diagram for the welding machine that created the Tiger tank, Loot," he said. "See, the Germans were two or three steps ahead of the process we use. They tacked together homogenous rolled nickel-steel plates that nothing short of a point-blank hit from an antitank shell could crack. You with me so far?"

"I think so," I said.

I could see Grandfather looking at us from the kitchen, his expression bemused. He was almost ninety, his eyes like blue milk, his calves swollen into eggplants.

"Before the war, we were still laying natural gas pipe bolted together at the joint, Lieutenant," Hershel said. "I've got seventeen of these German arc welding machines located. It's just a matter of transporting them into the country. I got a deal on a fleet of army-surplus flatbeds, too."

"It's Weldon," I said.

"Yes, sir. I can get us German steel that we can use as center cutters on our own ditching machines. The next step is obtaining patents for the modifications on the arc welders. Sir, you have no idea how big this can be."

I nodded. "There's a hurdle we haven't gotten to yet, isn't there?"

"Yes, sir. A big one. We need thirty, maybe forty thousand dollars to get out of the chute." He looked straight ahead, his face tight.

Rosita was standing between us, gazing at the designs of the welding machines. "Who are the people selling you the machines?"

"Krauts," he said.

"Were they members of the Nazi Party?" she said.

He kept his eyes on the table. "They could have been. I didn't ask. For me, the war is over, Miss Rosita."

"I've got an uncle who's a wildcatter," I said.

I heard Grandfather work his way into the room on his walking canes. "Satchel, did you sustain an appreciable amount of brain damage while you were over there?" he said.

WE ATE DINNER late that night, and Rosita said little at the table. Upstairs, she put on her nightgown and lay down on the mattress and turned on the bed lamp. It was ceramic, its white glaze painted with green and purple flowers. She touched the flowers with the tips of her fingers.

"Is something bothering you?" I asked.

"Those machines have blood on them."

"They're just machines. They're neither good nor bad."

"You've given up your plans to enter graduate school, haven't you?"

I didn't answer.

"You have the soul of a poet," she said. "You'd be a wonderful teacher."

"The GI Bill pays eighty-five dollars a month for a married man. Can you imagine living in New York on that?"

"We can move to Austin. You can attend the state university."

"Hershel and I are going to see my uncle Cody tomorrow afternoon. I want you to come with us."

"You don't need me for this."

"I want you to understand my family. Some of them have led violent lives. I'm not like them, but that doesn't mean I don't love and admire them. Uncle Cody left home when he was twelve years old and became a vagabond. In a freight car outside St. Louis, he offered to share his food with two drifters. They thanked him by taking his food and trying to rape him. He killed both of them with a pocketknife. In New York, he was a bodyguard for Owney Madden, the man who owned the Cotton Club. Today he's a wealthy oilman. I'm going to ask him what he thinks of Hershel's plans."

"Why are you telling me all these things?"

"I'm not sure, Rosita. My family is different. We were never spectators."

She turned on her side, her back to me, her hip rounded under the sheet. Her shoulders were white and as cool and smooth to the touch as marble.

"You're not going to say anything?" I asked.

"You don't realize the gift you have."

She reached out and clicked off the lamp.

CODY HOLLAND'S RANCH, one of several he owned, was a long drive, almost to the Gulf of Mexico, a spot he'd obviously chosen to create the home and the life he had never enjoyed as a boy. It was almost dark when we passed Goliad, the site of the execution of 350 Texas soldiers under the command of James Fannin on Palm Sunday, 1836. A winter storm was building in the south as we pulled up to a brightly lit diner on the highway, within sight of Matagorda Island. The palm fronds down by the beach were whipping in the wind against a black sky that rippled with electricity.

My uncle had not invited us to his home. He was an untrusting man, unpredictable, sentimental, often controlling and quick to anger. He was also feared. Oddly, though, I had never felt uncomfortable around him. I think I saw the orphan in his eyes, because like my mother, Cody was one of the children Grandfather had let founder by the wayside.

Rosita and I and Hershel and my uncle sat in a cigarette-burned red vinyl booth in back and drank long-necked Jax beer and avoided talking business until after we had finished eating. Hershel's level of ill ease was palpable. His face had an oily shine; he constantly touched at his mouth with a folded paper napkin and rubbed his neck, as though he wore a serf's collar. "Is the fishing right good down here?" he said.

"Speckled trout and gafftop catfish, mostly," Cody said. He was built like a door. His hair was wavy and black, silver in places; he looked directly into people's faces whether they were offended or not.

"I'd like to get in on that," Hershel said. He stared down at the steak gravy and blood and pink-edged remnants of the T-bone on his plate, unable to think of anything else to say.

The waitress put the check on the edge of the table. It stayed there, absorbing the wet rings left by our beer bottles.

"What's this pipeline venture you've got in mind?" Cody asked.

In the background, somebody dropped a nickel into the jukebox. Harry Choate's famous recording of "La Jolie Blon" began playing.

"I've got a way to put pipe in the ground that will stay there a hundred years without a leak," Hershel said. "I'm talking about the same weld that held the King Tiger tank together. I was doing both tack and hot-pass welds when I was sixteen years old, Mr. Holland. It's something I always had a talent for."

"Is that a fact?" Cody said.

"Yes, sir, you can take it to the bank," Hershel said.

There was a pause. "Why don't you tell me about it?"

Hershel's passion was that of a true believer, in the same way that the Puritans saw work as a virtue and idleness as sin and failure as a preview of perdition. Hershel had probably never heard of Cotton Mather, but in a large crowd, one quickly would have recognized the other.

While Hershel talked, Cody wrote on a paper napkin. Then he shook a Lucky Strike out of a pack and lit it, looking at the figures on the napkin, without offering a cigarette to anyone else. "What's your feeling about all this, Miss Rosita?" he asked.

"How about not addressing me as though I'm a character in *Gone With the Wind*?" she replied.

Cody removed a piece of tobacco from his tongue. "You seem like an intelligent woman. I want to know what you think."

"I think Hershel is a good man. I think you're fortunate that he's come to you rather than to someone else."

"I didn't get that."

"You're rude and you're arrogant, Mr. Holland. You radiate a sense of self-satisfaction that's hard to take."

Cody tipped the ashes from his cigarette on the side of his plate. I took the dinner check from the table and put it in my pocket.

"Give me that," Cody said.

Rosita, what have you done? I thought.

"This is the way I see it," Cody said, placing the napkin he had doodled on in front of Hershel and me. "Thirty to forty thousand won't cut it. You'll need bulldozers and side booms, and you want to buy them, not rent them. At the least, you'll need seventy thousand dollars. I'll lend it to you at four percent interest. I'll need eighty percent of that to be guaranteed by collateral. Since you don't have any, you'll have to factor me in as a fifty-one-percent partner. I don't know if that suits y'all or not."

"I might have to study on that, Uncle Cody."

"You don't want a relative as your partner? You just want to borrow his money?"

"I wouldn't put it that way."

"You know who's funding the major drilling around here now?" he said. "It's not the banks; it's insurance companies. Talk to those sons of bitches."

"I'd appreciate it if you wouldn't use that language in front of my wife," I said.

He tapped the ashes off his cigarette again, his expression neutral. He looked out the window. "I wouldn't want to get caught on the highway in that storm."

"Grandfather said if we went to the bank, he'd put up the ranch as collateral. Except the ranch just isn't worth the kind of money we need."

Cody put out his cigarette on his plate. Waves were capping out on Matagorda Bay, exploding in geysers of foam against a jetty that looked like a long black spinal cord protruding from the water. "He said he'd do that?"

"Why wouldn't he?" I replied.

"Tell him it's not necessary."

"What isn't?" I asked.

"He doesn't need to put up the ranch. Not with the bank, not with me. I don't need a percentage of your company, either."

"Do we got us a deal, Mr. Holland?" Hershel said.

"You deaf, son?" Cody said. He got up from the booth and placed three ten-dollar bills by the cash register and walked out into the rain. He turned around and looked at us, the rain clicking on his hat. "Y'all want to come up to the house?"

AT SUNRISE THE next morning, I fired up the woodstove in the kitchen and began cooking a large breakfast for everyone. Grandfather was the first to come downstairs, sitting down heavily at the breakfast table, his chin razor-nicked, a piece of bloody toilet paper stuck to it. I poured him a cup of coffee and placed the cup on a saucer and set the saucer and cup in front of him. He poured coffee into the saucer and blew on it, then drank from the saucer. I had told him late the previous night of the agreement we had struck with Uncle Cody. Grandfather had said nothing in reply.

"You want a pork chop or ham with your eggs, Grandfather?" I asked.

"Whatever you're fixing."

"You're the one who has to eat it."

"How's Cody doing?"

"He sure has a pretty home."

"You got to see it?"

"He invited us over after we had supper with him. No one can call him ordinary."

"Cody doesn't forgive. He harbors resentments. I stole his childhood, Satch, just like I did your mother's."

"I don't think they see it that way," I lied.

"I want you to listen to me about the oil people you're fixing to involve yourself with. Give them the chance, they'll tear you boys up. They might be from Texas, but they're not our kind of people. They'll wave every flag they can get their hands on and tell you they're patriots. Don't be taken in. They're not political. They're just downright mean."

Chapter 8

SPRING CAME EARLY in 1946, the year that arguably marked the inception of the New American Empire, and with it came the development of our company, which Hershel insisted on naming the Dixie Belle Pipeline Company. We underbid two contractors in Louisiana, and by April we were cutting a right-of-way through wooded areas north of the Atchafalaya Basin. The night before the first weld was made on our first pipe joint, we celebrated by going to a Cajun dance hall in Opelousas.

It was hot and smoky inside the hall, ventilated by two huge window fans, the dance floor crowded, the walls scrolled with neon beer signs. Through a serving window, I could see three black men French-frying potatoes in chicken fat, their skin glistening with sweat. Hershel danced with his wife, Linda Gail, then asked Rosita to dance, and I was left alone at the table with Linda Gail. She had a small gap between her front teeth and the solid physique and round face of a farm girl; her auburn hair was full of curls that looked like springs, her eyes as serene and one-dimensional as a cloudless sky. Nonetheless, she was a pretty girl and, I suspected, more intelligent than she seemed at first glance. "Have you ever been to River Oaks?" she asked.

"In Houston?"

"That's the only River Oaks I know of. Did you ever live there?"

"No, I grew up in the country, far west of there."

"I can't imagine anybody having that much money, can you?"

"I guess some people have it and some don't."

"Hershel thinks the world of you."

"He's pretty hard to beat himself," I replied.

"He gets impressed too easily. That's how people take advantage of him."

A black man put a tray of French fries on the table. She picked up one and put it in her mouth and watched the black man walk away. "Do you think they wash their hands?"

I looked at her awkwardly.

She laughed. "Got you. You need to develop a sense of humor. Nobody in a place like this washes their hands. Oh, look, thank God, the band is taking a break. I thought my ears were going to start bleeding. You'd think they'd try to learn English, at least enough to sing a song. Will you order me a whiskey sour? I'm going to drop a nickel in the jukebox. Jesus, it's hot. A person could make a fortune selling deodorant in this place."

She walked away, pulling her blouse off her skin with the tips of her fingers and shaking it to cool herself. There were four men drinking beer at a table not far from the jukebox. Linda Gail positioned herself in front of the jukebox and read the song titles while she smoothed her dress against her hips with the heels of her hands. One of the men at the table got up and stood behind her. He wore a soiled dress shirt and a beat-up fedora and was unshaved and had a long face and narrow shoulders. Linda Gail propped one arm on top of the jukebox and leaned down, as though examining the selections more closely, the orange and green and red glow of the plastic casing marbling the tops of her breasts.

"This is quite a place," Hershel said when he and Rosita returned to the table. "Where's Linda Gail?"

I could see the tall man looking down at Linda Gail's breasts, his three friends at the table enjoying the show. "I think she went to the ladies' room," I said.

"I guess we have to get up pretty early tomorrow," Hershel said. "Y'all had enough for tonight?"

"Linda Gail said she wanted a whiskey sour."

"She likes mixed drinks, all right. Growing up in the Assemblies of God has a way of doing that to you."

I saw Linda Gail turn from the jukebox and head back toward us. "Let's have one more round, then go," I said.

I have always believed that women have a much more accurate sense about other women than we do. I think the same is true of men: We know things about our own kind that women do not. The things we know are not good, either. There are feral creatures among our gender, throwbacks to an earlier time, and as a man, you know this as soon as you are in their proximity. For that reason I have never subscribed to the notion that we all descend from the same tree. There are gatherers and there are hunters. The inclination of the latter is always in their eyes.

The waitress brought us another round. Linda Gail sipped her drink, her eyes roving around the dance hall. "Hershel promised to take me to Mexico City to see a bullfight," she said. "But here we sit."

Hershel scraped his thumbnail on the label of his beer bottle. "We'll be going there directly. You'll see," he said.

She lifted her gaze toward the ceiling, as though barely able to suppress her exasperation. She looked at Rosita. "Do they have bullfights where you come from?"

"Yes, in Spain there are many bullfights. But I've never seen one," Rosita said.

"Why not?"

"I guess I never had the opportunity."

"You think they're cruel?" Linda Gail said. Without waiting for a reply, she said, "If I was a bull, I'd rather die that way than be ground into hamburger. Well, Mexico City awaits us, if we can get out of this mud hole. I thought Bogalusa was bad."

Hershel drained his beer glass. "Let's hit the road. I'm going to officially burn the first stringer-bead rod at 0800. Watch out, Standard Oil. Here comes the Dixie Belle Pipeline Company."

I saw the man in the fedora approaching our table. His sleeves were rolled up to his elbows, exposing the tattoos on his forearms.

We had made a serious mistake in granting Linda Gail's request for one more whiskey sour. "Howdy," he said.

I looked up into his face. It was furrowed and grainy and as brown as a tobacco leaf, his eyes playful. Hershel's back faced him. "How you doin'?" I said.

"Are y'all visiting?" he asked.

"No, we're not," I replied.

One of the buttons on his shirt was missing, and I could see the flatness of his stomach and a black swatch of his chest hair. There was a soapy yellow cast in his shirt, as though it had been washed in a lavatory.

"Let me know if you need anything," he said.

"We will," I said.

"I'm from here'bouts," he said.

"I had that sense," I said.

Hershel turned his head and looked up at the tall man, then back at me, his gaze locked on mine.

"Well, let's get on it," I said. I stood up and pulled back Rosita's chair. I could feel the tall man's eyes peeling off the side of my face.

"You don't have to run," he said. "The band is gonna be playing three more hours. You ought to have some more of those taters cooked in chicken fat. They oil you up."

"You know how it is when everything is early to bed and early to rise," Linda Gail said, fixing her dress.

I wasn't sure if she was mocking him or us.

"I hope you're not rushing off because of me," he said. "I just wanted to say howdy. People say howdy to visitors where y'all come from, don't they?"

"Yeah, we do. Then we say adios," I said.

We went outside into the coolness of the night, under a canopy of stars. Out in the darkness were piney woods, and dirt roads lined with live oak trees and thousands of acres of green sugarcane, and a gigantic swampland that smelled of spawning fish and drilling rigs that leaked natural gas like soda bubbles.

"I know that guy," Hershel whispered as we walked toward the car.

I started to look over my shoulder.

"Don't turn around," Hershel said. "He and his friends are behind us. He was the guy on the bus when you picked me up in Kerrville."

"Are you sure?"

"I remember his tattoos. He's got a naked woman on his left forearm."

"Hold up there!" the tall man said.

We put Rosita and Linda Gail in the car and closed the doors. The tall man and his friends were walking toward us, crunching across the gravel. "I just wanted to tell you something," he said to Hershel. He put a cigarette in his mouth and cupped the flame of a Zippo around it. He snapped the Zippo shut with his thumb, his face disappearing into shadow again. "I was scoping out your lady by the jukebox. You've got yourself a real nice piece of tail there."

I heard Hershel step forward. I put my hand on his wrist and held it tight. "This is St. Landry Parish," I said to the tall man, although my words were really addressed to Hershel. "It's a corrupt place. The cops protect the whorehouses and the gambling joints. You wouldn't start trouble with us if you weren't operating with permission. Go back and tell the guy who sent you here it didn't work. Don't misunderstand the gesture, either. Stay away from us."

"You're pretty clever," he said. "Except you're all wrong. I used to see that girl in the car around Bogalusa. She was anybody's punch. I never tried it, but I heard she could buck you to the ceiling. You boys enjoy yourself."

I stepped in front of Hershel.

IT WASN'T EASY to get him into the car and away from the man who obviously wanted to engage us in a situation we couldn't win. But finally, he listened to me, probably because in his mind I was still his commanding officer. A thunderstorm broke on our way to the motor court, drumming so loudly on the car that we couldn't talk. In the rearview mirror, I could see Linda Gail staring out the window into the darkness, lost in thought. I wondered if she was thinking about the mansions in the River Oaks section of Houston or about a matador saluting her with the ears and tail of the bull that had been sacrificed in her honor. I wondered if she was indeed a dissolute country girl from Bogalusa. But as we all learn in our misspent excursions down the wrong highway, profligacy and innocence tend to be bedfellows. I think that Linda Gail belonged to the vast hordes who believed in what we call the American dream, a fantasy somehow linked to the magical world of Hollywood and the waves crashing on the rocks at sunset along the beaches of Santa Barbara.

Back at the motor court, I realized Rosita had been more upset by our confrontation in the parking lot than I had expected. I walked down to the office and got a Coca-Cola and a container of chipped ice and went back to the room and poured a glass for her and put an aspirin in her palm. "Who was he?" she asked.

"Who cares? If I hadn't stopped Hershel, he would have spilled that guy's guts on the gravel."

"Hershel says this man was following him."

"Hershel gets emotional and doesn't always see the world correctly."

She sat down by the window and pulled back the curtain and looked at the rain dancing on the motor court's driveway. "I saw men like that march through Andalusia with their tassels bouncing on their hats. They were merciless. They all had the same lean and hungry look, the kind a wolf would have. I believe Hershel."

"Time to go to sleep, kid," I said. "We're the good guys. The good guys always win."

We went to sleep with our heads on the same pillow, our brows touching. I woke at three A.M. and saw her sitting at the window again, flashes of lightning reflecting off her face. "Did something wake you?" I asked.

"It was only the wind swinging the sign in front of the office," she said. "It was a rainy night like this when the Gestapo raided the apartment building where we were living. We thought we were safe because of the rain. The Gestapo would not leave their collaborator mistresses to go out in the rain in order to arrest a bunch of pitiful, frightened Jews, would they?"

"Don't talk about it, Rosita."

"I was there," she said. "I will always talk about it. I will talk about it until my mouth is stopped with dirt."

I lay back down and closed my eyes and tried to lose myself inside the drumroll of the storm on the roof and the rain gutters spouting into the driveway, flowing like a river into the street, the surface of the water crosshatched with pine needles and green leaves and camellia petals, as though the earth were attempting to cleanse itself of the attrition caused by those who were supposedly its stewards.

IT WAS COLD the next morning when Hershel and I drove out to the right-of-way we had cut through the heart of the forest. The trees were dripping, a band of light the color of yellow ivory trapped on the horizon under thunderheads that sealed the sky like the lid on a skillet. Our pipe had been dropped in segments along an open trench as far as the eye could see. There was no sound in the forest except the dripping of the trees and occasionally a dirt clod rolling into the rainwater at the bottom of the ditch.

Then our crew began to arrive. Most wore long-sleeved shirts to protect their skin from the mosquitoes. Most were gypsies by choice and the kind of men you meet on the edges of an empire in the making. They were brave and stoic by nature, and never complained of the conditions or the risks they took, and considered time in the military part of the ordinary ebb and flow of their lives. They were also incurably improvident, obsessed about matters concerning women and race, often went by their initials, and never used last names. They worked seventy-hour weeks as a matter of course and looked upon a conventional job in an industrial plant as little more than a vacation.

Hershel turned around his cap, put on a welder's mask, and clipped a stringer-bead rod into the electrode holder of a rebuilt Nazi welding machine. Then he knelt down by a pipe joint and began a tack weld on the first of two hundred joints we would complete that day, the ball of reddish-yellow flame working its way around the circumference of the pipe. When he stood up and lifted the shield off his face, he was grinning so widely that I could have counted his teeth. "We just do'ed it, Loot," he said. "Great God Almighty, we have done do'ed it."

The weeks and months that followed were marked by no incidents of significance. I was surprised by how easily everything went. In reality, the rules on a pipeline or an oil rig are draconian and simple and cultural in nature rather than legalistic: If you show up late, you're fired; if you show up drunk, you're fired; if you sass the crew boss, you're fired; if you screw up a weld, you're fired; if you're fried or wired or hungover and tired, you're fired. We didn't have to let one man go. We had no trouble with the union and no accidents on the job. Compared to life in the army, the work was a breeze. Rosita flew back to the ranch and visited me on the weekends at the motor court in Opelousas.

I rarely saw Linda Gail. I didn't know if that was good or bad. Regardless, I didn't ask Hershel about her and decided to forget about the marital problems of others and about the implications of our encounter with the tall man in the parking lot. The Dixie Belle Pipeline Company was a success, and our profit margin on our first contract was far more than I had anticipated. We were receiving calls from Houston and Dallas about pipelines that would run from Oklahoma to the refineries of Texas City down on the Gulf. We were already talking with two drilling companies about laying undersea pipe for wells being drilled offshore.

Hershel bought a Cadillac convertible. Rosita and I went marlin fishing in the Yucatán. We swam in the mornings with dolphins in water that was as clear as green Jell-O, the coral reefs waving with gossamer fans, the sand white and striped with the torpedo-shaped shadows of lemon sharks that swam harmlessly past us.

It was wonderful to be with Rosita in a country where people cooked fish over open fires at sunrise on the beach. It was time to let the war and the slave camps and the burned cities of Europe slip into memory. We were in the springtime of our lives; the world had survived and was still a place of tropical rain forests and flowers floating on waves along our shores and sunsets that were like a metaphysical representation of the Passion of Christ. America had entered a new era; for good or bad, we were the new pilgrims, our gaze fixed on not one but two hemispheres.

We opened an office in Houston and bought an oil field supply yard in Beaumont. A national business magazine did a feature on our welding machines. Then a very improbable event occurred in our lives: We were invited to have lunch at the River Oaks Country Club with Roy Wiseheart.

It was October, and we were living in a rented two-story home that had been built in the 1880s in the Heights section of Houston. The house had a wide, columned porch and a big yard and flowerbeds and shade trees; it was located on a street divided by an esplanade and lined with Victorian homes similar to ours. It was a fine place to live, and I wish I could go back in time and freeze-frame that fateful afternoon when I returned home from the office and picked up the afternoon newspaper from the lawn and tucked it under my arm before going into the house. The light was golden in the trees, the smell of the chrysanthemums as heavy as gas in the cooling of the day; across the street, two boys were throwing a football back and forth. It was a portrait of traditional America that may have been a fiction, but if so, it was a marvelous one. Then I walked through the living room and into the kitchen, and Rosita told me of Wiseheart's phone call.

"You're sure that's the name he gave you?"

"No, I made it up, Weldon."

"Sorry."

She handed me a slip of paper. "I wrote it down. The number is at the bottom. Do you know him?"

"Not personally. He invited Linda Gail and Hershel, too?"

"He said he was inviting you and me and 'Mr. Pine and his wife.' I told him I didn't know if you were going to be in town Saturday. Would you answer my question, please? Who is he?"

"One of the richest men in the United States. Don't worry about it. I'll take care of it."

"Take care of what?"

"You know, *it,*" I said.

Chapter 9

FIVE MINUTES LATER, I came out of the den and went into the kitchen. "What's for dinner?" I asked.

"You talked to Mr. Wiseheart?"

"Briefly."

"Would you stop whatever it is you're doing?"

"What am I doing?"

"You're really frustrating to talk to. You turned down his invitation?"

"I told him we were tied up. We always color-match our socks on Saturday. It's high priority. I think he understood."

"Why is this man such an ogre to you?"

"He's known as an anti-Semite and an all-around son of a bitch." I removed the top from a pot on the stove and looked inside it.

"You're turning down the invitation because of me?"

"We don't need guys like Wiseheart in our lives," I said. "Let's eat on the screen porch. It's a fine evening."

Two hours later, Hershel's black Cadillac pulled up in front of the house with Hershel behind the wheel. Linda got out and headed up the walk, her expression as flat and filled with portent as an overheated pie pan. "Hello, Linda Gail," Rosita said, opening the screen door. "You look very nice."

"Would you kindly tell me why you have turned down an invitation for the four of us to the River Oaks Country Club, an invitation I already accepted?"

"I didn't know Mr. Wiseheart had called you," Rosita said.

"His wife did. She seemed very polite and cultured. I assumed we were all going. She called back and said it was too bad y'all wouldn't be available and that perhaps we could do it another time. Fat chance."

I walked into the living room from the kitchen. Hershel had followed his wife inside. He was trying to smile in the way people do when a situation is so intolerable and without solution that you wish to flee the room.

"It was me who turned down the invitation, Linda Gail," I said. "I don't think this is a man to get mixed up with."

"Who are *you* to make decisions for what *we* do?"

"I didn't," I replied.

"We should have called you, Linda Gail," Rosita said.

"Well, 'shoulda coulda' seems a poor excuse, if you ask me," Linda Gail said, on the verge of tears. In my mind's eye, I saw a little country girl in a dime store being pulled away from a display counter her mother couldn't even afford to look at.

Rosita turned around so I could see her face. She raised her eyebrows.

"I'll call Mr. Wiseheart back now," I said. "Is noon on Saturday fine with everyone?"

Linda Gail pulled a Kleenex from her purse and dabbed it at her nose. "I always have hay fever in the fall," she said. She squeezed the Kleenex into a ball and dropped it back into her purse. "Yes, noon on Saturday is just fine, thank you very much."

THE COUNTRY CLUB'S main building was palatial, the St. Augustine grass a deep blue-green, more like an inland Mediterranean bay than a lawn. The red clay tennis courts, the swimming pool, the manicured golf course seemed testimony to the secret rewards that awaited the adherents of a benevolent patrician deity. "Oh, my," Linda Gail said in an almost erotic tone as we drove through the gates.

"Yeah, this ain't no hog farm," Hershel said.

"Would you not talk like that, please?" she said.

The dining room that had been reserved by Roy Wiseheart and his wife, Clara, overlooked a tennis court where two players in white trousers, one of them a world-ranked professional, were whocking the ball back and forth, glazed with sweat, both playing with smiles that could have been part of a toothpaste promotion. Our table was covered with immaculate Irish linen and set with silver bowls of red roses and Flora Danica dinnerware. The Wisehearts greeted us at the doorway as though our arrival marked a special occasion. Neither seemed embarrassed by their theatrical behavior. I remembered Grandfather's warning about dealing with people who were not our kind.

The differences between the husband and the wife were soon apparent. Roy Wiseheart was trim, his hair copper-colored and neatly combed, his handshake controlled, his eyes clear, his appearance younger than his years, his expression marked by curiosity rather than by design. There was nothing relaxed about his wife. At the table, there was a tic in her cheek, an irritability in her eyes that gave you the sense that you were the cause of her unhappiness. The fingers of her right hand were constantly moving, the thumb touching each of the tips. She also gave you the disquieting conviction that whatever you said next would prove an unfortunate choice.

She had gold hair and wore a brocaded white dress with small gold buttons. More important, she wore white gloves that she didn't take off. She kept looking sideways at Rosita.

Her eyes were a liquid blue, her face unnaturally pale to the point of being bloodless, the cheeks rouged. She ate in very small bites, as an anorexic might. She tried to feign interest in the conversation, but her eyes dulled over whenever she looked down at her plate. I had the feeling that Roy Wiseheart's marital situation was one no man ever wants to find himself in.

"This is sure a nice club," Linda Gail said. "This dishware is something else, too."

"We're happy you could join us," Wiseheart said. "Mrs. Holland, you have a hint of a British accent. Were you educated overseas?"

"I grew up in Spain. I had a British tutor. My father was a linguist at the University of Madrid."

"Really? How did you come to meet Mr. Holland?"

"He rescued me from a rather bad situation."

"And what was that?"

"Hershel was there, too," Linda Gail said. "If we're going to tell our stories, let's tell the whole thing."

"Beg your pardon?" Wiseheart said.

"I was in the camps," Rosita said.

"You were a prisoner of the Nazis?" he said.

"You could call it that."

"Could we change the subject?" Clara Wiseheart said, drinking from her water glass as though cleansing her throat of an unwelcome taste.

"I hope y'all like Houston. It's an up-and-coming business community," Wiseheart said. "I expect one day it will be like New York City on the plains."

"It's mighty big, that's for sure," Linda Gail said. "I bet the jobs go begging. In Bogalusa you could either work at the gin or slaughter chickens."

Clara Wiseheart touched her temple as though a vein had burst inside her head. She gestured at the waiter. "Please serve dessert now and bring coffee for those who are having it," she said. Then she stared out the window at the tennis courts, as though willing herself through the glass.

Wiseheart turned his gaze on me and Hershel. "You fellows have gotten the attention of quite a few people. They say your welds may be the best in the business. If you ever think about expanding or merging, I'd like to talk over a couple of possibilities with you."

"Merging with your corporation?" Hershel said.

"You'd still be in charge of your company. You'd just be under a bigger umbrella. Small business is old business."

"What do you think, Weldon?" Hershel said.

"We're loners, Mr. Wiseheart," I said.

"Nobody is a loner in the oil and natural gas business," he replied.

Clara Wiseheart opened a cigarette case that was either sterling silver or white gold. "Can we talk about financial matters somewhere else?" she asked.

"I'm like you, Clara," Linda Gail said. "I can't get my mind focused on business matters. Know why? My father owned a dry goods store and talked about nothing else. My mother would stuff cotton balls in her ears when he'd get started."

Clara Wiseheart's back straightened. "Excuse me a moment," she said. She went out the door, lighting her cigarette, her hand trembling.

Linda Gail looked about uncertainly. "What I meant is a lot of business things are surely over my head," she said. "I hope I didn't say anything wrong."

"Clara has migraines. It has nothing to do with our conversation," Wiseheart said.

"You want me to go talk to her?" Linda Gail asked.

"That's very kind, but you don't need to do that," he said. He pushed away his plate and looked at me. He smiled good-naturedly. "My analysts say those modifications you did on those German machines are extraordinary. Maybe my people could replicate them, maybe not. I'm an oil producer, not a welding contractor. I hear you all might start up a drilling operation. Come in with me and I'll back your play. I mean to the hilt. You can write your own ticket."

Hershel waited.

"We're not interested," I said.

"You're sure about that?"

"Sure as God made little green apples."

"Do you mind telling me why you're so resistant to a perfectly reasonable business proposal?" Wiseheart asked.

I held my gaze on his and said nothing.

"Say something, Hershel," Linda Gail said.

"Weldon got us the capital, hon."

"You're the one who got the welding machines. I think we owe Mr. Wiseheart an answer to his question," she said. "I think it's impolite to turn into a possum on a gum stump when somebody just wants information from you."

I stood up and put my hand on the back of Rosita's chair. "Thanks for the lunch. Please tell Mrs. Wiseheart good-bye for us."

Wiseheart lifted his hands in resignation. "It's been my pleasure," he said.

Clara Wiseheart was nowhere in sight when we walked out of the clubhouse. I could hear Linda Gail breathing through her nose. "What in the name of Sam Hill has got into y'all?" she said. "Do you realize what you just threw away?"

"It's all right, Linda Gail," Hershel said.

"It is *not* all right," she replied. She looked at the marble floors, the high ceilings, the huge bouquets of flowers on the tables, with the expression of a woman being driven from Eden. "Weldon Holland, I can't believe what you just did. Who put you in charge?"

"I don't think you quite appreciate Mrs. Wiseheart's estimation of us," I said.

"So she's a little snooty. If you want snooty, go back where I grew up," Linda Gail said.

Trying to understand her statement was like tying a knot inside your head.

"There's a reason she wears gloves," Rosita said.

"Yeah, *what*?"

"She doesn't want to touch people like us, Linda Gail," Rosita said. "Maybe she doesn't want to touch a Jew who was in a death camp. Or maybe she just doesn't want to touch the silverware the Negroes have touched. Maybe she doesn't like being seen at the same table with what she would call 'common people.' The possibilities are many."

"I don't think that's true at all, not for one minute," Linda Gail said, pouting. "If you ask me, some people have wild imaginations."

IT WASN'T OVER. As I was to learn, patience and latitude and even humility are paradoxically the handmaidens of wealth, because virtue is costly only for those who own nothing else. It was a warm Sunday night, the pecan and live oak trees perfectly still, black-green against an autumnal moon. Fireflies were lighting in the darkness, like cigarettes that sparked and died inside their own smoky tracings. Roy

Wiseheart pulled a red and metallic-gray Packard into our driveway. I went outside before he had a chance to cut his engine. I leaned down to the passenger window. "We're done, sir," I said. "That's an absolute."

"How about giving me a chance to talk?"

"Nope."

He held up his hand, his fingers spread. "Five minutes," he said.

"I don't like your politics, and I don't like your racial attitudes, Mr. Wiseheart. I don't like the way your wife was looking at Mrs. Holland, either."

"My wife lost her sister to Huntington's disease and thinks she'll die the same way. She has an obsession with germs. She's erratic and unpredictable and tried to burn our home down. Her behavior has nothing to do with you, your friends, or Mrs. Holland." He turned up the underside of his wrist and glanced at his watch. "I'm flying to our home in the Bahamas in one hour. Do you and your wife want to come? I'm madly impressed by both of you."

"No, thanks."

"The fishing is great. Get in. What have you got to lose?"

"I think I'll say good night instead."

His hair was neatly clipped, his face egg-shaped without a sag in it, his complexion flawless. He had the confidence and serenity of a man who understood the world and did not contend with it. He turned off his engine. "There are no secrets in our line of work," he said. "You and your partner are laying the underwater line to the first oil rig to drill more than one mile from the American shoreline. The rig is being towed into place as we speak, over in Louisiana, south of Vermilion Parish. In ten years that part of the Gulf will be lit with oil rigs from one horizon to the other. You and Pine can be stringing pipe to every one of them."

"You hire industrial spies, Mr. Wiseheart?"

"I don't have to. They come to my office every day. I throw most of them out. You say you don't like my politics? Would you care to explain to me what my politics are?"

"Thanks for coming by," I said, and started to walk away.

He got out of the car, a bottle of champagne in his hand. "I bought this for my brother-in-law's birthday, but he hates my guts and told me to get out of his house. So I'm going to drink it for him. Join me."

"I'm a closet teetotaler."

He broke the neck off the bottle on the car bumper, the foam running down his hand and wrist. He poured into his mouth, staining his chin and shirt. "If I just swallowed a piece of glass, it's your fault," he said. "Come on, take a drink. You're a bloody fire-eater. Don't pretend you're not. I can see it in your eyes. We're cut out of the same stuff."

I had to concede he put on a fine show. "We're fixing to have some pie and go to bed," I said.

"No matter whether we ever do business or not, I want you to understand something. I didn't know about your wife's background. I'm sorry if I offended you all in any way. I'm not an anti-Semite. There might be people in my family who are, but I'm not one of them."

"Fair enough," I said.

"One other thing: Neither Truman nor Roosevelt would bomb the train tracks going into the extermination camps. You didn't happen to vote for that pair, did you?"

"I can't remember."

"You like motion pictures?"

"Anyone who doesn't like motion pictures is probably spiritually dead."

"I make them. Check it out," he said. "See you around, Mr. Holland. For reasons of personal integrity, you just turned down a fortune. If I had ten like you, I could own half the country."

I TOOK A PECAN pie and a bottle of milk out of the icebox and fixed plates for Rosita and me at the kitchen table while I told her everything Roy Wiseheart had said.

"He's a man who gets what he wants. He'll be back," she said.

"He's not totally unlikable."

"Are you rethinking his offer?"

"I don't see the advantage. There's another problem, one I didn't mention. A friend of mine flew with Wiseheart in the South Pacific and told me a disturbing story about him. The squadron leader's plane was hit, and Wiseheart was supposed to escort him back to base. Instead, he went down on the deck after another kill. The plane he splashed turned out to be an unarmed trainer. Two Zeros came out of the clouds and blew the leader out of the sky."

"That's a terrible story."

"Maybe he thought he was protecting his leader. But my friend said Wiseheart had four kills and needed a fifth in order to be an ace."

"What's the expression your grandfather is always using?"

"Don't borrow trouble."

"Good words to remember. Let's go upstairs."

The house had a big attic fan. When we shut all the windows except the one in our bedroom and turned on the fan, the entire house creaked, and within minutes our bedroom was airy and cool. There was a magnolia tree in full bloom outside our window, and I could hear raindrops ticking on the leaves. Rosita undressed with her back to me, then got under the sheet.

"You're still shy with me," I said.

"That's what you think, buster."

"You've been watching too many American movies," I said.

She looked into my face. "Did you have a bad dream last night?"

"I dreamed about Hershel. He was buried alive and I couldn't pull him loose from the ground."

"Are you worried about him?"

"I'm worried about his wife."

"She's not a bad girl."

"She's easily used. Most Southerners are. We give power to the worst among us."

Rosita turned off the light on the nightstand and pulled the sheet off her. "Come here," she said.

"When did you start giving orders?"

"Just now."

"Bad idea," I said. I got up from the bed and took a pair of scissors out of the desk drawer. "Don't go anywhere."

"What are you doing?"

"I'll let you know."

I went downstairs in my pajamas and into the backyard and cut a huge yellow rose from a bush and went back upstairs and sat on the side of the bed and laid the rose on her stomach.

"Why did you do that?"

"I felt like it," I said. Then I kissed her on the mouth and forehead and on each of her eyes.

She rested her hand on the back of my neck and gazed into my face. "You're an honorable and brave man, Weldon. For that reason you'll always be feared and rejected by the world."

"I don't think the world is particularly interested in people like me."

"Hershel isn't educated, but he understands the goodness in you. It's not the kind of goodness that people acquire. It's of a kind that certain people are born with. Hershel will always remain loyal to you. His vulnerability lies in his belief that people with education and money are better than he is. He doesn't understand that he's the same good man you are."

"You're pretty smart."

She lifted a lock of my hair from my eye and pushed it back over my forehead. "People will try to use your goodness against you," she said. "I made you accept the invitation to the country club. I was foolish. Regardless of what Wiseheart told you, I saw the look in his wife's eyes. It was iniquitous. We never should have had contact with either of them."

"We won't be seeing them again."

"They want what you have. They may never use it, but they need to own it. They cannot allow others to think their power is limited."

I picked the rose up from her stomach and put it in her hair. I kissed her stomach. "I love you," I said.

Then I kissed her all over, and when she tried to get up and hold me, I pressed her back down on the bed and entered her, her eyes closing and her mouth opening. I heard the trees moving in the wind outside, brushing wetly against the eaves of the house. I felt her hands kneading the small of my back, running up and down my ribs, her breath on my cheek, her tongue on my neck, her thighs like long golden carp. Her climax was gradual, like a swell building in the ocean, then cascading onto a beach, and seconds later sliding back into the surf, only to crest again and again and again, as steady as the movements of the tide, a tiny cry leaving her throat each time she pressed her stomach into mine.

To make love with Rosita Lowenstein was to enter a Petrarchan sonnet. I told her she was probably the only woman in the world who made love in iambic pentameter, and the Lowenstein sonnet always ended with a rhyming couplet, one that left me weak and breathless. To make love with Rosita was not a sexual act; it was a sacrament.

After she fell asleep, I went downstairs with my notebook and wrote these words: *Lose the entire world if you have to, drive your car off a cliff, gamble away a fortune in Vegas, single-handedly invade the Soviet Union, but never let go of Rosita Lowenstein. Never, never, never.*

NEW YEAR'S DAY of 1947 seemed like the beginning of another celebratory season. Hershel had always said he could not only smell money but he broke into a sweat when he was about to make it. I had come to believe him. Hershel sweated and the money rolled in. One offshore drilling rig after another punched into a pay sand, and the gas flares burning far out on the horizon gave witness to the birth of a new secular religion. We had arrived, and the technological reach of our nation knew no bounds. The bejeweled refineries along the Texas coast, smoking like an outer-space facility inside the great American night, were not a blight but a continuation of Walt Whitman's ode to American promise. The displacement of an emerald-green swampland of sawgrass and cypress and gum trees was forgotten in the sacrifice that had to be made for the greater good.

The brothels of Port Arthur, Texas City, and Galveston never closed. A bottle of cold beer, served in an illegal gambling joint on the beach, was twenty cents. A paper plate full of boiled shrimp was thirty-five. And we were part of it all. A dance orchestra played under the stars on the amusement pier that extended into Galveston Bay, the waves bursting against the pilings beneath our feet. We flew to Fort Lauderdale and hit quinellas and even the daily double at the racetrack as a matter of course.

We became like the Las Vegas gambler who discovers against a backdrop of purple mountains and the glitter of the Strip that he has been painted with magic by a divine hand. His prescience is in his walk and his benevolence toward his fellow man. He knows which cards will slip stiff and shiny out of a six-deck shoe; the dice he rolls bounce off the felt backboard in slow motion, the red dots freezing at seven or eleven, one pass after another, as though they're loaded and incapable of forming any other combination.

Bankers wanted to lend us money. We turned them away. We were invited to visit Saudi Arabia and passed. In April Grandfather took a fall, and Rosita and I flew back to the ranch and helped my mother care for him. We knew he had recovered when we caught him saddling his horse at five in the morning.

We drilled our first well outside New Roads, Louisiana. The seismic reports were all good. Then we began a second one less than a mile away. Hershel said it was a sure bet. "We're holding four aces, Weldon," he said. "There's a pay sand down there that people are not going to believe. All those dinosaurs have been waiting millions of years for me and you to turn them loose."

In June our geologist declared both wells dry holes, what are called "dusters" in the oil business. We were standing by the first rig at high noon, in one-hundred-degree heat, the sun white and boiling overhead. I could feel sweat crawling down my sides. I got two bottles of Dr Pepper out of the cold box in my car and popped off the caps with my pocketknife and handed one to Hershel.

"It's down there, Weldon," he said. "I never felt so strong in my life about something."

"I believe you," I said, adjusting my hat so the shadow fell across my face. "Let's go back to that café on the highway and have us some dirty rice and a chicken-fried steak."

"How bad are we hit?"

I didn't want to tell him. "Our level of liquidity won't be quite the same for a while. We'll adjust and get by. We're still the boogie-woogie boys from Company B."

"Next time I have an opinion on something, don't listen. Last week I told Linda Gail I'd be buying her a home in Bellaire."

I put my hand on his shoulder. His shirt was dry and hot, as though it had just been ironed. His eyes were a few inches from mine. I could feel his blood humming through my palm. "This stuff isn't diddly-squat," I said.

"I hate to disappoint Linda Gail," he replied. "It makes me feel plumb awful."

Chapter 10

WE HAD BID on three jobs, counting on capital we thought was ours. Overnight we discovered we were leveraged to the eyes. The bankers who had wanted to lend us money, bankers we had rebuffed, now treated us with caution. One loan officer said he would like to "revisit" our situation in a year or so; another wanted an audit; a third pressed my hand warmly and said, "I'm a Texas A&M grad myself. I like your ideas. I bet you have a bright future once you get your reversals behind you."

Rain was pouring down at our house, flooding the street and washing over the gutters onto our lawn, when a taxi splashed into the driveway and stopped under the live oak nearest the porch. A man I never wanted to see again got out and ran through the puddles, an umbrella over his head. I met him at the front door. He was folding his umbrella, the brim of his hat dripping.

"Major Fincher?" I said.

"At least you haven't forgotten me," he said. "I'm changing planes for the Islands and thought I should come out to see you."

"Come in," I said, pushing open the screen.

Inside, his gaze roved around the living room. As long as I could remember, Fincher had been looking at something other than the person he was addressing. "You got a fine place here," he said. "I hear you married that lady you rescued."

"We rescued each other. But yes, you're correct. I married her."

"Damn fine. Good God, that's a gulley washer out there, isn't it? You have a drink? We hit a storm outside of San Antonio. Is that the little lady in the kitchen? I'm sorry to bust in on you like this, Weldon, but sometimes I miss the old days. Damn me if I don't, war or not."

"Have a seat, Major. I'll see what we have in the cabinet."

"None of that formal stuff. The army is the army. Peacetime is peacetime," he replied, sitting in a stuffed chair. When Rosita came out of the kitchen, he rose from the chair. "You're everything your husband said you were. I'm Lloyd Fincher. Weldon and I were in some rough spots together."

"It's a pleasure to meet you," she said.

For just a second, or maybe a hundredth of a second, I saw his eyes drop to her breasts and hips. It was one of those instances when one man immediately knows the thoughts and makeup of another man, and from that moment on he never thinks of that man in the same fashion. Fincher wiped rainwater off his forehead and looked around the room again. "Well, this does beat all," he said. "Who thought we'd make it plumb to the Elbe and end up in one piece and rendezvousing in the Heights?"

I fixed him a drink and wrapped it in a napkin and handed it to him. I had put aside most of my resentments from the war, particularly ill feeling toward the incompetents who never should have been promoted into positions of authority. It was hard, however, to forget that Fincher had been part of an investigation into Rosita's past.

"Did you finally get your Silver Star?" he asked.

"Yes, I did."

"It was an honor to put you in for it. There's another reason I came out to see you. A friend of mine at the National Bank of Commerce said you were looking for a loan. Maybe I can help out."

"In what way?"

"Oil exploration isn't being financed by money from the banks, son. It's coming from insurance companies. Mine is one of them."

"I didn't know you were in the loan business."

He mentioned the name of an infamous wildcatter, an uneducated, brawling alcoholic who grew up dirt-poor within a few miles of Spindletop and was now one of the most cost-efficient oil producers in the business. The man was also building a luxurious hotel, one with a huge turquoise pool shaped like a shamrock, at the bottom of South Main Street. "Every dollar going into that hotel went across the top of my desk first," Fincher said. "Know why we lend money to a violent drunk who can't walk down stairs and chew gum at the same time? If you sent him into a desert with a bucket and a shovel to find water, he'd come back with a bucket full of oil. That's you, Weldon. You've got the same kind of initiative. Except you're intelligent and educated, and you've got manners and breeding on top of it."

"We just brought in two dusters."

"If it weren't for dusters, everybody would be in the oil business."

"Can you stay for dinner?" Rosita asked.

"Major Fincher has to catch a plane," I said.

He finished his drink, the ice cubes clinking when he set it down. He studied the glass as though he couldn't see his thoughts clearly.

"You're the right man for the times," he said. "My friend building the hotel belongs to another era. When he figures that out, he'll probably become born again or stick a gun in his mouth. The big money is in oil, Hollywood, and technology. But you've got to have a brain. I knew it in the Ardennes."

"Knew what?"

"The Germans weren't going to kill you. You were fixing to walk into history. I'm willing to bet the ranch on it."

"Thanks for coming by," I said.

He removed a business card from his shirt pocket and wrote his home number on it and put it on the coffee table. "How's Pine doin'?"

"Hershel's the best there is."

"They would have eaten up him and his welding machines if you hadn't been on board."

"Who would have eaten him up?"

"Good Lord, son, who do you think? The boys in Houston and Big D are putting a man in the United States Senate who used to be an elevator operator. Pine isn't equipped to deal with men like that. You can. You got the smarts and the education, and you're not afraid. Can I use y'all's bathroom?"

"It's at the back of the hall," I said. "I'll call a taxi for you."

LINDA GAIL STOOD on the gallery of a country store north of Bogalusa and watched a black man crank the handle on the gas pump and begin fueling her car. The evening sun was red inside the dust from the fields, the cotton leaves wilted in the heat, the air close with the odor of herbicide and hot tar. On the far side of the road, three men with a camera on a tripod were filming several figures in the distance who were hoeing out weeds in the cotton rows. Linda Gail fanned herself with her handkerchief and went back inside the store and bought an Orange Crush at the counter. A soot-stained Confederate flag was tacked by all four corners to the ceiling, puffing and rippling in the breeze created by an oscillating fan mounted on the wall.

She asked the owner where the restroom was. "Out back. The latch is broken, but there's a rock you can push against the door," he answered.

The aggregate of the restroom's interior was revolting, the heat stifling. When she was finished, she tried to wash her hands. The handle on the faucet squeaked dryly when she turned it, and it left a rusty smear on her palm. The bottom of the lavatory was matted with dead flies, the sides striped with noxious minerals that abided in the water. She walked around the side of the building to the gallery, trying to forget the experience of using a public restroom in the place where she'd grown up. The black man had just started up a gasoline-powered air compressor. "Your tires is low, ma'am," he said. "I'll be done in a minute."

One of the men who had been filming the workers in the field walked toward her, an expensive camera hanging on a cord from his shoulder. He was tall and had a thin black mustache and wore two-tone shoes and a long-sleeved white shirt with pale silver stripes in it. He touched the brim of his panama hat. "Would you mind if I took your picture in front of the store?" he said.

"What for?"

"We're making a documentary."

"A documentary on what?"

"The agrarian culture of the South. Small-town hospitality and that sort of thing. You'll probably see it as a short in your local theater. Are you from close by?"

"I live in southwest Houston."

"Just visiting, huh?"

"I have a family member in a retirement home here. Why do you want to photograph me in front of an old run-down store?"

He held up his camera and looked through his lens, pushing up the brim of his panama. "You're photogenic. The wide-brim flowered hat is perfect. So is the light. Do you mind?"

"I'm not sure. Who did you say you were?"

"Jack Valentine. I'm with Castle Productions."

"Castle Productions? I never heard of it."

"It's a forgivable sin," he said.

"Well, I guess it wouldn't hurt anything."

She heard him clicking the shutter, advancing the film by pushing a lever with his thumb, moving quickly from one angle to the next. "Wonderful," he said. "Now turn your head toward me. No, don't turn your body, just your head. Look straight at me. That's fine. You must have done this before."

"Not often."

"I'm going to bring the Bolex over here. I just want you to walk back and forth on the porch. We'll be recording, too. I'll ask you a couple of questions. Say whatever is on your mind. Smile, look gloomy, pout, whatever you feel like."

He was going too fast for her. "You'll bring the what?"

"The sixteen-millimeter. You put me in mind of Miss Garland. The same smile, the same freshness, the same country-girl innocence. See? You're blushing."

"Judy Garland? That's silly."

"I worked with her on two pictures. What's your name?"

"Linda Gail Pine."

"Are you married, Miss Linda?"

She realized with a flush of guilt that she had been hiding her left hand and her wedding ring in the folds of her dress. "My husband is Mr. Hershel Pine. He's from a plantation family in Avoyelles Parish. He's president of the Dixie Belle Pipeline Company."

"If he doesn't object, we're going to get you on film."

The black man turned off the compressor. "It's a dollar thirty-two for the gas, ma'am. You can pay inside. Right now you're ready to go."

She stared at her car, and at the molten redness of the sun, and at the cinnamon-colored dust that was rising into the sky like a veil obscuring all the mysteries she should have been privy to. The smell of herbicide made her eyes water. The workers in the fields were still chopping with their hoes among the cotton plants even though the hour was late. Then she realized these were not ordinary workers. They were convicts, and their warders were picketed on the edge of the field, dressed in khaki, mounted on horseback, each armed with a shotgun he rested across the pommel or butt-down on his thigh. The words Hershel had said to her days ago were as audible inside her head as if he were standing five inches from her ear: *We just cain't live as high up on the hog as we thought, hon. It's not so bad. Worst comes to worst, we can live at my folks' place till Weldon and me get on our feet again.*

"The windows are thick with dust," she said to the black man. "Please wash them. In fact, throw a whole bucket of water on them." She turned to the man with the pencil-line mustache. His eyes were blue-green, the color eyes she imagined a Spanish buccaneer would have. "Will there be any remuneration for these pictures?"

"Quite possibly," he answered.

She touched at her brow with the tip of her handkerchief and tilted up her face so it caught the sunset. "I'm at your disposal, sir."

TWO WEEKS LATER, on our pipeline right-of-way south of Beaumont, I smelled alcohol on Hershel, the boilermaker variety, heavy levels of it deep down in the lungs and the blood and the lining of the stomach. It was six-thirty A.M., the sun not over the trees, the air still blue, ground fog billowing out of the woods. He was smoking a Camel, turning his face to exhale, as though protecting me from the smoke. His eyes were as rheumy as broken eggs.

"What time did you go to bed?" I asked.

"The baseball game was on. It couldn't have been too late." He flicked his cigarette into a pool of water and coughed into his hand. Up ahead, the welder on the tack rig was starting his first weld of the day. We were working extralong days, paying out large sums in overtime, trying to meet our contractual deadline.

"What's going on, Hershel?"

"I ran into a couple of guys in a hotel bar. I showed some bad judgment, that's all."

"What were you doing at a hotel bar?"

"Linda Gail and I had a fight. She went out to Hollywood for a screen test."

"There's a thermos of coffee in my pickup. We'll talk about this later."

I began walking down the right-of-way alongside pipe that was propped on skids all the way to a saltwater bay. Up ahead, I could see two tack-welder rigs and one hot-pass rig moving up the line, the welder's helpers yanking up the steel pipe clamp that acted as the ground, and running with it after the truck; then the welders crouched again, their shields down, the arc crackling alight when the stringer-bead rod touched the metal.

The oil boom broke the back of the Southern plantation system and was a godsend for working people. There was a tradeoff, though. A mistake on a drilling or seismograph rig or a pipeline could cost a man a limb, an eye, or his life. It happened in a blink, and it happened with regularity. That's why there were no second chances in the oil patch.

I looked over my shoulder at Hershel. He was sitting in the passenger seat of my pickup, holding the plastic thermos cup to his mouth with both hands. He looked back at me, shamefaced. At noon I told him I would buy him lunch. We made it about three miles down the highway.

"Stop the truck," he said.

"What's wrong?"

"I'm about to puke my guts. I've never been so sick in my life."

He got out of the vehicle and walked through a field of buttercups into a grove of live oaks, clutching his stomach all the while, his face beaded with sweat. He sat down in the shade, his back against a tree.

I squatted down next to him. "Some people have a violent reaction to alcohol," I said. "It doesn't mean they're weak-willed or lacking in character. In my family, it's like matches and gasoline."

I could see he wasn't listening.

"She called me paranoid," he said.

"Why would she do that?"

"Because I don't trust these film people. Because I saw that guy again."

"Which guy?"

"The one we had trouble with at the dance hall in Opelousas. The one who's been following us around."

He was wearing a straw cowboy hat. I took it off his head and placed it crown-down on his lap. He lifted his eyes to mine. His face was beet-red, his breath rank. "Don't do this to yourself," I said.

"I won't," he said, his hands knotting.

"Let Linda Gail have her way. If this Hollywood overture isn't on the square, she'll let it go. But it has to be her choice. In the meantime, we keep the cork in the bottle." He didn't reply. I fitted my hand on his shoulder and looked into his face. His shoulder bone felt as sharp as a knife. "Do we have a deal?"

"Yes, sir. How far in the red are we?"

"Seventy-six thousand dollars, plus what we owe my uncle."

"We're still afloat, though?"

"We lost the contract for the job in East Texas. I couldn't pay the up-front money on the pipe. We're in danger of having our welding machines confiscated."

He looked seasick. "All because of those dadburned wells outside New Roads. It eats my lunch thinking about it."

I picked up his hat and put it on his head. "They can kill us, but they can't change us."

"I think it's like Linda Gail said."

"What did she say?"

"We chopped a hole in the bottom of our own boat."

I felt like telling him to kick Linda Gail Pine in the butt. Instead I waited until I had showered and put on fresh clothes and eaten dinner, then I called Lloyd Fincher in San Antonio, my throat so dry I could hardly speak when he picked up the phone.

"There's some static on the line. I can't hear you," Fincher said. "Who is this?"

"Weldon Holland, Major."

"I declare. What can I do for you, son?"

ROSITA AND I checked in to the Menger Hotel, close by the Alamo and the River Walk, the night before we were to meet with Lloyd Fincher and his attorney. The hotel was built in 1859 and had inlaid ivory-colored and royal blue marble floors and potted palms and slender white columns with gold trim in the lobby, and a balcony that wrapped around the atrium and allowed the visitor a wonderful overview of the hotel's interior, which looked more like ancient Rome than modern-day Texas.

I threw our bag on the bed. Through the window, I could see the facade of the Alamo's chapel, the building that had served as an infirmary during the siege of the mission in 1836. I opened the French doors and stepped out on the balcony. "Jim Bowie died right there," I said to Rosita, pointing at the chapel. "He was bayoneted to death on his cot. Davy Crockett probably died by the barracks wall."

Rosita didn't reply. I stared at the plaza. I had been there many times and had always walked away with the same sensation. I felt that the spirits of the 188 men and boys who had died after thirteen days of siege were still among us, their ashes under the stones we walked on, their voices whispering to us in the wind, should we ever choose to listen.

"Are you worried about tomorrow?" Rosita asked.

"I'm gambling on Fincher, a man who got a lot of GIs killed at Kasserine Pass."

"That was then. This is now," she said.

"That's what I tell myself."

"You've done all you could to raise money, Weldon. Everything you've done is for Hershel. I just wish he understood that."

"If it wasn't for Hershel's welding machines, we'd be living on the GI Bill. Let's go to a restaurant on the river and get something to eat."

"Just wait a minute. The real question is whether this man Fincher is honest or not," she said. "Do you believe he's honest?"

I could hear the music in the outdoor cafés along the River Walk. I didn't want to think or talk about Lloyd Fincher. I didn't want to believe I had deliberately put myself in a relationship with a man for whom I had no respect. I hadn't slept in three nights. "Sometimes you have to do business with the devil," I said.

"He's not that bad, is he?"

"Probably not. But I wouldn't count on it."

She put her arm in mine. "We'll always be together, no matter what happens," she said. "You've always done the right thing, Weldon. That's all that counts."

When I needed someone to back my play, Rosita Lowenstein never let me down.

We walked along the river's edge under the cypress and willow trees, over the pedestrian bridges, past a gondola filled with mariachi musicians wearing white sombreros and brocaded jackets and trousers. Up ahead was a tree with the bark and long thin leaves of a willow, but it was blooming with clusters of purple flowers that trailed in the water. I did not know its name. "What a beautiful tree," I said.

Then I realized that a few feet away from the tree, Hershel and Linda Gail were sitting at a table with Lloyd Fincher and a heavy-set peroxide-blond woman in an orange sundress. Her skin was like tallow, with the kind of tan you see on people who sunbathe in the nude. Fincher stood up, a bottle of Corona in his hand, his face flushed, as though he had run upstairs. He had on a tropical shirt printed with parrots and flowers that he wore outside a pair of pleated white slacks. A saucer of salted limes and a silver flask in a leather case sat in the middle of the table. "Hail, Sir Weldon, and hail your ladyship," he said. "We're rewriting the outcome of the Alamo. Help us clean Santa Ana's clock."

There was a glass of iced tea in front of Hershel, and a plate with three tacos and a scoop of avocado salad, but no bottle of beer. *Good for you, Hershel,* I thought.

"We're taking a walk," I said.

"Definitely not. You have to sit down," Fincher said. "Travis is mortally wounded and the little brown buggers are coming over the wall. Time to give them a face full of chain and grape and send them back across the Rio Grande. We used to have a cheer in high school: 'Two bits, four bits, six bits a peso. All good pepper-bellies stand up and say so.'"

"Don't offend him," Rosita whispered.

"What's that?" Fincher said.

"We'd love to join you," I replied.

"Damn straight," he said. "How about two fingers of Mexican kickapoo juice with a Corona chaser? It'll set you right. This is my friend Paula. She used to throw the shot put. Right, baby? She can still throw it, too, I'm here to tell you."

Linda Gail turned around in her chair and smiled at us. She had tinted her hair a darker shade; her curls covered the back of her neck, the way an antebellum girl may have worn them. "I'm going to be in a motion picture," she said.

"That's grand," Rosita said.

"I counted my lines in the script. I have a hundred and two," she said. "That's what most actors do, count their lines. I'm just happy to be in the film."

Fincher remained standing until Rosita and I had sat down. "Linda Gail was starting to tell us about her experience in Hollywood," he said. "What's the name of that company?"

"Castle Productions," she said.

"That's right," he said, his eyes unfocused. He sat down unsteadily. "Like moats and drawbridges and that sort of thing." He looked into space, a bead of light in his eye, a faint smile on his mouth.

"You know them?" she asked.

"Not really. I'm not too up on the film world," he said. "Truth is, I was never big on movies. How do you like staying at the Menger? Did you know Lillie Langtry and Robert E. Lee stayed there?"

"Are you talking to me?" Linda Gail asked.

"Who else, Hollywood lady?" Fincher said. "Theodore Roosevelt organized the Rough Riders here."

"Well, I hope they all flushed the toilet before they checked out," she said.

I had to hand it to her.

Fincher continued to get drunker and louder. His arm was draped over the shoulder of his girlfriend, his armpit dark with perspiration. He had become bored with the conversation. He waved his free hand at the air. "I never told you two guys I was sorry you got left behind at the Ardennes," he said. "Actually, I thought a bunch of y'all might have hightailed it."

"Excuse me?" I said.

"The woods were swarming with deserters. Everybody made a big deal out of that Slovik kid going before a firing squad. I personally think he had it coming, although I wasn't unsympathetic with his situation. Considering what those Tigers did, I might have bagged it, too. Our headquarters got the crap knocked out of it. When we retook the area and didn't find y'all's bodies, I figured maybe you'd surrendered or headed over the hill for parts unknown."

"That's not what happened, though, is it?" I said.

"No, you ended up with the goddamn Silver Star," Fincher said. "Where's that waiter?"

"But you're saying you thought Hershel and I were deserters?"

"No, what I said was the woods were full of them. And I think Eddie Slovik deserved death by a firing squad." Fincher's girlfriend was trying to shush him, to no avail. "What did you think I was trying to say?" he said to me.

"I guess I misunderstood you," I replied.

He hiccupped and let his eyes settle fondly on Linda Gail. "Castle Productions, you say?"

"Yes, sir, that's the name of the company. You have it absolutely right," she answered.

He squeezed his girlfriend against him, then looked back at Linda Gail. "Think you can get roles for the likes of us?" he said. "I bet it's more fun out there than three monkeys trying to hump a football. You never know which way the dice are coming out of the cup, do you?"

He laughed to himself. I had no idea at what.

Chapter 11

HERSHEL AND I signed all the loan documents the following morning, and Fincher's attorney presented us with a check for two hundred and fifty thousand dollars. I tried to forget the events of the previous evening. I told myself that Fincher's boorish behavior was indicative of his kind and didn't necessarily mean he served a corrupt enterprise. But one detail would not go away: He seemed intrigued by the name of the production company Linda Gail had signed a contract with, at the same time disclaiming any knowledge about the movie industry or serious interest in it.

He and his girlfriend had taken adjoining rooms down the veranda, and had not checked out yet. I tapped on his door. "I need to talk to you a minute about last night, Lloyd," I said.

"That business about deserters? I got tongue-tied, that's all. Too much flak juice."

I stepped inside the room without being asked. The French doors to the balcony were open. Outside, on a table, were two half-empty Bloody Marys, celery stalks sticking out of the crushed ice. Earlier a bellhop had told me that a child had fallen into the river and was thought to have drowned. "Last night you seemed quite interested in Linda Gail's contract with a film company called Castle Productions," I said.

"You lost me, son."

"You've heard of that company?"

"I could have. I don't remember. What's the problem?"

"You seemed to be enjoying a private joke about it."

He removed a pocket comb from his slacks and combed back the hair on the sides of his head. "We didn't give you enough money?"

"I'd just like a straight answer."

"I don't have any idea what you're talking about, Weldon."

"Roy Wiseheart told me he makes movies."

"He and his father own half the planet. Why should you be surprised they're in the movie business?"

"Does Roy Wiseheart own Castle Productions?"

"Ask him. I never met the gentleman."

"Maybe I think too much, huh?" I said.

"I wouldn't say that. You can't be too careful in business."

I went out on the balcony. Down below, two divers in wet suits and air tanks were climbing out of the river. An ambulance was parked close by, its back doors yawning open. An overweight Mexican woman was crying inconsolably, reaching out for a gurney that a paramedic was pushing toward the ambulance. Behind me, Lloyd Fincher put on his aviator glasses to protect his eyes from the glare. He screwed a cigarette into a gold holder. He stepped next to me and lit the cigarette, then dropped the burnt match over the railing. In profile, I could see the tiny red veins in the whites of his eyes, the discoloration of his skin from the booze still in his system, his down-hooked snub of a nose that reminded me of a sheep's. I wondered who Lloyd Fincher was.

"A fine day," he said. He took a puff off the cigarette holder and exhaled the smoke into the breeze.

"It's too bad what happened down there," I said.

"Pardon?"

"The little boy," I said.

He looked at me, then at the ambulance. "What happened?" he said.

"I thought you were watching."

He leaned over the rail to see better. "I was watching the skywriter. Look." He pointed upward. A canary-yellow biplane was writing the word "Pepsi" in smoke against a sky as flawless as blue silk. "That pilot's an artist, isn't he?"

He continued to enjoy his cigarette and watch the biplane climb straight up into the sky. I didn't know what to say. I believe there are people among us who are not simply insentient but are also incapable of thought. Lloyd Fincher was one of these. I left him to his reverie and started toward the door.

"Weldon?" he said behind me.

I turned around.

"Watch yourself," he said.

"Regarding what?"

He drank the ice melt and remaining vodka and tomato juice out of his glass. He bit off a piece of celery and chewed it. "Whatever comes down the pike," he replied. "It's a nest of vipers out there. Maybe that's why I have to get laid almost every day. It keeps my mind off things."

ROSITA AND I stayed over an extra night and ate in an outdoor Mexican restaurant on the River Walk, by an arched stone bridge and a cypress tree whose leaves resembled green lace. I paid the mariachi band twenty dollars to play "San Antonio Rose" so we could dance under a full moon to Bob Wills's signature song in front of the Alamo. I didn't think those who died within the mission walls would find us disrespectful; in fact, I believed their voices whispered to us and told us to celebrate the lives that had been given us and the love we shared. They also told us to treat the world as a grand cathedral and to give no sway to either death or evil men who sought to spread their net over the globe.

I am almost sure I heard them say all those things.

FIVE DAYS LATER, deep in a Louisiana swamp, Roy Wiseheart rode a cream-colored gelding, sixteen hands high, down our pipeline right-of-way. When he dismounted, he removed his Stetson hat and wiped a mosquito out of his hair. "I knew you and Pine would pull it out of the fire," he said, shaking my hand. "By God, it's good to see you, Holland. You're the real deal."

"I didn't quite catch all that," I said.

He told me he had heard by chance that we were laying a pipeline across the Atchafalaya Basin to a refinery in Texas, and that a friend in Morgan City had lent him the horse and a trailer and a pickup. I wanted to believe him. He was handsome and clear-eyed and apparently humane and, for a rich man, egalitarian in his attitudes. I had never spent much time thinking about the very rich, primarily because I hadn't known many. Those I knew came from old money and had always struck me as bland and obtuse and dependent upon servants and usually given over to vices that were adolescent in nature, particularly in their sexual lives, about which they seemed to show terrible judgment. In the town where I grew up, my grandfather was considered well-to-do. In reality, we barely got by. Once, when I asked him about the importance of money, he replied, "It won't buy happiness, but it'll keep a mess of grief off your porch. Rich or poor, everybody gets to the barn. It can be a hard ride, too."

I always thought that statement summed up the human condition better than any line I ever heard. Death was the great leveler. Whenever I was tempted to compare my lot with others', I tried to remember Grandfather's words. I wondered if this wasn't one of those moments.

"What's the 'real deal'?" I said to Wiseheart.

"You don't rattle. You refinanced yourself, and you're back in the game. I admire that."

"How do you know these things?"

"Come on up to the highway with me. I want your advice about something."

"You need to explain how you know about my financial situation."

"You think a blabbermouth like Lloyd Fincher can keep a confidence? Wake up."

"What do you want advice about?"

"It's not about business."

"Will you answer my question, sir?"

He looked sideways and blew out his breath. "It's personal as it gets. Call it a spiritual problem."

"I'm probably not your guy."

"Then to hell with you."

"Say again?"

"You don't understand English?"

"I want to make sure I heard you right before I knock you down."

He smiled, pointing his finger at me, as though tapping on the air. "See what I'm saying? You've got moxie, bud."

WE DROVE IN his truck to a ramshackle roadhouse set back in a grove of live oaks and slash pines not far from the edge of a vast swamp. The sky had darkened, and the air smelled of ozone and brass and fish that had died from the explosive charges set off underwater by a seismic rig. The roadhouse was attached to a six-room motel that had already turned on the neon tubing that ran along the eaves. A gleaming purple Lincoln Continental, with whitewalls and wire wheels, was parked in front of the last room on the road.

"Is that your vehicle?" I asked.

"How do you like it?"

"Has anyone told you this is a hot-pillow joint?"

"I like to check in on the folk and see what they're up to."

"The *folk*?" I said.

He was laughing. "You're the perfect straight man," he said.

The roadhouse was almost empty. We sat at a table in front of the window fan and ordered a plate of boudin and two bottles of Dr. Nut. Wiseheart watched the waitress walk away from the table. "Is this place really a cathouse?"

"That's its reputation."

"What an irony. You know what I want your advice about?"

"No clue."

"You ever stray?"

"From what?"

"You know what."

"My marriage vows?"

"Boy, you're fast as lightning."

"That's why you got me here? I can't believe this."

"My wife has multiple mental problems. I won't go into detail. Put it this way: Her father liked little girls. One night he decided to drive himself and his wife off a cliff into the Atlantic Ocean. Since the night her parents died, my wife has been an ice cube."

I was trying to signal the waitress to bring the check.

"I say something wrong?" Wiseheart asked.

The shadows of the fan blades were rippling across his face. The impropriety of speaking about his marital problems to someone he hardly knew seemed totally lost on him. I started to speak, but he cut me off. "I got into a sexual relationship with another man's wife," he said. "I don't feel good about it. I've had a dalliance here and there, but not with a married woman."

"Then get out of it."

"Hell hath no fury," he said.

"What do you want from me?"

He folded his hands on the table and looked out the window at the swamp and the thunderheads building in the south and the wind straightening the moss in the trees. "I just wondered what you thought of me."

"Why should you care about my opinion?"

"I know your war record. You were at Omaha Beach and the Bulge. You heard the story about the Nip trainer I shot down at the expense of my squadron leader?"

I looked away from him.

"I had four kills. The trainer gave me five and the status of an ace. All I saw was the rising sun on the fuselage. I thought it was a Zero. I didn't realize my mistake until I was down on the deck. I took out the trainer anyway. When it caught fire, I saw the pilot's face. He looked like he was seventeen. When I climbed back upstairs, it was too late to help Captain Levy."

"You thought you were protecting him. As far as the Japanese trainee is concerned, maybe he would have flown a kamikaze into the side of an American battleship."

"Not everybody thinks that way."

"They weren't there. They've never paid any dues. They have no idea how you think when other people are trying to kill you. What if the trainer had been a Zero and gotten on your leader's tail?"

"You're a good guy, Holland."

"There's nothing exceptional about me. Regarding that other matter, my advice is to bail out."

"Which matter is that?"

"What do you think?"

"Oh, the marital question. I don't know about that. She's quite a gal."

"I'm done on this."

He beamed. "I nailed you again. That's three times. I have to invite you to one of our poker games. God, you're fun."

I've always subscribed to the notion that we can never really know the soul of another. I didn't know whether Roy Wiseheart was tormented by his conscience or his ego. Maybe a little of both. Or was he simply a manipulator? I went to the bar and paid our check. When I returned to the table, he was staring out the window at the rain dimpling the water in the swamp. "Know why I stay at a place like this?" he asked.

"No, you're a mystery man."

"My room doesn't have a phone. Nobody knows who I am. I fish at sunset and sunrise for big-mouth bass. I caught an eight-pounder right by that clump of flooded gum trees."

"I need to get back to the line," I said.

"They're going to get you."

"That's the second time in less than a week someone has delivered me a vague warning. Who are *they*?"

"Take your choice."

"Why am I a threat to anyone?"

"You're a water walker. Guys like you cause trouble. You're not a team player. Wait till you meet some of the Saudis. Some of them should be forced to wear full-body condoms."

"I can take care of myself."

"They'll crush you and Pine. They'll bankrupt your family and turn you against each other, they'll take away your home, they'll ruin your name. They can make a speed bump out of a guy without breaking a sweat."

"My grandfather knocked John Wesley Hardin out of the saddle and kicked him in the face and locked him in jail," I said. "I put a bullet in the back of Clyde Barrow's automobile, with Clyde and Bonnie Parker and Raymond Hamilton and his girlfriend inside. I was sixteen. What do you think of that?"

He didn't answer my question. Maybe with the rain tinking on the fan blades, he couldn't hear everything I said, or maybe he was unimpressed by the rural and violent world in which I had grown up.

We walked outside just as the rain cut loose. Then a strange event occurred that made me realize Roy Wiseheart would never be a quick study. A bolt of lightning struck a cypress tree not twenty yards from us, splintering the trunk, cooking the leaves, boiling the water around the roots, filling the air with a thunderous clap that was like someone slapping the flats of his hands on my eardrums. Mud and water and the detritus of the tree showered down on our heads. Wiseheart never moved. He stared at the smoke and flame rising from the base of the tree, his expression composed. "Incoming," he said. "Told you. We're on the wrong side of things, Holland."

I wanted to get a lot of distance between me and Roy Wiseheart.

ONE MONTH LATER, the right-of-way flooded and we had to shut down the line for five days and return to Houston. On a fine summer evening, I drove to Hershel's home on Hawthorne Street to talk over an offshore pipeline south of Lake Charles. I caught Hershel and Linda Gail unawares, in the midst of moving. "Where are you going?" I asked.

"Into our new home," Linda Gail replied. "In River Oaks."

I looked at Hershel. He grinned and glanced away.

"River Oaks?" I said.

"Is something wrong with that?" Linda Gail said.

The dead-end street where they were living was beautiful, lined with bungalows and two-story brick houses and green lawns and shade trees. On the other side of the cul-de-sac were a canebrake and a huge pasture with live oaks in it that must have been two hundred years old. Beyond the pasture, against a salmon sky, you could see the neon-striped tower of a theater called the Alabama. The ambiance was a fusion of the pastoral and the urban South, in the best possible way. "Why would you want to leave?" I asked.

That was a mistake.

"Maybe it's none of your business, Mr. Weldon Avery Holland," she said.

"He's just kidding, Linda Gail," Hershel said. "Tell him what we're doing. He has a misunderstanding."

"I don't see any misunderstanding at all," she said. "We're moving into an elegant neighborhood. Are you suggesting we don't belong there, Weldon?"

"I like the bungalow y'all have, that's all. This street puts me in mind of Norman Rockwell. There's a watermelon stand just yonder on Westheimer, under those live oaks. There's a firehouse on up the street, and an ice cream parlor and a grocery that has all its produce and fruit out on the porch. I always liked this part of Houston."

"Well, I'm sure *The Saturday Evening Post* would love your endorsement," she said. "If it will make you feel better, we are not buying the house in River Oaks. It is being lent to us by Jack Valentine. He's the documentary director who arranged my screen test at Castle Productions."

"It's a rent-with-option-to-buy deal, Weldon," Hershel said.

"I need to talk with you about laying some pipe in Calcasieu Parish," I said.

"Do y'all have to do that now?" Linda Gail said.

"Yeah, we do, Linda Gail," I said.

"Let me ask you a question," she said. "Please be candid in your response, too. Where would you be without Hershel's welding machines?"

"Sweetheart, don't be saying something like that," Hershel said.

"I would appreciate your not telling me what to say and what not to say," she replied.

I should have left. But business was business, and principle was principle. "How about I buy y'all some ice cream?" I said.

"I'll be in the house, packing," she said. "Jack will be here in twenty minutes with the van. Try to be of some help, would you, please, Hershel?"

She went into the house, a brick one-story bungalow covered with English ivy, and flowerbeds filled with roses and blue and pink hydrangeas. Hershel got into the car with me. I didn't start the engine. "This won't take long," I said. "We can probably get the contract for that well going in the south of Calcasieu Parish. We can also get in on the drilling."

"I don't know, Weldon. We got burned pretty bad at New Roads."

"I've talked to the geologist. I went to school with him. I trust him. He says the odds are one in three we'll punch into a dome."

"You call it."

"Nope. Dixie Belle is a partnership."

"I'm not thinking too clear right now. I thought this house in River Oaks might make Linda Gail happy. But nothing makes her happy. She's always mad about something."

"Sorry to hear that."

"What do you reckon it might be?"

I shook my head and didn't reply.

"We went to the public pool, and she told me to wear canvas shoes till I got in the water. I asked if she didn't like being seen in public with a man missing three of his toes. She said she was concerned for the children at the pool."

I looked through the windshield at a rainbow that seemed to dip into the pasture. Clouds that resembled lavender horsetails were scattered against the sun's afterglow. *What a perfect evening,*

I thought, wondering why we often substitute pain for the fruits of heaven and earth. Cruelty comes in many forms, but the level of injury in Hershel's eyes was one I'll never forget. "You should have received the Silver Star instead of me," I said. "You're the best line sergeant I ever knew, and one of the best human beings."

"Maybe she was telling the truth. Kids get shocked easily. My right foot looks like the flipper on a seal."

"You want to go in on the well?"

"Hell yeah, I do," he replied. He patted his hands up and down on his knees. "Weldon?"

"What is it?"

I knew what was coming. I wanted to get out of the automobile and begin walking back to the Heights before he said it. But I was trapped in my car with no way to exit the situation. I could see the neon-lit tower of the movie theater against the paleness of the sky, like a beacon telling us of the promise that awaited us in America's Babylon by the sea. "You think Linda Gail is having an affair?" he asked.

"I wouldn't have any way of knowing something like that," I said. "I recommend getting those thoughts out of your head."

A few minutes later, the documentary-maker named Jack Valentine arrived with a moving van and three workmen, and the Pines began moving their furniture out of the bungalow on Hawthorne in preparation for their new life in a sprawling oak-canopied green arbor across town, one where moat and castle were norms and even moth and rust and decay were given short shrift.

THE HARDEST AND dirtiest work in the oil patch is done by the crews who cut right-of-ways and build board roads in swampy terrain. Imagine walking in a flooded woods dense with mosquitoes in hundred-degree heat, hacking your way through air vines and cypress and gum and willow trees, always watching for a cottonmouth moccasin that might drop from a branch on your neck or sink its fangs in your wrist when you reach down to move a log. Your boots are encased in mud up to the ankles; your clothes are sopping with sweat; gnats get in your nose and mouth; leeches attach themselves to your calves; your eyes burn. If you drink all the water in the canteen, you're out of luck. Your face feels poached, out of round from all the mosquito bites. The air smells of humus and carrion and water grown stagnant inside the mud; there is a rawness to it that is like the odor of birth or fish roe or leakage from a sewer line. Through the trees, you can see waves smacking against a sandbar out on the bay, but there is no wind inside the woods, no breath of fresh air, no movement of any kind, and the hottest part of the day is ahead.

We were cutting a right-of-way through the southern tip of Calcasieu Parish when an old yellow school bus with Texas plates lumbered along the levee and stopped just above a dry spot that our brush gang and board road crew were using as a staging area. A man dressed in a cowboy shirt and straw hat and khaki pants stuffed inside rubber boots swung off the bus and approached me, the string and tab of a Bull Durham tobacco sack hanging out of his shirt pocket. The bus was packed from stem to stern with dark-skinned Mexicans. Not one of them got up from his seat to stretch or get a drink from the water can or relieve himself in the bushes.

"Well, we made it," the man said, extending his hand. "Tell me where you want them at."

"I don't know what you're talking about," I said.

"I got thirty-two men waiting to clear brush and lay board road."

"Not for me, you don't."

"You're with Dixie Belle?"

"I'm half owner. Somebody gave you a bum lead. We've got our own people."

One of his eyes was watery and had no color and kept blinking, like an injured moth. He took a handkerchief from his pocket and pressed the moisture out of it. "We drove all the way from San Antone. I think you're mixed up."

"No, I'm not the one with the problem. You've got the wrong address."

"Hang on. I've got the paperwork on the bus."

"Don't bother. Obviously, a mistake was made. But that's it. This conversation is over."

"Sir, don't turn your back on me. Sir? *Sir,* did you hear me?"

I turned around. The men on the bus were all looking at me through the windows. "Who do you work for?"

"Minuteman, Incorporated."

"I've heard about you," I said. "This isn't your fault. But you need to leave now. I'm sorry about your men. There's a campground outside Lake Charles where they can shower and rest up."

"You think we're just gonna drive off?"

"Unless you want the mosquitoes to start eating on you."

I walked away. A couple of minutes later, I heard him start up the bus and clank the transmission into gear. "What was that about?" Hershel said.

I told him.

"How did he get our name? How'd he know where we were?" he said.

"You got me."

"He's out of San Antonio?"

"Yeah, same place Lloyd Fincher lives," I replied.

That night the phone rang in my motel room. I hoped the call was from Rosita. It wasn't. "What the hell is going on over there, Weldon?" Fincher said.

"How you doin', Major?" I said.

"Not very well. I just heard from a labor office we use. Minuteman is their name."

"How'd you get my number?"

"From your wife. You told the crew leader to get lost?"

"No, I told him he'd made a mistake."

"You didn't get my message that these guys were headed over there?"

"No, I didn't. When did you become an executive with our company?"

"Maybe you don't quite understand the nature of our arrangement. Our loan agreement guarantees us one percent of Dixie Belle's profits as long as the contract is in effect."

"That's right," I said.

"If you look carefully at the paragraph that details assignation and management of those profits, you'll see my company has a fiduciary trust mandate. In other words, we have a managerial responsibility to protect our stockholders' investment. We sent you a tremendous cost saver today. You refused it. We've got us a problem here. Now, what the hell are you going to do about it?"

"Minuteman hires wets for minimum wage or less. So far, we have a good relationship with the union. We don't want a picket line in front of the job."

"If you breach the terms of our contract, we can call in the loan."

"Then do it. We'll declare bankruptcy and your company won't get five cents."

"Remember what I told you in that tuberculosis sanitarium in France? Don't be a hardhead. People will beat on you enough without you helping them."

"Hershel and I know how to lay pipe and make money, Major. Stay out of the oil patch, and we'll stay out of the insurance business. Don't try to pull some kind of contractual flimflam on us again."

I eased the phone back into the cradle, the side of my face tingling. Then I let out my breath and tried to decompress. What's the old lesson in the army? Don't make enemies with anybody in records. What's the larger lesson in an organization? Don't humiliate bureaucrats whose careers are characterized by mediocrity. It may take them a while, but sooner or later, they'll park an arrow between your shoulder blades.

I called Fincher back. "Lloyd, you're looking out for your company's investment. I can understand that. But union trouble could tear us up. It's not worth it. Let's put this behind us."

I could hear ice cubes clinking in a glass and a woman's voice in the background.

"Did you hear me?" I said.

"Yeah, that's a good attitude, son," he said. "No need to call back.

I'm kind of tied up right now, get my drift? One day I'll stop flying the flag, I guess, but not for a while."

"Good night, Lloyd."

"Weldon, tell me you're not going to be an ongoing pain in the ass."

"I wouldn't dream of it," I said.

Chapter 12

IT WAS SUNDAY night when I got a phone call in Houston that reminded me of a line in the Bible: There are those who are made different in the womb. I had heard the voice before. It was full of rust, the words coming from a place where humanity and pity had never taken hold. "Bet you don't know who this is," the voice said.

"The Cajun dance hall outside Opelousas. You and your friends followed us into the parking lot," I said.

"You got a good memory, boy. Got a business deal for you."

"What's your name?"

"I'll tell you when we meet. You know where the Bloody Bucket is at?"

"No."

"I'll give you directions."

"I think it's better that you not call here anymore."

"Your wife like her new piano? What was that piece she was playing about five minutes ago? 'Clair de lune'?"

On the corner, at the end of the esplanade, there was a telephone booth under a streetlamp. I thought I could see a man's silhouette inside.

"Cat got your tongue?" the caller said.

"Tell me where you are," I said.

I took my raincoat out of the hallway closet and went upstairs. Then I came back down wearing the coat. Rosita was still playing the piano. "Where are you going?" she asked.

"Some fellow wants to talk to me about a business deal. I'll be back shortly."

"Why are you wearing your raincoat?"

I put my right hand in the pocket, adjusting the weight of the coat on my shoulders. "It's fixing to rain."

She looked out the window. A solitary raindrop struck the glass. "Don't be long. It's Sunday. You need to relax a little more, Weldon."

Geographically, the distance from our neighborhood in the Heights to the Bloody Bucket was no more than two miles. In terms of the cultural divide, the distance could not have been greater. It was a beer joint that prided itself on its violent clientele. The women were either masochists or over-the-hill whores; hardly a man drinking in there had not been in Huntsville or Sugar Land. Houston cops didn't enter the Bloody Bucket except in numbers, usually with a baton hanging from the wrist.

The interior was painted red and black; the only illumination came from the neon beer signs on the wall behind the bar and the electrified rippling colors inside the casing of the Wurlitzer and the tin-shaded bulb hanging above the pool table. My caller was sitting in a booth by the entrance to the women's restroom, his hands folded on the tabletop, a cigarette burning in an ashtray inches away. I sat down across from him. "What's your name?" I said.

"There's coat hooks by the door if you want to hang up your coat," he replied.

"I'm fine. Are you going to tell me who you are?"

"Harlan McFey. I'm a private investigator. Want to see my ID?"

"No."

"Why not?"

"Because you can buy one at any pawnshop on Congress Street. You fond of looking in people's windows, Mr. McFey?"

"If the occasion demands it." He took a puff off his cigarette and returned the cigarette to the ashtray. He opened a manila folder on the tabletop. "We got a four-inch file on you and people of your acquaintance. I'm willing to share it. I'm also willing to share information on the man who hired me to bird-dog you and yours. Here's for openers." He handed me the top torn half of a blown-up black-and-white photograph. "She's enough to make any man forget his Christian upbringing. If we can come to a business agreement, I'll show you who's underneath her. Believe me when I say it's not her husband."

In the photo, Linda Gail's head was tilted back, her mouth open in the midst of orgasm, her bare breasts as taut as cantaloupes. I pushed the photo back across the table. "What are you after?" I said.

"A percentage of that offshore well y'all are drilling south of Lake Charles."

"Is that all?"

"I've been picking up rich men's crumbs all my life. I think it's time I get in on the entrée."

"Let me tell you what you're going to get out of this, Mr. McFey. With luck, you'll stay alive. If you show this photo to Hershel Pine, he'll probably kill you. If he doesn't, there's a good chance I will."

He picked up his cigarette from the ashtray and took another puff, squinting as he did, breathing the smoke out of his nose before he stubbed out the cigarette. "You and me go way back; you're just not aware of it. I know that Bonnie Parker and Clyde Barrow and Raymond Hamilton and his girlfriend came to your house in 1934. I was a guard in Eastham Pen when Bonnie and Clyde shot their way inside the gates and killed a guard. That guard was a friend of mine. So I made a point of talking to Raymond before he died, reminding the boy of his sins and what was awaiting him when he met Old Sparky. I also watched him ride the bolt. You know what those boys mean when they say 'ride the bolt,' don't you? I know everything about your wife, too." He lit another cigarette and waited for me to speak.

"I've run across my share of white trash, Mr. McFey, but I think you've set a new standard," I said.

He smiled while the bartender served him a bottle of Pearl off a circular tray. He poured his glass full and salted the foam. He took a sip and wiped his mouth, then licked the salt off the web of skin behind his thumb and forefinger. "I've got some other things here that might interest you. Your daddy left y'all in '33, didn't he?"

An electric fan on a stanchion was blowing across the tops of the booths. Nonetheless, I could feel the temperature rising in the room, my body heat intensifying inside the raincoat. I touched the back of my neck. My skin seemed on fire. "It's warm in here, isn't it?" I said. I pulled my raincoat off my right arm and let it flop on the seat, my hand resting on a hard lump inside the pocket. "Would you repeat what you just said?"

"Your father went to parts unknown and never came home," he replied. He slipped an eight-by-ten off a stack of photos and set it in front of me. He placed a penlight next to it. "Take a look and tell me what that is."

The photograph showed an excavation dug around a section of pipe buried five feet deep in the ground. "That's called a bell hole," I said.

"When there's a leak in the pipe, it's got to be dug up and re-welded on the joint, right?" he said.

"Yes, the hole around the joint has the shape of a bell, hence the name. What does this have to do with my father?"

He placed another photo on top of the first one. "See anybody in that group you recognize?" He tilted his glass and emptied it, the salt draining down to the edge. "Come on, boy, who do you see?"

There were four men digging inside the bell hole. They were all thin, their stomachs flat as shirt board, their clothes loose on their bodies. They looked like Depression-era men who might have climbed out from under a boxcar. One of them was wearing a slug cap and staring straight at the camera, as though bemused, as though he didn't belong there.

"That's my father."

"Thought you'd be interested."

"Where did you get this?"

"Out of a company file."

The furrows in McFey's face resembled erosion in a pan full of dirt. His eyes contained a darkness I had seen in few men. A canine tooth shone just behind his lip. "Maybe I shouldn't show you this last one, but here it is. The explosion down in that hole flat blew them to hell. You can see the smoke rising off what's left of their clothes."

My left hand was crimped on the edge of the photograph; my right hand held the penlight. I felt a tremolo in my fingers that I could hardly control.

He said, "As I understand it, when a bell hole blows out, it's for one reason only: Somebody at the pump station left the shutoff valve open. Am I correct on that?"

"That's right."

"These photos were taken for a company magazine article. After the explosion, they got buried in a file cabinet. They probably could have handled a negligence suit for pennies, but the man who owns that company knows how to make the eagle scream."

"You need to tell me the company's name, Mr. McFey."

"Mine to know, lessen we strike us a deal."

I got up from the booth and draped my coat over my forearm. I put on my hat. Three motorcyclists were drinking at the bar, their bare arms swollen with gristle and wrapped with hair. Someone was playing a pinball machine, smashing its corners with the heels of his hands. "How long were you outside my window?"

"I wasn't. I was standing on your front porch. I was gonna ring the bell, then decided to call instead."

"I see. You're no voyeur?"

He put the photos back in the manila envelope and closed it. "I can make your life easier. Take it or leave it."

"My guess is your employer fired you, Mr. McFey. I have the feeling you're not particularly employable right now."

He looked up at me, the corner of his mouth wrinkling. "You're not curious about who Miss Linda Gail was entertaining?"

I went out into the sudden coolness of the wind and the smell of rain and the heat lightning coursing through the clouds. I put on my raincoat and stood in the doorway of an abandoned brick building three doors down from the beer joint. Ten minutes later, Harlan McFey walked out on the street and blew his nose in a handkerchief. He looked in both directions and replaced his handkerchief in his pocket, then walked to a darkened filling station on the corner where he had parked his car. He never heard me until I was two feet from him. I shoved him inside his car.

"Do you know what I'm holding?" I asked.

He stared at my hand. "A Luger."

"If the Waffen SS captured you with one of these, they shot you with it. My wife was a guest of the SS. Did you discover that in your research?"

"Yes."

"What else did you learn about her?"

"She's a Red."

"Is there anything you want to tell me?"

"No."

"Do you believe I'm capable of killing you?"

His eyes left mine. He looked at nothing. I hit him across the bridge of the nose with the butt of the Luger. He made a muffled sound that could have been a word but probably wasn't; he bent over, cupping his nose with both hands, blood dripping on the front of his shirt.

"Do you want to tell me who you work for?"

"No, sir," he said.

"It doesn't matter. I already know. If you come near my wife or me again, I'll shoot you through the face." I caught him by the necktie and pulled him out on the concrete. I removed the photo of my father wearing his slug cap and threw the rest of the folder down a storm drain. I squatted next to McFey. "Are you all right?"

"What do I look like?"

"You watched Raymond Hamilton die in the electric chair?"

"Yes, sir."

"Just to see him suffer?"

"I just wanted to tell him something."

"What?"

"How Bonnie and Clyde died. How she screamed like a banshee when they capped her. I wanted him to know they hurt like hell."

I walked away and left him bleeding on the concrete. I don't know if men are evil by choice or if some are born without a conscience. I suspected Harlan McFey knew the answer. I didn't think he would ever share it with the rest of us.

I WAS DUE BACK on the job Monday morning, but I called Hershel and put him in charge and, after breakfast, headed straight for Roy Wiseheart's home in River Oaks. On a street of mansions, I passed the home of which Linda Gail Pine was so proud. It was couched on a small, treeless lot. With its flat roof and off-white hand-grimed stucco walls, it could have been a store that sold used automobile tires. I wondered if she had knocked on the neighbors' doors to introduce herself, or brought them a home-baked pie or wildflowers she had picked in a vacant field. Her gladness of heart, the rural innocence that dwelled alongside her obtuseness toward her husband's adoration, made me grieve, if only for a moment, on the pain and disappointment that were waiting for her in the wings.

Roy Wiseheart and his wife lived on an estate that even by River Oaks's standards was so majestic and massive in its architectural dimensions that you got lost looking at it. Its fluted columns were three stories high; its white paint glowed like a symbol of capitalistic purity inside a bower of towering oaks. The ambiance of lichen-stained stone birdbaths and tarnished sundials and hanging trumpet vine and roses that climbed up trellises to the second story were all part of an antebellum stage set that had no relationship to the rough-hewn legacy of Sam Houston. Even the carriage houses and the servant quarters were made of soft antique brick that probably came from historical teardowns in the Carolinas. As I stood on the breezy porch and rang the chimes, I felt like I was about to walk through a doorway into the classical world, and once there I might not want to leave it.

Roy Wiseheart pulled open the door, smiling broadly, as though I had walked in on a joke he had told to someone else. "Holland, you rascal! You won't believe who I just got off the phone with," he said. "Come in, come in! This is hilarious."

He walked toward the breakfast room, talking over his shoulder. "You just missed Whorehouse Harlan by three minutes. I'm talking about McFey, the guy who tried to shake you down." He laughed so hard he had to sit down. " 'Whorehouse' is his nickname. Know why? He had venereal disease of the face. That's how he got those furrows in his skin. Guess under what circumstances he contracted it? The key word is 'under.' "

"I'll pass."

"He says you broke his nose."

"I doubt that."

"Holland, you're heck on wheels. God, I'm glad you dropped by."

Through the French doors, I could see flowers blooming in the shade of the live oaks, the potted Hong Kong orchids beaded with dew on the brick terrace, the swimming pool that looked as blue and cool as a Roman bath. His breakfast table was set with warmers containing ham and bacon and biscuits and redeye gravy and scrambled eggs. "Eat up," he said.

"I already ate. How do you know McFey?"

"He was a bird dog for my father. My father fired him a couple of years ago. You hit him in the nose with a Luger?"

"Probably. I have blank spaces in my head sometimes. Why's he calling you now?" I said.

"He's trying to sell information. Plus, you scared the crap out of him."

"Information about what?" I asked.

"You, your wife, any dirt he can dig up. He's a scavenger. Nobody takes him seriously."

"I do," I replied.

He leaned out of his chair and hit me on the arm. "Sit down. At least have some coffee. You're a breath of fresh air. Most of the people I know have the thinking power of cinder blocks." He folded a strip of bacon inside a biscuit, then took a bite of the biscuit. His eyes brightened as though he were examining a thought in the back of his mind. "Did you think Harlan was working for me?"

"You were the first person to show an interest in our welding machines."

"And you think I hire dimwits like McFey to represent me?"

"You said he worked for your father."

"My father employs people a Bedouin wouldn't shake hands with." He picked up an ornate silver coffeepot and filled a cup. He set the cup and a spoon on a saucer and handed them to me. "Come on, Holland. You're a good judge of people. I'm not a back-shooter. I like the hell out of you."

"I think McFey wants to hurt Hershel Pine."

"In what way?"

I kept my eyes on his. "Maybe he'll try to mess up Linda Gail and Hershel's marriage."

"I hear she's doing just fine. She's got a role in a western being filmed in New Mexico. The director says she's a natural."

"How do you know all this?"

"I own part of the company that signed her up. I told you I'm in the movie business, didn't I?"

"Yes, you did. Do you know Linda Gail very well?"

His cheeks were rosy. He smiled with his eyes, the way a woman would. "What are you asking me, my friend?"

"I'm not sure," I said.

"Don't let McFey get to you. He's fun to laugh about, but under it all, he's an evil man. The oil business is full of low-level operatives like him. If the money is right, they'd kill the president. That's not hyperbole. See what happens if Truman tries to get rid of the oil depletion allowance. It's the biggest corporate swindle in the history of American taxation, but nobody dares touch it."

I wasn't interested in his politics or his cynical statements about the corrupt empire that he both served and was empowered by. "You've got quite a place here," I said. "It's enough to make a Bolshevik out of a fellow."

"I've got an extra swimsuit that should fit you. How about it?"

Autumn was on the wind, and the sky had turned a hard blue, like an inverted ceramic bowl. Red and yellow oak leaves tumbled onto the shimmering silklike surface of the pool; even the sun seemed captured by the inviting quality of the water, like a wobbling yellow balloon just beneath the surface. "Why not?" I said.

"That's the spirit, by God," he said, slapping me on the thigh.

"Who's that down there, Roy?" a harsh voice called from the landing at the top of the stairs.

"Mr. Holland dropped by, Clara. Everything is fine," Wiseheart replied. "We'll be in the pool."

"Is he with someone?" she said.

"No, he's come to talk about a business matter."

I set my cup quietly in the saucer and rose from the table. "I'd better be going," I said.

"No, dammit, you will not." He walked through a hallway to the foot of the stairs. "Go back to bed, Clara. We'll go to the club for lunch. Do you understand me? Everything is grand."

"Send Pepe up," she said.

"What for?"

"I want him to massage my back. My sciatica is particularly bad this morning."

"Right away, dear," Wiseheart said.

"Is your wife bothered by the prospect of Rosita being here?" I said.

"No. I give you my word," he replied. "Clara has convinced herself that Communist agents working for the government are about to turn the IRS loose on us. Come on, be a good fellow and stay with me. The water is fine."

He was right. Ten minutes later, I was floating facedown on an air mattress in the middle of the pool, my arms trailing in the coolness of the water, my back warm under the sun, the oak limbs rustling overhead, a vague and sleepy erotic sensation spreading through my loins. Was there a sybaritic element in Wiseheart's environment that made me feel the way I did, the sensations a visitor to the Baths of Caracalla might experience? Wealth buys insularity, and together the two guarantee secret access to all the forbidden pleasures the world can offer. What better example of satiating one's repressed desires and celebrating the self than the place I was enjoying?

Wiseheart sprang from the diving board and plummeted to the bottom of the pool, as sleek and graceful and hard-bodied as a porpoise. When he surfaced, his face was inches from mine, his breath sweet from a piece of mint on his tongue. "It's like a bit of the ancient world, isn't it?" he said, as if reading my thoughts. "It's not easily given up, either. It's not unlike the allure of a woman's thighs."

"What are you trying to tell me?"

"We're in the midst of creating an empire. Our virtues are those of pagans, not Christians. Once you admit that, you'll be surprised how many of your inner conflicts will leave you."

"I don't have inner conflicts."

"You will," he said.

I wondered if he was speaking of the affair he was having with another man's wife; I wondered if the woman was Linda Gail Pine.

He pushed off from my air mattress and dove to the bottom of the pool, not surfacing for almost two minutes, gasping for air, eyes wide, like a man with an invisible cord strung round his throat. "See? I'm more fish than mammal," he said. "Don't get caught up in rules, Holland. Accept the spoils of war. If you don't, someone else will. Just don't take a tour of a Saudi jail."

"You've seen one?"

"I keep a short memory about those kinds of things," he replied. "Hey, the world is a lovely, exotic brothel, in the best possible way, if a fellow wants to have a run at it. Regarding Linda Gail Pine, I know what you were thinking. Forget it. I may be a bastard, but I wouldn't lie to a man like you, one I respect."

He began swimming laps, taking long strokes, breathing with his mouth turned to one side, his tanned body slicing through the water. I was twenty-nine. He was about thirty-five. His body was as supple as a teenager's. In terms of real age, he was a whole generation older than I. He pulled himself up on the side of the pool and sat on the tile, his legs hanging in the water, strands of his coppery hair in his eyes, his profile as handsome and ethereal as a Greek god's.

"Why are you looking at me like that?" he said.

"I think you may be from an earlier time."

"Like one of those fellows with a washboard brow flinging a javelin at mammoths?"

"More like a Byronic figure swimming through a wine-dark sea," I replied.

"What I wouldn't trade to have your gift for language. I majored in geology. We used to say, 'Six months ago I couldn't spell "geologist." Now I are one.' You dream about the war much?"

"I dream about the death camp where I found my wife."

"You're lucky."

I got off the air mattress and stood up in the shallows. I pushed the mattress toward the deep end and watched it bump into the concrete drain gutter. "I guess I didn't understand you."

"My squadron leader's kite burned. He was trying to get the canopy open. I saw his face when he went down. He was alive inside the flames. I swear he looked straight at me, like he wanted to tell me something."

"Tell you what?"

"That he understood. That it wasn't my fault."

His eyes never blinked. They were red from chlorine, glistening with moisture.

"I tried to get a guy out of a Sherman that was on fire," I said. "The plates burned my hands. I gave it up. We didn't create those events, Roy. They were imposed upon us."

"That's the first time you called me by my first name. Know the real reason I want to go into business with you?"

"No, I don't."

"You need somebody to save you from yourself. It's you who's out of the past. What's the title of that great French ballad? *The Song of*

Roland? That's you, Holland. No matter what you say, you hear the horns blowing along the road to Roncevaux."

The wind gusted across the surface of the pool, wrinkling it like old skin. My blood ran cold. Could Roy Wiseheart see into my soul? Were he and I more alike than I wanted to concede?

Chapter 13

THE NEXT MORNING I drove to Lake Charles and took Rosita with me because I didn't want her home alone with the likes of Harlan McFey roaming around, perhaps seeking revenge. Before I left the house, I picked up the morning newspaper from the lawn and stuck it in my coat pocket without looking at the front page. Hershel met us at the motel on the south end of town, out by the lake. The air was cool, the sun buried inside rolling clouds that reminded me of the dust storms in the early 1930s. Waves full of sand and tiny nautical creatures were scudding up on the shoreline, then receding into the water. I thought I could smell gas on the wind from the swamp, a hint of early winter and a drawing down of light from the shingles of the world. Hershel was standing in the porte cochere, staring at the southern horizon, his face as hot as a lightbulb. "I've got us a boat. Let's get out to the rig," he said. "These guys aren't listeners."

"You have to explain that to me."

"This bonehead driller didn't have the blowout preventer on. He said the dome was at least another two thousand feet, if it was there at all."

"What does the geologist say?"

"Same thing. They're down in the mouth about our prospects. I told them if they didn't get the blowout preventer on, the sky was going to be on fire tonight."

"It's down there?" I said.

"I could smell it."

I didn't want to think about the two dusters we brought in outside of New Roads, a direct result of Hershel's conviction that a huge pay sand lay under our feet.

"Come on, Weldon. We need a diplomat. If those guys don't get the blowout preventer on, every guy on the floor is going to be incinerated."

"Let's don't get out of the paddock too fast on this one, Hershel," I said.

His face was stretched as tight as a helium balloon, his system hitting on all eight cylinders. "It's going to blow. I've never felt so strong about anything in my life. I'm sweating all over."

"I believe you, Hershel," Rosita said, placing her hand on his arm. "Can I come along?"

I saw the rigidity leave his face; he smiled.

The boat was a sixteen-footer with a console and a canvas top and two big outboard engines. The sky was darkening, the barometer dropping, the groundswells in the Gulf long and green and as flat as slate, tilting sideways, as though the horizon were out of kilter, then suddenly cresting in waves that could cover the gunwales. Each time we slid down the far side of a wave, cascades of foam slapped across the windshield. If Rosita had any fear, it never showed.

When we climbed aboard the rig, the clothes of the floor men were flattening against their bodies; they looked like men on the deck of an aircraft carrier. I had to yell for the geologist to hear me: "Mr. Pine believes we need to get that blowout preventer in place!"

"Pine is an interesting guy!" the geologist yelled back.

We climbed the ladder into what was called the doghouse, with the geologist and tool pusher and driller and two men who were majority stockholders in the company. Even though I had introduced Rosita as my wife, they kept looking at her out of the corners of their eyes, as though they had to remind themselves who she was or why she was there. Through the windows I could see the long gray-green, mist-shrouded coast of Louisiana, a strip of barrier islands and swamps and bayous and flooded trees that seemed left over from the first days of Creation. Above me, the derrick man on the monkey board was leaning out into space on his safety belt, racking pipe, his hard hat cinched with a strap under his chin. Down below, around the wellhead, I could see the roughnecks on the floor wrestling with the drill bit and the tongs, the oiled chain whipping around the pipe. They never missed a beat, never looked up in apprehension or fear when lightning struck the water or thunder boomed on the horizon.

None of the men in the room was sympathetic with Hershel's point of view—namely, that he knew more about drilling for oil than they did. The tool pusher took me aside. He had a round, clean-shaven face that was bright with windburn; he wore an insulated long-sleeved denim shirt and khakis that were hitched up high on his stomach. He glanced at his wristwatch, then glanced at it again.

"Are we taking too much of your time?" I asked.

"No, I appreciate y'all's concerns," he replied. "But that man over yonder drilled an offshore well about six miles from here in 1937 and went ninety-four hundred feet before he hit a pay sand. He's also the majority stockholder in this company. If I was y'all, I wouldn't be telling him his business, Mr. Holland. Another way of putting it is Mr. Pine is becoming a king-size irritant."

"Hershel's instincts are usually pretty good," I said, trying not to remember New Roads.

"Religion is for the church house. Instinct is for the horse track. This here is a dollar-and-cents environment, Mr. Holland."

I felt Rosita next to me, felt her arm slip inside mine, her hip touch against mine. "How's your overhead so far?" she said to the tool pusher.

"Couldn't be better. This whole job has been smooth as Vaseline."

I looked him in the face to indicate my feeling about his metaphor, but he didn't catch it.

"Which would be more costly?" Rosita asked. "Taking a preventive measure now or incurring a couple of dozen lawsuits?"

"Believe it or not, little lady, we've considered all the possibilities."

"Are most of those men out there Cajuns?"

"Quite a few. Yes, ma'am." He was looking straight ahead, visibly tired of the subject.

"How would you like explaining yourself to a jury made up of your employees' relatives?"

The tool pusher's eyes clicked sideways, fixing on hers. "Fellows, could I have your attention a minute?" he said to the other men in the room.

THE BLOWOUT PREVENTER went into place. Offshore rigs were primitive in those days, lacking the galleys and living areas they contain today. We ate supper on a shrimp trawler anchored to the base of the rig and pitching against the rubber tires hung from the stanchions. I say "we." Hershel ate nothing more than a piece of buttered white bread while he drank black coffee so hot it would scorch the paint on a fire truck. No one was happy with us; installing the blowout preventer was time-consuming and expensive. We had a minority interest in the rig but had prevailed over people with far greater experience in the oil field than we had. As the hours worn on, I became convinced our victory was Pyrrhic and once again Hershel's prophetic gifts would prove illusory.

The three of us slept on narrow bunks inside a small cabin on the trawler. It was cold at sunrise, the early sun a paradoxical burnt orange inside black clouds that looked like smoke from a batholithic fire under the Gulf, the waves three feet high and hitting the trawler's wood hull with the steady bone-numbing rhythm of a metronome. Hershel was undaunted. He shaved with cold water and dried his face with his shirt, his eyes jittering. "Let's go up to the doghouse," he said.

"I think we'd better stay out of there," I said. "I think if the wind drops, we should head for shore."

"Trust me on this, Weldon."

I have, I have, I thought. But I kept my own counsel. Rosita and I went to the galley to eat breakfast, depressed with our prospects, bored with the routine, anxious to get back on land. "I wonder what's going on in the world," she said.

I remembered the morning paper I had picked up from the lawn and stuck in my coat pocket. "I'll be right back," I said. I went to our cabin and returned to the galley, flipping open *The Houston Post,* glancing at the headlines above the fold. Then I sat down across from Rosita and flipped the paper over and looked at an article at the bottom of page one. Hershel had gone up to the doghouse.

"Weldon?" she said.

"What?"

"Your face is white."

"Remember the man I went to see Sunday night?"

"What about him?"

"He was killed by a hit-and-run driver."

"I'm sorry."

"Don't be. He was a blackmailer."

"He was trying to blackmail you?"

"The issue involved Hershel and Linda Gail. He also had two photos of my father. One showed my father just before he was killed in an explosion down in a bell hole. Another showed his body right after the explosion. All these years Grandfather and my mother and I had no idea what happened to him. The man's name was Harlan McFey. He was a detective. I had hoped to find out who he was working for."

"Is that why you went to see Roy Wiseheart?"

"Yes, I thought maybe he'd hired McFey. He said McFey had worked for his father but was fired two years ago."

"Go back to what you said about Hershel and Linda Gail."

"She's probably having an affair."

"How do you know?"

"McFey had a photo of her in a compromising situation. Half of the photo was torn off. I don't know who the man is. I thought it might be Roy Wiseheart. I talked to him about it. I believe what he told me. I don't believe he's romantically involved with her."

"You have to leave this alone, Weldon."

"Just walk away?"

"Linda Gail has the mind of a child. Nothing you can do will change that. She's Hershel's responsibility."

"I need to find out the circumstances of my father's death. I have to find out why he didn't write or tell us where he was."

"But you have to leave Linda Gail and Hershel's marital problems out of it."

"Okay, General Lowenstein."

"You want a slap?"

I looked out the porthole and saw two strange phenomena occur in a sequence that made no sense. The wind dropped, and instead of capping, the waves slid through the rig's pilings like rippling green silk. Then the surface quivered and wrinkled like the skin on a living creature. I unlatched the glass on the porthole and looked up at the roughneck on the monkey board. He had unhooked his safety belt and stepped out on the hoist, one hand locked on the steel cable, and was riding it down to the deck, rotating his arm in a circle, like a third-base coach telling his runners to haul freight for home plate.

"Oh, boy," I said.

"What?" she asked.

"You have to see this. There's nothing quite like it."

We climbed the ladder onto the floor of the rig. I could smell an odor similar to rotten eggs leaking off the wellhead. The tool pusher and driller and Hershel were coming out of the doghouse. An unshaved roughneck with a beer barrel's girth was dancing by the wellhead, joyfully pumping his loins against the air, his tin hat cocked on his head.

I could feel a vibration through the soles of my shoes, then the pipes on the wellhead began to sweat in drops that were as big and bright and wet to the touch as a bucket full of silver coins lifted from a sunken galleon. Every connector pipe was as cold as an ice tray fresh out of a freezer. The driller dipped a board into a can of turpentine and lit it and touched the burning end to a flare line that immediately erupted in flames reaching a hundred feet into the sky.

The confined eruption of oil and natural gas and salt water and sand through the wellhead created a level of pressure and structural conflict not unlike an ocean channeled through the neck of a beer bottle. The molecular composition of the steel rigging seemed to stiffen against the sky. A hammer fell from somewhere in the rigging, clanging through the spars as loudly as a cathedral bell, but no one paid any attention, even when the hammer bounced off the roof of the doghouse.

"Wahoo!" Hershel said, jumping up and down on the deck. "Wahoo!" He began singing the lyrics from a song I'd heard beer-joint bands play for years: " 'Ten days on, five days off, I guess my blood is crude oil now. I reckon I'll never lose them mean ole rough-neckin' blues.' Lord God in heaven, we're rich, Weldon!" Then he shouted again: "Wahoo!"

He wasn't through. He stood on his hands and walked across the deck.

"Did you ever see a happier man?" Rosita said.

"Never," I replied.

"The private detective killed in the hit-and-run?"

"Yes?"

"Don't let his evil live beyond the grave," she said.

THE WEEKS FOLLOWING the completion of the rig were grand. We paid down our debt to Lloyd Fincher's insurance company and started up another pipeline in Victoria, Texas, and one in Lottie, Louisiana. Linda Gail and Hershel painted their humble house in River Oaks, and she applied for admission in the River Oaks Country Club.

Rosita and I went back to Grandfather's ranch and planted a windbreak of poplar trees on the north side of the house, and bought my mother an automobile and hired a man to teach her how to drive. We celebrated Grandfather's ninetieth birthday with a three-layer cake that had white icing and pink candles. Among his friends at the party were old men who had been drovers on the Goodnight-Loving and the Chisholm Trail, and twins who had gone up Kettle Hill with Fighting Joe Wheeler.

I did not know how to tell Grandfather or my mother about my father's death. My mother was not stable and never would be. My father and Grandfather had never gotten along. My father was also a Holland, but a distant cousin, one who Grandfather claimed was a woods colt and not a legitimate member of the family. He had resented my father's drinking and blamed it for my mother's mental and emotional problems. For many years, Grandfather had been a master at transferring his guilt onto others. But I felt he had come to accept responsibility for his wayward life and for neglecting his children, and I didn't want to open old wounds by telling him or my mother that my father had found work but hadn't cared enough about his family to send money home or tell us where he was.

Or maybe I couldn't face the fact that my father's first love was alcohol and that everything else, even his son, was secondary.

I tried. Right after Grandfather's birthday party, he and I were sitting on the porch in the sunset, our newly planted poplars green and stiffening in the breeze, the underbelly of the rain clouds as red as a forge. He was drinking his coffee from the saucer.

I told him what I had learned of my father's fate from McFey. He didn't speak for a long time. "It was him in the photographs? You're sure?"

"Yes, sir."

"How do you feel about it?"

"I'd like to get the people who caused the accident. I'd like to get the ones who covered it up."

"That's not what I meant. You feel he betrayed you?"

"I don't know if 'betrayed' is the right word."

"He couldn't call y'all collect and tell you he was okay and coming home directly? That's not betrayal?"

"Yes, sir, I wondered why he didn't do those things."

"Maybe he didn't get the chance. There'd be no reason for him not to contact you. His grievance wasn't against you and your mother. It was against me. What's the name of the company he was working for?"

"I don't know. The private detective was killed by a hit-and-run driver the day after I met him."

"That's pretty convenient for somebody, isn't it?" he said.

"I'd say so."

"You cain't do what you're thinking."

"What am I thinking?"

"Same thing you did when you put a bullet in the back of Clyde Barrow's stolen automobile."

"McFey knew all about that. He was a guard in Eastham Pen."

"Why didn't you say so, Satchel Ass? String the phone out here and bring me my address book."

"Would you not call me that awful name?"

"I'll think about it."

I went inside the house and brought out the telephone on a long cord. I also brought him the black notebook by which he kept in contact with his shrinking army of old friends. Then I went out in the vegetable garden and began hoeing weeds out of the rows, the sun melting inside its own heat on the earth's rim. When I went back on the porch, Grandfather was wearing his spectacles, looking at the piece of notepaper he had written on and torn from his book.

"One friend of mine knew McFey at Eastham," he said. "He says McFey was a harsh shepherd and made life as miserable as possible for Clyde Barrow. Barrow may have been raped at Eastham. Maybe repeatedly. A former Ranger told me McFey went to work for the Coronado Oil Company."

"Coronado is owned by the Wiseheart family," I said.

"Well, McFey got himself fired for padding his expense account."

"How long ago?"

"Two or three years back."

"That coincides with what Roy Wiseheart told me."

"According to my friend, McFey was always bragging on his access to rich people." Grandfather looked again at the page he had torn from his notebook. "He did chores for Clara Wiseheart. That's Roy Wiseheart's wife, isn't it?"

"Yes, sir, it is," I said, feeling my face constrict. "What kind of chores?"

"That's what I asked. Know what my friend said? 'When you work for somebody whose family owns a quarter of a billion dollars, you do whatever they tell you.'"

"That's what the Wisehearts are worth?" I said.

"You got it wrong. Her family is the one with the big money. Roy Wiseheart married up."

I sat down on the steps. It had been a wet summer, and the pastures and the low-lying hills were still green. The last of the sunlight was glinting like a red diamond at the bottom of the sky, and hundreds of Angus were silhouetted in its afterglow. Grandfather maintained that our land had been soaked in blood, first by Indians, then by Spaniards, then by Mexicans and white colonists, then by Rangers who virtually exterminated the Indian population after Texas gained its independence in 1836. I picked up a piece of dried mud from the step and tossed it out on the flagstones. "Blood and excrement," I said.

"What's that?"

"That's our contribution to the earth."

Grandfather removed his spectacles and rubbed his eyes. "You feel your friend Wiseheart took you on a snipe hunt?"

"That's close."

"It doesn't change what you are. The shame is on him. Those people aren't worth spitting on, Weldon. The Hollands are better than that bunch any day of the week and twice on Sunday. I'll tell you something else, too. Since you were a little boy, I knew you'd be the one to shine."

I went into the house and got a carton of peach ice cream that Rosita had brought home that afternoon. I brought out two bowls and two spoons, and Grandfather and I ate the entire carton, down to the bottom, under the porch light, while stars fell from the sky.

LINDA GAIL PINE had hand-dropped invitations to her lawn party through the mail slots of her neighbors' homes, up one side of the street and down the other. Many of the neighbors were people she had never met. For these, she had written a special note at the bottom: "Let's not be strangers." To some, in order to vary her language, she wrote an extra note: "We've heard so many good things about you. Bring children if you like."

She rented lawn furniture and strung bunting from the eaves of her house to the overhang of live oaks that grew in the neighbor's yard. She hired a catering service and set up a bar under the gas lamp by the back fence and made sure the two bartenders arrived wearing white jackets and red bow ties and razor-creased black trousers, because that was what the bartenders had been wearing at a garden party she attended in the Hollywood Hills.

That morning she and Hershel had received a letter from River Oaks Country Club, telling them their application for membership had been rejected. She dropped the letter in front of him on the dining room table. "What did you put on the application form?" she asked.

"Our income for last year. That's what they seemed most interested in. I guess it wasn't enough."

"What about all the equipment you have? What about the oil well you just brought in? That's not enough?"

"They're snobs, hon. We're working people."

"I'm an actress and going back to a film location in three days. You're the founding executive of a national company. How dare they write us a letter like this?"

"To hell with them."

"I'm going to make them eat their words. They're not going to treat us like this, Hershel."

The lawn party was to begin at five P.M. Rosita and I drove up at five-fifteen. There were no cars parked in front; the only car in the driveway was Hershel's black Cadillac. We walked around the side of the house. Linda Gail was rearranging chairs in the backyard, her face pinched with anger. Next door a bunch of teenagers were diving in a swimming pool that glowed with a smoky green aura from the underwater lighting. She walked into the bamboo that grew along the fence and snapped her fingers at the swimmers. "Please tell the adult members of the household that I'm sorry they cannot attend our party," she said. "Also tell them the noisy behavior of their ill-mannered children is not appreciated."

"This is going to be awful," Rosita whispered.

"Yes, it is," I replied. "Talk to her. I'll be back in a minute."

"Where are you going?"

"Probably firing in the well."

I went inside and used the phone in the bedroom. The wallpaper and bedclothes and padded furniture were a blend of pale blue and pink and silver that reminded me of a child's nursery. I dialed Roy Wiseheart's home number.

"Hello?" he said.

"I need to clear up something," I said.

"Holland?"

"I've been told that Harlan McFey was an employee of your wife."

"Oh, McFey again. Use your judgment, partner. Why would my wife have anything to do with a man like that?"

"You tell me."

"Okay, I'll ask her, if that will make you feel better. Maybe he worked for one of her family's companies. You know how many people they employ?"

"You said you had no connection to him. Were you lying to me?"

"No, but I'll tell you what. The next time I see you, I might just punch you in the nose."

"Save the martial rhetoric. Just answer yes or no. Did you lie to me?"

"No, I did not."

"Did you get an invitation to Linda Gail's lawn party this evening?"

"If she sent one, I never saw it."

"Oh, she sent it, all right. You would have been at the top of her list."

"Well, I didn't get it, or at least I didn't see it. So how about giving it a rest?"

"What are you doing right now?"

"Talking to you, which I wish I wasn't doing. Give me the address. Remind me in the future not to answer my telephone on Saturday afternoon."

I told him where the house was. Then I said, "You have a lot of friends here'bouts. I bet they'd love to come over."

"Are you serious?"

"I've got faith in you. You can do it. Make us proud."

He hung up. At 6:05 his Rolls-Royce pulled into the Pines' driveway; his wife was not with him. Four couples from the neighborhood arrived; then others, people who drove modest automobiles. In the next hour, I met a golf pro, an accountant, a stockbroker, a social secretary, a cattleman, an Episcopalian minister, a female tennis champion, and an amphibian charter pilot who wore a patch over one eye. All of them seemed overjoyed to be invited to the home of a Hollywood actress who was a friend of Roy Wiseheart's. Linda Gail was ecstatic. From across the yard, Wiseheart toasted me with his champagne glass.

I couldn't help but feel a great sense of kinship and warmth toward him. Random acts of charity define few of us, and seeing them in a man of his background made me think that the possibilities of goodness are at work in everyone, even those with whom we associate an avaricious and profligate ethos. Then I saw his eyes shift from me to Linda Gail. She was wearing a sundress, her shoulders smooth and tan and muscular, the tips of her dark brown hair burned almost blond, her breasts and hips tight against her dress when she reached up to retie a strip of bunting to the gas lamp.

I had no doubt that something unexpected happened inside Roy Wiseheart. Maybe it was because he had acted in a charitable way toward her and he now saw her in a different light, or maybe he was entering that time in a man's life when he falsely perceives his youth slipping away. The look on his face did not involve lust or desire; nor was it one of acquisitional need. I think he saw Linda Gail Pine as a rebellious and petulant and vain girl who needed a protector and was nothing like the women he had ever courted or slept with. She was also brazen, the kind who would incur a thousand cuts to prevail over an adversary. And she was very good to look at, with her countrywoman's breasts and the childlike joy in her eyes.

There was only one problem with Linda Gail: She was married. I walked across the St. Augustine grass and placed my hand on Wiseheart's arm. I could feel the body heat trapped under his sport shirt. "Thanks for doing what you did," I said.

"Nothing to it," he replied.

"Hershel is my closest friend."

"I gathered that."

"I'd like for you to be the same," I said.

He turned so I would have to take my hand from his arm. His face was no more than six inches from mine. To this day, I don't believe I have ever looked into a pair of more intelligent and perceptive eyes, nor had I ever met a man who was more aware of nuance than he. "I'd like that," he replied.

I gazed at the wire fence and bamboo that separated Hershel and Linda Gail's property from the next-door neighbor's. "Did you ever live in a neighborhood that didn't have fences?" I asked.

"Nope."

"I guess setting boundaries is what civilization is all about. We set boundaries, and then we have to live within them. It doesn't seem fair, does it?"

He was drinking a Scotch and soda. He rattled the ice cubes in the glass and watched Linda Gail carry a huge tray of baked Alaska from the kitchen to a serving table. "I never gave it much thought," he replied. "Did you ever see a creamier dessert? I get hungry looking at it."

Chapter 14

ROY WISEHEART CALLED me at home Monday morning. "You tell me what to do and I'll do it," he said. "Just don't lay your damn recriminations on me later."

"Excuse me?" I said.

"Evidently, your friend Hershel has gone back to the job site in Louisiana. In the meantime, his wife has gotten herself into serious trouble nobody needs. The police called me from the River Oaks substation on Westheimer. I also got a call from the manager at the country club. We've got about thirty minutes before she's packed off to the city lockup. You don't want to think about the women in the downtown jail on Monday morning. Got all that?"

"No."

"I'll have another run at it. Take notes if you like," he said.

Linda Gail had dressed in a pink suit with a narrow-waist coat and a skirt wrapped tightly around the hips, and a pink pillbox hat with a black feather in the band, and ankle-strap patent-leather black shoes, and white gloves that went to the elbow, not unlike Clara Wiseheart's. She had gotten in her waxed black Cadillac and driven to the River Oaks Country Club, where she walked directly into the manager's office and asked, "Who the fuck do you think you're dealing with?"

While two security personnel stood outside the door, Linda Gail was assured that her application for membership would be reviewed, that all consideration would be given to her, that no bias or insult was intended by the letter of rejection.

"I think you're under a misimpression," she said. "I didn't come here to negotiate with you. You've already indicated what you think of us. I would just like you to be a little more specific. Are we not cultured enough for you? Do you not like the wax job on my automobile? Should we work on our diction? What exactly is it that puts your nose so high in the air?"

The manager, who used a feigned British accent that came and went with the occasion, was beginning to lose his composure. "Frankly, our membership is based primarily on income, Mrs. Pine. Most of our members are millionaires. You're not."

"You're correct. I'm merely a film star and have never owned a string of filling stations," she said, rising from her chair. "If you haven't heard of Castle Productions, you will. We will be filing suit against you and your ersatz accent and your dump of a country club for slander and besmirching my name and my professional reputation. By the way, there's dandruff on your collar."

She walked down the carpeted hallway to the front entrance, her little purse gripped in front of her like a family coat of arms. It should have been over. With a phone call or two from Roy Wiseheart, the country club probably would have been glad to admit the Pines. But Linda Gail in motion was like an artillery shell. The law of gravity would have its way.

In this instance, that meant Linda Gail getting into her Cadillac and backing into the grille of an Oldsmobile. Rather than get out and examine the damage, she shifted the hydromatic transmission into low and drove away, tearing the bumper loose from the Oldsmobile and T-boning a Buick at the end of the aisle.

"So it's a parking-lot car accident," I said to Wiseheart. "Her insurance rates will go up. Hershel has had worse problems."

"You didn't let me finish. She slapped a cop in the face," Wiseheart said. "You don't slap a Houston cop."

"I guess that puts things in a different light."

"Do you want me to go down to the police station by myself, or do you want to come, too?" he asked.

When I arrived at the substation on the edge of River Oaks, Roy Wiseheart was sitting down in a small room with a uniformed police officer. The officer dwarfed the folding chair. His head was the size of a cider jug, his hands as broad as baseball mitts, ridged with knuckles that resembled lead washers. Wiseheart leaned forward and cupped his hand on the officer's shoulder. "She and her husband are church people. Mr. Pine was at Kasserine Pass and Omaha and the Bulge," he said. "I'm sure Linda Gail feels like hell about this. Officer, they're just getting started here in Houston. They're a little bit insecure. That's why she was carrying on the way she did. The girl is scared."

"She's insecure because she owns a Cadillac?" the policeman said.

"I bet they busted their piggy bank to buy it at a used-car lot. She's got a chance at a movie career. Do you know what this will do to her? I saw the Globe and Anchor on your arm. I flew with Pappy Boyington. How about it, gunny?"

The policeman stood up. He wore a sky-blue uniform with black flaps on the pockets. The back of his neck was thick and pocked with acne scars. "My wife belongs to the Northside Church of Christ," he said.

Wiseheart nodded reverentially.

"They could use some he'p," the policeman said.

"I know exactly where it is. They're fine people," Wiseheart replied. "If you'll give me the name of your pastor, I'd like to give him a ring."

Ten minutes later, Wiseheart and I and Linda Gail were back on the sidewalk, across the street from an enormous high school whose lawn was shadowed by live oaks. Linda Gail's face looked glazed, as though she had just walked out of a meat locker into a warm room. Her Cadillac had been towed.

"How did you know Hershel was at Omaha Beach?" I said to Roy.

"You must have told me," he replied.

If I did, I had no memory of it.

"I guess that winds things up here," he said, looking up and down the street. He tapped his palms together, his fingers spread, his eyebrows raised. "Can I give you a ride?" he said to Linda Gail.

"That's very nice of you," she replied.

"I'm going right by your house," I said.

"On your way to the Heights?" Wiseheart said.

"I'm supposed to see a friend in River Oaks," I lied.

"Well, it's been quite a morning. I hope everything turns out all right for you, Linda Gail. Call me if I can help in any other way."

"Thank you so much. I'll be forever in your debt," she said.

I opened the passenger door of my car for Linda Gail to get inside. She tried to look straight ahead and not let her eyes follow Wiseheart's Rolls, but there was no mistaking the resentment she felt because I had not let Wiseheart drive her home.

Neither of us spoke. When I pulled into her driveway, I heard her take a breath as though resuming a routine that was unbearable.

"Do you want to say something to me, Linda Gail?" I asked.

"Thank you."

"I didn't mean that."

"Then what *did* you mean?" she asked.

"Are you and Hershel having problems?"

"That's none of your business."

"He loves you."

She didn't seem to hear me. She stared wanly at the front of her house. "I know what it looks like now. I couldn't put my hand on it, probably because I wouldn't let myself admit it."

"I don't know what you're referring to," I said.

"My house. It looks like the public restroom on West Venice Beach. I was there just last week. Now I'm here."

"Hershel said you made him wear slippers at the public pool."

She turned her head and looked at me like someone awakening from a dream. "What did you say?"

"I don't think you know how he lost part of his foot. He and I walked in snow up to our knees in zero-degree weather. He carried Rosita in his arms while his right foot was so swollen with frostbite that he couldn't unlace his boot."

"He told you I asked him to wear slippers at the pool?"

"His feelings were hurt, Linda Gail."

"I didn't want the children staring at him. I didn't want to correct them in front of him. So I tried to avoid an unpleasant situation that would embarrass him. Did that ever occur to you?"

"Did you tell him that?"

"What good would it do? Talking to either of you is a waste of time, particularly you, Weldon. Do you think it's wrong to want a better way of life? I never want to go back to the house I grew up in. If you'd lived in my house, you wouldn't want to, either. During the Depression, we glued cardboard soles on our shoes."

"Hershel is a good man. I'm not sure what Roy Wiseheart is," I said.

"I want to hit you. Instead, I'm going to forget everything you've said. I'm flying on a private plane tonight to Albuquerque. Tomorrow I'll be on location, and none of this will have happened. Goodbye. Thank you for calling Roy."

I wanted to tell her that Rosita's family had been exterminated by the Nazis, and that I had pulled her from under a pile of corpses, and that Rosita didn't feel the world owed her anything as a consequence. But I didn't. For some reason I thought of Bonnie Parker and the way her smile reminded me of someon: opening a music box. I guess I tried to remind myself that most people, no matter how offensive they might be, are doing the best they can at the time. It's a hard precept to follow, and I was certainly not good at it.

So here's to you, Linda Gail, I thought. *You've wrecked three cars, struck a behemoth of a Houston policeman in the face with your bare hand, and are on the edge of entering an adulterous affair with a man married to probably one of the most vicious women in Texas, and it's not even noon.*

I COULD NOT GET the photograph of my dead father out of my mind. My father was an eccentric man who drank too much and wanted to be a journalist but instead went to work in the oil field. Every night he came home and washed his hands with a brush and Lava soap, as though trying to scrub the oil-and-natural-gas business out of his life. Aside from his drinking, he was good-natured and generous and treated all people equally; he was honest in his dealings with others and deserved better than dying in a bell hole explosion and having his remains disposed of anonymously, his family left to wonder what had happened to him.

Somebody owed me an answer. I wasn't sure who. I'd learned a lesson in the Ardennes. When we went up against the panzer corps, we were not fighting only German armor. We had also taken on Stonewall Jackson. Erwin Rommel and his colleagues in martial mischief had studied Jackson's Shenandoah Valley campaign and had used Tiger tanks in the same way Jackson used cavalry. How egregious can the ironies of history be? Out there in the snowy forests south of the Belgian border, the right-hand man of Robert E. Lee was guiding the Waffen SS against his countrymen, some of them probably descendants of the Confederate soldiers who were with him when he died at Chancellorsville.

Jackson's strategy, as he explained once, was simple: "Mystify, mislead, and surprise." I thought I might give it a try. I drove back home and ate lunch on the screened porch with Rosita. It was Indian summer, the air tannic with the smell of burning leaves. "I'm going to the office of Dalton Wiseheart this afternoon, then I should head on over to Louisiana," I said.

"Is that Roy Wiseheart's father?" she asked.

"He's supposed to be quite a character."

"What are you doing, Weldon?"

"The detective who showed me a death photo of my father worked for him. Mr. Wiseheart needs to be made accountable."

"I'll go with you."

"It's better you don't."

"Try to stop me."

The reddish-brown light that lived in Rosita's eyes never changed. It didn't diminish; it didn't intensify. Every time I looked into her eyes, I thought about the light of the world that Jesus mentions in the Gospels. Dark memories never had their way with her; anger never made her its captive.

"What are you thinking about?" she asked.

"I feel sorry for Hershel. I think Linda Gail is going to destroy both of them."

"Whatever they do, they won't destroy us," she said. "Do you hear me, Weldon? That can't happen."

DALTON WISEHEART OWNED an office building in downtown Houston but did most of his business on the veranda of the Rice Hotel, where a personal bartender fixed mint juleps for him and his friends while they decided the future for arguably hundreds of thousands of people. His origins and background and education were at odds. He grew up on a large wheat farm on the Texas–New Mexico line, not far from the original XIT Ranch. Journalists liked to use terms such as "homespun" and "pioneer patriarch" in describing him. They took little note of his degrees from Georgia Tech and MIT. They also failed to remember a statement he made about his method of dealing with troublesome people. For clarity of line, it had no equal: "Make them wince."

I don't mean to fault journalists. Like most people who worked for others in that era, they did as they were told. Besides, Dalton Wiseheart's appearance was deceptive. When we walked out on the veranda, he was dozing in a swayback straw chair, his booted feet up on the rail, a battered cowboy hat over his face, his body half in shadow. One of his aides touched him on the shoulder and told him we were there. His face was as plain as a bowl of porridge. The nose was bulbous and pitted, the teeth long, the bottom lip protruding, as though snuff were tucked inside it. He wore khakis and a long-sleeved denim shirt and wide suspenders, and he had a stomach that made me think of piled bread dough. He took a dark blue handkerchief out of his pocket and blew his nose in it. "I hate to sleep during the day," he said. "I wake up with a head full of cobwebs. You're Roy's friend?"

"Weldon Avery Holland," I said. "This is my wife, Miss Rosita."

"Forgive me for not getting up. I'm about half fossil these days," he said, his gaze lingering on Rosita. He wiped at his nose with his wrist. "What's this about?"

"A private detective named Harlan McFey. A hit-and-run driver killed him in north Houston," I said. Down below I could hear the traffic in the street, a policeman blowing a whistle at an intersection.

"Yes, I remember him," Wiseheart said. "He was a bird dog for anybody who'd throw him a bone. Here, sit down. Why are you coming to me about him?"

"My father was killed in 1934 at the bottom of a bell hole in East Texas. McFey had a photograph of his body. The company my father was working for covered up his death."

"My son sent you to me to help find information on your father? That doesn't make much sense."

"McFey worked for you, sir, at least until two years ago. He also worked for your daughter-in-law, Roy's wife."

He rubbed the back of his neck and picked up his julep glass from the floor. "Y'all want a drink?"

"No, thank you," I said.

"Good for you. Roy's wife is a different kettle of fish. That's all I have to say on the subject."

"Were any of your companies laying pipe in East Texas in '34, Mr. Wiseheart?"

"Probably. You think my people had something to do with your daddy's death?"

"That's what I'd like to determine," I said.

Others around us had stopped talking. A white-jacketed black waiter had brought another julep on a tray and was standing motionlessly next to Wiseheart's chair. "Set it down," Wiseheart said.

"Yes, suh," the waiter replied.

"Now go back over there by the bar."

"Yes, suh."

Wiseheart turned back to me. "How'd you make my son's acquaintance?"

"He wanted to buy out my company."

"I remember the name now. You're the one with the welding machines. They say your welds never leak. I'm happy for your success, son, but our visit is over. No offense meant. I've got a mess of work to do, more mess than work."

"Somebody sicced McFey on us. If it wasn't you, who do you think it was?"

The awning above the veranda was riffling in the breeze. Wiseheart watched a pigeon glide out of the sunlight into the shadows; his eyes shifted to Rosita, his mouth wrinkling at the corner when he grinned. "What are you?" he asked.

"Beg your pardon?" she said.

"You're either European or British. Which is it?"

"I grew up in Madrid. You might say I'm Spanish. Some of my family came from Germany."

"You're a handsome woman. I think your husband is a fortunate man. Now I need somebody to prop me up behind my desk so I can get some work done."

With the passage of years, I've learned that age can be used as either a sword or a shield. Dalton Wiseheart was a master at both.

As we walked to our car, Rosita put her arm in mine. "Want me to go to Louisiana with you?" she said.

"I'd like that."

"Leave that man alone," she said.

"He'll be hearing from me again."

"Why?"

"Because he's a liar from his hairline down to the soles of his feet," I said.

"You underestimate him."

"About what? My father's death?"

"Lying is probably one of his virtues. If he had his way, I'd be a lampshade."

HERSHEL AND I had bought a half interest in a doodlebug rig, a seismograph drill barge with propellers that allowed it to move from location to location, where it would be anchored to the floor of a river or bay with four hydraulic pilings. Once the drill site was established, a long, flat powerboat strung recording cables in both directions from the barge, sinking the instruments to the bottom of the river or the bay. After the exploratory hole was drilled, the deckhands would begin building explosive charges from cans of dynamite that screwed together end to end in sticks of six. A can of primer was attached to one end and screwed into a second and third stick. Then a nitro cap and an electric wire were attached to the last can and the charge dropped down the hole, the cap wire slithering through the driller's hands as it disappeared inside the pipe.

That's when everyone went to the stern or got on the jug boat, and the shooter would holler "Fire in the hole!" and twist the switch on the detonator. The explosion was so powerful, it would slam the iron hull of the barge against the water and send a geyser of sand and brackish water high into the air and often break dishes and cups in the galley. Seconds later, a huge dirty cloud of sulfurous yellow smoke would rise from the water and drift back through the barge; if you breathed it, the inside of your head would ache for the rest of the day.

The seismograph crew was working deep in the Atchafalaya Basin, an enormous watershed composed of marsh, saw grass, cypress swamp, rivers, networks of bayous that didn't have names, inland bays, and miles and miles of flooded tupelo gums and willow trees. The crew worked ten days on the water and five days off. The work was hard and physical and sometimes dangerous; in the summer the crew did it under a blistering sun, and in winter they lived in wet clothes from sunrise to sunset, wading through waist-high swamp while they strung electronic recording cable from a spool on their backs. They were brave and hardworking and never complained about the food or the low pay; most of them had soldiered all over the world and were carefree and irresponsible in the way that children are. When it came to women and matters of race, they had the lowest self-esteem of any group I have ever known. They also got in trouble, often for reasons that made no sense other than a desire to see how much harm they could do to themselves.

Morgan City, down on the coast, with its Spanish-tile roofs and stucco buildings and palm trees and stilt houses along the Atchafalaya River, looked like a conduit into a nineteenth-century Caribbean postcard, a place where anonymity and a self-congratulatory paganism were a way of life. The bars and the brothels never closed.

Slot and racehorse machines were everywhere. The Cajun girls were beautiful and often illiterate and believed any story told to them. Fugitives from the law only had to step on a boat to find themselves one week later in Brownsville or Key West or on the Mexican coast, eluding the law like a cipher disappearing inside a bowl of alphabet soup. What better place for a man who believed he had run out of options?

Hershel and I had nothing to do with hiring the crew on the doodlebug barge we had bought a half interest in. That didn't mean we weren't responsible for what they did. He and I were in the pilothouse on the barge when one of the drillers got into it with a jug hustler on the deck. The party chief was away on the quarter boat, and we were the only form of authority on the barge. I had seen the driller in action before. His nickname was Tex because he had the word "Texas" tattooed in large blue letters across his back, not unlike the food-dye lettering on the rind of a smoke-cured ham. A geologist nobody liked had flown his pontoon plane right over the top of the barge, causing everybody to scatter except Tex. He climbed up on the drill with a monkey wrench, and when the plane came in for another swoop, he threw the wrench, barely missing the windshield and the geologist's face.

Hershel went down the steel ladder from the pilothouse onto the deck and approached the driller. The jug hustler had offloaded a crate of cap wire from the jug boat by throwing the crate over the gunwale onto the deck, not knowing that a vial of nitroglycerin was inside each spool of wire. Four feet away, stacked against the pilothouse, were 160 pounds of canned dynamite and primers. Hershel talked to both men. All the while, Tex kept rotating his head, looking everywhere except at Hershel.

"So that's it. Let's get back to work," Hershel said.

"I don't want to get to Glory in pieces," Tex said.

"Neither do I," Hershel said.

"Then this little pipsqueak here needs to stop putting others at risk."

"He didn't know about the nitro caps. Now he does," Hershel said.

"I didn't see your signature on my paycheck, sir." Tex was barechested and had a sculpted upper body that was as hard and tapered as a cypress stump. He rotated his head again, his eyes empty.

"The party chief isn't here. So I'm the skipper until he gets back. Tell me if that doesn't quite sit right."

"I was looking for a job when I found this son of a bitch."

"The jug boat is going to the levee for supplies at fourteen hundred. You can be on it if you want."

Tex looked at his nails. "I don't give a shit one way or the other."

Hershel nodded as though in appreciation of a profound concept. "I'll have your drag-up check ready by the time you pack your duffel. Get off the barge."

"This is a hard-boiled outfit. Got a man lecturing and firing people and talking military language like he's Dwight Eisenhower, with a foot that looks like a duck's."

I went down the ladder. "You're gone, buddy. Not at two but right now. Got it?"

Tex picked up his shirt from the deck rail and drew the sleeve up one arm, his eyes never leaving mine.

"Is there something you want to say?" I asked.

He scratched his head. "Let me think. No, not right now. I'll catch y'all later, though," he replied. "Like the ole boy says, you'll know when it's my ring."

In the early A.M., three days later, someone broke into the cast-iron lockbox where we stored the nitro caps and the detonator on a sandbar three hundred yards from the barge. The thief built a stick of at least twelve dynamite cans and blew the pilothouse into smithereens. The most likely suspect was our friend Tex.

The same day, the cops picked him up dead drunk in a mulatto brothel on the north side of Lafayette. He claimed he had little memory of anything he had done during the last forty-eight hours. We thought we had our man. The problem was the family who ran the brothel. They were glad to see Tex taken away. He had passed out in the trailer behind the brothel after he had spent all his money, and they hadn't been able to get him out. They didn't like him, and because they were protected by the Mafia in New Orleans, they didn't fear him. The point is, they had no reason to provide him an alibi. They said he had been at the brothel, in one stage of debauch or another, from before the time of the explosion until the sheriff's deputies had arrived.

Rosita and I went back to Houston for four days. I called Lloyd Fincher in San Antonio and told him what had happened.

"Why are you telling me?" he said.

"Do you think the Wisehearts or their minions are capable of something like this?"

"I know nothing about them and don't want to. Am I clear? I have no opinion on the subject and nothing to say about it. What the hell is wrong with you?"

He hung up. It was 1:13 P.M. Four hours later, he pulled into our driveway. I went outside to meet him because I did not want him in our house. Our pecan trees were swollen with wind, the candles inside carved Halloween pumpkins flickering on front porches up and down the street. "You drove here from San Antonio?" I said.

"I didn't feel good about hanging up on you," he said. "But you shouldn't be talking about certain things over the telephone."

"You think there's a wiretap on your phone?"

"Hershel Pine and you have underbid Dalton Wiseheart's companies on three jobs I know of. You and your wife went to the Rice Hotel and called him to task in front of his employees. I'm surprised he didn't have your house blown up. I need a drink. I need a shower, too. Mind if I wash up and change clothes inside?"

"How do you know all this?"

"Did your mama drop you on your head? Can I use your shower or not?"

"Go right ahead."

"I'm going to take you and Rosita to Garth McQueen's hotel opening tonight," he said. "I want you to meet McQueen. Watch everything he does and listen to everything he says. Make a study of it."

"He's a man to learn from?"

"No, do just the opposite of what McQueen does. He's going

down in flames. Jesus Christ, boy, I need to keep you on a short leash. It's beyond me that people can believe in the intellectual superiority of the white race."

I thought one of us had to be mad, most probably me, since I was listening to advice given by one of the men responsible for the military debacle at Kasserine Pass, a man I would allow to shower in my house.

Chapter 15

THE PARTY AT the hotel at the bottom of South Main Street might have been called grandiose and vulgar, but in its way it reflected the times in which we lived. Inside its crassness was a kind of meretricious innocence, one you might associate with a nation's inception or perhaps its demise, like the twilight of the gods or an antebellum vision borrowed from the world of Margaret Mitchell.

The party overflowed from the pool into the downstairs rooms and lounges of the hotel; the balconies were filled with celebrants, too. Hollywood movie stars, country music artists, congressmen, cattlemen with barnyard detritus on their boots, and ordinary people who had been handed an invitation by Garth McQueen in his famous lounge mingled as equals, all somehow part of something larger than themselves, the evening sky striped with scarlet clouds that resembled a celestial flag.

Across the street was a pasture where red Angus grazed among oil derricks whose pumps moved methodically up and down, backdropped in the east by black clouds that crackled like cellophane. The smell of gas on the wind was not suggestive of the season; it was the smell of money, and the thunderstorm building in the sky was a symbol of the power inherent in a bountiful universe waiting to be harvested.

Rosita and Lloyd Fincher and I were crowded among the guests standing by the pool. Ten feet away I saw a man in a checkered sport coat and a loud tie pick up a drink from a tray and hand it to a woman in a strapless silver evening dress that exposed the tops of her breasts and was as tight as tin on the rest of her. "That's Benjamin Siegel," I said.

"Who?" Rosita said.

"He was a member of Murder, Incorporated," I said.

"And that's Virginia Hill with him," Fincher said. "Want to meet them?"

"No," I said.

"I don't blame you. He scares the hell out of me," Fincher said. "There's McQueen at the table on the platform. Look who's with him."

"Is that Linda Gail?" Rosita asked.

"She's on her way up," Fincher said. "On jet-propelled roller skates. That gal's a rocket."

"Where's Hershel?" Rosita said.

"In Louisiana," I said.

Linda Gail's presence at the party didn't bother me. Nor did the fact that she was at a table with Garth McQueen and Jack Valentine. I was bothered by the fact that Roy Wiseheart was sitting next to Linda Gail, his hand on the back of her chair. I had a sick feeling in the bottom of my stomach that wouldn't go away.

"Where are you going?" Rosita said.

"To have a chat," I said.

"With whom?" she said.

"I'm not sure."

"Hold up, Weldon," Fincher said.

I ignored him and worked my way through the crowd to the far end of the pool. If I thought I was about to embarrass Roy Wiseheart, he quickly proved me wrong. He caught me before I reached his table, clamping his arm around my shoulders. "Fincher got you out here after all, did he?" he said.

"How'd you know?"

"I told him to bring you and Rosita. He didn't think you'd come."

"You know Fincher personally?"

"Everyone does. He's a bank. Did you see Bugsy Siegel and his girlfriend over there?"

"Did you bring Linda Gail here?" I asked.

"No, she's with this Valentine character. Talk about grease-balls."

"How did you end up at her table?"

"Garth invited me. Give it a break, will you?"

I didn't know what to say. "Is your wife here?"

"Are you kidding? My wife wouldn't sit down in a public restaurant unless the chairs were sprayed with DDT. Come on, Garth has heard a lot about you."

"Maybe I shouldn't intrude."

"He'll be disappointed. Do it as a favor to me. He's not a bad guy. Then I want to get some advice from you."

Whether he was lying or not, I never knew anyone who was better at getting others to do his will. I stepped up on the platform and shook hands with McQueen. He was a large man, with craggy good looks and no fat on his body and a voice that was like a dull saw cutting through a dry board. Journalists loved him because of the fights he picked in his own lounge and the caricature he created at his own expense. All in all, though, he was a likable fellow, and I suspected that, like many men of humble origins, he had learned to say as little as possible and let his reticence be interpreted as a sign of wisdom. "You're in the movie business?" he asked.

"No, I'm part owner of a pipeline company," I said.

"Oh," he said, seemingly unsure of what he should say next. "I met Jack Warner recently."

"Really?"

"He told me this story. You know who William Faulkner is?"

"I've read two or three of his books," I replied.

"Warner took Faulkner and Clark Gable duck hunting. When Gable was introduced to Faulkner, he said, 'It's nice to meet you, Mr.

Faulkner. What line of work are you in?' So Faulkner says, 'I'm a writer. What line of work are you in, Mr. Gable?'"

McQueen waited, unsure of the effect of his anecdote. Wiseheart and I laughed. No one else did. Linda Gail probably knew who William Faulkner was, but her eyes were focused on me. No, "focused" is not the right word. "Smoldering" is more accurate, and I doubted if she cared two cents whether she made a good impression on Garth McQueen.

"Where is Rosita?" she said.

"She wandered off with Lloyd Fincher. I'd better be getting back. It's good meeting you, Mr. McQueen."

I should have walked away. But I couldn't. No matter what Linda Gail did, I could not think of her as a villainess. I believed she was infatuated with Wiseheart and he was infatuated with her, regardless of what either of them said. In her own mind, she was guilty of no wrongdoing. The pantheon of gods and goddesses that surrounded her, here in the hotel and in the Hollywood Hills, was as real as the temples and the hanging gardens of Babylon. The deities looking down at her from their niches might have been of human creation, but to her, they obviously represented the grace and perfection that awaited those who believed and were willing to take risks.

That said, I could not forgive Linda Gail for the way she treated her husband's affections; nor could I forgive her indifference toward the unhappiness she caused him. "Are you expecting Hershel?" I said.

"He's out of town," she replied. "You didn't know that?"

"I thought he might be back today. Can Rosita and I offer you a ride home?"

"I'm with Mr. Valentine. Thank you just the same," she said.

Valentine stood up from the table and arched back his shoulders. "I got to see a man about a dog," he said. "How about you, fella? I want to tell you about a project I've got in mind."

I had to use the restroom anyway. Maybe it was time to have a talk with the man who had started Linda Gail's film career. We walked through the ballroom. On the bandstand, a country musician named Moon Mullican was playing a song on the piano titled "I'll Sail My Ship Alone."

"Let's fill up the tank before they run out," Valentine said, stopping at the bar. He ordered two mint juleps. His mustache was so thin, it looked like grease pencil. His tin-colored suit and open-necked white snap-button shirt hung on his body as loosely as clothes on a hanger. He kept drumming his fingers on the bar, like a man whose clock spring was wound too tight. He was looking across the room at Benjamin Siegel and Virginia Hill. "I don't know why they let riffraff like that in here."

"I'd lower my voice if I were you," I said.

"He bought the house next door to Jack Warner," he said. "I heard Warner browned his shorts."

"What was the project you wanted to tell me about?"

"Siegel's got the unions tied up so he can extort the studios."

"The project?" I said, trying to get his attention back on track before we had trouble.

"I'm getting some money together in order to make a documentary about drilling in the Louisiana swamps. It's going to show all the good that's being done there. I'd like to get you in on it."

I watched the bartender pour from a bottle of Jack Daniel's into two paper cups filled with crushed ice. It seemed more than coincidence that Jack Valentine was soliciting me in the same way he had solicited Linda Gail. "I'll think about it," I said. "Right now I need to go to the restroom."

"Did you know Roy Wiseheart keeps a fuck pad here?"

"No, I wasn't aware of that."

"In one of the penthouses. He uses his wife's money to cat around on her. I'm surprised he doesn't charge his rubbers to her pharmaceutical account."

I picked up my drink and walked into the restroom. Seconds later, he came in behind me. He set his drink on top of the urinal next to me and unzipped his trousers. He let out a sigh as he relieved himself. "Don't get me wrong about Wiseheart," he said. "Everybody's human. Once you accept that, you make it work for you."

"I don't know if I follow you."

"Look at Linda Gail. She's standing on the front porch of a general store in a backwater shithole, with that innocent look on her face and a hush-puppy accent, and she gets hit by lightning."

"I guess she's a lucky girl."

He looked sideways at me, his hand cupped on his phallus. "Luck doesn't have anything to do with it, Holland."

I went into a stall to get a piece of tissue and came back out. Valentine was washing his hands and examining his teeth and nostrils in the mirror.

"I'm not good at code," I said. "What was that last remark?"

"About luck? I guess it's a matter of definition. I was at the store. She was at the store. I clicked the camera a few times, and she was off and running."

"It wasn't a chance meeting?"

"You've heard the stories about somebody getting discovered at a soda fountain on Hollywood Boulevard?" he said. He took a long drink from his julep. "Believe me, it doesn't happen."

"Somebody sent you to find her?"

"What difference does it make? The girl has talent. She's also a realist. She knows people need to make concessions. That's what I mean when I say everybody's human. I poled her the same day I photographed her."

"Say that again?"

"You heard me. At a motel in Bogalusa. That broad is one great piece of ass."

My fist caught him squarely on the mouth and knocked him to the floor, his head bouncing off the rim of the urinal. He stared up at me, his wrist running with blood when he pressed it against his bottom lip.

I washed my hands in the lavatory and went outside, almost colliding with Siegel and his girlfriend. They stepped back, smiling, amused rather than polite. "Blow your horn so we'll know you're coming," Siegel said.

"You're Mr. Siegel, aren't you?" I said.

"I was when I got out of bed this morning."

"My name is Weldon Avery Holland. I just knocked a man down in the restroom. He called y'all riffraff. That's not why I knocked him down, but I thought you should know."

"You're kidding me, right?" Siegel said.

"I think he's looking for his tooth in the urinal. He said you use the unions to extort the studios in Hollywood."

"You get off a spaceship?"

"Check it out," I said.

Siegel pushed open the restroom door and looked inside. He let the door swing back in place. "Who's the guy?" he asked.

"His name is Jack Valentine. He's with Castle Productions. He says you live next door to Jack Warner but Warner hates your guts."

"Do you believe this guy?" Siegel said to his girlfriend.

"He's just having fun. Keep it in your pants, Benny," she said.

"That's what you're doing. Playing a joke?" Siegel said.

"Not me. Not with you. I know better."

"Yeah?" His eyes were a piercing blue and reminded me in their intensity of the warning light I used to see in Grandfather's. "Have a drink with us."

"My wife is waiting on me."

"Go get her," he said.

"Can't do it."

"No, you need to sit down and have a drink."

I shook my head.

"Virginia says I'm full of shit," he said. "Is that what you're saying? I'm full of shit?"

"It's an honor to meet both of you," I said. "Miss Virginia, you have the same shade of hair as Bonnie Parker."

Her mouth opened. "That hag who smoked cigars?"

"She wasn't like that. I knew her. She was my first love. I was sixteen. I put a .44 round through the back window of her automobile. Clyde Barrow was driving."

"I've got to get to know this guy," Siegel said. "Go find your wife. We'll get us a table."

"What I told you about the fellow in yonder is straight up. He did a serious wrong to a friend of mine. That's why I knocked his tooth out. I hope y'all enjoy your stay in Houston. I'm sure I'll see you on another occasion."

Jack Valentine opened the restroom door, a wadded-up paper towel pressed to the corner of his mouth. He stared stupefied into Bugsy Siegel's face.

"Get back inside the john," Siegel said, pushing him in the chest. "I've got some movie ideas I want to talk over with you."

ONE WEEK LATER, I was back on the pipeline in Louisiana, down by Grand Isle, deep in bayou country. A singular phenomenon that occurs on a pipeline has always intrigued me and made me wonder not only about the molecular structure of steel but the physical composition of the universe. It has also made me wonder if atoms are more akin to living tissue than inert matter. When the pipe joint is welded, it rests on wood skids that elevate the pipe three or four feet from the ground. As the tack and hot-pass welding crews move down the line, they create a long snakelike creature, sometimes with a thirty-six-inch girth, that weighs thousands of tons, resting all day and night on the skids, right next to the trench dug by the ditching machine. The pipe, which is black and wrapped with a heavy protective coating of tarpaper, absorbs heat during the day and cools during the night. At about eight-thirty A.M., when the day begins to warm, the pipe will jump forward, like a snake shedding its skin, toppling the skids as far as the eye can see. The same constriction and expansion occurs in winter, although sometimes not as dramatically.

The illusionary nature of steel doesn't stop there. The welded pipe is put into the ground by a side boom, which lifts it in the air and lowers it into the bottom of the trench. When the pipe is swung over the trench, it bends like soft licorice. Seconds later, down in the trench, it resumes the rigidity that characterized it before it was hoisted.

Watching this take place in the early-morning hours, in a swamp that was probably like the genetic soup from which we originated, made me wonder if the laws of physics were all they were stacked up to be. But speculation on the nature of creation is a luxury reserved for scholars. The rest of us have to deal with one another and ferret our way through the snares and pitfalls that we create for our fellow man. If I doubted that lesson, I was about to relearn it.

This particular morning it was cold enough to wear a canvas coat and gloves. Fog was rolling off the bay and lay three feet deep on the ground, as white and thick as newly picked cotton; the segments of pipe on the skids were beaded with drops of moisture as big as half dollars. Two men parked a Plymouth on the right-of-way and walked toward me, the fog puffing around their knees. I had no doubt they were lawmen, although I didn't know what kind. One was short, one was tall. The short one was overweight and wore a windbreaker and a rain hat and had an unlit cigarette in his mouth. "Are you Mr. Holland?" he said.

They had walked directly from their car and had passed several members of the crew without asking where they might find me. "Do I know you?" I said.

They opened their badge holders and gave their names, but I didn't catch them. "You're feds?" I said.

"Thought you might be able to help us out," the tall one said. His face was lean, hollow-cheeked, as though some of the bone had been removed. One eyebrow was scarred, as if a piece of string had been drawn through it. He wore shined tan shoes speckled with mud. "Can we sit down somewhere?"

"Not unless you want to sit on the pipe and get your trousers dirty," I replied.

He had an eight-by-ten envelope in his hand. He took out a photograph and handed it to me. "Are these friends of yours?"

"No."

"But you know them?"

"I know who they are. I ran into them by accident."

"You know that's Ben Siegel and Virginia Hill?"

"I bumped into them at a hotel opening in Houston. Literally. They asked me to have a drink with them. I turned down the offer. What's this about?"

"Benny is a pretty crazy guy," said the man in the rain hat. He lit his cigarette and took it out of his mouth. "You punched out a guy in the crapper?"

"Must be a slow day at your office," I said.

"Humor us and answer the question, please."

"If a guy named Jack Valentine says I knocked his tooth out in a hotel restroom, he's probably telling you the truth," I said. "What else would you like to know?"

"Your wife's application for admission to the United States contains perjured statements," the tall man said. "The marriage certificate you provided is not a legitimate one."

"You're saying she's here illegally?"

"I didn't say that. An immigration officer might," the man in the rain hat said.

"The certificate is signed by a priest," I said. "The marriage is recorded in the Hotel de Ville in Paris."

"Immigration says the good reverend is a defrocked drunk," the tall man said. "You have another problem. You didn't get permission to marry from your commanding officer."

"I think you need to talk to Major Lloyd Fincher about that. He lives in San Antonio. I'll give you his number. Were you all following me or Siegel when you took this photo?"

"Don't flatter yourself," said the man in the rain hat.

"That's what I thought. So why is my wife a problem for you?"

"She didn't mention to you that she's a member of the Communist Party?"

"That's because she's not."

"Her whole family was," he said. "She's related to Rosa Luxemburg. They don't come any redder than Red Rosa Luxemburg."

"You're full of it, bub."

"I wouldn't take that attitude," the tall man said. "Your wartime service is being reexamined. There's speculation that you were actually a deserter. You and Eddie Slovik didn't take off on your own, did you?"

I could feel my right hand opening and closing at my side. Slovik was the only American soldier shot for desertion during World War II. I looked at the whiteness of the fog at the base of the trees, the bright sheen on the trunks, the water dripping off the canopy. I thought of Tiger tanks smashing through a medieval forest, the tree trunks snapping like matchsticks. "I'd like to know the basis of your statements about me and my wife."

"The only witness to your flight from the Ardennes Forest was Sergeant Hershel Pine. It's funny that you two ended up business partners in the States. It's coincidental that he gave you a partnership in his welding business, a guy with a degree in history and no experience in engineering?"

"I think I'm going to get back to work now," I said. "There might be some coffee up there in the welding truck. Help yourselves." I walked away.

"Does your wife belong to a cell here?" said the man in the rain hat.

"A *what*?"

"You have a hearing problem?"

"You keep your lying mouth off my wife."

"Is that a threat?"

I walked toward both of them, my palms tingling. I could see Hershel strolling along the edge of the trench, a shovel propped across his shoulders, his arms spread on the handle. He smiled as the sunlight broke on the tops of the trees. I cleared my throat and leaned to one side and spat. "That's my sergeant coming. He lost half his foot walking out of the Ardennes. Show him some respect. Regarding me and my wife, do your worst. We're not afraid of you."

THAT NIGHT I couldn't sleep. Rosita lay inside my arms in our double bed at the motor court, her eyes closed, her breath rising and falling on my chest. The neon sign in front glowed in a red blush through the window shade, and I could hear the sound of the surf in the distance and the dripping of the rain on the camellia bushes outside. I had not told Rosita of my encounter with the federal agents. I finally drifted off to sleep, then woke with a start, the way you do when you dream about a doorbell ringing or the klatch of a Bouncing Betty when a man steps on it.

I sat up on the side of the bed, staring at the red glow on the shade.

"What is it?" she asked.

I told her about the feds and everything they had said.

"Do they want to talk with me?" she said.

"They're out to harass us. Nothing we say will change their agenda."

"Why do they care about us?"

"They don't. They're just carrying out somebody's orders. I suspect Dalton Wiseheart made some phone calls. It's the way he operates. Grandfather warned me about him."

"What did he say?"

"That guys like Wiseheart aren't political. They're just mean."

She sat beside me and put her hand inside my thigh. "*No pasarán,*" she said.

"You got it, kid," I said.

She took my hand in hers. "What do you think they'll do now?"

"Maybe they'll go away."

"You know better."

"They'll try to separate us. They'll smear our names."

"All because we offended that old man on the balcony?"

"Bullies create object lessons," I said. "If we weren't the target, it would be somebody else."

She stood up and took off her nightgown in front of the window shade, her body silhouetted against the red glow of the motel sign.

"You're the most beautiful woman on earth," I said.

"You think so?"

"Helen of Troy might have been a contender, but I think you've got her beat."

She knelt behind me on the mattress and squeezed my head against her chest and kissed my hair and ran her hands down the sides of my face. "Oh, Weldon," she said.

The register in her voice had changed. I felt her tears on the back of my neck. "What's wrong, kid?"

"I don't deserve a man like you."

"Never say that, not under any circumstances."

"Your goodness fills my life. You fill me with light when you're inside me."

"It's the other way around. I'd only be half a person without you. You're my sister and lover and wife and mother and daughter and all good things that women are. No one could ever take your place. There's a glow on your skin. You smell like flowers in the morning. I have romantic dreams about you every night of my life."

She folded her arms across my chest, her mouth against my ear. I could feel her heart beating, her breath on my cheek. I got up from the bed and undressed and lay down beside her. I kissed her stomach and her breasts and her mouth. "I'll never let anyone hurt us," I said.

"It's you they want to destroy, not me. They'll go through me to get to you, but I'm of little interest to them. Be careful of Roy."

"He's probably a womanizer, but I don't think he's an evil man."

"The men who murdered my family were baptized Christians. No one ever called them evil, not until people saw what they had done. Shakespeare said the Prince of Darkness is always a gentleman."

"Did you hear a sound outside?" I asked.

"No."

"It must be the wind."

"I'm sure it is," she said. "Even if it's something else, we don't care."

We made love the way friends and kindred spirits do, rather than husband and wife or lovers. Rosita was my navigator and conscience and the source of my strength. She was my Ruth, my Esther, my

Jewish warrior queen out of the Old Testament. She smelled like the ocean when she made love. Her skin was warm and cool at the same time, her hair fragrant with an odor like night-blooming flowers, her legs long and strong and warm against mine, her mouth wet against my ear.

When we reached that heart-twisting moment that is like no other experience on earth, I felt released from all my problems, as though I were gliding through a starry galaxy that trailed into infinity. I was determined that I would never allow anyone to harm my heroic Jewish wife, who I believed was descended from the House of Jesse.

At four A.M. I heard someone tip over a tin bucket in the driveway. I peeked through the edge of the window shade and saw a man in a hooded raincoat standing five feet from my automobile, looking straight at me.

I slipped on my khakis and my half-topped boots and went outside, my Luger in my right hand. The driveway was empty, the night still except for the water ticking in the trees. Only three blocks away, under a full moon, I could see the Gulf of Mexico and the alluvial flow of yellow mud from the mouth of the Mississippi channeling its way along the coastline, waves crashing in a ropy froth on a barrier island that a dredge boat was hauling away for construction material.

The man by my automobile had disappeared. Had he placed an explosive charge under my car? Or slashed my tires? Or played the role of voyeur and watched my wife and me during sexual congress?

This is how it will go, I thought. *They'll wage a war of gradual attrition that is the equivalent of death in the Iron Maiden. Their resources will be suspicion and anxiety and inculcation of self-doubt and feelings of personal violation. Like the blindfolded man being broken on the wheel, we will never know where the next blow is coming from. And the men behind all this will do it with a phone call they'll forget about two minutes after they hang up.*

"I think you're still out there, within earshot," I said. "I've killed men against whom I had no grievance. Think what I'll do to you."

There was no answer except the wind blowing in the trees, shaking hundreds of raindrops on a pond that glistened in the dark.

Chapter 16

THE NEXT EVENING Hershel knocked on my motel door. He had a six-carton of Jax in one hand and a greasy brown paper bag in the other. He was smiling awkwardly, shifting his weight from one foot to the other. "Is Rosita here?" he said.

"She went to buy groceries in Golden Meadow," I said.

"I didn't see the car and thought you might like to have some beer and cracklings with me."

"Sure, I would. Come in."

"In the fall we always made cracklings and boudin and had people over to eat on the gallery," he said. "You ever do that?"

"Yeah, my grandfather was big on barbecues. We had some fine times."

I knew something else was on his mind. I guess for Hershel I would always be the lieutenant, the man who had pulled him from a collapsed foxhole and could do no wrong.

"Did something happen today?" I asked.

"Linda Gail called from Houston. She was pretty upset. It's this guy Jack Valentine. Remember him? We got our house in River Oaks through Jack."

"I remember him well."

"He told Linda Gail this crazy story. He says you attacked him at the hotel opening Lloyd Fincher took y'all to."

"I wouldn't phrase it that way."

"He also says you turned Bugsy Siegel loose on him."

"That last part is pretty accurate."

"You didn't punch Jack in the mouth?"

"I flattened him."

His eyes went away from mine. "What for?"

"He got out of line."

"What'd he say?"

"What difference does it make? He's coarse and vulgar and treats other people like they have the same frame of reference he does."

"He says he told a joke in the restroom, and for no reason you blindsided him."

"He told me Roy Wiseheart kept a hotel room for his trysts. I didn't want to hear any more of his ugly stories about other people. He kept at it, and I lost control. It was a foolish thing to do."

"You poleaxed a guy over something he said about Roy Wiseheart?"

"I'm a little foggy on what happened, Hershel. I don't handle alcohol well."

"This doesn't sound like you. You handle your liquor just fine."

"Valentine is a bum. Let it go."

"Is he the guy?"

"What do you mean by 'the guy'?"

"The guy sleeping with Linda Gail."

"He was half in the bag. He made a loose remark. I'm not even sure what it was. I hit him. If I had it to do over, I'd walk away and not pay him any mind."

"He said something about Linda Gail?"

"Ask Valentine."

"You're my friend, Weldon. I'm asking you."

"A man like that has no credibility. Why should we care what he says or doesn't say?"

I took the beer opener out of his hand and snapped a cap off a Jax and drank.

"What did he say about her?"

My blood was throbbing in my wrists. "He said he slept with her. He said it happened on the same day he filmed her on the front porch of the general store."

I saw the lump in his throat and the color draining from his cheeks. "You weren't going to tell me? You were going to let me walk around not knowing while this kind of thing was going on behind my back?"

"I considered the matter closed."

"You believed him, or you would have told me he was spreading lies about her."

"Don't let a guy like this hurt you, Hershel. Two federal agents accused Rosita of being a Communist. You think I believe them? You think I'm going to empower J. Edgar Hoover's errand boys?"

"You're saying he was just drunk and shooting off his mouth?"

"I don't know. Give Linda Gail a chance. Talk with her. And stay away from Valentine."

"You know what would happen to a guy like that where I grew up?"

"Yeah, I do. And I don't agree with it."

"At the least, he'd get the skin taken off his back."

I wasn't getting anywhere. Hershel had gone into a mind-set I had known all my life. F. Scott Fitzgerald once said that no one could understand the United States without understanding the graves of Shiloh. The penchant for vigilantism and the slaying of our brothers went all the way back to the colonial era. I had no doubt the hot coals out of which we forged our country were still glowing in the breast of my friend Hershel Pine. I could see his confusion growing in the silence, his forehead knitting.

"People make mistakes," I said. "Too much to drink, wrong situation and wrong people, a decision made in anger after a domestic fight, who knows what? A person makes one bad choice at an intersection and spends a lifetime grieving over it."

"You're saying forgive Linda Gail?"

"I'm saying we should have the willingness to forgive. That's ninety percent of the battle. You're not even sure she did something wrong."

He sat down at the writing desk. His forearm lay across the bag of cracklings he had brought. He seemed to have forgotten where he was or why he had come to my room.

I opened another bottle of Jax and pushed it in front of him. He watched the foam run over the lip and down the neck, without picking up the bottle. "She was too young to get married," he said. "I'm seven years older than she is. I came home a cripple. That's a lot for a girl in her teens to deal with. Maybe that's the way I should look at it."

I hoped one day Benny Siegel would run into Jack Valentine again and put a bullet in him. I looked through the window at the Gulf. The western sky was aflame, seagulls hovering like sketch marks above the surf. "There's Rosita," I said. "Why don't the three of us have a seafood dinner at the café?"

"You meant what you said?"

"I'm not sure what you're referring to."

"That maybe all this is smoke. That Valentine was drunk and trying to mess us up."

"Yeah, it could be that simple," I said, avoiding his eyes.

"Okay," he said, and took a deep breath, like a man stepping out of a bathysphere. "Okay. Right. I get myself wrapped in a knot sometimes. I'm glad I talked with you."

I prayed silently that our conversation about Linda Gail was over. I also prayed that I would not have to tell him another lie.

"You wouldn't lead me on, would you?" he said. "Everything you told me is on the level?"

"I don't know the truth about anything," I said. "You and I were spared at the Ardennes. Maybe it was for a reason. Maybe we'll see the reason down the track. That's the way I look at it."

Before he could speak again, I went outside and helped Rosita unload the automobile.

Later that night I got my notebook out of my suitcase and wrote down a line I remembered from the Book of Psalms: *For, lo, the wicked bend their bow, they make ready their arrow upon the string, that they may privily shoot at the upright in heart.*

Then I added my own words: *Lord, deliver up poor Hershel, because some very bad people are fixing to eat him alive.*

GRANDFATHER WAS AILING, and Rosita and I flew back home to see him. He had reached a stage that elderly men enter when they see specters, sometimes those of old friends, beckoning to them from a shady copse or a roadside cemetery overgrown with mesquite and blown with dust and tumbleweed. His pale eyes seemed distracted, his attention drawn by voices or the sounds of cattle moving in large numbers across a river that had turned bloodred in the sunset, sounds that no one else heard. He slept with his Colt 1860 Army revolver, five chambers loaded, the hammer resting on the sixth chamber, which was empty.

My mother asked him why he needed his revolver.

"So I'll be ready for him when he comes," he replied.

"Ready for whom?" she said.

"Death."

His ankles and feet were so swollen that he had to wear extralarge rubber boots resembling the ones Frankenstein's monster wore in the movies. Our family doctor forbade him to get on a horse, or to drink whiskey or smoke a cigar or pipe, or to ingest sugar in any form.

For Grandfather, that meant he should fire up his pipe right after breakfast, have a bowl of homemade ice cream incised with a half dozen Oreo cookies for lunch, drink a glass of straight whiskey by three P.M., and saddle and get on his horse.

"You have to stay off him, Big Bud," my mother said. My mother called him by his nickname, I think, because she could not bring herself to accept him as her father. But how could I judge her and her siblings when I could not forgive my own father for abandoning his family? I felt sorry for Grandfather. I believed he was truly contrite. Unfortunately, nobody was interested in his contrition.

"You don't need your horse. I drive an automobile and can take you wherever you want," my mother said.

"Emma Jean, go fix yourself a pork chop sandwich or a bowl of grits with a big piece of ham hock," he replied. "Pour some redeye gravy on top. Try to gain some weight, or tie a rock to your ankle. You're skin and bones. A puff of wind would blow you off the planet."

"I have the fragility of a dandelion?"

"That cuts to it."

"You're not going to talk to me like that, Big Bud."

"You're absolutely right. I'm going out the door and ride my horse," he said.

Some might say Grandfather's stubbornness about his horse was motivated by denial of his physical infirmities. They saw only the outside of Grandfather. When he rode into the woods, his rubber-booted feet wedged so tightly in the stirrups that sometimes he had to pull his right foot out of the boot to dismount, he was not simply resisting the earth's gravitational pull. He was riding back through a doorway in time to a place that had nothing to do with the airplanes and motorized vehicles and telephone wires and radios that surrounded him now. In his way, I think he had already taken leave of us.

The woods in late autumn had become his private sun-dappled cathedral, one that contained presences antithetical to the conventional notion of a church. In the columns of light filtering through the canopy, he may have seen the ghosts of John Wesley Hardin and Bill Dalton and Quanah Parker. The saloon girls might have been there, too, most of them as small as Orientals, wearing dresses as tight as sealskin. There was a free lunch on a bar, a faro table, a rotating wheel with numbers on it, men who wore bowler hats and carried derringers under their sleeves, vaqueros and cowboys with coiled lariats hanging from the shoulder, bowie knives on the belt, some wearing wide-brim tall-crown hats that cost a week's wage.

They didn't care if he wore a badge or not. They were all cut out of the same fabric, or they wouldn't have chosen to live and die and be buried in a godforsaken landscape where their grave markers would soon be gone. Susanna Dickinson, the only white adult survivor of the Alamo, was in the cathedral, too. Grandfather knew her when she lived in Austin; she had told him what really happened inside the walls on the last day of the siege: the Mexican soldiers who were so numerous coming over the walls they fired into one another; the drunk Texas soldier who hid in the rubble and begged and was executed; the stench of the bodies piled like cordwood and burned.

Grandfather's stories were wonderful. He said the horns of the cattle glowed with electricity when a storm was in the offing. With the first pop of lightning, the herd would stampede and flow like a brown river through the ravines and dry washes of the Arbuckle Mountains, trampling wagons and tents into splintered wood and strips of canvas.

I don't think he rode into the woods in anticipation of his death. I think he went there in preparation for his return to an era that, for him, had always existed just the other side of the horizon. Others watching him ride along the river's edge saw an old man who was not willing to let winter have its way. I think Grandfather did not see the woods or the river but had already begun his journey on an infinite plain, one unmarked by fences or human structures, one whose mesas and buttes and dead volcanoes and ancient riverbeds antedated the arrival of man and even the dinosaurs. For the first time in his life, he no longer carried the thick gold pocket watch he had bought in Mexico City in 1910.

The snake was a diamondback, the kind of rattler that usually hid in rocks and sunned itself on hillsides and wasn't drawn to dank woods piled with autumn leaves. Just as Grandfather's horse stepped across a log, the diamondback made a sound like seeds rattling inside a dried poppy husk, then popped Grandfather's horse on the fetlock. The horse crashed through the trees and brush and raked Grandfather out of the saddle on an oak limb.

We found him by flashlight two hours later. He had been stirrup-drug twenty yards across hard ground. His eyes were closed, his face spotted with drops of mud that looked like insects. I could not feel a pulse in his throat; I placed my ear against his chest. His skin was as cold as marble. Then he moved. "Is that you, Weldon?" he whispered.

"Yes, sir."

"You were always my son rather than my grandson. You know that, don't you?"

"I do."

"Is that your mother behind you?"

"Yes, sir, she's right here."

"You don't look anything like a dandelion, Emma Jean," he said. "I just cain't keep my mouth shut sometimes. You cut a fine figure. You always did."

He came back from the hospital the next day with a diagnosis of a concussion and three broken ribs. We made a bed for him on the front porch so he could be outside during the day and visit with friends who dropped by; we also brought the mail and newspaper and his encyclopedias to him. I went to town and bought six Mexican dinners to go, although there were only four of us. That's because Grandfather could eat more Mexican food than any man I knew. I sat on the porch with him and watched him eat a tamale soaked in frijoles wrapped with two flour tortillas, and chase it with a glass of buttermilk. "Where are the pralines?" he asked.

"The doctor says no sugar. He says if he catches you on your horse again, he's going to shoot the horse, then you."

"Telling a ninety-year-old not to eat sugar is like telling a death-row inmate to beware of uncooked pork."

"Some people are trying to bushwhack me, Grandfather," I said.

"What kind of people?"

"The kind you warned me about."

"Those big oilmen?"

"That's the bunch. I think Dalton Wiseheart might be involved."

He looked at the dirt road that led into our property and the crows perched on our fences and the trees in the woods that were becoming more skeletal with each sunset. "I don't think you could pick a worse enemy. How in God's name did you get mixed up with a bucket of pig shit like that?"

"I think somebody is trying to break up my business partner's marriage. And I think somebody has turned the feds loose on Rosita."

"Can you prove any of this?"

"No, sir."

He put his empty plate on a chair and sat up on his pillows. He was wearing his beat-up Stetson, his shirt unbuttoned on his hairless chest. "Draw a line in the sand. But don't tell anybody where it is. Don't let your feelings show. Don't let others know you've been hurt. No matter what they do, don't react until they come over the line. Then you drop them in their tracks."

"It's 1947, Grandfather."

"It certainly is," he said.

I waited for him to go on. But he didn't. A few minutes later, he closed his eyes and went to sleep. After sunset I turned on the porch light and covered him with a blanket. At ten P.M. I woke him and took him inside and helped him into his bedroom. As he sat on the side of his bed, he looked dazed and unsure where he was. I got his pajamas out of the dresser drawer.

"I dreamed we were at the county fair," he said. "You and me and Emma Jean and your father. It was 1925. You were seven years old. You were afraid when I put you on the carousel. So I got on it with you."

"I remember that," I said.

"We rode it together, didn't we?" he said.

"Yes, sir, we surely did," I replied.

"I'm proud of you, Satch," he said.

I TRIED TO GET information from the Houston Police Department about the hit-and-run death of Harlan McFey. The detective I spoke with wore a vest without a coat and polished needle-nosed boots and a delicate silver chain that held his necktie in place. He had Indian-black hair that was neatly clipped and shiny with oil. He had put aside a magazine when I entered his office. The windows were open, a hot wind blowing from the street, a fan rattling on the wall. He looked from me to his magazine and back to me. He poked his tongue into his cheek. "I haven't figured out why you're here," he said. "You were an acquaintance of the deceased, not a member of the family?"

"No, I'm not a member of McFey's family. No, I would not call myself an acquaintance."

"So what would you call yourself?"

"Someone he wanted to blackmail or extort."

"Blackmail about what?"

"Any lie he could think up."

"Please explain to me why you're concerned over the manner of his death."

"McFey had been in the employ of Dalton Wiseheart."

He laughed. "The oilman who does business on the veranda of the Rice Hotel? That's who you're trying to tie the tin can on?"

"You think that's funny?"

"No, I don't." He opened a folder on his desk. "McFey came out of a bar and was crossing the street to his car. A truck hit him and kept going. There was one witness: a Mexican kid who shines shoes in the beer joints on the north side. He didn't get a plate number, and he couldn't describe the truck except to say it didn't have its lights on."

"Does the last detail seem significant?" I asked.

"Not necessarily. It was twilight." He closed the folder and tilted back in his swivel chair.

"I have a feeling this isn't going anywhere."

He laced his fingers behind his head. "If you find out anything, let us know."

"Is that a joke?"

"A feeble attempt at one. You've got an attitude, and it's not helping your cause. Anything else?"

"Yeah, I think you've found the right line of work."

AFTER I LEFT the police department, I started to drive back to the Heights. It was Friday, and I had been working at home, with no plans of returning to the job site in Louisiana for another week. I had gotten nowhere in my attempt to find out whom McFey had been working for, or where my father had died. I stopped at a drugstore and called Roy Wiseheart's house. His wife told me he was at a boxing gym downtown.

"Roy is a boxer?" I said.

She hung up.

I suppose I should not have gotten more involved with him than I already was. But so far, he was the only conduit I had into the mystery surrounding my father's death. Second, I wanted to believe he was not having an affair with Linda Gail. Or maybe I'd learn they'd made a brief mistake and had put it behind them. It happens. The world doesn't end. Hadn't I told Hershel as much?

The gym was in a borderline neighborhood between the business district and a decayed residential area that was mostly black and Mexican. I saw Roy on the far side of the gym. He was wearing a pair of scarlet Everlast trunks and a sweat-streaked jersey, the sleeves scissored off at the armpits. He was hitting a speed bag with such precision and force that the bag was a black blur, the rat-a-tat-tat rebound like a machine gun.

"How'd you know I was here?" he said.

"Your wife."

"I'm surprised she'd admit I was here. I've got some extra gym clothes in the car. You want to work out?"

"I need another favor. I tried to get some information from the Houston Police Department on McFey's death. I hit a dead end."

He began unwrapping the leather bands on his gloves. "Nobody is going to help you with McFey, Weldon. He was disposable, a wad of soiled Kleenex. Who knows, maybe he was working for himself. Watch this." Using his bare fists, he hit the heavy bag with a combination of punches that sent it spinning on its suspension chain. "Hang around. I'm about to go three rounds with this fellow who was supposed to be the middleweight champion of Huntsville Prison."

"Did your father tell you Rosita and I went to see him at the Rice Hotel?"

"No, he didn't. My father and I were never close. You know who my brother was?"

"No."

"He was a fighter pilot in Europe. He had nine kills when a couple of Messerschmitts nailed him. He's buried in Germany. My father always felt the wrong son came back home."

I lowered my eyes, my hand on the chain of the heavy bag. His confessional tone made me trust him less. I looked up at him. "Are you on the square, Roy?"

"Regarding what?"

"My friend Hershel."

"You think I'm milking through his fence?"

"Jack Valentine said you keep a fuck pad."

"I'm disappointed to hear you use language like that."

"Are you sleeping with Linda Gail or not?"

He said something I didn't expect: "If I had my way, I'd be you. I wouldn't be married to the woman I live with, and I wouldn't have my father's last name."

"You always seem to slip the punch," I said.

"Slipping the punch is the name of the game," he replied. "Come on, you can be my cut man. Check out that guy's skin. It's luminescent. It reminds me of an exhumed corpse. He could pass for a human slug. This is going to be great."

"Why don't you say it louder?"

The ex-convict boxed under the name of Irish Danny Flannigan. His body was free of tattoos and wrapped like latex, his armpits shaved, his lats as ridged and hard as whalebone. He was flat-chested, his small eyes buried deep in his face. He danced up and down in his corner, rotating his neck, waiting on Roy. I had no doubt he was the kind of man you never provoked or underestimated.

"I think this is a mistake," I said.

"Don't be hard on him. I bet he's a fine fellow," Roy replied.

Flannigan worked his lips around his mouthpiece and hit himself in the face with both gloves, *pow, pow,* to show his indifference to pain and his frustration with the delay.

"Sorry to keep you waiting," Roy said, climbing into the ring. "Tell me what to do. I'm a bit new to this."

"There's the spit bucket on the apron in case you want a drink," Flannigan said.

"Really?" Roy replied. "Oh, excuse me. You meant that as a joke."

"Let me know if I hurt you, and I'll back off. Or tell the ref. You look like a bleeder. We try to screen out the tomato cans here. You a bleeder, pal?"

"That could be. I hope not," Roy said.

A Mexican kid pulled the string on the bell, and Irish Danny Flannigan jabbed Roy once in the forehead, once on the eye, then hit him with a right cross that folded Roy's face against his shoulder and bounced him off the ropes. The next blow caught Roy square on the nose and splattered blood all over his chest and shoulders.

"You all right?" Flannigan said, stepping back. "Maybe you ought to go lie down. You don't look too good."

Roy swung at him and missed. Flannigan hit him with a combination of blows that were devastating, pinning him against the turnbuckle, working on his rib cage and face and then his rib cage again, hooking him under the heart, the kind of blow that's like a piece of broken wood traveling through the vitals. Roy was bent over, trying to cover up, blood running from his nose over his upper lip.

A referee got between the two of them. Other fighters in the gym had stopped their workout to watch. I climbed up on the apron. "How about it, ref?" I said.

"You want to stop, Mr. Wiseheart?" he said.

Roy showed no sign that he'd heard the referee. He went into a crouch, his gloves in front of his face, his elbows tucked in. He took two shots in the head for each one he threw. Flannigan didn't try to hide his intentions; he was going to break every bone in Roy's face. Then I realized I was about to see a side of Roy Wiseheart I had not seen. When the bell rang, he didn't go to his corner. The referee tried to grab his shoulder, but Roy pushed him away.

Flannigan realized the game had changed, and turned around and faced Roy. "This is the way you want it? Fine with me," he said. "Which funeral home does your family use?"

Maybe it was luck. Or maybe Roy was faster and smarter in the ring than anyone had thought. He feinted with his right, as a novice would, then shifted his weight and fired a left straight from the shoulder into Flannigan's jaw, knocking his mouthpiece over the ropes. Flannigan was stunned. Somebody in the back of the gym laughed. Flannigan came back hard, windmilling his punches, sweat flying from Roy's hair with each impact. By all odds, either from the number of blows Roy took or out of self-preservation, he should have gone down. Flannigan knew it, too. He acted as though he had won the fight and started through the ropes for the dressing room. Roy picked up a wood stool from the apron and brained him with it.

It didn't end there. Roy climbed out of the ring with Flannigan, flinging the stool at his head and missing, then pulling off his gloves and clubbing Flannigan in the face with his bare right fist, squashing his nose, splitting his eyebrow. Flannigan toppled into the metal chairs, the spit bucket rolling across the floor. I had never seen anything like it. Flannigan's people had to form a human wall to protect him.

I got in front of Roy, my left hand pushing against his sternum. His stench was eye-watering. "Where are your clothes?" I said.

"In the car. The locker room here is full of cockroaches."

I shoved him ahead of me, out the door.

"Jesus, what's the hurry?" he said.

"Are you out of your mind?"

"I had a blackout or something. It's a gym. What's the big deal? The guy had it coming."

"You could have fractured his skull."

"What I said in there? You don't hold it against me, do you?"

"Said what? What are you talking about?"

"I said I was disappointed by the remark you made. You know, about my keeping an apartment for romantic interludes? You used a vulgar term for it. That's not you, Weldon. Fellows like you set the standards for the rest of us. I was just surprised, that's all. I didn't mean to hurt your feelings."

I couldn't begin to explain what went on inside Roy Wiseheart's head.

He felt his jaw before he got in his Rolls-Royce. "Boy, that guy's got a punch." Then he laughed.

ON THE WAY home, I stopped at a neighborhood drugstore for a box of aspirin. In those days we seldom locked our cars or homes. Perhaps we felt that the slaughter of thirty million people had somehow driven evil from our shores and that V-J Day marked the restoration of the isolationist policies we had clung to during the prewar era. Didn't our prosperity indicate as much? Wasn't there a divine hand at work in our lives?

I sat at the soda fountain and drank a cherry milk shake and listened to Hank Williams on the jukebox and tried to forget the bloody business I had witnessed at the boxing gym. The doors of the drugstore were open, and the interior was breezy and cool, the comic books on the magazine rack ruffling. Across the street, stubborn kids who refused to go with the season were playing baseball in a park, the pitcher taking an exaggerated full windup before his delivery, smacking the ball into the catcher's glove as fast as a BB. I watched a seedy man wearing a hat and wire-framed dark glasses ride a bicycle past the window on the sidewalk. He was also wearing cloth gardening gloves. A moment later, I saw him stop his bicycle and look directly at me. His face was expressionless, like a death's-head, his mouth small and downturned at the corners, his face as deeply lined as a prune. He tossed a package wrapped with twine and brown paper through the open window of my automobile.

By the time I got outside, he had rounded the corner and disappeared on the other side of the baseball diamond, like a satyr working his mischief among the innocent and seeking another vale in which to play. I got behind the wheel and picked up the package from the passenger seat. It was thin, perhaps fifteen by fifteen inches in width and breadth, the paper stiff and neatly folded on the corners, the twine snipped and tied in a square knot.

I opened my pocketknife and cut the twine and peeled back the paper gingerly. There were no wires, no capsules containing explosive gelatins, no suspicious devices that I could see, only a square tin box. At the bottom of the lid was a small German swastika. I took off the lid and removed a reel of movie film from the box.

There are times in your life when you know, without any demonstrable evidence, that you are in the presence of genuine evil. It is not generated by demons, nor does it have its origins in the Abyss. It lives in the breast of our fellow man and takes on many disguises, but its intention is always the same: to rob the innocent of their faith in humanity and to destroy the light and happiness that all of us seek.

To watch the film was to do the bidding of iniquitous men. To destroy it was to preempt any chance of finding out who had sent it. I drove to a photography store owned by a family friend who had been a member of the OSS and had parachuted into the Po Valley in the last days of the Italian campaign. "Can you put this on a projector?" I asked.

"Yeah, but I'd like to know what for," he said.

"An anonymous person dropped it on the seat of my automobile. I have no idea what's on it."

My friend tapped his fingernail on the tin container. "I've seen these cans before. They were carried by German army combat photographers, sometimes by guys who worked for Joseph Goebbels. Some of them shot footage in the camps, then doctored it. You don't want to see the footage that wasn't doctored."

"I walked into a camp right after the SS pulled out. I'm not worried about the content of a newsreel, doctored or undoctored."

He placed the reel on a projector in the back room and aimed it at a small screen on the wall. His thumb rested on the switch. "Is there a reason I should leave?"

"None that I know of."

He clicked the switch. The footage was in black and white and set in a large room with three beds in it. At first the lens was partially blocked by a man who had a head like a white bowling ball and a thick neck spiked with pig bristles. He wore suspenders and jackboots and was drinking from a stein and eating a sausage, his porcine face split with a grin, his tombstone teeth shiny under a lightbulb suspended from the ceiling. Two naked young women were sitting side by side on the edge of a bed, their faces turned from the camera. One had her arm around the waist of the other.

An SS colonel walked past the lens, his shoulders erect, a cigarette held in front of him, the way a European gentleman would smoke. The two women were taken to separate beds, where one was slapped repeatedly in the face by the man with the beer stein and the other was systematically degraded and mounted by the colonel.

"I don't think this is the kind of crap either one of us needs to see," my friend said.

"I'll watch it by myself," I replied.

"Turn it off when you've had enough. We need to find the guy who left this in your car."

I didn't answer. He started to leave the room. Then we saw another woman appear on the screen. She was wearing a dress that went almost to her ankles, and a Spanish blouse, and pearls around her neck, and a white rose in her hair. I felt as though a sliver of ice had been pushed into my heart.

"I'm going to turn it off, Weldon," my friend said.

"Leave it alone."

"Don't do this to yourself, buddy."

"I'm fine. I appreciate the help you've given me. I'll let you know when I'm finished."

He closed the door behind him. I could hardly bear to look at the screen. Rosita was undressing directly in front of the camera; then she and the SS colonel re-created all the fantasies that a perverse and misogynistic and depraved sex addict was capable of imagining. The film lasted nineteen minutes. When the colonel rose from her body, she washed him with a towel and a pan of water while he combed his hair in a mirror.

I took the reel off the projector and replaced it in the tin container. Then I sat down in a wood chair, staring at the floor, a train whistle blowing inside my head. When I closed my eyes, I saw a snowfield under a blazing moon and a primeval forest that was dark and green and pure and smelled of colossal trees reaching into the clouds, the way the earth probably smelled before the first man despoiled it with his scat.

I got up and tucked the container under my arm and walked out to my automobile with the precision of a drunk man making his way along the edge of a precipice. I heard my friend calling to me from the door of his shop, but the words were like the underwater sounds you hear in a swimming pool when you have caught your foot in the drain and think you are about to drown.

Chapter 17

THE PHYSICIAN HAD told Linda Gail the sedatives would allow her to sleep without dreaming and to arise rested and fresh in the morning. But that was not how she felt now. The light outside was brittle and harsh, the inside of the house too warm, even though she had opened all the windows. Her skin was clammy, her breath sour, her coffee cup trembling on the saucer when she set it down.

She had awakened in the predawn hours from a harrowing dream, one in which she was covered with tentacles that searched in the cavities of her body and wrapped around her chest and face and squeezed the light from her eyes.

All of this was Jack Valentine's fault. After he had filmed her on the gallery of the general store, he had taken her to dinner and then to a private club in Bogalusa. She had never had a vodka Collins. The cherries and orange twists and crushed ice and the sweetness of the mix were wonderful. Perhaps she drank three. Or was it five? Her throat was cold, her skin warm, her nipples hard. When he placed his hand on her thigh under the table, she clasped it as she would the hand of a friend. He told her what the ocean looked like from the deck of a house on the cliffs of Malibu. He showed her the photographs in the celluloid windows of his wallet: Jack Valentine standing next to Tom Mix, both of them wearing tall-crown snow-white Stetsons; Deanna Durbin handing him a Coca-Cola on a tray;

Bob Steel showing him how to load a six-gun. She hardly remembered what occurred later at the motor court.

Or at least that was what she told herself. In the middle of the night, she had gotten up and gone to the bathroom and realized that something terrible had happened and that she was in a place she had never seen and that there were scratch marks on the tops of her shoulders and a soreness inside her like a shard of broken glass. Her stomach was nauseated, the backs of her thighs shaking, her face a bloodless white balloon she hardly recognized in the mirror.

She told Valentine at breakfast that they were adults who had made a mistake and they would treat their situation as such. That's what adults did, didn't they? Whatever had occurred was the result of circumstances that were unplanned and nobody's fault. They would remain friends. He was a nice man. If he didn't wish to introduce her to his fellow directors and producers in Hollywood, she wouldn't hold it against him.

While she spoke to him across a plate of eggs and greasy bacon that made her sick to look at, he gazed out the café window, a merry gleam in his blue-green eyes, eyes she had associated with a buccaneer on the Spanish Main.

"Do you find this humorous?" she asked.

"I guess I shouldn't suggest the hair of the dog that bit you," he replied.

"I think I'll go now," she said. "You can leave me out of your documentary. I'm going to erase the last twenty-four hours from my memory and restart my life without any of this in it. Good-bye, Mr. Valentine."

He clenched her wrist as she started to rise from the chair, his eyes still focused out the window. "You're going to Hollywood, and the world is going to be your oyster. It's your destiny, Miss Linda. You've got it all. Do you have any idea what the average Gump would pay to see a sweet-faced girl like you in a negligee?" He held up his thumb and index finger an inch apart. "You're that far away from having your name on every marquee in the country. Don't throw it away."

Now it was obvious that Hershel knew of her infidelity and that

Valentine had sullied her name with anyone he could. She could have confessed, but she saw no reason that she should carry the responsibility, or the odium, for an act that was not the result of a conscious choice. Plus, she would hurt Hershel, she told herself. Yes, she needed to protect Hershel.

There was a problem in her thought processes. After she and Valentine had left a cottage party on the beach north of Malibu, he made another pass at her, this time for a go-round in the backseat of his convertible. He had been smoking marijuana and drinking whiskey and had put his arm around her shoulders and was walking her toward the sand dune where his vehicle was parked, as though their coupling were a foregone conclusion. "We'll do it au naturel, out in the fresh air," he said.

"Who the hell do you think you are?" she replied. "You're drunk and you smell bad. As far as skill in the sack is concerned, your reputation among the extras is between a D-minus and an F-plus. You avoided getting an F only because of the Japanese rubbers you supposedly use."

"You're fast on your feet, kid. But there's a little matter you've never latched on to. Do you believe you got your contract because of your brains or the space between your front teeth? The people who wanted your name on a contract had other reasons, and it wasn't that heart-shaped twat, either, although they'll probably get to it eventually."

He got in his convertible and drove away, stranding her on the beach. The wind was cold and blowing hard, full of sand that stung her eyes and invaded her person. The ocean was as black as satin, lustrous when the moon peeked out from a cloud, the waves welling over the rocks along the shore, forming pools where trapped baitfish skittered like handfuls of silvery dimes thrown on the water. One hundred yards away, the party at the cottage was still in progress. Should she go back and ask for a ride from people she hardly knew, signaling to all of them the squalid nature of her relationship with a man like Jack Valentine?

She walked up the incline among huge wind-sculpted formations that resembled abstract works of art and came out on the highway and began walking back to Los Angeles, ignoring the backdraft of trucks that sucked past her. At dawn a police cruiser picked her up and a patrolman drove her home. He was young and had olive skin and a dimple in his chin and sun-bleached hair and was obviously impressed when she told him about her acting career. "Sounds like you're on your way," he said.

"I bet you're from the South," she said. She was riding in front with him.

"You caught my accent, I guess," he said.

"No, I can tell because you're a gentleman. They seem in short supply out here. I grew up on a plantation in Louisiana. All the young men I knew were very much like yourself—courteous and genteel. You've been terribly kind."

"Can I buy you breakfast?"

She touched his arm. "Another time. I think I'm going to sleep for a week," she said. "You've been quite *gallant*." She let her eyes linger on his.

"Here's your place," he said. "That's Muscle Beach down yonder. I'm gonna take my little boy swimming there one day. Don't be walking on the highway again, you hear? There's people here'bouts that don't care two cents for the welfare of others."

When she got back to Houston, the first person she called was Roy Wiseheart. "Jack Valentine said I was given a contract at Castle for ulterior motives."

"He's a gofer and a public fool and one cut above a pimp. He shouldn't be allowed around you."

"Why would he make up a story like that?"

"Because he's jealous. You're going to be a star. Valentine used to clean dog poop off W. C. Fields's lawn. Anthony Quinn lived next door. Valentine thought he'd hit the big time when he was allowed to clean both their yards. This is the guy you're taking seriously. Where are you?"

"At home," she said, her mouth suddenly dry. "I just got back to town."

"You're alone?"

"Yes," she replied, trying to control the beating of her heart and the catch in her throat.

"Are you sure you're all right?" he asked.

"Hershel will be back this weekend. I'll be fine until then."

"You don't sound like it. Would you like me to come over?"

"I wouldn't want to impose on you."

"Stay there."

Her fingers were shaking when she set the receiver back in its cradle.

When he arrived, he was wearing a white suit and an open-necked crimson silk shirt and shined loafers. He was holding a bottle of nonalcoholic champagne in one hand and a 78-rpm phonograph record in the other. His cheeks were like apples, his skin glowing, his hair barbered and wet and neatly combed.

"Do you have a phonograph?" he said.

"Yes, right there," she replied, pointing at the walnut-encased combination radio and record player she and Hershel had just bought.

He opened the top of the console and slipped the 78 out of its paper jacket onto the flat on his hand. She had closed all the curtains, and when the record began to play, she felt that she and Roy Wiseheart had become the only two people on earth.

"That's Bunny Berigan," he said.

"What's the name of the song?"

"'I Can't Get Started with You.' You have some glasses?"

"Roy?" she said.

He looked at her, his face warm. "You don't like champagne?"

"I'm weak. I want to do right, but most of the time I don't."

"You're stronger and braver than I, nobler, and much more gifted than you think. Don't ever speak badly of yourself."

He slipped his right arm around her waist and lifted her right hand in his, his body barely touching hers. "I wish I married someone like you, but I didn't. That doesn't mean I can't be your friend. The movie business is full of bad people, individuals who are far worse than Jack Valentine. They're cruel and unscrupulous when they don't have to be. Do you know why they're cruel?"

"No."

"They have no talent of their own. They have to steal it from others. They don't deserve their success, and they know it. They're always frightened someone is about to catch on to them. Six months ago some of them were pumping gasoline in Peoria."

"I don't understand you. You're so wise, yet you seem so unhappy."

She felt his fingers spread across her back, his breath like a feather on the side of her face. "I think I used up all my luck in the South Pacific. I don't worry about it, though. We're born and we live and we die. What we do along the way isn't that important."

"You shouldn't say that."

He released her hand and held her with both arms, his cheek against hers. Her temples were pounding.

"I'm not a philanderer," he said. "I take care of my wife, but I don't love her. By the same token, I try not to cause grief in the lives of others. I haven't always done the right thing."

"You're not causing grief," she said. "Not to me."

She felt his arm tighten around her back. "I wish we'd met earlier."

"What are you saying? I'm confused. What do you mean? Are you here to tell me you shouldn't be here?"

He stepped back from her and removed the needle from the record and replaced the record in its jacket. He picked up the champagne bottle from the coffee table. "Drink a glass with me."

"Whatever you want."

"Do you like Weldon?" he asked.

"Sometimes I do. I don't think he likes me."

"He's going to get hurt. When that happens, he'll need his friends."

"You're saying I'm not one of them? You're here about Weldon Holland?"

"I'm telling you that you're swimming among a school of piranhas. I don't want to add to your burden."

He popped the cork on the champagne bottle and filled two glasses. The door to her bedroom was open, and through it she could see the mix of pinks and blues that resembled a child's playroom.

"Call me again if you have trouble with Valentine or anyone else," he said.

"You're going?"

He touched her hair and cheek in a way that reminded her of how she had touched the sleeve of the policeman who drove her home in Los Angeles. "You're a beautiful woman," he said. "Keep being who you are, Linda Gail. Be true to thine own self." He set down his glass and opened the front door, then looked back at her. "I can't wait to see your first film."

He eased the door shut, letting the lock click quietly into place, as though not wanting to disturb the solemnity normally associated with a church. She could not remember when she had felt so foolish.

NOW HE WAS at her house again, this time without invitation or a phone call. When she opened the door, she couldn't believe what she was looking at. He was carrying his clothes and wearing only boxing trunks and a jersey that was dark and soggy with sweat. "Do you have room for a wayfaring stranger?" he asked.

"You look like you were hit by a manure truck. Is that blood on you?"

"I went a round or two with a fellow at a gym. It's nothing. Is Hershel home?"

"He's out of town."

"Do you mind if I use the hose in your backyard?"

"No, you cannot. What happened?"

"This fellow was rude and things got a bit out of hand. I'm sorry to be a bother."

"What fellow?"

"He was in prison. I thought I'd go a few rounds with him. Weldon was there. I could have gone to his house, but I didn't want to upset his wife."

"I hate to ask this question, but why don't you go to your own house?"

"Because I have a problem and I need to talk to somebody about it. I don't trust many people. You're the exception."

"Where are you trying to take us, Roy? What are you trying to do to me?"

"If you want me to leave, I will. Let me be honest. I saw your husband's pickup was gone. It was also gone yesterday. So I came here and knocked on your door."

"You've been spying on my house?"

"I'll see you another time."

"No, you won't. Get in the shower," she said. "Give me your clothes. All of them."

When he hesitated, she grabbed him by the jersey and pulled him inside.

While the shower water pounded inside the bathroom, she sat in a chair and tried to think. In three days Hershel would be home. She had already resolved that she would make a clean breast of her bad behavior with Jack Valentine. Again and again, she had gone over the words she would use. She was drunk when she went to bed with him. She might even admit that she had been drawn to Roy Wiseheart when Hershel was away, and had danced with him in the living room. Nothing really bad had happened, but she was sick with fear and guilt just the same. She would promise never to be unfaithful again, not even in thought. She would be a good wife and go with Hershel wherever he went, even if she had to give up her career.

Her contrition was sincere, her words from the heart. Except for the last part. Her breath came short when she thought about turning down a costarring role that had been offered to her. There was another consideration, one she pushed away from the edges of her conscious mind: She had never loved Hershel Pine.

She had met him at a dance when she was sixteen and he was about to be shipped overseas in advance of the invasion of Italy. He was handsome in his uniform and the center of attention among all the local boys who had never been farther than two parishes from their birthplace. The following night Hershel took her to a movie and an ice cream parlor in Bogalusa and kissed her under a magnolia tree in the park. In the moonlight he became a French legionnaire, a Roman centurion, a British officer in a pith helmet firing his pistol at the Fuzzy Wuzzies attacking the walls of a desert fortress. Hershel

Pine was her deliverance from the small-town world of cotton gins and five-and-dime stores and wood-frame heat-soaked churches that groaned with organ music and warnings of eternal perdition.

Roy Wiseheart was dressed in slacks and a golf shirt when he came out of the bathroom, one eye almost shut, the lumps on his face as big as bumblebee bites, the cuts clean of blood. "Sit down," she said.

"What are you going to do?" he asked.

She took bottles of iodine and peroxide out of the medicine cabinet and went to work on the damage done to him in the ring, boiling out each cut with the disinfectant, painting it with iodine. "Ouch," he said, squinting.

"Does that sting?" she said.

"Yes."

"Good."

"You have a rough side to you," he said.

"You don't know the half of it."

"I tried to kill that kid," he said.

"He doesn't sound like a kid to me."

"I not only tried to kill him, I enjoyed it."

"Stop talking about it. It's over."

"I've done it before."

"Fight someone?"

"Gone after someone with a purpose. Done serious injury."

"Is that what you came here to tell me?"

"No. I came here to tell you something else. I abandoned my squadron leader when he was limping home. I did it so I could get another kill and be an ace. Two Zeros lit him up. He was trapped in his cockpit. He burned all the way down."

She placed her hand on the back of his neck. It was as warm as a woodstove. "Maybe you were trying to protect your friend. That would be anybody's first instinct."

"My brother was an ace. I wanted to be one, too. I sacrificed another man's life to satisfy my ambition."

"I don't know about military things, but I don't think you should blame yourself. Wouldn't your friend tell you that if he were here now? He must have been a good man or you wouldn't feel remorse. A good man would forgive you. Are you saying he's not a good man?"

He looked up at her. "Run that by me again?"

She repeated her words. She could see the shine in his eyes. She stroked the back of his head. He stood from the chair, and took the bottle of iodine and the towel from her hands, and set them on the chair. He put his arms around her and kissed her on the mouth. Then he buried his face in her hair, squeezing her body into his, running his hands down her back and sides, kissing her neck. She could feel his manhood swell against her.

"Roy—" she began.

"I love you," he said. He pushed her arms around his neck and spread his fingers on her rump and lifted her against him. "You have the loveliest figure on earth. Your skin feels like silk. I'm sorry for the way I'm behaving. I think about you all the time."

"It's all right," she heard herself say.

He unbuttoned the top of her dress and bit her shoulder. "Can we go in your bedroom?"

"Yes."

"You're not expecting anyone?"

"No. I want to be with you. I want to help you leave behind all those bad memories from the war."

"You're sure this is what you want?"

"Yes, it is. It's the way it's meant to be, or it wouldn't be happening," she said.

"This isn't the first time I've done this," he said. "But it was different. It was selfish. That's not the way I feel about you."

She took him by the arm and led him into the bedroom. "Get undressed. It'll be all right. Don't worry anymore."

He hesitated, and she realized he was looking at a framed photograph of her and Hershel on the dresser. "You don't have to feel guilty," she said. "Anything that happens here is my responsibility, not yours. You don't know the whole history."

"History of what?"

"It doesn't matter at this point," she said.

She turned off the light and pulled back the bedcovers and threw all the pillows except one on the floor. She hung her dress over a chair and removed her underthings with her back to him, then turned around. His face softened, like warm wax changing shape. She pushed him down on the mattress and spread her knees, straddled his thighs, and placed his hands on her breasts. Next door she could hear someone bouncing up and down on a diving board, then springing and flattening on the water. "I just want to ask one thing of you," she said.

"Anything," he replied.

"Don't talk bad about me later. Like men do when they brag to others. Don't ever do that to me."

"I wouldn't."

"I want you to hold me and kiss me when it's over. I want to see you in other situations also."

"Whatever you want, Linda Gail."

She made a cradle of herself and leaned down and kissed him and put her tongue in his mouth.

"You're the most wonderful woman I've ever been with," he said.

She reached down and placed him inside her. She shifted her weight back and forth and crunched her stomach and rotated herself until she saw his eyes go out of focus. She had never felt such power in her life. It was like the first time she walked into the waves at Santa Monica, the water sliding above her thighs, the foam wetting the tops of her breasts, the gulls wheeling overhead as though in tribute to her, the suntanned boys on Muscle Beach setting down their iron weights to gaze upon her. Now, when she came with him, she went weak all over, her neck stretched back, a ragged sound bursting from her throat. Then she came again and again, something she had never done, as though an entire race were being conceived inside her, as though at that exact moment she was silhouetted against a molten sun descending into the ocean, the palm trees stiffening into black cutouts against a flaming sky, her nails digging into his arms on a beach where there was not another human being.

Later, they lay side by side, their bodies damp with perspiration. As he fell asleep, she stroked his forehead with the tips of her fingers and idly stared at the ceiling. Then she kissed his shoulder, enjoying the warmth of his skin and the hint of salt on it. A great and restful fatigue seemed to settle upon her and quiet all the turmoil and anger that lived inside her. Just before she nodded off, she thought she heard wind blowing in a seashell and waves sliding back from a precipitous shoal gnarled with crustaceans. Out in the swells, she saw herself mounted on a porpoise that would take her to a coral kingdom beneath the sea. It wasn't simply a dream. She had earned her place in the Pantheon. Today was just the beginning.

Chapter 18

OUR DRIVEWAY WAS unpaved. Maybe that seems a silly observation to make in regard to the place where we lived in the Heights in the year 1947. But it was one detail of many I noticed on that late afternoon when I parked my car next to our screened porch and wondered how I should confront Rosita with the movie reel that sat in a tin box on the seat to me. The grass was a pale green, the chrysanthemums blooming in the flowerbeds, the driveway little more than a pattern of white rocks, like an ancient road protruding from the dirt, the lawn scattered with pecans in their husks.

There was another detail about our neighborhood that I had not given great weight to, and that was the absence of fences between the houses. It was an era of trust, of a boy on a bicycle sailing the evening paper up on the porch, radios in a window blaring with the overture from *William Tell* at six-thirty Monday through Friday evening all over the land. I didn't want to go inside. I didn't want to hurt my wife. I didn't want to discover she was someone other than the truthful person I thought she was.

She was making sandwiches in the kitchen, trimming off bread crusts on a chopping board. She glanced at me and at the can in my right hand, then resumed slicing. "Where have you been?"

"Somebody dropped a movie reel in my car. I took it to a photo shop owned by a friend and watched it."

"Your friend didn't have a telephone?"

"I asked my friend to leave the room while I watched it."

"It must have been interesting material."

I set the can on the drainboard. "There's a swastika on it."

"Get it away from me."

"Have you seen a film can like this one?"

"Not that I remember."

"You're in the film, Rosita."

"How nice," she said, the blade of her knife moving along the edges of the bread. "Now take it out of my sight, please."

"You didn't have to hide your past from me."

"No one has any idea what went on in the camps," she said. "You couldn't begin to understand what they did to us and what we did to one another."

"Why didn't you tell me about the film?"

"Because it's inconsequential in terms of other things that happened."

"You told me you spat in an SS colonel's face when he asked you to be his mistress."

"Because that's what I did."

Then I spoke the worst words that ever passed through my lips. "That's not what you're doing in the film."

She set the butcher knife down and stepped back, as though untangling herself from thoughts she didn't believe herself capable of. "Do you want to know the colonel's name?"

"No."

"Why not?"

"Because if I find out who he is and learn that he's alive, I'll go wherever he is and kill him."

"Tell me what you think you saw."

"*Think* I saw?"

"Tell me!" She shoved me in the breastbone.

"I won't discuss it."

"You watched him fuck me. What else did you see?"

"Don't you use that language."

She hit me again in the chest, harder this time, knocking me backward. "Tell me!"

"I just want you to explain how it happened. You were well dressed. You were wearing pearls. You had a white rose in your hair."

"You're shocked because of what you saw. I was the person he used and degraded while others watched. How do you think I feel?" This time she made a fist before she hit me. "There's no way I'll ever wash him off me."

"I saw the whole reel. You acted like you were his lover."

"Because he told me he'd spare my family!" she said.

She slashed at my face, kicking my shins, her thumb reaching for my eyes. I grabbed her with both arms and locked my hands behind her back and lifted her into the air, carrying her into the living room while she fought.

"I understand," I said. "I was in an artillery barrage that I would have killed my best friend to get out of. I apologize for hurting you. We have to find out who put the reel in my car."

"Put me down, Weldon. Put me down or I will kill you."

"I will. Don't hit me again. Roy Wiseheart said somebody would ruin our names and turn us against each other. That's what they're doing to us now. But we're not going to cooperate with them."

She started to raise her fists again.

"Did you hear me?" I said, taking her by the wrists. "We're stronger than these men are. Whatever you were forced to do in that camp has nothing to do with who you are. Whatever happened back there is nothing more than a decaying memory. It has no substance other than as a reminder that you were willing to undergo a torment worse than death to save your family." I could barely restrain her; she had the body and strength of a woman who had done hard physical work all her life. "Don't fight me, Rosita," I said. "Nothing can ever come between us. I'm going to find the men behind this. It's just a matter of time."

"And do what?" she asked.

"It'll be a memorable day in their lives."

I saw the heat go out of her face, the brightness fade in her eyes. "You were a soldier, but you're not a violent man," she said. "You must never become one."

I released her wrists. "You don't know me."

"Don't do their bidding. That's what they want. They'll put someone in your path who's dispensable. They destroy people's souls. That's how they work. They're cowards, all of them."

"Grandfather went after Pancho Villa. These guys don't make the cut." I put my hands on her shoulders and tried to make her smile.

"You don't know your enemy," she said.

"What do you think life was like at Saint-Lô and in the Ardennes?"

"The men who put that film in your car are far worse. They're your countrymen, too. They have greater power than the Nazis because you don't believe they're among us."

"Could be," I said. "But you and I are going out for dinner. Then we have a date upstairs. And no one, and I mean no one, will ever harm you again."

I went into the kitchen and picked up the film can from the drainboard and wrapped it in tinfoil and electrician's tape, then got a shovel out of the tool closet on the back porch.

"Where are you going?" she said.

"To bury this," I replied. "Maybe it'll stay in the ground forever. If I find the men behind it, I'll dig it up and pack it down their throats with a broom handle. That's not a metaphor."

MYTHOS IS USUALLY created to justify the self-indulgence of those who control the lives of others. Dalton Wiseheart's reputation as an iconoclast was no exception. The supposedly humorous stories told about him were not funny. He called up people in the middle of the night and forced them to make business decisions when their minds were fogged and their defenses weak. He took his private plane to pick up business associates in New York or Los Angeles and have them flown to a hangar in a remote section of Nevada or Utah. After he concluded his business, he flew away and let them get home on their own.

He carried a sack lunch to his office. At Christmastime, he gave bottles of deodorant to black employees. One night a year he rented every girl in Norma Wallace's brothel on Conti Street in New Orleans. He watched 1930s black-and-white Mickey Mouse cartoons at a drive-in theater on South Main, where admission consisted of the ten cents a patron was required to spend on a mug of root beer. He left nickel tips at Jimmy's Coney Island and used a water witch to drill for oil. He spent twenty-six hours at a Reno poker table, then put his six-figure winnings in a canvas bag and stuffed it in the poor box of a rundown church on the edge of town.

He had no pattern. That was obviously his goal. No one knew his thoughts or plans. He could buy a banana republic with a personal check or take a nap in his car at a traffic light; one had about as much importance as the other. Grandfather always said the man to kill you will be the one taking out your throat before you realize you're wearing a red bib. I think Grandfather may have had Dalton Wiseheart in mind.

I wanted to find Dalton and ask if he had seen my wife's degradation on the film that he or his minions had gotten from a British or American intelligence agency. I wanted to ask what it felt like to be a coward and a character assassin. I wanted to humiliate him in public and tell him I couldn't do him physical harm because of his age; otherwise, I would probably take a whip to him.

My head was filled with my own vituperative rhetoric, repressed anger turning in my chest like a set of kitchen knives. Wealth buys not only control and transcendence but inaccessibility. Dalton Wiseheart had turned to smoke.

I tried to get to him through Roy. His wife hung up on me again, and his secretary told me he had left for Los Angeles on the Sunset Limited.

"Oh yes, I think I remember his mentioning that," I said. "Can you give him a message?"

"He's still on the train."

"Is he staying at the hotel he normally uses?"

"Nice try," she replied.

A week passed. I worked out of our office downtown and left

Hershel in charge of our projects in Louisiana. Then I received a call I didn't expect. "This is Jack Valentine," the voice said. "I need to talk with you."

"You want to have another get-together with Bugsy Siegel?" I said.

"Siegel is dead."

"What?"

"Somebody shot him through his window in Beverly Hills. His eye was blown out of his head. The photo was in the paper. Maybe he wasn't so tough after all."

"Why are you calling me?"

"We're on the same side. We can help each other."

"Wrong on both counts," I said.

"Wait till you hear what I have to say. That cunt is in the middle of it."

"What did you say?"

"I'm talking about Linda Gail Pine. Get off your high horse. They're going to cook the flesh off your bones, Holland. I know who's going to do it, and I know how. You want to talk or not?"

Valentine gave me the name of a bowling alley. I found him in the lounge. He wore a fedora and a brown shirt with a red-and-silver-striped tie, zoot trousers hitched up on his sides. He was drinking a beer at the bar. A pinball machine was dinging just inside the door, the maple-floored bowling lanes echoing with the explosion of wood pins. I sat down on a stool next to him. "You always hold your business meetings here?" I said.

"Some people have electronic ears, know what I mean?" he replied. "You ever hear a clicking sound on your telephone?"

"Somebody has my phone tapped?"

"What do you think?"

"I think I don't trust you."

"Linda Gail got me fired."

"How?"

"Through Roy Wiseheart."

"Too bad."

"I want my job back. He's your friend. I'll give you his number. You get me my job back, I'll give you everything you want."

"What is it you think I want?"

"I know all their secrets. I know who's blackmailing who, I know who's screwing who. I know they're going to hang you up by your scrotum."

"Can you tell me why 'they' want to do that?"

"You grew up down here, right? A coon gets out of line, they give him a warning. Next time around, they take the skin off his back. He does it again, they bounce him off a tree limb. Hollywood works the same way."

"What do I have to do with Hollywood?"

He shook his head as though he had been talking to someone of diminished capacity. "I hear you got a private screening of your wife's film talents. That was for openers, Holland."

"You know about the Nazi film reel?"

"Word gets around."

He was smirking. I picked up his bottle of beer and poured it on his fly. "You don't want to come near me again, Mr. Valentine."

When I walked out of the lounge, the sound of the bumpers on the pinball machine seemed to have crawled inside my head, growing louder and louder, turning to flashes of light behind my eyes, reaching a crescendo that left my ears popping.

LINDA GAIL'S AGENT was Morton Lutz and had been introduced to her by Roy Wiseheart. Roy said "Moe" was a rare man in Hollywood and would not deceive or cheat her. He lived in Pasadena with his wife and five children and looked like a pink whale stuffed inside a three-piece suit with a red boutonniere in the lapel. When he smiled, which was most of the time, his eyes disappeared inside his face. Moe told Linda Gail she was a "nice goil." They were standing in the garden outside the Beverly Hills Hotel, waiting to go inside and sign a contract whose content made Linda Gail's head swim.

"I'm nervous," she said.

"What's to be nervous?" he asked.

"I don't understand how the contract works. I'm being sold to Warner Brothers?"

"Something is happening here that doesn't happen often," he replied. "It's all because of Roy Wiseheart. Castle Productions is letting you go to a studio that is going to pay you ninety thousand dollars a year. Warner Brothers is very happy to do that. What does that tell you?"

"I don't know."

"It tells you if you belong to a church, put something extra in the basket."

"I feel funny calling you Moe."

"If you don't call me Moe, I won't know who you're talking to. Where would that leave us?"

"I'm getting a break because of Roy?"

"Call it that. Castle is letting you go because of him. The money Warner Brothers is paying for your contract is not a break and not connected to him. That's the kind of money you're worth. This bunch doesn't spend money to give people breaks or make them feel good. The money gets spent to make more money."

There was a newspaper folded in his coat pocket. He moved into the shade under a palm tree and put on his reading glasses. "You're in Louella Parsons's column this morning," he said.

"I don't believe you."

"This is what she says: 'Linda Gail Pine is the freshest and brightest thing since the invention of flowers and sunshine.'" He lowered the newspaper. "You're so innocent, butterflies light on your hair. Look." He used the back of his hand to lift a Mourning Cloak butterfly off her shoulder. He set it down in a flowerbed. "You ready to go inside?"

"What do I say?"

"Nothing. You'll go home rich. In a week you'll be famous. After that, who knows?"

"What's that mean?"

"We'll talk," he said.

She thought he was about to make another joke. But he didn't. And his smile had disappeared.

The signing of the contracts inside the meeting room was formal and perfunctory; it reminded her of people meeting at a bus stop and exchanging pleasantries and disappearing ten minutes later into their own lives.

She had lunch with Moe in the dining room. Through the window, she could see the golf course and the swimming pool and the shade trees and the cottages where the most famous celebrities in the world stayed. "You waiting for Roy?" he asked.

"Yes, he said he would meet us."

"He called and said he got tied up. I forgot to tell you."

"Oh," she said.

"It's just as well."

"Why?"

"Because I got to tell you a couple of things," he said. "These are not things meant to offend you. So when I say them, they are not directed at you. These are the rules that apply to everybody out here. It doesn't matter who. You can do almost anything you want in this town, and that means sleep with almost anybody you want to, but you got to be careful. You know what John Huston always says? You got to respect your audience. That means you got to look and act like the sweet goil that lives next door. The goil next door doesn't wake up in the morning not remembering where she left her panties."

"I'd prefer you didn't talk to me like that."

"I'm not saying these things about you. I'm talking about the rules. There are two things out here you don't go near. Narcotics is one. For you I don't think that's going to be a problem. You know what the other one is, don't you?"

"No," she replied.

"Some of the writers here are Reds. At least they pretend to be. Most of them read *The Wall Street Journal* every morning. You know any Communists?"

"In Bogalusa, Louisiana?"

"That's what I thought. Good for you. You and your husband are busted up?"

"Pardon?"

"That's what Roy said. Maybe I got it wrong. There he comes now, on the edge of the pond in the golf course, splashing his trouser cuffs. That's what I call a different sort of guy. A war hero blasting Japs out of the sky, more money than King Farouk, a face that melts the ladies' hearts, and not one friend he didn't have to buy."

"Say that again?"

Moe got up from the table and squeezed her hand. "Be nice to each other," he said. "But be nice to yourself first. Out here, people don't die. After they're used up and don't have any box office value, they get jobs as doorstops."

FOR HER BIRTHDAY, I gave Rosita a customized 1946 cherry-red Ford convertible, one with whitewall tires and a starch-white top. She loved her car and found every excuse to drive it. One Friday while I was at the office, she drove out to South Main to visit the library at Rice University. On the way home, she stopped at Bill Williams's drive-in restaurant, right across the boulevard from the university. Just before turning off South Main, she saw a Houston police cruiser in her rearview mirror. The cruiser turned with her and parked under the canvas awning, six spaces down. She thought nothing of it.

She ordered a box of fried chicken and a carton of French fries and a carton of coleslaw to go. Thanksgiving was one week away. A marching band was practicing somewhere across the boulevard, the bass drum booming behind the hedges and live oaks on the Rice campus. The sky was a flawless blue, the sunlight in the trees like gold dust sprinkled in the branches, the wind balmy, the awning flapping above her head. The jukebox was playing Glenn Miller's "In the Mood" through the loudspeaker on a silver pole that supported the canopy. She flashed her lights to get the carhop's attention and ordered a bottle of Lone Star to drink while she waited on the chicken.

After she finished the beer, she set the bottle on the metal tray the carhop had placed on her window. The policeman got out of his vehicle and went to a pay phone attached to the side of the restaurant and made a call. He seemed to be looking at her from behind his shades, the receiver small in his hand. He pulled a cigarette from a package of Pall Malls with his lips.

After she paid for her order, she started the convertible and drove back onto South Main. Within seconds she saw the police cruiser in her rearview mirror. She turned off the boulevard and went through a residential neighborhood and entered Hermann Park. The cruiser followed. The park was shaded by pines and live oaks and landscaped with dales and small hills and wildlife trails; it was curiously empty. She knew she had made a mistake leaving the boulevard. She looked again in the mirror. The cruiser was ten yards from her bumper. She pulled off the asphalt onto the grass and got out. The cruiser stopped also. The patrolman cut his engine, flipped away his cigarette, and opened his door. "Get back in your vehicle," he said.

"Why are you following me?" she said.

He was standing behind the open door of the cruiser. His sleeves were rolled, the tops of his arms covered with swirls of dark hair, his brow furrowed, like that of a man whose temper and passions were on a short leash. His eyes moved up and down her body, seeming to take note of her slacks and rayon shirt and the bandana tied in her hair, as though he were looking at an alien or an aberration. "Get in your car and stay there, with your hands on the steering wheel."

"Not until you answer my question."

He closed the door to his cruiser and walked toward her. She could see her reflection in his shades, trapped, small, insignificant. "You'll either get in your car or be arrested," he said.

"What is the matter with you? Why are you doing this?"

He stepped closer, his body blocking out the sun. "Put your hands on the fender."

"Do you have me mixed up with someone else?"

He fitted his hands on her shoulders and turned her sideways. "Lean on the car."

"No."

He slid his right hand down her spine, flattening his fingers on her shirt, pressing it against the sweat that peppered her back, moving her forward. "Now spread your legs," he said.

"*What?*"

"Do as you're told. Spread your legs."

"I will not. You will not treat me like this."

The thumb and index finger of his left hand tightened on her shoulder bone. "Are you carrying any weapons?"

"No. You're hurting me."

"Lean against the car."

The pain traveled along her shoulder into her neck, causing her left side to wilt. She felt her eyes watering. "Let go of me," she said. "You've mistaken me for someone else. I haven't broken any law."

"You made an illegal lane change. You went through a red light. You smell like you've been drinking."

She widened her feet, her hands now on top of the fender. He loosened his left hand but let his thumb rest on the back of her neck, kneading her skin. Then he ran his right hand inside her thighs. "You bastard," she said, turning around.

He grabbed her by the shoulders again and shoved her against the car, hard, jolting her teeth. "What's that on your breath? Mouthwash?"

"I had one beer at the drive-in. You saw me drinking it."

"Do you want to empty your pockets, or do you want me to do it for you?"

"You have no right to do this."

"Last chance."

She pulled her pockets inside out, her face hot with anger and shame.

"That's a good start," he said. "Now give me your driver's license and registration."

Her hands were shaking when she took her wallet from her purse and removed her driver's license and handed it to him.

"Thank you," he said. "Now give me your registration."

She leaned over the seat to open the glove box.

"Hold on there," he said, leaning on top of her, his hand reaching past her, his loins touching her buttocks. "I don't want you pulling a surprise on me." He popped open the glove box and raked the contents on the floor. "Pick it up."

"Pick what up?"

"Are you deaf? You don't speak English?" he said, his breath on her neck.

"You're not going to get away with this."

He backed out of the seat and came around to the other side of the convertible. He opened the door and grabbed her by one wrist and dragged her onto the grass, twisting her arm. "You think you can threaten a police officer?"

"I did no such thing."

"Oh yes you did, lady. You were asking for this when you turned in to the park."

"Liar."

"Just keep talking," he said, rolling her onto her stomach, pressing his knee into her back. He cuffed her wrists, pushing the steel tongues deep into the locking mechanism, bunching her skin. He pulled her to her feet, his fingers sinking deep into her upper arm.

She fought with him and tried to kick his shins. He wrapped his arms around her and lifted her into the air, his mouth against her cheek, close to her ear, his phallus hard against her rump. "You're quite a handful," he said. "Maybe after this, you'll learn not to drink and drive."

Chapter 19

My anger didn't serve me well at the police station. Rosita had been placed in the drunk tank. The charges included driving under the influence, resisting arrest, and threatening a police officer. Her bail had not been set. I couldn't get her out of the tank, and I had been allowed to talk to her through the bars for only five minutes.

"She has to stay in there until tomorrow morning?" I said incredulously to a desk sergeant.

"She has to be arraigned. That's how it works. She's from overseas?"

"Why do you ask?"

"Maybe they do things different there."

"What are you saying?"

"If you don't agree with the system, change it," he said, resuming his paperwork.

When you live in a democracy, there are certain things you believe will never happen to you. Then a day comes when the blindfold is removed and you discover the harsh nature of life at the bottom of the food chain. I could hear myself breathing; my skin felt dead to the touch; I had never felt as inadequate in dealing with a situation. "What's the arresting officer's name?"

The sergeant looked up again. "Slakely," he said.

"Is he in the building?"

"Possibly."

"I want to talk to him."

His eyes drifted down the hallway to a coffee room that had a Coca-Cola machine and a table where several cops were sitting. "He's a hard-nose, but the people he brings in usually deserve it," the sergeant said. "Do yourself a favor. Get a lawyer. Don't pick a fight with the wrong guy."

"Thank you," I said.

He didn't answer, nor did he look up from his paperwork again. I walked to the doorway of the coffee room. I didn't have to guess who had put my wife in jail. He was eating a sandwich, his long legs splayed, his fingers covered with grease and crumbs. He was the only man in the room whose eyes immediately met mine.

"Are you Officer Slakely?" I said.

He stopped chewing and set down the sandwich. "What can I do for you?"

"Why did you make up those lies about my wife?"

"Who says they're lies?"

"I do."

"This is a restricted area."

"The city attorney's office is right down the hall. I come here all the time." I dropped a nickel in the Coca-Cola machine. I pulled a Coke out of the slot and stuck the neck in the bottle opener and pried off the cap and set it in front of him. "Do you other fellows want one?" I asked.

They looked at me, blank-faced.

"Your wife is in jail for a reason. You're not making things easier for her," Slakely said.

"I pulled her out of a pile of corpses in a Nazi death camp. She spat in the face of an SS colonel. The only reason she didn't do it to you is she didn't want to bring down trouble on me."

"Who do you think you're talking to?"

"A cop who's for sale."

"You'd better haul your ass out of here."

I nodded. A jar of tomato sauce sat on the table in front of him, a steak knife inserted in it. I looked at his throat, the malevolence in his eyes, and the ignorance and hostility and fear that lived like a disease in his face. "You violated her person, didn't you?"

"She told you that?"

"She didn't have to. It's written all over you. I'm going to expose you for what you are, bub. I've never met a cockroach that did well in sunlight."

I heard his chair scrape back as I walked out of the room. But he didn't follow me into the hallway, and I knew I probably would not see him again. Like all of his kind, he would disappear and be only a footnote in a script written by someone determined to ruin our lives. I wished Grandfather were with me. I wished he could tell me what to do. I wanted the moral clarity and violent alternatives available to him when he took on John Wesley Hardin in 1881. The advent of modernity had empowered the bureaucrat and the coward and the bully, and I would not see my Jewish girl from the Book of Kings until morning, when she would be led into court handcuffed to a chain, her hair in disarray, her clothes grimed from sleeping on a floor stained with spittle and cigarette butts and the overflow from a broken toilet.

HER BAIL WAS three thousand dollars. Her car had been towed to an impoundment, the bumper bent out of shape, the fender scratched by the wrecker's steel hook. When we came home, she immediately went into the shower, and I put her soiled clothes in the washing machine. I opened all the windows in the house, inviting in the sunshine and the wind and the smell of burning leaves as a way of counteracting the pall that seemed to be settling on our lives.

Our attorney, an old family friend named Tom Breemer, found out that during the Depression, Slakely had worked private security for a fruit company in California and had been involved in the shooting death of a labor organizer.

"How'd he get out of it?" I asked.

"The records disappeared. He was a chaser in a navy brig during the war. He's been divorced twice. Colored people get off the street when they see him coming. He worked vice in Galveston. That's the long and short of it."

"Somebody is paying him to hurt us," I said.

"Maybe, maybe not. This is going to be a tough one, Weldon. There's a witness. A woman riding a bicycle said she saw Mrs. Holland try to kick Slakely."

"That was after he brutalized her."

"I'll try to get the charges reduced," he replied. "That's about as good as it's going to get."

After I hung up, Rosita came out of the shower, a towel wrapped around her.

"How do you feel?" I said, trying to smile.

"I'm fine."

I sat with her on the side of the bed. Through the window, we could see the tops of trees swaying above our neighbors' roofs and a plane towing a Burma-Shave ad across the sky. "We may have to pay the fine and be done with it," I said.

"Do you know where he touched me? Do you want to know what he did to me with his penis?"

"We'll get him, Rosita. We'll get the person who hired him, too. We just need to get the court situation out of the way."

She pulled her hand away from me. "By giving in to it? That's how we get it out of the way?"

"I'm trying to be realistic. Rhetoric doesn't help. Those charges could get you up to a year in jail."

"You don't realize how your words hurt me."

The doorbell rang downstairs. Our bell was an old one, installed in the 1920s, the kind you twisted. I don't know why I thought of that; maybe I associated it with an earlier time, when I delivered newspapers in a small Texas town and I had no consciousness of the evil that men can do to one another.

The bell rang again. I went downstairs and opened the door. No one was there. I saw a kid on a service cycle drive away, his lacquered-bill cap low on his eyes, his cavalry-like breeches puffed around the thighs. A flat cardboard mailer addressed to Rosita lay on the doormat. I carried it upstairs, tapping it against my leg.

"What's that?" she asked.

"It's for you. The return address says 'Blue Bird Record Company.'"

Her face showed no recognition. She removed the towel wrapped around her body and dressed with her back to me.

"You want me to open it?" I asked.

"No, I'll do it."

"I confronted Slakely yesterday. If I had my way, I'd shoot him."

"He's a functionary."

I had run out of words. "I'll fix us something to eat," I said.

I went downstairs and began making sandwiches and a salad. I kept hoping she would join me of her own accord, slicing tomatoes and bread crust and cucumbers, smiling and talking at the same time, ignoring my cautionary words, as was her way.

Twenty minutes passed. I took an ice tray from the freezer and cracked it apart in the sink. I filled two glasses with sun tea and inserted sprigs of mint in the ice and lemon slices on the edge of the glass. I could hear no sound from upstairs. "Lunch is ready!" I called.

There was no response.

I dried my hands on a dish towel and gazed out the window at the sun spangling inside the trees. I saw my neighbor's vintage automobile parked on an unpaved driveway, just the other side of our unfenced yard. For a second, the year was 1934 again and I was looking at the stolen vehicle driven by Clyde Barrow and Bonnie Parker. I'm hard put to explain why I would associate that particular moment with the arrival in our lives of the Barrow gang. I think it was because I had never understood them, or perhaps I had never understood what they represented. Some considered them nothing more than pathological killers. Grandfather believed they were lionized by J. Edgar Hoover for political reasons. Others saw them as products of their times. I guess I believed they were all three.

But why would I dwell upon them now? The answer was simple. Something far more wicked than a group of semiliterate, small-town bank robbers was wrapping its tentacles around Rosita and me and also Linda Gail and Hershel Pine. Worse, the people trying to hurt us were using the law to do it.

Rosita was sitting on the bed, wearing only her skirt and bra. The cardboard mailer was on the floor. She had opened it with a pair of scissors that lay beside her. A ten-by-twelve-inch black-and-white glossy photograph rested on her knees. Her eyes were wet when she turned and looked at me. She picked up the photo with her left hand and held it in the air, waiting for me to take it.

"What is it?" I said.

"It's self-explanatory."

Even as my fingers touched the edge of the photograph, I knew what it showed. Or at least I thought I did. I saw Linda Gail propped on top of her lover, her breasts bare, her face gone weak with orgasm. It was the same photo Harlan McFey had shown me, except the bottom half of his copy had been torn off. "This is a trick photograph," I said.

"That's not you putting the blocks to her? That's the term for it, isn't it?"

"That's my face. I suspect someone photographed me at a distance and superimposed one negative on another."

"I can see the scar on your chest. That's the shrapnel wound you received at Saint-Lô."

"Somebody photographed me at a beach or at a swimming pool. Don't buy into this, Rosita."

"I've been too kind," she said.

"I don't understand."

"Linda Gail is not the eater of the apple. She's the serpent in the Garden, but she's too stupid to know it. Her selfishness and vanity and ambition are at the center of all this. She's manipulative and treacherous. I hate her."

"This isn't like you, Rosita."

"Stop it. If they sent this picture to me, who else do you think they've sent it to?"

I stared at her. In my mind's eye, I saw Hershel opening a mailer similar to the one on the floor and pulling a ten-by-twelve glossy from it. I went downstairs and called our office in Baton Rouge. The phone rang a long time before the secretary picked up, out of breath.

She was an elderly lady who had graduated from Millsaps College in Mississippi. "I'm sorry. I just went outside to get a delivery," she said.

"Where's Hershel?" I said.

"He left late yesterday for Houston. He was planning to go back today, but he said he had everything tied up here, so he was leaving a day early."

"Was he all right, Miss LeBlanc?"

"He seemed quite happy. Is something wrong?"

"Not at all. You said you just had a delivery?"

"Yes, a beautiful bouquet of flowers. They're from Mrs. Pine. The card is tied on the vase. I couldn't quite help seeing what's on it. I hope Mr. Pine won't be mad at me."

"What does it say?"

"You're sure it will be all right for me to do that?"

"Yes, it's fine, Miss LeBlanc."

"It says, 'I just signed a contract made in heaven. Love, your Louisiana sweetheart.' Isn't that wonderful?"

"I'm sure it is," I said. "Have there been any other deliveries or important mail I should know about?"

"None that I can think of."

"I ordered a phonograph record from the Blue Bird Company. Did you receive a package that might have a record inside it?"

"No, nothing like that. I'm so happy for Mr. and Mrs. Pine. They're such a fine young couple."

I eased the receiver back into the cradle, hardly aware of what I was doing.

I dialed the office downtown. Hershel had not checked in. I asked the secretary about special deliveries we might have received, or packages that might contain a phonograph record. There had been none. I called Hershel's house in River Oaks.

"Hello?" he said.

"How you doin'?" I said.

"Everything is great, except I overslept."

"That's good. You need some extra sleep."

"I just got off the phone with Linda Gail. Wait till you hear this. She got a five-year contract with Warner Brothers. She's going to star in a movie about the French Underground. My little Linda Gail is an actual movie star."

"That's something, isn't it?" I said.

"All those worries I had, they didn't mean anything, did they?"

"I guess not."

"She's flying in tonight. Let's go out on the town."

"We've had some trouble, Hershel," I said. I told him what had happened to Rosita.

"Who's this cop?" he asked.

"He's not important. It's the people who hired him we have to nail."

"In the meantime, this guy needs to be taken off at the neck."

"That's what they want."

"You think this bastard is working for Dalton Wiseheart?"

"That'd be my bet."

"I feel awful about this, Weldon. I wish I'd been there."

"Let me call you later."

"Tell Rosita we're all on her side. Linda Gail will tell her the same thing."

"I'll tell her, Hershel. You and Linda Gail take care."

"It's y'all I'm worried about, not us," he replied. "Don't do anything without including us in. We got us an agreement on that? We'll always be Rosita's friends. We'll back your play, whatever it is, Loot."

I went back upstairs. Rosita had finished dressing but had not put on any makeup. "You don't look well," she said.

I sat in a chair by the window and told her of my conversation with Hershel.

"He has no idea what's going on, does he?"

"None at all."

"Why didn't the people who sent us the photo also send one to Hershel?"

"You already know why," I said.

"They didn't want to use all the knives in the set. They want you to live with the knowledge that at any given moment they can destroy Hershel's marriage. They also want to make you party to the deception of your best friend."

"That's exactly what they're doing."

"Maybe you should tell Hershel and show him the photo."

"The photo of Linda Gail looks like it was taken in a motel. In all probability, it was taken the night she got drunk and allowed herself to be seduced by Jack Valentine. Should I tell Hershel that?"

"I think we have to let go of Linda Gail. Her choices are always about herself. She won't change. She seems incapable of understanding how much injury she's done."

I couldn't argue with that logic. "I'm going to destroy this photograph," I said.

"They have others."

"Good," I said. "One day I'll catch up with the people who took them. When I do, I won't feel any qualms. They'll get the reward they've earned."

"I don't want you to talk about killing again."

"What do you think I did in the war?"

"The war is over."

"It's never over. You enlist and you fight it for the rest of your life. I'm going to make these people pay for what they've done. There's a difference between justice and vengeance."

She walked toward me and placed her hand on my forehead, as though checking to see if I had a fever. "Don't you ever start thinking like that," she said. "Don't compromise yourself because of scum like these people. Do you hear me, Weldon?"

That was Rosita Lowenstein in full-frontal attack mode. It was a state of mind I had learned not to challenge. I put my arms around her, crossing them behind her back. I could smell the fragrance in her hair and the heat in her skin. I looked her in the eye. "Straight shooters always win," I said.

She buried her face in my neck, her fingers kneading my arms, her bare feet standing on the tops of my shoes. I swore I would get every one of them, one at a time or all at once; it didn't matter.

I KNEW I COULD not get close to Dalton Wiseheart on my own. But maybe there was another way into his inner circle, I told myself. He might have an enemy who would be only too glad to help undermine the outer wall of the fortress. Wiseheart had made a remark about his daughter-in-law, Clara. What was it? She was a different kettle of fish? I wondered in what way.

While Rosita took a nap, I drove to the far end of River Oaks, where Roy and Clara Wiseheart lived amid a level of Greco-Roman glory that Nero would have envied. Her name had been Harrington before she married. Her family had made its money in rice and cotton in the early part of the century, then doubled its wealth during the Great War by growing beans for the government and investing the profits in the demand for explosives. Unlike many of their peers, the Harringtons were reclusive and generated no mystique about their personal lives. They were rich and gold-plated against the minuscule concerns of ordinary people, and that was all that mattered. What else did anyone need to know?

I pulled into the driveway and walked across the lawn toward the porch and the massive three-story columns at the front of the house. I had no idea if anyone was home. Nor did I have a plan. During the drive from my house to the Wisehearts', I had decided to approach whoever was home in the most honest fashion I could. If I was rebuffed, at least I wouldn't have to resent myself.

I saw her in the side yard, weeding the garden on her knees. She was wearing cloth gloves and denim pants and a straw hat and a gray work jacket with big pockets for garden tools. "How are you, Miss Clara?" I said, lifting my hat.

"Roy is in Los Angeles, Mr. Holland," she said.

The sunlight was not kind to Clara Wiseheart. The foundation on her skin was cracked, the wrinkles at the corners of her eyes showing through like cat's whiskers. I realized she was at least a decade older than her husband.

"May I talk to you?" I asked.

She inserted her weeding trowel in the dirt. "About what?"

"My wife was arrested on false charges. She was molested by the arresting officer."

One of her eyes was smaller than the other, an intense blue, triangular in shape. "Why would you want to tell me about something like this?"

"Because I think Dalton Wiseheart is trying to injure us. Because I want to make him accountable for the evil deeds I think he's done."

She got to her feet and brushed off her knees. "Follow me."

I walked behind her into the backyard. The swimming pool had been drained, and pine needles and oak leaves were stuck to the bottom and the sides like crustaceans. The air was cold in the shade and smelled of gas and herbicide and a moldy tarp carelessly piled against the pool house. The yard seemed marked by neglect and the onslaught of winter or, better said, the ephemeral nature of life and our inability to deal with it.

An old hand-crank record player had been set on a low brick wall that bordered an elevated flowerbed. It had a fluted horn on it and a record mounted on the turntable.

"Sit down," she said.

The chair was hard and cold to the touch, the glass tabletop the same. She sat across from me, her triangular-shaped eye watery. She took a drink from a coffee cup that smelled of liqueur, her gaze never leaving my face. "Why would I be your confidante regarding the character deficiencies of Dalton Wiseheart?"

"I'm not asking that of you. I'm telling you of the harm I believe he's done to an innocent woman. I want to talk to him. I want him to look me in the face and tell me he's not responsible for hiring an evil man to commit sexual battery on my wife and put her in jail."

"Dalton plays the role of an avuncular wheat farmer for journalists stupid enough to write about him. He has squandered millions buying professional baseball and football teams. He also spends huge sums trying to control an electorate that, in my opinion, shouldn't be allowed to vote. Dalton is a bumbling idiot and should be treated as such."

"Do you think he's capable of paying a Houston police officer to hurt my wife?"

"I feel sorry for you," she replied.

"Oh?"

"Is he 'capable' of hurting your wife? He's capable of anything. He used to make his son beat him."

"I don't know if I heard you correctly."

"When Roy didn't fulfill his father's expectations, Dalton would lie across the bed and make Roy whip him with a razor strop to demonstrate how much pain his son was causing him. You ask what he's capable of? The answer is anything."

"I see," I replied, not knowing what to say.

"I doubt that. You've entered a world you have no knowledge of. You remind me of the man who was king because he had one eye in the kingdom of the blind. Isn't that the kind of place where you grew up? A kingdom of blind people where the gentry have the astuteness of Cyclopes? It must be harrowing to find yourself in an environment where you're never sure whether you should go to the front or the back door."

"I've never had anyone say something like that to me," I said, getting up to go. "This has been quite an experience."

"Don't put on self-righteous airs with me, Mr. Holland. You brought Mrs. Pine into our lives. I know my husband's propensities. He has the appetites of an adolescent. When they wane, he comes back home, repentant and talking about tennis and his coin collection, just like a little boy. Next time he'll be at it with the maid. She would be the logical step down from your business partner's wife."

I looked again at the hand-crank record player. Normally, I would have thought it was completely out of place. In this instance I did not. I had come to think of Roy and Clara Wiseheart as people who lived inside an inner sanctum where the difference between death and life was hardly noticeable; it was a place where the bizarre and the pathological were norms.

"I'll find my way to my car," I said. "No need to see me out. I'm sorry I intruded upon your privacy."

"You wanted to be a gamesman," she said. "Now you are. Enjoy it. An actor I knew before I met my husband once called it a 'divine and sweet, sweet sewer.' That was right before he killed himself. Maybe you won't drown in it, Mr. Holland. Your friends probably will."

As I walked away, I heard her start up the phonograph. I turned around, the air even colder now, the leaves of a transplanted swamp maple lit like fire against the sun. "Is that Bunny Berigan?" I asked.

"It's 'I Can't Get Started with You.' Roy gave it to me on our second date. I guess I still have my sentimental moments."

Are we our brother's keeper? Her face was a Grecian mask of callousness and cynicism so blatant, you wondered if it was pretense. Did she fear the Great Shade? Did she know the last names of her servants? Did she ever experience joy? As I looked around, I wondered if I was standing inside a necropolis. That night I wrote these words in my journal: *Dear Lord, Thank you for my dear wife. Thank you for the wonderful life you've given us. God bless all those who work and play in the fields of the Lord. This is Weldon Avery Holland signing off again. Amen.*

Chapter 20

LINDA GAIL'S FLIGHT back to Houston had been canceled because of bad weather, so she took a cab to Union Station and bought a stateroom ticket on the Sunset Limited, an expenditure she previously would have thought unimaginable. It was late afternoon when the train pulled out of Los Angeles, and in no time she found herself gazing through the lounge window at orange groves and palm trees and painted deserts and a red sunset that seemed created especially for her.

She ordered a glass of sherry and took her fountain pen and monogrammed stationery from her bag and began writing Hershel a letter she would ask the conductor to mail at one of the stops. When she thought about Hershel, she had to reconstruct her mental fortifications one brick at a time so an inconvenient truth or two didn't steal its way into her peace of mind. It was a difficult task. He would never be able to understand the complexity of her situation, she told herself. Why burden him unnecessarily? She had made a conscious choice to enter into an affair with Roy Wiseheart, that was true. Yes, it was morally wrong and indefensible and even treacherous, but it had happened. That was it, it had happened. Things *happened*. Passive voice. And there was nothing to do about it. So enough about that.

She had stayed true to Hershel when he was overseas, hadn't she?

There had been temptations, many of them, potential boyfriends lurking around the edges of a dance floor or looking at her from a back pew in the church. What about Hershel? No French or Italian girl ever tempted him? Had anyone thought of that?

People were weak, she told herself. Her infidelity didn't mean she was indifferent toward him. He doted on her and would give her anything she wanted. She wasn't unappreciative. It wasn't his fault that he didn't understand the creative world and the people who dedicated themselves to the arts and humanities and the making of great films. There was a simple way of putting it all in context: She had grown up in a place where she didn't belong, and she had finally found her milieu. It was no one's fault. That was life.

Dear Hershel, she wrote in a navy blue calligraphy that had been the envy of everyone in her high school English classes, *I'll probably be home before you receive this. But no matter. I just wanted to organize my thoughts and put them down on paper for you to look at. I've been thinking about building a home in Santa Monica, not far from the ocean. I think my commitments are going to keep me there much of the time. Would you object if I talked to an architect? A small house on one of the bluffs would be a grand place for you to relax, and it wouldn't cost much. It's not Malibu.*

The train pulled into a biscuit-colored stucco station covered with a Spanish-tile roof and surrounded by an oasis of date palms that reminded her of an illustration from the *Arabian Nights*. She could see the ice and mail wagons on the loading platform, and the marbled pink and purple stain of the sun's afterglow on the hills and desert floor, and car lights tunneling through the dusk out on Highway 66. She looked down at the flowery design on the borders of her stationery, and the blue swirls in the letters that comprised the words she had written to her husband, her heart becoming sicker and sicker at the betrayal she was making a systemic part of her life.

She had to stop this self-flagellation, she told herself. Adults needed to behave as adults and deal with the world as it was. Guilt solved nothing. She began another paragraph.

I think from a financial perspective, the investment would be a good one. One home in River Oaks and another by the beach in Santa Monica! Who would have ever believed that? It's funny how things work out. Remember when we met at the dance? Boy howdy, life can be a jack-in-the-box, can't it?

She felt her face shrink at her hypocrisy. She tore the stationery into strips and put them in her bag just as the train jolted forward and two men in suits and fedoras, one of them with a Graflex Speed Graphic, entered the lounge and sat down on the horseshoe-shaped couch across from her. The photographer raised his camera and popped a flashbulb in her face.

"Good heavens, who are you fellows?" she said innocently.

"We almost got you at the airport, but you were too quick for us," the other man said. "Can you give us an interview?" He held a notebook and pen in his right hand.

"Who's it for?"

"It's a wire story about the new girl at Warner Brothers," he said.

"Anything to pass the time. Can I buy you boys a drink?"

She was surprised by her ease and familiarity with the press. Well, why not? That was Hollywood. They were all part of the same culture, weren't they? Others didn't understand what it was like out *there*. The weather was beautiful. It seldom rained, although the bougainvillea and orange trees seemed to bloom year-round. The actors and producers and directors and news reporters and the army of people behind the camera were guests at a party that never ended, one that began with a mist-shrouded sunrise over the Santa Ana Mountains and at night was domed with the constellations and rimmed by waves that created a sensation like an erotic kiss when they surged around her thighs.

The two journalists sitting on the pale blue vinyl couch seemed like pleasant and considerate men, not lighting cigarettes without asking permission, the man with the Graflex dropping his used flashbulbs in his coat pocket so the porter would not have to clean up after him, both of them smiling good-naturedly. She particularly liked the older man. He said his name was Jimmy Flynn and that he had worked for several of the studios as a publicist and had been a correspondent during the war at the Battle of Monte Cassino and a friend of Ernie Pyle's. He was handsome and dignified and wore a wedding band and addressed her as Miss Pine.

"Actually, I'm married," she said.

"Out here, all actresses are eternally Miss," he said. "What profession is your husband in, Miss Pine?"

"Do we have to go into that?"

"Not if you don't want to," he said.

"He's from an old plantation family in central Louisiana. But he's in the oil business these days. He has his own company."

"How do you like being with Warner Brothers?"

"It's wonderful. Everyone has been very nice, Mr. Warner in particular."

"I think I remember reading about your husband," Jimmy Flynn said. He set down his pen. "He created a big breakthrough in natural gas technology, didn't he? Something to do with welding machines."

"That's correct, he did."

"His business partner is a man named Holland?"

"Yes, that's true," she said.

"They call themselves the Dixie Belle Pipeline Company."

"It's not what they call themselves. It's the name of their company."

Outside the window, she could see the headlights of the vehicles on Highway 66 veering angularly into a stretch of desert that was white and cratered and devoid of vegetation, even cactus.

"It's quite a story, if I remember it correctly," Flynn said. "They were in the war together. Mr. Holland brought back a girl who was a prisoner of the Nazis. She's related to Rosa Luxemburg. Her father was a Communist."

Linda Gail's smile had faded. "I don't know anything about that," she said.

"Her name is Rosita. To your knowledge, is the wife of your husband's business partner a Communist?"

"I don't know why you're asking me this. I don't know her."

"Not at all?"

"I have met her, but I do not associate with her. Does that answer your question?"

"You didn't know she was a Communist?"

"If I knew that, I would have reported her to someone."

"Really?" Flynn said. "You're a tough lady. She's tough, isn't she, Quinn?"

"Real tough," the photographer said, blowing his cigarette smoke out the side of his mouth. "One more before we go, sweetheart. You don't mind, do you?"

He didn't wait for her answer or let her recover her composure. He popped the flashbulb three feet from her face. Even after they were gone, her eyes were filled with receding rings of red light, as though she had stared too long at the sun.

I WENT BACK TO work on the pipeline down in the Louisiana wetlands close to Grand Isle, and took Rosita with me. We stood on an oil platform at the southern tip of the state and gazed at the slate-green surface of the Gulf, the wind cold and smelling of salt and leakage from a well. Winter was on its way; the sky was black with thunderclouds and empty of pelicans and gulls. In the distance, I could see gas flares burning on three wells and lightning striking the water on the southern horizon, like gold wires without sound. Behind me was the largest and grandest watershed in North America. I wondered how long it would remain as such. Not far away was one of the channels our company had cut from the Gulf into freshwater swamp and marshland. The deleterious consequences had not been instantaneous, but their growing presence couldn't be denied.

The tide was coming in, flowing like a river through the pilings under our feet. The grasses along the edges of the channel had turned yellow and, in some areas, brown and could be torn loose from their root systems in the sediment like handfuls of human hair. That's an unpleasant simile to use, but to me it seems appropriate. The tupelo cypress and willow and gum trees and cattails and bamboo were being killed slowly through their root systems, the leaves in old-growth trees dying first. Ironically, the saline was reconfiguring the very channels that carried the salt water into the swamp. One of the first channels we had cut was no longer a straight line. Its banks had eroded and collapsed in places, and it had taken on the shape of a huge sulfurous-colored slug that a giant had stepped on.

The damage wasn't confined to saltwater intrusion. Our bulldozing and dredging operations had dammed up streams and caused stagnation in ponds that were now coated with mosquitoes and a thick bacterial film as thick as paint dried on top of a bucket; you could pick it up like a tattered, soggy garment on the end of a stick.

It wasn't good to brood upon the excesses of the Industrial Age, I told myself. Give unto Caesar. That was the latitude given to us by Our Lord. The earth abideth forever, said the writer in Ecclesiastes. Who was I to argue with Scripture? Unfortunately, my debates with myself on these matters were becoming more and more frequent.

"There's Hershel," Rosita said.

He was walking down the right-of-way toward the platform, wearing a slouch hat and khakis and a navy blue corduroy shirt and his old field jacket. I had no idea why he had come down to Grand Isle. My puzzlement wasn't lost on him.

"I had to get out of Houston. I guess I'm just not good at big cities," he said. "Let's go up to the café and have some étouffée."

But Hershel was a poor actor. During lunch, he seemed to catch about half of what either Rosita or I said. "You'll have to excuse me," he said. "My father isn't doing well. I thought I might go up to the farm and spend a couple of days with him."

"That'd be fine, Hershel," I said. "Everything is on track at both offices."

"He wants to go squirrel and bird hunting," he said.

"Pardon?" I asked.

"My father. He wants to get out his twenty-gauge and make a squirrel-and-robin stew and shell pecans and make a pie. It's funny how old people retreat into the past, like it can bring back their youth. I think this might be his last Christmas."

I nodded as though in sympathy, but in reality I believed Hershel was talking about himself, not his father. Then I asked a question I should have left unsaid. "How is Linda Gail?"

He looked at me like a man trapped under an airless glass bell. "Did she call?"

"No," I replied. "I thought she was about to start work on a new film. It's about the French Underground, isn't it?"

"She hasn't told me a lot," he said. "I know what I read in the papers."

Rosita set down her knife and fork. "It's nice to have you here, Hershel," she said.

Her words could have been snowflakes sliding down window glass.

THAT EVENING HERSHEL rented a room at the same motor court we were using, way up the two-lane, surrounded by cypress and oak trees hung with Spanish moss. The clouds were lit from behind by the moon, the bamboo that grew along the flooded roadside clattering as loudly as broomsticks. I never knew a more haunted land or one that was more beautiful. I tapped on Hershel's door.

"It's open," he said from inside.

When I opened the door, he was removing his clothes from his suitcase and laying them out on his bed, his back to me. He didn't bother to turn around. On top of his neatly folded shirts was a 1911-model army-issue .45 automatic.

"When did you start carrying a gun?" I asked.

"Recently," he replied.

"What for?"

"You never know."

"Never know what?"

"When you might need one."

"Did you come here to talk about something, Hershel?"

"She wants to build a house in Santa Monica. I told her we don't have that kind of money. She said our house in River Oaks looks like a filling station. She doesn't like our snooty neighbors, either. She says they're too stupid to know what it means to have a contract at Warner Brothers."

"Maybe she's got a point. I mean about your neighbors. It might not be a bad idea to own a home in Southern California. A lot of people say that's the place to be."

"You think so?"

"It's a cinch that any land you buy there will go up in value."

"Except I think she wants to build the house for herself. I don't think she wants me out there. I embarrass her."

I couldn't meet his eyes. "How could anybody be embarrassed by you? You were at Kasserine and Salerno and Omaha and Saint-Lô and the Bulge. Don't talk about yourself like that, Hersh."

"She just got back from Los Angeles. I made dinner reservations for us at the San Jacinto Inn. I filled up our bedroom with flowers. She told me she had a stomachache. Then told me it was her time of the month."

"I'm sorry to hear that."

"There's something else I got to tell you. A guy from a wire service called me. He asked if Linda Gail and I were friends with a Communist by the name of Rosita Holland."

"What did you tell him?"

"I said if he was calling Rosita a Communist, he was a damn liar. I'm correct on that, right? Rosita was never a Communist?"

"Would you feel differently toward her?"

"I don't know."

"That's not a good answer."

"Maybe her family was. That doesn't mean she is," he said.

"What if I said she was?"

"Then she wouldn't be Rosita. Why are you talking to me like this, Weldon?"

"Because she's my wife. Because people are trying to hurt her, and my friends are either behind her or they aren't, no matter what her politics were."

He sat down on the side of the bed. He was in his socks and undershirt, and there was a V-shaped area of tan below his neck. The top of his forehead was pale above his hat line, and the effect made him look older than he was. There was a strange cast to his face, like that of a man who had seen into the future and realized the Fates had perpetrated a terrible fraud. He picked up the .45 from his stack of shirts and opened the drawer on the nightstand and placed the

.45 on top of the Gideons Bible inside the drawer. "I had a peculiar experience today," he said.

"How's that?"

"I was looking at one of our welding machines. I saw a swastika inside the frame. It was like the Krauts were telling us they were still with us, they weren't going to forget."

"Forget what?"

"That we made our money off their invention. That we owe them. That maybe we weren't supposed to come home."

"I'll see you tomorrow," I said.

"Linda Gail is in the sack with another man," he said.

"Sometimes we have to let things run their course. That's a tough lesson, but it's the way it is."

I could see his face darken, his restraint beginning to slip. "What would you do if it was your wife?" he asked.

"Leave my wife out of it."

"I thought you might say that," he replied, his jawbone flexing.

"I'm worried about you, partner."

"Don't." He closed the drawer hard, with the heel of his hand.

"You shouldn't take your anger out on the wrong people," I said.

"Is Rosita a Communist?"

"I won't answer that question."

"I know she's not. But what if you knew she was a turncoat? How would you feel, Loot? How would you like to be deceived by the woman you love?"

I didn't have an answer for him.

"See what I mean?" he said. "I was a virgin when I married Linda Gail. I've never wanted another woman. You ask why I'm carrying my forty-five? I think I might shoot myself for being so damn dumb."

"I don't think that's what's on your mind."

"It's my upbringing. If a badger digs under your back fence, you deal with it."

I didn't want to hear any more. Hershel had said he planned to visit his father on their farm. I had never met his family, but I knew their frame of reference well. Whether Hershel knew it or not, he was rejoining his family and the culture they represented without ever stepping out of the motor court. I clicked off the light switch for him on my way out.

ROSITA AND I returned to Houston two days later. Historically, in the long and weary traditions of warfare, snipers were treated as ignominious individuals who seldom became prisoners of war. The degree of enmity directed at them was for a reason. A successful sniper destroyed morale, robbed exhausted soldiers of the few hours of sleep they were allowed, and inculcated feelings of nakedness and vulnerability in a foot solider that can only be compared to having your skin stripped off with a pair of pliers.

A single sniper could influence the behavior of hundreds or even thousands of troops, whether he was close by or not. We didn't salute in combat zones or silhouette on a hill or wear good-luck pieces or watches or rings that reflected light. We believed in the three-on-a-match warning passed down from the Great War. (The first and second man who lit his cigarette off the same match would probably be all right; by the time the third man lit up, the crosshairs of a scoped rifle would be on his face.) An effective sniper did not simply command territory; he lived in your mind like a parasite, sapping your energies, eating away at your nerve endings.

The people trying to hurt us operated in the same fashion. We did not know who or where they were, but they could reach out and touch us any time they wished. We were blindfolded, groping about in the darkness, waiting for them to strike, while they stood faceless in the sunlight and enjoyed our plight.

We had been home three hours when I saw a police cruiser pull into our driveway, a uniformed officer behind the wheel and a middle-aged woman in the passenger seat. The woman got out and walked across the grass to the front porch, her plain black bag hanging from her shoulder, her dark suit too tight for her body.

As adherents of a Judeo-Christian ethos that teaches us not to judge, we have a tendency to shut down our instincts and avoid first impressions that are cautionary in nature. But as I review my own experience, I have to conclude that my choice not to pet a junkyard dog was probably a good one, and I should not have been surprised at the irritability of a black-garbed, wimple-encased two-hundred-pound Catholic nun on a one-hundred-degree sidewalk when I asked for directions to the San Jacinto Battleground. Of course, those are facetious examples. There was nothing humorous about the encounter I was about to have.

The woman who knocked on my door wore no expression, unless you counted the flat stare in her eyes and the bitterness around her mouth. She seemed to radiate the kind of repressed animus that has no origins, the kind that is probably pathological and characterizes functionaries who serve perverse abstractions created for them by others. When we meet people of this kind, we assume their source of discontent has nothing to do with us, and hence we're often incautious in dealing with them. I was not the exception. She said her name was Lemunyon and that she was a probation officer assigned by the court to make a recommendation regarding the charges against Rosita.

"Recommendation about what?" I said through the screen.

"I've called three times to make an appointment. No one answered," she said. "So I came out. May I come in?"

I pushed open the door. "Sit down," I said.

"Is Mrs. Holland here?"

"She went to the store."

"I also sent a letter and asked that you call me."

"We were out of town. We haven't had time to open the mail."

"Out of town?" she said, sitting down in a stuffed chair but touching it first, as though it might have dust on it.

"Yes, my company has several pipeline contracts in Louisiana. I'm over there two weeks out of four."

She looked at a spot midway between her chair and me. "You're telling me you and your wife were in the state of Louisiana?"

"That's what I said. Excuse me, but I don't understand what you're doing here."

"Obviously," she said, looking around the room, as though its old furniture and bookcases and dark drapes and big globe mounted on a stand were an extension of an attitude she couldn't piece together.

"I'm doing a background report on your wife. She can be tried for misdemeanor battery or for felonious assault. Do you know the difference between the two?"

"Yes, I believe I do."

"You believe?"

This time I didn't speak.

"Do you know the penalty for felony assault on a police officer?" she said.

"My wife did not assault anybody," I said.

"She just goes out of state while she's on bail?"

"I didn't know there was a proscription on the bail. The prosecutor knows our attorney. We were a phone call away."

"She left the state. What is it you don't understand about that?"

I wasn't sure what "that" was. But I knew I had made a terrible mistake. The anger I saw in her eyes had nothing to do with the issue at hand. Rosita and I were a personal affront to Miss Lemunyon and the system that validated and empowered her. I thought of the nurse who came to our house with a psychiatrist in 1934 and took away my mother. I also thought of the death camp where I had found Rosita. Deviants and monsters ran the camps where families were sent up the chimney or turned into bars of soap, but they would have been powerless without the clerks who sat anonymously behind typewriters and gave them bureaucratic legitimacy.

"The fault is mine, Miss Lemunyon," I said.

"What do you think 'bail' means?"

"I don't understand the question."

"Do you think it means permission to do whatever you want?"

Any answer I gave her would be the wrong one. I knew that. I also knew it was too late to turn the situation around. "Would you like to talk to our attorney? Maybe he can assure the prosecutor's office that Mrs. Holland had no desire to be a fugitive."

"She's an alien?"

"A resident alien, that's correct."

"Her file has been flagged."

"Flagged?"

"She's come to the attention of the FBI. Where did you go in Louisiana?"

"Down by the coast."

"You were there for business purposes, and you took her with you?"

"Yes, that says it."

"I want to see the letter I sent you."

"I'm sorry, you've lost me."

"You said you had not opened it. I want to see it. It should be in your mail."

"You're right," I said.

I found her letter among a stack of unopened envelopes on the dining room table. I showed it to her. She placed a business card on the coffee table. "I want her in my office by eight-thirty tomorrow morning."

"We'll be there."

She got up from the chair. She brushed at her skirt and straightened her jacket. "Don't get the wrong idea," she said.

"Pardon?"

"There's a chance Mrs. Holland might not leave the building. I haven't made up my mind yet," she replied.

LINDA GAIL MET Roy in the lounge at the Shamrock. After they had a drink, he went up to the penthouse; she followed him twenty minutes later. From the balcony, she could see the nocturnal glow of the swimming pool and, across South Main, the oil wells that pumped night and day, as steady and reassuring as the beat of the human heart. Roy turned down the lights and undressed her and laid her down on the bed, then sat beside her and looked into her face. "You like the hotel?" he asked.

"Of course."

He put his mouth on hers. His lips were cold from the whiskey and soda he had been drinking. He tried to put his tongue inside her mouth.

"Roy?" she said, turning away on the pillow.

"What?"

"Nothing."

"What is it?" he asked.

She shook her head and smiled. "You know me. I'm just funny sometimes."

He undressed and got under the sheet; he molded himself against the curve of her buttocks, his hands slipping around her hips. "Is there something you want to tell me?" he asked.

"No, I just have moods. It's a silly way to be."

"If you have a problem, I'd like to help."

"Eventually, we all die and then nothing makes any difference. So why talk about it?"

"We're not going to die now, though. Why not enjoy the party in the meantime?"

"You're right," she said.

She went through it with her eyes closed, her senses dead, her face slanted away from the hardness in his jaw. Minutes later, she felt him rise from her and his weight lift off the bed. She kept her eyes closed and turned toward the wall and pulled the sheet up to her shoulder. She heard the blender flare to life, the grinding noise as invasive as a dentist's drill. He sat down next to her. "I made you an orange frappé," he said.

"Put it on the nightstand, would you?"

"You weren't quite with it tonight."

"Thanks. A girl loves hearing she's a bad lay."

"I wondered if it was because of something I said or did."

She felt for his hand and squeezed it but did not look at him. "You're fine."

"Then tell me what it is."

"It's a funny feeling I have. Like things are coming apart. Like birds are all flying from a tree. The way they do at sunset."

She heard him set down the glass he was holding. His hand was ice-cold when he touched her shoulder.

"Do you want me to call the hotel physician?" he asked.

"I'm not sick. I just feel strange. We start production in Mexico in five days."

"I thought you were making a movie about the French Resistance."

"There're flashbacks in it. About the Spanish Civil War. The male lead is based on André Malraux."

"I just don't follow you, Linda Gail. I don't know what we're talking about."

"I'll be playing in scenes about the Spanish Civil War. I'm the lover of an aviator fighting for the Republic."

He turned her on her back so she was forced to look into his face. He was wearing a blue robe; his hair was combed and shone like bronze in the subdued light of the apartment. His expression was full of pity. "I've heard that everyone at Warner Brothers is delighted to have you on board."

"I told some newspapermen on the train that I didn't know Weldon Holland's wife. No, that wasn't how I put it. I told them I didn't associate with her. I said if I knew she was a Communist, I'd report her."

"She isn't a Communist, so what does it matter?"

"I lied. I think they wanted me to. Then they could treat me like I was dirt."

"Give me their names."

She sat up, the sheet gathered in front of her. "I have to get into the shower. Turn around, please."

"Is Jack Valentine involved in this? He's been telling people you got him fired."

"That's not true," she said.

"I know that. But somebody should have taught Jack Valentine a lesson a long time ago."

"I have to go into the bathroom. Look the other way."

"You're my girl, Linda Gail. Do you think you have to act shy? Why are you doing all this?"

"Hershel knows I'm cheating on him. I don't know what's going to happen, that's why. You don't know the kind of world we come from."

"The way I see it, a cuckold invites his fate."

She got up, the sheet wrapped around her, and started toward the bathroom.

"People break their vows for a reason," Roy said. "None of this is your fault. It's not mine and it's not your husband's. It just the way it is. Come back to bed."

She stood in the center of the room, the sheet trailing off her body. The rug was tan and thick and soft under her bare feet, the glassware and bottles behind the bar sparkling. The curtains on the French doors were gauzy and rose-tinted and transparent, filtering the light but preserving the view for the occupants, who were located so high in the sky that their privacy could never be violated.

"You want me to come back to bed?" she said. "That's what's on your mind? A more successful go-round?"

"I could make love to you five times a day, Linda Gail. It's an honor to be with a woman like you."

"I don't think it's an honor at all," she replied. "I think we're all cheap goods."

She walked to the French doors that opened onto the balcony, seventeen stories above the swimming pool shaped like a four-leaf clover. Clutching the sheet to her chest with one hand, she depressed the brass lever on the door with the other.

"What are you doing?" he said.

"Nothing," she replied. "I'm doing nothing at all."

She stepped out on the balcony and let the sheet fall from her body. She raised her arms straight out from her sides and stood on her tiptoes, her head tilting back, her eyes closed. She could feel the wind in her hair, her nipples hardening, the pores of her skin opening in the warm air. Across the boulevard, the oil wells were clanking up and down, the rhythm not unlike the sounds created by copulation upon a noisy mattress spring. She stepped up on a footstool beneath the retaining wall, then on a table, as gracefully as a woman ascending a winding staircase, and with one push she was up on the wall, the evening star winking conspiratorially at her.

For just a moment she thought she heard multitudes of people crying out in alarm, yelling at her, reassuring her that she was loved. She leaned forward, the night air sweet with the smell of flowers and chlorine, the promise of eternal summer sealing her eyes, quieting her heart, anointing her brow.

That's when she felt Roy grab her with both hands and pull her off the wall and carry her as he would a child back into the apartment.

"How do you like your girlie now, Roy?" she said. "Do you still like your little cutie-pie from Bogalusa, Louisiana? Tell me, Roy. Tell me."

Chapter 21

OUR ATTORNEY AND Rosita and I met with the probation officer Miss Lemunyon in her office at city hall at eighty-thirty A.M. the day after she told us Rosita might be rearrested for bail violation. Then she said she had to confer with her supervisor and left us in her windowless office for almost a half hour. Our attorney, Tom Breemer, told us that, in reality, Rosita had not violated the terms of her bail by temporarily leaving the state. The charges against her were misdemeanors that could be kicked up to felonious status, depending on what the prosecutor wanted to do, but nonetheless misdemeanors. Technically, we were in the clear. Then Tom added, "Unfortunately, these guys can elevate the 'resisting' charge to a felony, and you can spend weeks or months in jail proving you're right."

"What are we supposed to do?" I said.

"You want my honest opinion?" Tom said. He wore a clip-on bow tie and a seersucker suit and looked like a high school civics teacher.

"Go ahead."

"The arresting officer deserves a bullet in the mouth. Maybe that would have happened to him in your grandfather's time. It's not going to happen now. You provoked Dalton Wiseheart. This is the consequence. We plea out and hope that Wiseheart contracts bubonic plague. No, don't argue about it, Weldon. Count your blessings."

"I don't buy that," I said.

"You know why people say justice is blind? It's because it's blind," he said.

The door opened and Miss Lemunyon came in and sat rigidly behind her desk. "You can go," she said.

"That's it?" I said.

"No, that is not it," she said. "You have a court appearance in three weeks. One other development you might note: The Immigration and Naturalization Service has taken an interest in your whereabouts and your behavior, Mrs. Holland. Our office is at their disposal. Do you understand what I'm saying to you?"

"Yes, I think I do," Rosita replied.

"You're certain of that, are you?" Miss Lemunyon said.

"I won't knowingly cause you any more difficulty," Rosita said.

"I believe we're done here," Tom said, rising from his chair. "Thank you for seeing us."

Miss Lemunyon didn't reply. Her face contained a dry, colorless heat of a kind you associate with people for whom personal humiliation has been a way of life. These are the worst people imaginable to have as enemies. As we left the building, I felt something else needed to be said. It has always been my conviction that nothing is ever lost by appealing to reason in others. If it doesn't work, it doesn't work. You tried. I knew that's what Grandfather would say, at least when he wasn't loading a gun in preparation to shoot someone. I put Rosita in the automobile and went back inside the building. I tapped on the frosted glass inset in Miss Lemunyon's door. "Come in," she said.

"I'll make this brief," I said. "I think you're probably a good judge of character. Officer Slakely molested my wife. He's poor white trash and a liar and a coward. What he did to my wife, he's done to other women. Don't let him use you."

She looked at me for a long moment. I noticed for the first time there were no cuticles on her nails and that the sides of her fingers on her right hand were yellowed by nicotine. Her mouth worked without sound; then there was a dry click in her throat and the words finally came out, thick and ropy and barely audible. "How dare you speak to me like that," she said.

MY MOTHER WAS no longer able to adequately care for Grandfather, so Rosita and I brought him to Houston and put him in a back bedroom where he could see the esplanade and the baseball diamond and the trees and picnic shelters in the park. Grandfather didn't do well in the city. To him, sirens, traffic noises, the drone of airplanes, the quarreling of neighbors, and solicitors knocking on the door were acts of theft. I thought that, like many elderly people, he might retaliate by making life hard for others, but that proved not to be the case. Grandfather was a study in contradiction and unpredictability. He had killed a number of men, but he was not a killer. He could be visceral and coarse, but under it all he was a kind man. Rather than publicly rinse his sins, as many others were fond of doing, he wrote off his early years as "lively times." I loved Grandfather; it was a pleasure to have him in our home.

I didn't want to burden him with our troubles. He was a good reader of people, though, and I didn't fool him long. "I heard y'all talking. Those same oil people are out to get you, are they?" he said when I spread a quilt over him and turned on the electric fan.

"Yes, sir."

"Tell me about it."

"It's a long and dreary business, Grandfather. We'll just have to see it through."

"Tell me anyway. It's not like my schedule is overly crowded."

So I did.

"Suffering God, Satch, it sounds like they've tried everything except give you anthrax."

"They can do whatever they want. We'll do it right back."

"It's not always that easy. You trust Roy Wiseheart?"

"He's got sand, I'll say that."

"So did John Wesley Hardin. He was also a bucket of shit."

"Roy's not like his father. I think there's more than one person living inside him."

"I bet one of them is a coral snake."

I didn't reply. The sky was dark, and the bedroom was brightly lit by an overhead light. Grandfather's face looked soft and pink against the pillow, his thick hair a tangle of gray and white. Even in his nineties, he was a big and powerful man and not to be taken for granted. "Don't get slickered," he said.

"By whom?"

"I know your thoughts before you have them, Weldon. You're fond of Wiseheart. You both went to war. Like you, he was brave. But when push comes to shove, he'll stick with his own kind. It won't be because of love, either. It'll be about money."

"Your revolver is sticking out from under your pillow," I said.

"I saw some of Pancho Villa's boys outside the window last night. I'd hate for one of them to get the drop on me."

I looked over my shoulder and back at him.

"Been on any snipe hunts lately?" he said, his chest shaking with silent laughter.

BY THE TIME Linda Gail arrived on location in Mexico, she had done her best to forget what had occurred on the penthouse balcony of the Shamrock Hotel, seventeen stories in the sky. She wouldn't have really gone through with it, she told herself. She'd had too much to drink. If something hadn't happened, it was not meant to happen, and hence could not happen.

Liar, a voice said.

She saw herself plummeting past the rows of hotel windows, spread-eagled, naked, upside down. Oddly, the image disturbed her not because of the fate she had almost imposed upon herself but because of the grotesque and unseemly fashion in which she would have been remembered.

She determined she would no longer think about what *could* have happened. This was *Mexico*. This was *now*. Somehow she would find a way out of her problems. Who would have believed where she was today compared with one year ago?

The location was the most beautiful stretch of terrain she had ever seen, the topography and seasons out of kilter in a way that convinced her a remarkable change was about to take place in her life. The mountains were purple in the distance, the grass long and yellow in the fields, and the earth the color of rust where it had been plowed, the irrigation ditches brimming with water that looked like coffee-stained milk. On the long slope that led up to a dead volcano were orchards of walnut and avocado trees, and at sunset the Indians built fires in the shadows and roasted ears of corn in the coals like people from an ancient time.

The set was meant to replicate a Republican airstrip in Andalusia in 1936, complete with biplanes that had Vickers machine guns mounted on the fuselages. But to Linda Gail this enormous, fertile valley, containing livestock and tall palms with trunks that were as smooth as elephant hide, and clumps of banana plants and orchards bursting with bloodred peaches, had nothing to do with modern times. The mountains and the warm, dense air and the great freshwater lake nearby where Indians fished from boats made out of reeds convinced her she was standing in a legendary place that had been transported from the confluence of the Tigris and Euphrates rivers. If that was true, or even a possibility, it could mean that mankind was being given a second chance. And if mankind could have a second chance, why couldn't she?

Roy Wiseheart had shown up on the set out of nowhere, driving a British lorry, wearing an Australian flop hat and khaki shorts and a hunter's jacket with cloth loops for bullets, a scoped rifle jiggling in a rack behind his head. When he braked to a stop next to her, outside an airplane hangar, a cloud of dust floating across her and the crew and the other actors, she tried to pretend she wasn't angry that he was irritating everyone on the set at her expense. She glanced at the director. His name was Jerry Fallon. He had the leanness of a lizard, and his skin was just as rough. He removed his sunglasses and hung one of the arm pieces from his lip and stared at her and Roy, his nostrils dilating.

"What are you doing, Roy?" Linda Gail whispered.

"Seeing what you're up to," he said, getting down from the lorry. "I'm a co-producer now. Didn't Jerry tell you?"

"No."

"I want to keep an eye on my investment. You look outstanding. You see those World War I crates over there? One of them is mine. I'm going to take it up."

Her face was burning. She lowered her eyes. "I need to talk to you."

"About that little episode? Don't give second life to the shadows of the heart."

"Roy, I'm *working* now."

"Time for lunch, everybody!" he shouted. "Is that okay with you, Jerry?"

"No, you're a bloody nuisance, you fucking sod," the director said.

"Thank you," Roy said. "Come on, Linda Gail. I made up a picnic basket. Don't worry about Jerry. I was his wingman in the South Pacific. He's a Digger but a swell fellow. Right, you malignant wog?"

"Take a break, everyone. Be back at one," Jerry said. "Linda Gail?"

"Yes?" she said.

"I have high hopes for this next scene," he said. "We want it right. You with me, love?"

"Yes, I'm with you. I understand."

"Do you?" he replied.

Why had Roy done this to her? He drove them to an adobe ranch house at the base of the volcano. The bougainvillea reached to the roof; the latticework over the walkways was interwoven with wisteria that had just gone into bloom. "Whose place is this?" she asked.

"An absentee landowner. He rented it to me."

"Did you arrange this role for me?"

"I don't have that kind of power. Regardless of what people think, it doesn't work that way out here. You got it on your own hook."

"I don't believe you."

"Let's go inside. I've missed you terribly." He shut off the engine. "God, you're lovely."

"I have to work this afternoon," she said. "You heard what Jerry said. What are you doing to me?"

"To *you*?"

"I never know what to believe. I think maybe my whole career was bought and paid for. You made me look like a fool in front of the whole cast and crew. How did you suddenly become a producer of the film? You're on a first-name basis with my director. You seem to orchestrate everything you come near. You're everywhere and nowhere."

"I was on a first-name basis with famous actresses when I was ten years old. Sometime I'll tell you the names of some my father slept with."

"Did you buy me this role or not?"

"Let me tell you a story about Jack Warner. He once said, 'I've got the best scriptwriter in Hollywood, and I've got him for peanuts.' He was talking about William Faulkner. You know who else he said that about? *You*. In light of what you're going to make for him, he considers your salary peanuts."

"I don't believe you, number one. Number two, what if I said I want out of our situation?"

"You'd hurt me beyond repair. But if that's your choice, I'd honor it. Is that your choice, Linda Gail?"

She felt a great dryness come into her mouth. "It should be."

"How should I read that?" he said. "What does a statement like that mean? People are what they do. Not what they say or what they think. You're with me of your own volition. You've made a choice. We both have."

The sun went behind the clouds. She could see the wind scouring dust out of the fields, peaches thudding to the ground in an orchard, the parked biplanes straining against their anchor ropes. "I grew up in a fundamentalist church," she said. "So did Hershel. You don't know what that does to you. Maybe I don't have your strength. Maybe I'm one of those weak girls who always have to like themselves."

"Let's have lunch," he said.

"You want to have lunch?"

"Yes. Don't take all these things on yourself at one time. Whatever decision you make will be fine. If you walk away from me today, you'll always remain my girl. A man meets a woman like you once in a lifetime. Every day with her is a gift. Then one day the gift ends. I can't stand the thought of losing you, Linda Gail. But I can't control your emotions. Just tell me what you want to do."

She thought she would cry.

That wasn't what she did. Ten minutes later, she was in bed with him, his head buried between her breasts, a wave building inside her with such intensity that the moans she made seemed to come from someone else.

THAT EVENING JERRY Fallon came to her trailer, a new Airstream that had been brought from Guadalajara for her sole use. He was dressed in tennis shorts and a blue polo and a white cap and was carrying two bottles of Champale. "Where's the lover boy?" he asked.

"Roy?"

"I hope you only have two of them. Lovers, I mean."

"He had to go to Mexico City. He'll be back tomorrow."

"Nice of him to tell me. Want one of these?"

"No, thank you," she replied.

"I admire your abstinence. You're going to do great, love. You know that, don't you?"

"Why did you call Roy a sod today?"

"That's from our flying days. I used to call him a sod because he was anything but."

"He chased women?"

"Not too far. It was wartime. We'd get what we called 'seventy-two' in Pearl. The navy nurses were everywhere. Roy cut a wide swath."

"What do you want, Jerry?"

"Can I sit down?"

"Do whatever you want."

He was wearing shades and had the darkest tan she had ever seen; his arms and chest were covered with swatches of black hair, his fingers tapered, like a piano player's. He cracked the cap off a Champale bottle with an opener on his knife. He caught the foam on the web of his thumb and put it in his mouth. "You want to be shark meat?"

"Are you talking about Roy?"

"America is in love with Betty Hutton and Margaret O'Brien. They love Judy Garland. They love mythology, and the Puritan in them is still alive and well. Rob them of their myths and they'll tear you apart."

"You think I'm doing something wrong?"

"I'm saying don't get caught. Anybody who was on the set today could sell a very nasty story with one phone call. Wake up, doll."

"I don't like you calling me names."

"I'm assuming you're an adult. The space between your teeth is worth a million dollars. Roy is reckless. He thinks his crate should have burned with him in it. One day he'll find a way to do it. You want to ride it down with him?"

"He's suicidal?"

"No, he's worse. He wants the funeral of a Viking."

"I don't know what that is."

"He wants lots of companions for the trip across, a dead dog at his feet."

"You're upsetting me, Jerry."

"That's why I brought you a drink. Roy's box score is legendary. You drove off with him at lunchtime in front of a hundred people. You know what I heard one of the cooks say? This is from one of the *cooks*. 'Her husband and Wiseheart were both war heroes. Now they're sharing the same foxhole.'"

Her face was as hot as an electric iron, her head throbbing. "And what did you do about it?"

"I'm not worried about what two scullions say. Hedda Hopper is another matter. You know the fun she'd have with a juicy bit of news like this?"

"Roy and I are friends. You stop assuming things."

"When you came back from the hacienda, you looked like you'd forgotten to put your panties on."

"Don't you dare talk to me like that."

"I got a call from your husband fifteen minutes ago. He'll be here tomorrow morning. We're shooting the battle scene at first light. We don't need distractions, love. Now you clean up your act and get with the program."

"Hershel is coming *here*?"

"That's what the man said. Does he know about you and Roy?"

She sat down in a chair. Her ears were ringing, her stomach roiling. Jerry upended the Champale, the foam running through the neck and down his throat. He set down the bottle and looked her evenly in the face.

"I hate to see you foul your own nest," he said. "You've got it all, love. You don't need the wrong guy crawling around on top of you. Dump the bastard while you have the chance."

"Get out," she said.

Maybe she threw something at him. She couldn't remember. When she went to bed, the wind was buffeting her trailer, blowing dust devils out of the hills, dimming the stars that one hour earlier had glittered as brightly as electric bulbs in a theater marquee.

JUST BEFORE DAWN she woke from a dream in which wolves were sitting on tree limbs, their muzzles moist with blood. At first she thought the wolves were looking at her, a frightened, small girl unable to flee her attackers. Then she realized that was not the case at all. She was sitting on a tree branch among them. What did the dream mean? The answer wasn't long in coming. She was a kindred spirit, her agenda as predatory as theirs. Linda Gail Pine had taken on a new identity, one that was probably hidden inside her all her life.

The first scene Jerry shot the next morning involved a Heinkel coming in low, out of a watery yellow sun, bombing and strafing the airfield, the planted explosives geysering showers of dirt and rock into the air, the Heinkel's engines rattling the tin roofs of the hangars as it swept overhead, the bombardier hunched inside the Plexiglas nose cone, his face like a pig's inside the leather cap and goggles and fur collar on his leather coat.

The explosions were deafening, their aftershocks vibrating through the ground under Linda Gail's shoes. Curds of black smoke coiled out of giant smudge pots, powdering the air with soot and filling it with an oily stench that reminded Linda Gail of the refineries in Baton Rouge. A small tank clanked across the airstrip, a Falangist flag flapping from its radio antenna. After the driver got out, Jerry told a stagehand to fire a fully automatic weapon into the cupola so he could record the sound of live rounds ricocheting off the steel plates. Linda Gail found herself stepping back involuntarily, her arms folded across her chest, as the bullets whined into the distance and a German fighter plane streaked low overhead, the barrels of its wing guns flashing. Was this what Rosita Holland actually went through? Linda Gail looked around, wondering if any of the crew or cast sensed the fear that had invaded her body.

Jerry put his arm around her shoulders. "You ready?" he said.

"For what?" she asked, startled out of her reverie.

"You're about to witness the fascists executing Republican wounded. It's not your everyday event. You rush out to stop it. You're the Angel of Andalusia. The poor buggers just want to touch the hem of your garment and be made whole. Remember Scarlett O'Hara walking across a train yard filled with Confederate wounded begging for water? That's you, love."

She felt as if a piece of wire were being tightened around her temples. Jerry stepped in front of her, placing his palms on her shoulders, staring into her eyes. "Many women live inside you, Linda Gail. That's why you're going to be a great actress. Don't let anything get in the way of that goal. Give voice to those women who depend on you. You're a strong woman, a fucking Amazon. You could rip the head off a fascist officer and spit in it. Are you hearing me?"

"Yes," she replied.

"Then get on it. Don't let me down."

"I won't, Jerry."

"That's my girl," he said. He squeezed her against him. "Put the fear of God in them."

The cameras began rolling as she ran toward a rampart that had been overrun by soldiers who carried bayonet-fixed rifles and wore tasseled caps and rolled blankets tied across their chests. Republican wounded, some wearing French helmets, were lying on the ground, their hands raised futilely against the bayonets being plunged into their bodies. The barrel of a knocked-out machine gun was still smoking behind a wall of sandbags. Some of the wounded were teenaged boys, their faces terrified as they awaited their fate.

Somehow the scene taking place around her had become real, the screams of the dying and the smell of cordite and burning vehicles and the raw stench of blood no longer imaginary or a creation of Hollywood but part of an actual battle in 1936 that she had stepped inside and was participating in among her comrades, all of them scarred by poverty and hunger and oppression. She not only owned this moment, she had earned it and would never separate herself from its suffering and pain.

She shielded the body of a fallen boy. She shoved aside bayonets with her bare hands. She implored a fascist officer to show mercy and yelled in his face when he didn't. She had become more than the Angel of Andalusia; she was the Angel of Goliad whom she read about in high school, the Mexican prostitute who saved the lives of many a Texas soldier at the Goliad Massacre of 1836. She was no longer Linda Gail Pine.

The tears in her eyes were real. Her clothes were rent by the bayonets she shoved aside, the smears of blood and saliva on her hands and face and hair no longer cosmetic, the alarm she saw in the actors' faces no longer feigned. She beat her fists on an officer's chest and tried to gouge his eyes; she cursed and used words that were not in the script; she tore at her own skin with her fingernails as she recognized a dead boy who had sold goat's milk to her family in their village. The actors playing the roles of fascist soldiers shrank back, blinking, afraid she might blind them.

"Cut!" she heard Jerry yell.

The world seemed to stop, the people around her frozen inside a single frame of film, their mouths open in midsentence. When she tried to speak, no sound would come out of her throat. The land, the sky, the orchards in the distance, the insignias on the wings of the biplanes, all of them were drained of color, just as the dust-covered bodies on the ground were, all of it caught forever inside a photograph taken in a place she had never been.

She saw Jerry walking toward her, his hands outstretched. He lifted her in the air and spun her in a circle. "That was bloody fucking glorious!" he said, and kissed her on the cheek. "Ernest Hemingway couldn't hold a candle to what you just did! By God, you're a marvel!"

The wounded and the dead were rising from the ground as though a form of secular resurrection were taking place. Everyone in the cast and crew was applauding, as happy for her as they would be for themselves. The joy she felt was like nothing she had ever experienced.

HERSHEL ARRIVED AT noon in a battered taxicab he had hired in a coastal town fifty kilometers away. He was wearing a sport coat and slacks that didn't match, and carrying a canvas suitcase he had bought in an army PX, his serial number stenciled unevenly on the side. He was also carrying a cardboard tube, the kind that held architectural plans. She ate lunch with him in the outdoor tent that served as a commissary for the cast and crew, the canvas swelling and flapping in the wind, the mountains as blue as steel in the distance, the sun golden on the peach orchards. If anyone noticed Hershel and the conflict he was causing his wife, they pretended otherwise.

"I hope you don't mind me popping in like this," he said. "Does the director mind if I stay in your trailer?"

"I'm sure that will be fine," she said, avoiding his gaze.

"I have this architect friend in Baton Rouge. He made up some sketches."

"Sketches of what?"

"That house you want to build in Santa Monica. Is there somewhere we can go look at them?"

"I have to go back to work."

"I mean later."

"Whatever you want to do is fine, Hershel."

"There's nothing wrong, is there?"

"No, not at all. I said everything will be just fine."

His reddish-blond hair was freshly barbered, his face clean-shaven, his eyes clear and devoid of guile. "I saw that tank and those biplanes out there. Where'd y'all find that stuff?"

"A contractor supplies it," she answered. She tried to repress her irritability. It wasn't his fault he didn't know about these things. Why was she angry at him? "I'm sorry we're so busy now."

"I heard some people talking about how good you were this morning."

"Jerry helped me a lot with the particular scene. It involved the fascists killing the Republican wounded."

"You're talking about the Spanish Civil War? Rosita's father was mixed up in that, wasn't he?"

She started to reply and realized his gaze had drifted away, out the tent flap.

"Is that Roy Wiseheart yonder?" he asked.

"He's co-producer on the film," she said.

"I didn't know that."

"He just showed up out of nowhere. He surprised me, too."

"That boy sure gets around, doesn't he?" Hershel said. He took a bite of his hamburger, lowering his eyes, his meaning, if any, concealed.

She was sweating, the veins in her scalp dilating. "How can an architect in Baton Rouge sketch a design for a house on the cliffs above Santa Monica or Malibu?" she said. "What would he know about the soil or the building codes or anything, for that matter?"

"A house is a house. This one will be two stories. It'll have a baby room, too."

"A *baby* room?"

"We're not getting any younger." He waited.

"I don't know what to say, Hershel. You drop in with no advance notice and bring up these things in a public place and make decisions for me without asking—"

He was looking outside the tent flap again. "Wiseheart is getting into a biplane. That guy is something else."

She glanced at her watch. Twenty-three more minutes before she went back to work. Ten more minutes of Hershel and she would be exhausted. "I have a difficult scene to do this afternoon. I can't talk about these other matters now."

"What 'other' matters are you talking about? I just wanted to show you the sketches."

"This is the wrong place and the wrong time."

"We've got to make some choices about where we live. Our rental arrangement with Jack Valentine got canceled," he said.

"We're being evicted by Jack Valentine?"

"Not exactly. He's dead. He was beaten to death two days ago in Los Angeles."

She stared at him stupidly.

"It was in all the papers. Someone did him in with a lead pipe down in the colored district. The real estate agent said we have to either buy the place or get out. Maybe it's just as well."

"I can't follow all this. Just as well what?"

"It's just as well about the house in River Oaks. I don't think you like it there. I don't, either. River Oaks isn't our kind of neighborhood."

"Not our kind of *neighborhood*? I knew you'd say something like that. I just knew it."

"They look down their noses at us."

"Then fuck them."

"When did you start using that kind of language?"

"Just now."

"Where are you going?"

"To lie down for a few minutes. Maybe I'll take a sedative. Or maybe not. I'm very upset. It's not your fault. I was just telling you how I feel. But I can't take this anymore."

"I'll go with you."

"No. Finish your lunch."

"Do they have a doctor here?"

"For God's sake, sit down and give me a few minutes alone. Please do that, Hershel. Don't argue. For once, don't argue about things you don't understand."

She walked out the tent flap, avoiding the stares from the other tables, her magenta silk blouse rippling in the wind. She saw Roy Wiseheart's open-cockpit biplane lifting off the dirt runway, his goggled face turning toward her. He was grinning. As he flew past her, he waved and pointed upward, as though telling her his destination lay somewhere beyond the heavens, and his plane made of wires and struts and fabric would take him there. Then he began climbing almost straight up, higher and higher, until his plane became a black speck and seemed to dissolve inside the sun. She continued toward her trailer, trying to remember what Roy had said about Jack Valentine. He needed to be taught a lesson? Was that it? Yes, those were Roy's words.

She heard the plane's engine sputtering, as though the fuel line had clogged. She shielded her eyes and stared up at the sound, then saw Roy coming out of the west, over brown hills that looked like clay sculptures of a woman's breasts, his plane upside down. As he roared past her, low over her trailer, he let his arms hang loose from his body, his full weight hanging against the leather safety harness, his shadow and the shadow of his plane rippling like an effigy of a feathered serpent across a field of green corn.

Then she turned and saw Hershel behind her. He was watching the biplane disappear over the hills, a look of resignation on his face. "I didn't come out here to cause you problems, Linda Gail," he said. "I missed you, that's all."

Chapter 22

I CAN'T TELL you what evil is. I'll leave that to the theologians. But I can tell you what it looks like in human form. In this instance its name was Hubert Timmons Slakely, the uniformed cop who arrested and molested my wife.

We had left Grandfather at home and driven to a miniature golf course a few blocks away. There was still light in the sky, and it was cool enough for a jacket. The stars were out, and families were putting golf balls down felt-lined corridors into imitation greens outfitted with toy windmills and tiny bridges over watercourses and tunnels that plunked the ball into a cup. I had no reason to worry about Grandfather. He enjoyed listening to the radio by himself and reading his encyclopedias and putting up preserves from our garden or the vegetable market, and we had told the next-door neighbor where we would be in case of an emergency.

Earlier I'd said I didn't expect to see Officer Slakely again. I was dead wrong. Wicked men do not go away of their own accord.

Grandfather was sitting up in bed with his spectacles on, the King James Bible propped open on his stomach, when he heard the house creak and felt the air in his room decompress. Someone had just opened and closed the front door.

"Is that you, Weldon?" he said.

A tall man wearing a pearl-gray short-brim Stetson and a sharkskin suit and a black shirt with red flowers on it appeared in the bedroom doorway. His hands were big, the back of the right hand tattooed with a string of blue stars. He was smoking a cigarette. "Howdy," he said.

Grandfather nodded.

"Where's your ashtray?" the tall man asked.

"I don't have one," Grandfather replied.

"You must be the former Texas Ranger."

Grandfather didn't reply.

"I didn't figure you for a student of Scripture," the visitor said.

"I was looking for the loopholes."

The visitor's cigarette was almost down to his fingers. "I got to remember that one. Where's your grandson at?"

"He comes and goes. Mind telling me what the hell you're doing in our house?"

"I'm Detective Hubert Timmons Slakely of the Houston City Police Department."

"You knocked and walked in? Or you didn't bother to knock and just walked in?"

"I knocked and thought I heard someone say come in."

"Are you the one who arrested Rosita in Hermann Park?"

"It's my opinion she got herself arrested."

"When did you become a plainclothes?"

"I passed the test a few months back but only got promoted recently. It's a little late for me, though. I'm fixing to retire and buy a beach home down by Padre Island."

Grandfather worked himself up on the pillow, one hand propped behind him. The detective wore a half smile on his face. He unhooked the window screen and flipped his cigarette into the yard. "What's an old fart like you doing by himself?" he said.

"Listening to the radio."

"You *were* listening to the radio." The detective clicked it off. "When are they due home?"

"Who?"

"Your grandson and his wife."

"They didn't tell me."

"Then why did you just look at the clock?"

"I listen to *Lux Radio Theatre* every Sunday night."

"It's not Sunday."

"That's probably why it didn't come on. What do you want with my grandson?"

"I'd like to make things easier for him and the little woman." Slakely sniffed and pinched at one nostril. "What's that odor?"

"A pot of stewed tomatoes and peppers I have on slow boil."

"I think it's you. Somebody hasn't been taking care of you. You need somebody to wash you. You want me to take you to the tub and do it for you?"

Grandfather could see the neighbor's lighted windows through the live oaks and pecan trees in the side yard. He could hear music playing on his neighbor's radio and leaves tumbling across the yard, striking the screens.

"An old man is a nasty thing," Slakely said. "He yellows the sheets and leaves his stink in everything he lies on."

"How much do you want?"

"How much what?"

"Money."

"I was thinking more in terms of stock options. You know what? I'm going to bring a washcloth in here and wipe you down."

"Have you ever been shot?"

"A few have tried."

"I killed six men. I wish things had worked out otherwise. But they didn't give me much selection. Has it ever been that way with you?"

"Is there supposed to be some kind of message in that?"

"You could call it that. You're about two seconds away from getting your head blown off."

"Get up, old man. I'm taking you in the bathroom. I think you messed yourself."

Grandfather peeled the sheet off his hand and forearm. "I had it converted for conventional ammunition in 1880. I shot one of Bill

Dalton's gang off a windmill with it. He fell straight down into the cattle tank." He raised the barrel of the revolver so it was pointed at Slakely's face. He cocked the hammer with his thumb.

"It looks like a relic to me," Slakely said.

"If you can see into the chambers, you'll notice there's an 'X' cut in the nose of each round. It's more or less the equivalent of getting hit with four pieces of buckshot. The exit wound is the size of a silver dollar. In your case, there won't be an exit wound. Your skull and your brain matter will be on the wall."

"Hold on." Slakely stepped back involuntarily, trying not to raise his hand in front of him.

"I think you should not move around too much," Grandfather said.

"I just came here to talk, not for trouble."

"No, you're here to bring grief to innocent people. You put me in mind of an egg-sucking dog. There's no cure for your kind. Where's your weapon?"

"I'm not carrying one," Slakely said. He opened the flaps of his coat. His face was tight, the color gone, his pulse jumping visibly in his throat, like a damaged moth. "See? You need to put that thumb buster away."

"Where's your throw-down?"

"I don't carry one. I don't do that sort of thing."

"Pull up your pants cuffs."

Slakely tugged on his trouser leg, his face turned to one side, his forehead and profiled cheek shiny with moisture.

"Unstrap it with your left hand and let it fall to the floor," Grandfather said.

Slakely leaned over and released the strap on a small holster attached to his right ankle. It contained a .32 revolver. The sight was filed off, the grips wrapped with black tape.

"Step away from it," Grandfather said.

"Whatever you want. My visit here is according to protocol. There's no need for—"

"How many times have you planted one of those?"

"I never had to. I never shot anyone. Not as a police officer."

"I think you're a liar. Close your eyes."

"Why?"

"Because if I pull this trigger, I don't want to see the look in your eyes. The men I killed all had the same look when they died. They knew their lives and souls were forfeit and there was no way they could change what was about to happen. That's why I read Scripture. It allows me to forget that look. Then a simpleton like you shows up and taints my spirituality."

"I apologize."

"You've got another problem. Like most white trash, you're disrespectful to your betters and proud of your stupidity and ignorance. If you didn't have the nigras to feel superior to, most of y'all would kill yourselves. I'm done talking. You want to say anything before I shoot you?"

WE CAME THROUGH the front door seconds before Grandfather probably would have pulled the trigger. I wished Grandfather had killed him. There is no downside to the death of a man like Slakely, except the body is an insult to the earth in which it's buried.

"Get that gun away from him," Slakely said.

"What are you doing in our house?" I asked.

"I offered to take him to the bathroom. He pulled a revolver on me. This man belongs in an asylum."

"You didn't answer my question."

"I came here to make your problems go away. I'm not a bad man."

"Yes, you are," I replied.

"Tell him to point that gun somewhere else."

"Grandfather, it's all right," I said.

He rested the revolver on his thigh and released the hammer. "This boy strikes me as highly excitable. He doesn't seem to do well in manly confrontation. I think he should stick to abusing women and cripples and children and such."

I picked up Slakely's ankle pistol and holster and handed it to him. "Out of my house."

"You need to talk to me, Mr. Holland."

"I already know what you're going to say."

"I don't think you do."

Rosita was standing in the doorway, her eyes fixed so intensely on the back of Slakely's head that he seemed to feel their heat. He turned and looked at her. "We meet again."

"Say what you have to say," she said.

"I've got your husband by the short hairs. That's what I was gonna say. I can have the old man arrested for threatening an officer of the law with a firearm. Or I can forget all this and see that the charges against you are lost in the process."

"Get him out of here, Weldon," she said.

"You heard her, bub," I said.

"Suit yourself. I tried. Someday y'all will figure out we're all little people, even you, the big war hero."

Slakely walked back through the hallway into the living room. The porch light was on, and candle moths were bumping against the screen. The wind was blowing, and the live oaks and pecan trees in the yard were full of shadows that kept changing shape, the leaves spinning on the lawn and driveway. Slakely was only a few feet from the door. In seconds he would be gone and we would return to our lives, and in the morning I would call our lawyer and see what could be done about Slakely's invasion of our home. Then he turned around, like a man who can't leave a dice table or an unfinished drink on a saloon table or a situation in which his paucity as a human being has been exposed.

He was still wearing his Stetson, his hands opening and closing at his sides, the veins knotting like twine under the skin. "The old man says he killed six men. That's a lie, isn't it?"

"Yes, it is."

"That's what I thought."

"He killed eleven or twelve I know of. He killed some of them while he was blind drunk. He doesn't count the Mexicans he shot on one of Pancho Villa's troop trains. If you think he won't kill you, call up Frank Hamer and ask him about Grandfather's track record."

"Frank Hamer, the Texas Ranger who killed Bonnie and Clyde?"

"That's the one."

"My goddamn ass."

Rosita was silhouetted in the kitchen doorway, wearing an apron, a wooden spatula in her hand. Behind her, strings of steam were rising from Grandfather's pot of stewed tomatoes and peppers. Next to the stove was a white table lined with glass jars and brassy metal tops, a metal spoon inserted in each jar to keep it from cracking when the preserves were poured into it.

It's my belief that lust, greed, and violence die hard in all of us, whether we're Semites or Gentiles or pagans, river-baptized, born again, or redeemed by a blinding light on the road to Damascus. But there's another group in our midst. I believe some are born with the scales and the tailed spine of the four-footed reptilian creature with which we share a common gene pool. I never bore an animus toward the average German soldier; I did, however, toward the Waffen SS, and I was glad I had killed as many of them as I possibly could. I didn't think Slakely had twin lightning bolts tattooed under his armpit, but if he had, I'm sure he would have worn them with pride.

"It doesn't have to be this way," he said.

"Which way?" I said.

"Ten thousand dollars in cash or stocks. That's all I want. I'm putting myself in danger on your behalf. You haven't figured that out?"

"I'm going to get you," I said.

"You're threatening me?"

"It's not a threat. I'm telling you what's going to happen to you. You violated my wife's person. You invaded my home. You tried to degrade my grandfather. You think you're going to get away with that because you're a Houston police officer?"

He huffed air out of his nostrils. "Live in your own shit. You'll wish you never heard my name."

"I believe you," I said.

He went out the screen door and let it slam behind him. I saw Rosita go back into the kitchen and lift the lid off the metal pot on the stove and put on cloth gloves so she could begin filling the jars.

"Grandfather wants to do that," I said.

"He'll burn himself."

"Let him do it or he'll get riled up again. I'll go get him."

I went into the back bedroom to help Grandfather out of bed. I hadn't latched the screen or bolted the door. It would have made no difference, though. Hubert Timmons Slakely was a man whose greatest enemy was knowledge about himself. He had been humiliated and treated like the white trash he was. Under the bedsheet that hides the identity of every Ku Klux Klansman is a cretinous, vicious, and childlike human being whose last holdout is his whites-only restroom. He is pathologically incapable of change this side of the grave.

Slakely came back through the screen and entered the kitchen, his shadow falling across Rosita. "I'm on to you, Mrs. Holland," he said.

She stared at him without replying.

"You know what the Jewish piano is, don't you? The cash register. You're a kike. You won't let your husband's money get loose from your hands. Also, you're too dumb to see what you're doing to both y'all."

"Did you know it's rude for a man not to remove his hat in someone's house?" she said.

"Wait till you get up to the women's prison. I'll put some interesting notations in your jacket. There's a section for bull dykes. I'll make sure you get to meet them."

"I'm looking forward to it."

"One day somebody is gonna tear you and that smart mouth apart, woman."

"That's what you would like to do right now. But you won't because there're witnesses. A man like you doesn't care for witnesses. They're inconvenient when you arrest a street prostitute or a hapless Negro or a vagabond. You frighten the defenseless and impose your will upon them in order to hide the fear that governs your life. That's why I pity rather than hate you."

I put Grandfather in his reading chair and as I approached the kitchen doorway, I saw Slakely's right hand, the one tattooed with a chain of blue stars, curl into a fist. I had no doubt that a blow from a man of his size could crush the bones in her face or even kill her. But if I thought I needed to protect my wife, I was mistaken. Rosita Lowenstein Holland did not need protection. Her adversaries did.

"The Krauts should have melted you into a bar of soap," Slakely said.

He heard me behind him and glanced over his shoulder. It was bad timing for Hubert Timmons Slakely. The stewed peppers and tomatoes on the stove had become as thick as ketchup, bubbles rising like big red blisters to the surface. She flung the pot with both hands into his face, covering his eyes and nose and mouth like a wet red kerchief wrapped around the head of a mannequin. He screamed and pushed the heels of his hands into his eye sockets and crashed into the doorjamb, fighting his way blindly through the living room and down the steps into the yard. She wasn't finished with him. She went through the door after him and poured the rest of the pot onto his head and neck, then threw the pot high in the air and watched it bounce on the lawn.

"Voilà," she said. "There's a garden hose by the hydrant if you want to wash off. Thanks so much for dropping by."

I CALLED A SITTER for Grandfather, went upstairs, and packed a bag for Rosita, and drove both of us to Galveston before Hubert Timmons Slakely could return to the house with his colleagues. I rented a motel room right across from the seawall that had been built after the great hurricane of 1900. I had not told her I would have to leave her there and return to Houston. Rosita was brave and loving and honorable and all things that are good. She deserved none of the things that had been done to her. Leaving her alone was one of the hardest things I had ever done. But I had to distract the authorities from her and somehow neutralize the power we had given Slakely.

"You're leaving?" she said.

"There's a taxi on the way."

"I don't like being a fugitive, Weldon. We've done nothing wrong."

"They're not going to get their hands on you again. I'm going to call the state attorney. I'm going to the police station tonight and file a complaint. There's Grandfather to take care of, too. You'll have the car, but if you go anywhere, take a cab. Don't talk to anyone. I registered us as Mr. and Mrs. Malory."

"As in Thomas Malory?"

"Why not?" I said.

For the first time since we had left Houston, she smiled. Through the curtains, I could see the amusement pier extending from the beach into the surf, the waves bursting against the pilings. All of the rides and concession stands were closed for the season, the long row of windows in the seafood restaurant darkened. "Lie down with me before you go," she said.

I saw the headlights of the taxi turn off the boulevard into the motel. I went outside and gave the driver three dollars and sent him away. When I came back inside, Rosita had already turned off the lights and undressed and was lying on top of the sheet, one knee pulled up in front of her, her back propped against the pillows. "You look like a painting on the side of a Flying Fortress," I said.

"Maybe that's what I am."

I undressed and got in bed beside her. I put my hand inside the thickness of her hair and kissed her on the mouth. I did not believe then, nor do I believe now, that any woman in the history of the world ever made love like Rosita Lowenstein. It was total and complete and unrelenting, and even after I was physically spent, my desire for her never dissipated. I never knew a woman whose hair was both mahogany-colored and black, one color inseparable from the other, yet always changing, depending on the light. Nor had I ever known one who had eyes that shone like sherry in a crystal glass.

As I write these remarks, I know they are personal in nature and perhaps violate good taste and might be embarrassing to read. They may never be read by another. But they reflect my feelings about Rosita. She never had to seek modesty. It was built into her. Reclining nude on a bed, or making love with an almost animal pleasure, or creating an erotic moment unexpectedly in a conventional situation was simply the expression of who she was.

She never had fewer than three climaxes, and after each one she began all over again with such heat and energy that I thought my heart would fail. I buried my face in the sweat on her neck and the dampness in her hair, and could feel both an ache and a rhythm in my loins that I believed would never end, in the same way that you know your love for another person will never end. That's what it was like with Rosita Lowenstein. The two of us let go of the world and floated away to a kingdom under the sea where no one would ever disturb us again.

At three in the morning she bit me softly on the ear and released me and lay back on the pillow.

"This will be over soon," I said.

"No, it won't, Weldon. They're like the fascists. They torture with passion and murder with indifference."

"They messed with the wrong bunch."

"The Hollands?"

"Sure. You're a Holland, too. How's it feel?"

"You still believe there's light in all men. They know that about you. They also know you'll never change, that you'll always be bound by the restraints of conscience."

"You worry too much, kid."

She squeezed my arm and turned toward the wall, the sheet pulled over her shoulder.

I showered and dressed and called again for a taxi. As I drove away with the cabbie, I looked through the rear window at the darkened amusement pier and the great slate-green moonlit roll and pitch of the Gulf, and I felt a pang in my heart that I couldn't explain. Maybe it was because I felt the spring and summer of our lives had slipped away, as though a thief had sneaked onto the pier and clicked off the switch on the Ferris wheel before we could reverse the terrible attrition that time imposes on us all. Or did my sense of mutability have another source? In 1942 Nazi U-boats had lain silently in wolf packs under the Gulf, waiting for the oil tankers that sailed from the Houston Ship Channel and the oil refineries in Baton Rouge. Four of them had been sunk by depth charges and were supposedly scudding along the Gulf's bottom, some of the crew members still aboard, their uniforms and empty eye sockets strung with seaweed. I wondered if their time in history was about to roll round again, like Pharaoh and his chariots laboring up on the shores of the Red Sea, determined that God's chosen would never get away from the points of their spears.

Chapter 23

THE LOCATION OF the office I maintained in downtown Houston was one I had chosen for reasons that had nothing to do with commerce. The building was in a seedy area off Congress Street and looked more like a structure you would find in the New Orleans French Quarter or Old Natchez than in a commercial center. It was made of stucco and crumbling brick and had a courtyard and an upstairs balcony with Spanish grillwork. More important, one wall in the courtyard contained a wall within a wall, one constructed of heavy stones that were out of context, rocks not from the coastal plains but perhaps from the bed of the Comal or Guadalupe River or the rough terrain of the Texas hill country. Regardless of their origins, the wall within a wall resembled a mosaic, the rocks held together more by their weight and their chiseled shape than by mortar and plaster. According to the legend, three Texas soldiers had been executed against this wall by Santa Ana's troops just before Santa Ana was entrapped, not far away, in the San Jacinto Basin on April 21, 1836.

These three soldiers, who in all probability were boys, may have lost their lives hours before Texas won its independence. A Mexican lady used to run a flower stall between two buildings on Congress Street, right next to Eddy Pearl's pawnshop, and once a week I bought a bouquet from her and put it in a ceramic vase filled with water and set it in front of the wall within a wall.

I had already gone to the Houston police station and had just gotten off the telephone with an assistant to the state attorney in Austin when Roy Wiseheart stuck his head in my office door and said, "Buy you lunch, Lieutenant?"

"Another time," I replied.

He stepped inside without being invited and closed the door behind him. He was dressed in a powder-blue sport coat and a polo shirt and pressed gray slacks and oxblood tasseled loafers, his face fresh and ruddy, as though he had just come from his gym. Roy had a perpetual aura of youthfulness that made me wonder if there wasn't a bit of Dorian Gray in his glue. "You mad at me about something?" he said, pulling up a chair.

"No. Why do you ask?"

"Because you look like it," he replied.

I told him of Slakely's visit to our house and what Rosita had done. Roy's face was composed while he listened, not one hair out of place, his eyes never blinking or leaving mine.

"You want me to look into it?" he said.

"In order to do what?"

"I don't know. Blitz the sod, as Jerry Fallon would say. Your troubles make mine sound minor."

"What troubles?"

He looked through the doorway into the side office where my secretary was working. I got up and closed the door. "What's the problem, Roy?" I said, barely able to hide my impatience.

"I'm co-producing Linda Gail's movie. Her husband showed up on the set down in Mexico. I think he's got the wrong idea."

"Regarding what?"

"I guess there're rumors going around about me and Linda Gail."

"The rumors aren't true?" I said.

"I suspect it's a matter of how you look at it. Things happen on a set. I can't say I've always stayed on the straight and narrow."

"What kind of statement is that?"

"I know Hershel's background. He comes from a place where they lynch Negroes and castrate people—that is, when the family isn't diddling one another. Do I need to start carrying a weapon?"

"I feel like knocking your teeth down your throat."

"I don't think that's a very rational attitude. I don't want trouble with your friend. And I certainly don't want to hurt him."

"What do you call ruining a man's marriage?"

He rested his forearm on the side of my desk and gazed wistfully out the window. "Did you spend a lot of time with your father when you were a kid?"

"No, I spent it with my grandfather. My father died at the bottom of a bell hole."

"I think the time spent with one's father figure makes all the difference in the life of a young fellow, don't you?"

"What kind of boyhood do you think Hershel Pine had? Can you imagine the kind of public school he attended, the kind of medical care he had?"

"Actually, I envy a fellow like that. You know, growing up on a cotton farm and squirrel hunting and going to barbecues and fish fries and outdoor dances, things like that. There's something a bit grand about it. Its simplicity, I mean."

I realized I was sitting next to a man who had probably lived inside a soap bubble his entire life and had no idea what privation was, and no awareness of the travail that people of Hershel's background endured.

"Does Linda Gail plan to leave Hershel?" I asked.

"I really don't know. That's their business anyway. Why should we be discussing something like that?"

"*Why?* Because he worships his wife. Because he's coming apart. Because he stayed alive from Kasserine Pass through the invasion of Italy and France to the Ardennes Forest so he could come back to her."

"I see what you mean. Yes, he seems a good fellow. That's why I'm asking for your help. Come on, have some raw oysters and a beer with me."

"Let me tell you how I feel about your father, Roy," I said. "No man is more cowardly than one who uses a surrogate to injure others. That's what your father has done. My wife and I go from day to day wondering who your father will send next into our lives. Right now it's Hubert Timmons Slakely. Tomorrow it will be somebody else."

Roy looked at me a long time before he spoke. "My father doesn't care enough about people to hurt them. Why do you think you're so special?"

"His company was responsible for my father's death."

"He could settle your suit for pocket change."

"I'm not planning on suing your father. I want to see him in prison."

He pinched his eyes with his thumb and forefinger. "In the state of Texas? What world do you live in, Weldon?"

"The United States of America."

"You still have those oil leases around New Roads, Louisiana, don't you?"

"We brought in two dusters on those leases. They almost bankrupted us," I said.

"But you still have the leases?"

"What if we do?"

"I'd hold on to them. Will you talk to Hershel?"

"No, I will not. It's time you carry your own water, partner."

"You have it all, Weldon, but you don't realize it. Others covet what you take for granted. You're an honorable man. Your wife loves you. You're the captain of your soul. With time, others will take all that away from you. That's what you fail to understand. They don't want your possessions. They want your soul."

"And how will they take that from me?"

"They'll turn you into one of them. You'll wake up one morning and look at your reflection in the mirror and wonder what happened to the little boy in his white First Communion suit. See you around, Buster Brown."

I followed him into the street. The sunlight was cold and brittle, with a reminder of winter and the shortening of the days in the air. Leaves were scudding out of the alley next to Eddy Pearl's pawnshop. The Mexican woman who ran the flower stall was gone. "Come back here," I said.

"Not a chance," he replied.

I went back into the office but couldn't think my way through the exchange. Roy had made a cuckold of my best friend but had presented himself to me as a victim. He seemed genuinely concerned with my fate but remained firmly entrenched in the world of wealth and power that threatened to destroy Rosita in order to get to me. Last, and perhaps most tragically for him, he was brave but beset with guilt because his ambition may have cost a life.

I went into the courtyard and poured out the stale water in the vase of flowers. It was green in the sunlight and had a rancid smell when it struck the flagstones. I had never felt more alone and helpless, even at the Ardennes. I leaned against the wall with one hand. The stones were hard and gritty and cold against my palm. As the wind gusted across the rooftops, I heard a sound that was like the staccato popping of small-arms fire when first contact is made between two armies. But the series of reports was only an automobile backfiring on the street. I was almost positive about that.

I KNEW WHAT WAS coming next, in the way you know the next pitch is a slider when a left-handed pitcher mops the sweat off his brow and wipes the back of his hand on his pants and not his palm. Saturday morning I got a person-to-person call from Linda Gail. I could barely make out her words. "We're having a terrible electrical storm here," she said. "Can you hear me?"

"Barely. Where are you?"

"In Santa Monica. The sky is black. Lightning is striking the cliffs above the beach. I've never seen the sky this dark here."

"What do you want, Linda Gail?"

"You'd better talk to Hershel. He's acting crazy."

"You're just becoming aware of that?"

"I'd appreciate it if you'd moralize on your own nickel. Why do you think I called you?"

"Roy Wiseheart was in my office yesterday and was probably more candid about you two than he should have been."

"Roy came to you?"

"I've had to put Rosita in hiding. She threw a pot of scalding tomatoes and peppers in a police officer's face. If you want to have a dalliance with Roy, that's your business, Linda Gail. But stop dragging your problems into my life."

"I didn't call you because of me. I called because I'm worried about *you*. God, you make me angry. Sometimes I want to break my fists on your head."

"Somebody sent Hershel a photograph?"

"Yes, exactly. Do you know who's in it?"

"If we're talking about the same photograph, I've already seen it. It's a fake. Or at least part of it is."

I could hear her breathing into the phone, even though thunder was booming in the background. "You're talking about me in the nude?"

"Yes, I am."

I expected her to say something vitriolic, to take on the mantle of outrage that she was extraordinarily good at. But there were facets to Linda Gail that sometimes surprised me. "I hate myself for this. It's all my fault, Weldon. It's not Roy's or Hershel's or yours. Do you know about Jack Valentine's death?"

"I read he was killed in South Central Los Angeles."

"He was killed after Roy told me someone should teach him a lesson."

"That's probably just rhetoric."

There was a violent intrusion of static on the line. Then she said in an almost plaintive voice, "Weldon?"

"Yes?"

"The lightning is hitting the water. I've never seen it do that. The ocean looks like it's full of black oil and electricity. There's green vapor rising off the waves. It looks like the world is ending."

"It's an optical illusion."

"Do you believe in karma?" she asked.

"If there was such a thing as karma, most of the world's leaders would have leprosy."

"It isn't funny," she said. "Do you think I'm a bad girl?"

I couldn't think of the right words to use. "No, I don't think that."

"I'm afraid," she said. "For all of us. Roy says we're wayfaring strangers, like the Canterbury Pilgrims trying to wend their way past the Black Death. He says death is the only reality in our lives."

"Roy is a nihilist."

"Say it again."

"Say what?"

"That I'm not a bad girl."

"Good luck to you. I think you're a formidable woman with qualities that you don't give yourself credit for. Don't let Hershel get hurt any more than he already has."

The line went dead.

I DROVE TO HERSHEL and Linda Gail's box of a house a few blocks off River Oaks Boulevard without calling first or knowing what to expect. It was hard for me to think of Hershel as a possible adversary, perhaps a dangerous one. But in light of how human frailty and jealousy affect us all, I knew if he had received the bogus photograph, anything was possible. As I drove down the boulevard past some of the grandest mansions in the Western world and turned onto Hershel's street and pulled into the deep shade of his driveway, I smelled an odor that was like wet leaves burning in a barrel, and water that had gone sour in a pond, and moist dirt oozing with white slugs spaded up in ground that never saw sunlight.

Hershel was bare-chested and pushing a shovel deep into the soil with one booted foot, his back knotted and red and sweaty and powdered with dirt. His shirt and leather jacket hung on the back of a wood chair. He had torn the flowers out of the beds and stripped the climbing roses and the trumpet vine from the trellises and smashed the trellises into sticks. He dropped the shovel on the grass and began ripping divots out of the St. Augustine grass with a mattock, destroying the root systems, driving the mattock deeper into sandy soil and rock and a metal sprinkler line. Hershel was waging war on the environment that Linda Gail had been willing to trade her marriage for.

"What are you planting, farmer?" I said.

He looked up at me like a primitive creature hard at work in front of his cave. There was a crooked grin on his face, a liquidity in his eyes that I normally would associate with yellow jaundice. The knees of his canvas trousers were green with grass stains. "I'm putting in a vegetable garden."

"It's December."

"I know. I kind of got carried away and tore up Linda Gail's roses. She flat loves those roses. I'm sorry I did that."

"It's mighty cold to be digging a vegetable garden."

"I'm late this year. That's why I'd better get on it."

Behind him was an aboveground swimming pool constructed of a pipe frame and sheets of blue plastic, a garden hose hung over the rim.

"Want to take a dip?"

"What's that smell?"

"Linda Gail says the neighbor's cat drowned in it. I don't believe it, though. Cats don't fall into pools. A coon or a porcupine might do that, but a cat is too smart."

"Can we talk?"

"I don't know if that's a good idea."

"I'm going to explain some things that have happened. Put down the mattock and let's go inside."

"I like it out here just fine."

His chest and shoulders and upper arms were hairless and smooth, his nipples as small as dimes. The temperature must have been fifty degrees, but sweat was leaking out of his hair and running down the sides of his face.

"Did somebody send you a photograph?" I said.

"They sure did."

"With me in it?"

"Looked like you."

"It's a fake."

"That's not Linda Gail in it?"

"Yes, that's Linda Gail, and that's me. But the photos were taken separately and the negatives manipulated in a darkroom."

The head of the mattock was resting by his foot, his palm propped on the handle's nub. He looked at the rose petals and torn trumpet vines scattered on the grass. He had no expression, as though all his motors had shut down.

"Forget everything I just said. Do you think I would betray our friendship? Look me in the face and tell me you believe I would have an affair with your wife and then come here and lie about it."

"No, sir, you wouldn't do that."

"So let's put an end to this."

"Who was with her when that photo was taken?"

"I think it was Jack Valentine. I think he got her drunk and took her to a motel the same day he filmed her on the gallery of that general store outside Bogalusa."

"She's been having an affair. Not with Jack Valentine. It's that damn Roy Wiseheart, isn't it?"

"It's not my business."

His face tilted up into mine. I could see the grainy lines around his eyes and smell the damp earth on his skin. "He confides in you like you're his lost brother or something. He's told you about Linda Gail, hasn't he?"

"I say let both of them go, Hershel."

"You'd give a thief the run of your house?"

"They'll come to a bad end. If that's their choice, you have to honor it."

"Linda Gail was the only girl I ever wanted."

There were any number of things I could have said to him, to no avail. Hershel Pine was one of those who went down with the decks awash and the guns blazing.

"Rosita scalded the face off the cop who molested her. Dalton Wiseheart is doing everything he can to destroy us, Hersh. Don't help him do it. I'm done here."

"Don't go," he called.

I ignored him and drove away. I didn't get far. There are certain kinds of currency you acquire in life. Most of it is ephemeral. But friendship and faith in the unseen world and the commitment to be true unto thine own self are the human glue that you never give up, not for any reason. I turned the car around and went back to Hershel's house. His garden tools lay amid the havoc he had visited on his lawn and flowerbeds, but he was nowhere in sight. A small boy from next door was staring through the hedge, his face full of alarm. "What's going on, little partner?" I said.

The boy was not over eight or nine. His mouth was shaking. He pointed at the wood chair where Hershel had hung his shirt and leather jacket. The jacket lay on the ground. "Mr. Pine had a gun," the boy said. Then he ran for his back door.

I tried to see through Hershel's windows, but the shades were drawn. I went to the front door and eased it open. Hershel was sitting on a footstool in front of a gas-log fireplace. The logs were not lit. His 1911-model .45 automatic was propped on his knee. I took it from his hand and released the magazine and ejected the round in the chamber. I sat down in a stuffed chair next to the stool and placed the gun on the coffee table. "We survived the Tigers. We saved Rosita from a death camp. Are you going to let a Houston oil tycoon do us in?"

There were lines of dried sweat and dirt on his face. "Maybe if I'd spent more time at home, this wouldn't have happened."

"That's like trying to figure out how you got hit by a bus. The only thing that counts is you got hit by a bus."

My attempt at humor was in vain. He started to cry, his head down, his back shaking, and his hands hanging in his lap. I waited a long time before I spoke. "I may need your help."

"Doing what?"

"Killing at least one man, maybe two," I replied.

I NEVER THOUGHT I would have a discussion about the premeditated, cold-blooded murder of another human being. Hershel listened as though a stranger rather than a friend and business partner had wandered into his living room. Even to me, the words I spoke seemed to come from someone else. As repellent as they were, I meant every one of them.

When I had visited the Houston Police Department the previous day, hoping to sit down with the chief and explain why Rosita had almost burned the face off one of his detectives, I was told by a captain that I could either bring her in or be charged with aiding and abetting. I didn't believe him. I had learned long ago from Grandfather that a serious lawman never told you what he might do. He simply did it, and usually with his sidearm or a baton or a blackjack; the target of his wrath seldom knew what hit him.

When I talked with an assistant to the state attorney, I got a much better perspective on the strategy about to be used on my beautiful and brave and loving wife.

"Her case is being turned over to the Department of Public Health, Mr. Holland," he said.

"It's being what?"

"You asked me to make an inquiry, sir. I've done that. This office no longer has any jurisdiction in the disposition of your wife's case. Neither does the district attorney's office in Houston."

"That sounds like quite a coincidence."

"Considering the seriousness of the charges against Mrs. Holland, perhaps y'all should show a little gratitude."

"You bastards," I said.

After I left Hershel's house, I used a pay phone to check in with Rosita at the motel in Galveston.

"Are you coming down?" she said.

"After dark," I replied.

"You sound a little strange."

"I just left Hershel. He's not doing too well. Someone sent him that bogus photo of me and Linda Gail."

"I really don't want to talk about that," she said.

"I'm telling you what happened."

"That doesn't mean I want to talk about it."

The air inside the phone booth had become hard to breathe. The sunlight through the scratched and vandalized Plexiglas windows was smudged and ugly, stained with the smell of the diesel trucks and junker cars passing on Wayside Drive. "They want to turn us against each other, Rosita."

There was a pause. "When are you coming to Galveston?"

"After dark," I repeated.

In my own country, we were taking on the identity of fugitives, people who thought and behaved in surreptitious fashion and traveled by night. Where had we gone wrong? What were we turning into? I picked up a box of takeout Mexican food for Grandfather and drove to our house in the Heights.

I KNOW I'M REPEATING myself, but it's hard to explain how much I loved Grandfather. In the darkest times of my life, wading ashore at Omaha Beach or shrinking into an embryonic ball at the bottom of a foxhole while German 88s rained down on us, I thought of Grandfather and said his name over and over in my mind. Even when I rebelled against him as a boy, he was always my model. And what a model he had been: a compulsive gambler and womanizing alcoholic who had knocked John Wesley Hardin out of the saddle and stomped in his face as an afterthought, a man who read the encyclopedia every night of his life, a gunman who feared bloodlust and was the friend of professional killers with badges who considered him a colleague but had no understanding of him.

I set the kitchen table for the two of us and laid out our dinner.

"Did you remember the pralines?" he said.

"Yes, sir, I got you a mess of them."

"Are you going down to Galveston tonight?"

"I surely am."

He bit into a taco, the shell cracking between his teeth, his washed-out blue eyes never leaving mine.

"Would you not stare at me, please?" I said.

"What's fretting you, Satch? It's not just Rosita's situation, is it?"

"I talked earlier with Hershel Pine about killing one or two people."

The winter solstice was almost upon us. The sunset was a purple melt beyond the live oaks in the yard, the Christmas lights in the neighbor's house flashing on and off. I couldn't look at Grandfather's face.

"Anybody I know?" he asked.

"Dalton Wiseheart, for openers. I thought I might throw in Hubert Timmons Slakely for good measure."

He placed his taco on his plate and cleaned the corner of his mouth with his thumb. "Did you learn that from me?"

"Learn what?"

"That it's all right to shoot an old man or maybe one you have to sneak up on."

"They're turning Rosita's case over to the Department of Public Health. You know what for, don't you?"

"It doesn't matter." He lifted his finger at me. "You killed German soldiers in war because you had to, not by choice. Don't you dare let these worthless people make you over in their image."

"You were fixing to drop the hammer on Slakely."

"I wanted to do it. But I didn't."

"I wish you'd parked one right in his mouth."

"The men you kill stand by your deathbed. Did you know that? I've seen them. They're out there. Waiting on me."

"They're going to take Rosita from me, Grandfather."

He looked into space, a great sadness in his eyes.

Chapter 24

THAT NIGHT, AS I drove down to Galveston Island, I could not free myself of images that seemed to have nothing to do with my situation. The moon was up, the clouds lit like silver plate, the sand dunes on the roadside spiked with salt grass. When I passed a lonely filling station, I thought I saw a boxlike vehicle with a lacquered black top and fenders and a maroon paint job on the body parked at the pumps. It had white sidewalls and chromed-wire wheels. I was almost sure it was the 1932 Chevrolet Confederate, the same model driven by Clyde Barrow and Bonnie Parker shortly before they were cut into pieces by automatic weapons fire in Arcadia, Louisiana. I thought I saw a man wearing a slug cap fueling the tank.

Almost fourteen years had passed since my encounter with them. Was I imagining things, a man my age? Or did I want their ghosts to pursue me? Did I secretly admire their cavalier attitude toward the law, their indifference to the lives they took? No, that was not the case. My fascination was not with *them;* it was with Bonnie Parker. Someone from the car spat on Grandfather, and I had always prayed that it was not she. It was the kind of thing Clyde might do, or Raymond Hamilton, or Mary, with her cleft chin and mean-spirited, downturned Irish mouth. Miss Bonnie wouldn't do that, I told myself.

They had been despised by the law. The four lawmen who went after them never intended for them to survive the trap they created with a broken-down truck on an isolated piney woods blacktop. What had always bothered me most in the aftermath of Bonnie and Clyde's death was the newspapers' failure to mention they had shot their way into Eastham Pen to honor their word and free a friend, with nothing to gain and everything to lose. How many law-abiding people would be willing to do the same?

The odds were stacking up against Rosita. Her immigration status had become suspect; her father had been an official in the leftist government of the Spanish Republic; she was related to Red Rosa Luxemburg; and she had assaulted a plainclothes detective. I had no doubt the referral of her case to Public Health was an attempt to circumvent the legal process and place her in a mental institution.

Where do you go for help under those circumstances?

That night Grandfather had our maid, Snowball, drive him to a pay phone from which he called me at the motel. "Your old commanding officer was here," he said. "He gave me a number in Houston for you to call."

"Lloyd Fincher was at the house?"

"That's the one."

"What's he after?"

"He says it's got something to do with Garth McQueen. Fincher wants to he'p you."

"What's your opinion of him?" I asked.

"I'd say he's a ladies' man."

"He had a woman with him?"

"She put me in mind of a Yorkshire pig that's been shampooed at the county fair—pink all over and fresh-smelling as a rose. She had a laugh just this side of an oink. You gonna be all right, boy?"

I DIDN'T WANT TO have contact with Lloyd Fincher, but I didn't have a lot to lose. I drove down the boulevard and called him from the pay phone at the Jack Tar restaurant. Through the front window, I could see the waves crashing on the beach, sucking the sand backward in the undertow. "My grandfather says you want to talk to me," I said.

"Holland? Is that you?" he replied.

Who else would I be? I thought. "Yes, sir, what can I do for you?"

"I don't want to talk over the phone. Know what I mean?"

"No, I don't."

"Tell me where you are. I'll be there."

"I'm down on the coast."

"The coast, huh? Ten miles north of Galveston, there's a Pure filling station on the east side of the highway. Meet me at the diner next door in one hour."

"What's this about, Major?"

"I guess I'm trying to undo my sins. Who the hell knows? Life's a bitch, isn't it?"

The Pure station was the one where I thought I'd seen the 1932 Chevrolet Confederate. Was it coincidence? I had no idea.

The station was dark, but the diner was open when I pulled into the shell parking lot. The only automobile out front was a prewar Cadillac; the bottoms of the fenders had rusted into orange lace. The interior of the diner was dour, the menu written in chalk on a blackboard above the stove, the air smelling of grease and disinfectant. Fincher and his girlfriend were at a wood booth in back. She was just as Grandfather had described her—pink-complexioned and rotund and jolly and drenched in perfume. Her hair was dark red and tied with a pink scarf. Fincher introduced her as Norma, no last name. They had white coffee mugs and a plate of French-fried onions in front of them. He saw me glance out the window at the Cadillac.

"I picked that up just recently. I'm restoring it," he said.

"I see," I said.

"I heard about your troubles," he said.

"They'll pass."

"That's what Garth McQueen thought when he built that damn hotel. He went into catastrophic debt so he could erect a monument to himself and leave behind the raggedy little boy who used to tote water in the oil field. Now he's teetering on ruin."

"You came down here to tell me about Garth McQueen?"

"Garth shouldn't be in the hotel business. He should be drilling wells. I thought you might want to partner up with him. Wildcatting may have gone into history, but he's still the best there is."

"I have a partner. And I have a couple of other things on my mind right now."

"Have you been swimming at his pool?" Norma said. "It's shaped like a big four-leaf clover. We saw a gangster there. What was his name? Frankie something. Lloyd knows him. He was a friend of Bugsy Siegel."

"Frankie Carbo," Lloyd said.

"It's getting late, Major," I said.

"I made a mistake at Kasserine Pass and got a lot of men killed. I'm trying to do good deeds here and there to make up for it." He pushed a brass key across the table to me. "I've got a duck-hunting camp down by the swamp, southeast of Beaumont. The place is yours. For whatever purposes you need. You hearing me on this?"

"Can you tell me who's trying to hurt me and my wife?" I said.

He pinched his eyes. "Hell if I know. It's like the army. Somebody up top gives an order, and it gets carried out by people they never see."

I picked up the key and dropped it in my shirt pocket. "Why do they have it in for me?"

Fincher leaned forward. "You really want to know?"

"That's why I asked you the question."

"It doesn't have anything to do with you. It keeps their minds off the fact that they have to die and all their money is worthless on the other side of the grave. They can buy anything they want except a free pass from the Grim Reaper. It makes them madder than hell."

Norma turned and looked at the side of Fincher's face as though she didn't know him.

LINDA GAIL'S COSTAR had contracted dysentery in Mexico and had sidelined production back in the United States for almost two weeks. In Santa Monica, she stared out her picture-glass window at the bronze-skinned young men lifting weights on Muscle Beach. Many of them had peroxide hair and wore bathing trunks hardly more than G-strings. She wondered how many of them were as unfaithful as she. Jerry Fallon sipped from a vodka Collins at her wet bar. Down below, against the brick wall that surrounded her tiny garden and patch of lawn, the bougainvillea bloomed as brightly as drops of blood in the cool sunlit air. "You're going back to Houston?" Jerry said.

"Does that bother you?" she replied.

He pulled a cherry out of the ice in his glass and bit it off the stem. His mouth made a sucking sound when he swallowed it. "Yes, it does, love."

"You think I'm escaping the menagerie?" she said, turning around.

"As talented as you are, you share many commonalities with the girls we dig out of these small-town anthills you Americans are so fond of. You do grand for a while, then you start to grow a conscience. You look upon your former life as one of naïveté and goodness. The rest of the world thinks of these places as the cultural equivalent of Buchenwald. That's why all of you left. You might remind yourself of that."

"You know how offensive that is, Jerry?"

"You had a fling and your hubby found out about it. What did he think happens out here? This is Babylon-by-the-Sea. On a spring night you can hear the hymens snapping like crickets. Are you going to dump your career and go back home and serve your redneck friends beer while they tell nigger jokes?"

"That word was never used in our home."

"I'm afraid you're about to leave us in the lurch, love. It's in your eyes. You want it both ways."

Why did Jerry always make her feel like a child? "I don't know what you're saying," she lied.

"Your lover is a handsome war hero and millionaire movie producer. Except you can't have him and still be the virginal lass from Hushpuppyville."

She sat down next to him. He started to drink from his glass, but she took it from his hand and replaced it on the bar. "You drink too much," she said.

"I hope you don't divorce. Because if you do, I'll probably marry you, and you'll make my life a bloody hell."

"Don't flatter yourself. What you told me on the set in Mexico? That was true?"

"About your ability? There's no question about it. Everybody knows it. That is, everybody except you. I'm going to speak a bit coarsely here. Every man in this town wants to go to bed with you because you're beautiful. But that's just part of it. They want your talent. That also goes for the ladies who are AC/DC. They're like candle moths swimming around the light in the bottle."

"Where does that put *you*?"

"I'll probably be an asterisk by your name. You're a temptation, though. I'd love to have a run at you."

"Why didn't you ever try?"

He stood up from the bar and put his arm around her shoulders. "Come over here," he said.

"What for?"

He walked with her to the picture-glass window. "See all those guys lifting weights down there? They want power and success that will never be theirs. They'll sleep with men or women to get it. Or maybe to have the crumbs from under the table. By the time they catch on that they've been had, it's usually too late. When you get fucked out here, it's for keeps. And when it's over, you hate yourself for ever thinking you were the one in charge."

"I don't understand," she said, her cheeks already burning.

"You never fucked somebody cross-eyed, all the time telling yourself you were in control? You never told yourself you had sexual power over others that they couldn't resist? Because the day you did is the day you not only got fucked in spades but helped the other person do it."

She went into the bathroom and locked the door and sat on the side of the tub, her sobs muffled behind her hand, unsure for whom she was crying.

ON THE NIGHT flight to Houston, the plane hit a violent electrical storm, one as intense and terrifying as the storm Linda Gail had witnessed off Santa Monica Beach. The windows of the plane were streaked with rain, the clouds erupting with great yellow pools of lightning, the thunder crashing so loudly that drink glasses were shattering in the stewardess's compartment. The plane was dropping with such rapidity through the air pockets that she couldn't hear the engines. But she kept writing on top of a book balanced on her knee, the beam of a small nightlight aimed at her sheet of stationery.

Once again she was putting down on paper the words she needed to say to Hershel. This time she was determined to hold nothing back and accept the consequences of her behavior, whatever they were, and to let Hershel decide whether he wanted her. She didn't mention Roy's name. She simply stated that she had been unfaithful and the fault was hers alone. If there was any lie in her words, it lay in her statement that she loved Hershel (though she did, it was not in the way a wife or lover would).

As the plane slammed against the updrafts, spilling luggage and hatboxes into the aisle, she wondered if she had underestimated the storm's potential. The plane's wing lights were blinking, the clouds streaming through the propellers like black smoke, making her wonder if her eyes were playing tricks on her or indeed the engines had caught fire. When a stewardess was knocked to her knees, none of the passengers was willing to unhook a seat belt in order to help her up. The door to the pilot's cabin was swinging wildly on the hinges, but there seemed to be no one available to secure it. She pulled the curtain on the window and kept writing and tried to suppress the fear that caused her hand to tremble each time she reached the edge of the page.

The great challenge was not in admitting wrongdoing; it was incurring the possible loss of her career. What if her betrayal caused Hershel to ask her to quit Warner Bros. or to leave Hollywood? As soon as she posed the question in those terms, her ego immediately flared to life, burning like an indignant white flame in her chest. *You earned your career,* a voice said. *Why should you have to give it away?* Was she supposed to be a penitent the rest of her life?

She felt her fountain pen leaking across her hand. She had forgotten what the variations in a plane's cabin pressure could do to the rubber bladder in a fountain pen. The ink left a dark blue stain in the shape of a monkey's paw on her white dress.

Down below she saw a break in the clouds and the lights of a city spread across a prairie as flat as a breadboard. The pilot came on the intercom and announced that the plane would be landing at Lubbock, and all the passengers would be placed in a hotel at the airline's expense until the storm passed.

Three hours later, as the dawn was breaking coldly in the east, Linda Gail called Hershel at home. There was no answer. She called three times, then at eight-thirty A.M. she called the office in Houston. The secretary said he had not come in. Nor was he at the office in Baton Rouge.

She called Roy Wiseheart at his home. "Oh, thank heavens," she said when he picked up.

"Linda Gail?" he said, his voice dropping into a whisper.

"We had to make an emergency landing in Lubbock. Will you go to my house and check on Hershel?"

"Me?"

"I have no one else I can depend upon."

"Call Weldon."

"I already did. He's no help. He's a stick in the mud on top of it."

"You shouldn't have called here."

"I'm worried about what Hershel might do. He has a gun."

"He's a grown man. He needs to be treated like one."

"You were both war heroes. He'll listen to you."

"Do you realize how inappropriate this is?"

"*Inappropriate?* I'm talking about somebody's life."

There was a silence. "Tell me what you want me to do."

"Go to the house. If he's not there, try to find out where he is. You have resources that other people don't. Do I have to explain this to you?"

"I've got to go now."

"Don't you dare hang up on me. I'll call back. I don't care who's there, either."

"I'll do what I can."

"I want your word."

"I promise."

"You don't know how much this means."

"Are we still on?"

"On for what?"

"*On*. What do you think I mean? We also have to talk about the picture. I spoke with Jerry Fallon twenty minutes ago. He wants us back in Los Angeles in five days. So does Jack Warner." There was another beat. "Are you there?"

"Call me after you check on Hershel."

"Did you hear what I said? Jack Warner wants us both in L.A."

"I don't care what he wants. Find Hershel."

"I'll take care of it," he said. "Linda Gail, I can't simply turn my feelings on and off. I feel sick when I can't see you."

"I'm sorry if I've hurt you," she said.

"It goes a little deeper than that."

"What? Into your glands?" she said. "Goes deeper into *what*? How many people have to get ruined before you understand there are other people on the planet?"

"I don't care about them. I care about you," he replied.

THE PLANE TOUCHED down in Houston at two that afternoon. Linda Gail took a cab to the house and was stunned when she stepped out on the sidewalk. Her flowerbeds had been destroyed, the roses and trumpet vine torn from the trellises, holes chopped in the side lawn, dirt piled on the St. Augustine grass like strings of anthills. A plastic bag that had contained processed cow manure was impaled to the ground by the point of a mattock, the plastic rattling in the wind.

"You want me to carry your bags in, ma'am?" the cabbie asked.

"What?" she said.

"Your bags. You want them inside?"

"Leave them on the porch," she said.

"What porch you mean?"

"The *front* porch, the only porch. We don't have another porch," she said.

"Yes, ma'am," he said, laboring with her two bags to the concrete bib around the single step that led into the living room.

She took her house key from her purse but didn't insert it in the lock. Her Cadillac was parked in the porte cochere. A curtain rod on the front window was broken, the curtain sagging in the middle.

"Is everything okay here, ma'am?" the cabbie said.

"Yes, thank you," she said. "Why do you ask?"

"You look a little bothered, ma'am. Is there somebody inside you're worried about? I'm asking if you want a cop."

"No. You're very thoughtful. I'm a little tired. Long plane trip."

"You're a movie star. I saw your picture in *The Houston Post*."

"That's nice. I appreciate it," she said.

"Could I have an autograph? It's for my daughter."

"I'd be honored. What's her name?" she said, taking a piece of stationery and her damaged fountain pen from her purse.

After he was gone, she opened the door and looked at the living room. There was nothing out of place other than the curtain. She walked into the kitchen and the dining room and onto the sun porch. Everything was clean, intact, in its proper place. Then she went into the bedroom. The curtains were closed. When she clicked on the light, nothing seemed out of the ordinary. The ambiance of frilly rayon and puffy quilts and pink and silver and pale blue was as she had left it. Then she saw the marriage photo of her and Hershel in front of the Assemblies of God church in Cottonport, Louisiana. She had been wearing a white suit, a corsage on her shoulder; Hershel had been wearing his uniform, his new chevrons on his sleeve, his ribbons pinned to his chest. They were smiling into the camera, their hands joined. Except Hershel was no longer in the picture. The photo had been scissored in half, and now only Linda Gail remained inside the frame, her hands cut away just behind the knuckles.

The photos in their scrapbook, which had a velvet cover and a glossy plastic heart glued on it, had been altered in the same fashion. Each photo left Linda Gail by herself, sometimes smiling at someone who was no longer there.

She opened the top drawer of her dresser, where she kept a piece of framed ceramic that contained her handprint and Hershel's side by side, the only souvenir she brought back from their honeymoon in Biloxi. The ceramic had been broken neatly in half, all dust and fine particles and rough edges wiped clean. Her handprint had been refitted in the frame and Hershel's removed.

As she closed the drawer, she felt a level of loss and abandonment she hadn't thought possible.

She went back in the living room and sat down in a deep chair and called Roy Wiseheart at home. A woman answered.

"May I speak to Roy, please?" Linda Gail said.

"He's next door. Who's calling, please?"

"This is Linda Gail, Mrs. Wiseheart. I need to talk to Roy. Can you ask him to call me at home?"

"Regarding what, please?"

"I understand that Mr. Warner wants both of us back in Los Angeles. I don't know if I will be able to do that."

"Why don't you contact Mr. Warner and tell him that?"

"Would you deliver the message for me, please?"

"I certainly will. You must come see us more often. I hear so many wonderful things about you. How is your husband? I bet you two are having a jolly time with all your success. I have to admire your composure when you call here. Your gall is like none I've ever encountered."

After Linda Gail hung up, the side of her face felt as though it had been stung by a wasp.

SHE BRUSHED HER teeth and showered and put on fresh clothes and drove to Roy Wiseheart's house at the other end of River Oaks, where the homes were monumental and as ornate and brightly lit as antebellum riverboats, the moss-hung live oaks so stately and dark and mysterious that she wondered if any of the people living here were made up of the same blood and tissue and bone as she. In comparison, the homes of the plantation oligarchy in Louisiana seemed like worm-eaten facsimiles. She found that thought a bit consoling.

Clara Wiseheart had said Roy was next door. But which house? The sky was almost dark, the stars sparkling in the east. The house south of the Wisehearts' was lit only by carriage lamps. The one on the north was another matter. Through the French doors, she could see a Christmas tree that towered to the ceiling, its boughs ringing with tinsel and strings of colored lights that winked on and off. Out back, two men were playing tennis on a red clay court, whocking the ball back and forth in the cold air, their thick white sweaters buttoned to the chin, like early-twentieth-century college boys.

She knew one of them had to be Roy. Who else would play outdoor tennis at night in winter? Who else would wear long pants on the court, as though the year were 1920? Who else would try to insulate himself from his loveless marriage by turning profligacy and self-indulgence into a religion?

She had to admit she was drawn to his boyish immaturity, and the fact that in bed he could be sweet and caring. His reverential attitude toward her beauty and the way he touched her body and did everything she secretly wanted were confessions of his need and his adoration. These were things that shouldn't be taken lightly.

She could not allow herself these kinds of thoughts. She had made a resolution on the plane during the electrical storm, and she had to keep it and not think in a self-centered manner. She had called Roy profligate, but she knew that deep down inside Linda Gail Pine, there was a sybarite always thinking about one more bite of forbidden fruit.

She parked her car by the carriage house and opened the chain-link door to the court and stepped out on its hard-packed surface. Roy turned around and grinned broadly in surprise, his face hot and sweaty under the lights. She felt her heart quickening, the way it had at high school dances years ago when a boy visiting from Baton Rouge or Vicksburg caught sight of her and was obviously smitten by her looks. Then Roy refocused his attention on the game. His opponent threw the ball in the air and served it like a white rocket across the net. Roy backhanded the ball up the line, then charged the net before his opponent could recover, slashing the weak lob diagonally across the court.

"Got you!" Roy said. "Be back in a jiff." He walked toward Linda Gail, blotting his forehead with his sleeve. "What are you doing here, you lovely thing?"

"Wondering why you didn't call me. Wondering if you saw Hershel."

"I thought that might be it. Let's go in my friend's pool house. I need a drink. How'd you know where I was?"

"Your wife told me."

"You called Clara?"

"No, I called you. She answered. She mocked me."

"In an earlier incarnation, she likely ran a torture chamber for the Inquisition."

He opened the door to the pool house and let her walk in front of him, then pulled off his sweater and dropped it on the bar. His T-shirt was soaked, his arms shiny with sweat. The room was outfitted with a billiard table, a refrigerator, a rack of cue sticks on the wall, and a felt poker table with mahogany trim and leather pockets for chips. He sat down in a deep cloth-covered chair and crossed one leg on his knee. "Can you fix us a Scotch and soda? I'm running on the rims. You picked up some tan in Santa Monica. You look stunning."

"Did you see Hershel?"

"I banged on the front and back doors and looked through the windows. No one was there. I went back later and tried again. I talked to a neighbor who said he thought Hershel was out of town."

"When did you do all this?"

"This morning and at lunchtime."

"That's it?"

"What else was I supposed to do?"

She didn't have an answer. "Thanks for doing what you could. I don't know where he could have gone."

"Maybe to visit his family. These things always pass."

"These things?"

"Don't start. I didn't mean anything by it."

"Hershel isn't one to disappear without saying anything. Why didn't he tell Weldon or somebody at the office?"

"Maybe he did. Anyway, you've done your best. Time we talk about other things, namely ourselves. You know how I feel."

"Does your friend want a drink?"

"Don't shut me out like this, Linda Gail."

"I asked if your friend wanted a drink."

"No, he needs to sulk awhile. He does that every time I beat him. He was the clandestine Jew in our fraternity. I was the only fellow who knew he was Jewish. He's extra-sensitive, particularly when I hammer him on the court."

"Why would you want to belong to a fraternity made up of people like that?"

"All of the fraternities were like that. They still are. In Louisiana, a lot of Negroes attended your school and church?"

"None of us had choices about where we went. You did."

"How about that drink?"

She filled a tumbler with ice and three fingers of Scotch, then squirted soda into it and wrapped a paper napkin around it and handed it to him.

"You're not joining me?" he said.

"I have to find Hershel."

He leaned forward in the chair and circled her wrist with his thumb and forefinger. His grip felt like a wet manacle. "Stay. Please. I'll shower and change clothes, and we can go to a restaurant for dinner. There's so much to talk about. Everyone is excited about the picture. There are so many wonderful things waiting for you. I want to be there when those things happen, to help you, to be your friend in any capacity you wish."

"I betrayed Hershel and I seduced you," she replied. "Believe me, I'm not worth your concern."

"Give me a little credit. I don't get seduced," he said. "When you all got married, Hershel was a mature man and a combat veteran. You were sixteen and knew nothing of the world. You call that a level playing field? I doubt Hershel would."

"I'm not your intellectual match. Thank you for going by the house. I'll be seeing you on location, I guess."

He put his drink down on the floor and stood up. "Are you saying good-bye?"

"I don't know. Do you want to divorce your wife? Do you want to marry me and start spending the holidays with my relatives in Bogalusa? Would your father and his friends approve of me? Would your father have my Jewish agent in his house? Would he like Rosita?"

"I'd do anything for you."

"I think you probably would. You're quite a guy, Roy. The problem is, I've never figured out who you are. Maybe your wife has and sees a kindred spirit in you. That thought frightens me to death."

She went out the door and began walking toward her automobile. She heard the chain-link door on the tennis court swing open behind her. "Miss Pine?" a voice said.

"Yes?" she said, turning around.

"I'm Bill Green. I've always wanted to meet you," Roy's tennis partner said. His hair was as black and shiny as a raven's, his face fine-boned. "Wiseheart and I are old friends."

"He told me. You were fraternity brothers."

"That's why I have to teach the bum a lesson on the tennis court sometimes. He's a fierce competitor. I let him have that last point because you were watching."

"I see. It was nice meeting you, Mr. Green."

"You have to go?"

"Yes, I'm afraid so."

"Maybe Roy will go home, too. He's been here since this morning. I think he and Clara have had some choppy sailing recently."

"He's been here all day?"

"Yes, he's been a nuisance. He does this when he and Clara get into it."

"He hasn't gone anywhere else?"

"No, he's either been playing billiards or trying to hand me my posterior across the net."

"Mr. Green, this is very important. Did Roy talk to anyone today? Did he make a call inquiring about my husband?"

"I heard him call a policeman. That's not unusual for Roy. He's an honorary police officer. He likes to ride around in cruisers and that sort of thing."

"What did he say to the policeman?"

"Something about doing Roy a favor. I wasn't paying much attention."

"You've been very kind. Good night, Mr. Green."

Green glanced up at the sky. "There's a ring around the moon. We'll have rain. You know what they say about Texas. If you don't like the weather, wait five minutes."

"It was Missouri," she said.

"Pardon?"

"Mark Twain said that about Missouri, not Texas. It's funny how people get a quotation wrong, and then the misquote takes on a life of its own. It's a bit like most relationships. We never get it quite right. The fabrication becomes the reality."

Green nodded as though he understood. She walked away from the light that glowed through the windscreens on the court and crossed the lawn, the St. Augustine grass spongy and thick under her feet, the shadows of the camellia bushes and live oaks swirling and dancing around her. Her face felt cold and small, the skin shrunk against the bone. For just a second she thought she heard the mocking voice of Clara Wiseheart laughing inside her head.

Chapter 25

I HAD NO IDEA where Hershel had gone. I felt guilty for having spoken with him about the possibility of shooting Dalton Wiseheart or Hubert Slakely. My sentiments about Wiseheart and Slakely were genuine, but whether I would shoot a man in cold blood was a matter of conjecture. In part, I had confided in Hershel to get his mind off Linda Gail's infidelity. Just the same I felt irresponsible, and Grandfather hadn't helped matters by taking me to task for my careless words.

Maybe I had begun to see the world through a glass darkly. I tried to remind myself that even as a teenager I had seen goodness in Bonnie Parker and an appreciable degree of heroism in Clyde. Even Lloyd Fincher, upon learning of Rosita's jeopardy, had given me the key and directions to his duck camp southeast of Beaumont.

Besides my growing cynicism about the world, I had another problem: I had a business to run. In my low moments, I needed to remember what Rosita and I and Hershel and Linda Gail had accomplished. The Dixie Belle Pipeline Company was a huge success. We had contracts all over Oklahoma, Texas, and the Gulf of Mexico. Our welds were known as the best in the oil patch. When we dropped the pipe into the ground, chances were it would lie there a century without a crack forming in the joints. On top of that, we had the patent on the machines responsible for the welds' longevity.

I wouldn't try to go inside the head of a dictatorial anti-Semite like Dalton Wiseheart, but I suspected he considered us usurpers, the kind of irritant he normally bought or neutralized with no more than a five-second commitment of time. That his minions had to deal with us on our terms, after I had indicated to him that his company's negligence may have caused my father's death, was probably a bitter cup for him to swallow. Even worse, he probably couldn't stand the thought of the country becoming a Jeffersonian democracy.

Rosita and I checked out of the motel in Galveston and went to one of our job sites in Louisiana, right outside of Morgan City. I no longer thought about the particulars of our problems with the law. I believed Dalton Wiseheart's people had written the script, and there was little Rosita and I could do to change it. Cancer and lightning go where they want. So does political corruption. For me, there was one operative principle to remember: They were not going to lock up my wife again. If I had to shoot Dalton Wiseheart or Hubert Timmons Slakely, I would. In the meantime, my company couldn't run itself.

In the years immediately following the war, Hollywood and the drilling industry were probably the only two portals through which a believer in the American dream could wander and suddenly find himself among amounts of wealth and levels of power he never imagined. The prerequisites were few. A teenager who escaped a chain gang in Georgia and climbed off a boxcar in California to pick peaches later became the actor we know as Robert Mitchum. A gambler and occasional wildcatter who drew to an inside straight in a Texas poker game won a deed to a seemingly worthless piece of land that became the biggest oil strike in the United States since Spindletop. The success stories were legion. All you had to do was believe. It was like prayer. What was to lose?

I loved the work I did and took pride in it. I loved the smell of a swamp or a pine woods at sunrise. I tried not to think of myself as someone who was despoiling the environment. When we laid pipe through woods, we cleaned and reseeded the right-of-way and created a feeding area for wildlife and a firebreak and access road for firefighting vehicles. The wetlands were another matter. Nonetheless, we broke the plantation oligarchy's hold on working people, often paid no more than twenty-five dollars for a six-day week.

I wrote these words in my journal our first night back in the motor court outside Morgan City: *Dear Lord, I've been out of touch for a little while. Sorry for all my rhetoric about shooting people, even though I think some of them deserve it. Take care of Hershel, would you, and please help me take care of Rosita. As always, I pray that my sacrifice is acceptable in your sight. In truth, I feel powerless; hence I entertain all these violent thoughts and feelings.*

Christmas is three days away. Happy birthday in advance, in case I don't have time to say it later.

That night I began rereading *Le Morte d'Arthur.* For either a man or a boy, it was a grand and romantic tale about the chivalric world, the jingle of chain mail and the crash of two-handed broadswords on armor and shields rising audibly off the page. The irony lay in the fact that its author, Thomas Malory, had been a professional thug and full-time lowlife, more specifically a thief, a spy, an extorter, a rapist, and an assassin. He not only broke the law at every opportunity but did so with great joy. Apparently, the only times he was not committing serious crimes were when he was in prison or fighting as a mercenary in France or writing the greatest romance since *The Song of Roland*.

How could a man who was probably a sociopath draw on symbols from the subconscious and use Celtic legends with such passion and iconic meaning and artistic cohesiveness? Why was such an unlikely person chosen for such a gift?

It was not really Thomas Malory who was on my mind. Bonnie Parker and Clyde Barrow were. They were poor and uneducated and never succeeded in stealing over two or three thousand dollars in a bank robbery. John Dillinger once called them "a pair of punks who are giving bank robbery a bad name." Like Woody Guthrie's migrant farmworkers, they had come with the dust and gone with the wind. Why did they continue to intrigue and fascinate us? Was it because we secretly envied their freedom? Or was it because they got even for the rest of us?

I had confessed my feelings of powerlessness in my journal. There was a paradox in my confession. My epiphany about my lack of power in dealing with the system had come to me in peacetime, not during the war. At Normandy and at the Ardennes Forest, I had felt empowered, not the other way around. I could kill my enemies at will. If I so chose, I could destroy myself inside a firestorm, perhaps saving the life of another. I lived under the stars and in the snow and in windblown forests like a druid hunting animals with a sharpened stick. I lived one cold, foggy breath away from the edges of eternity; the trappings of civilization meant no more to me than stage props.

I had fallen asleep with my book in my hand. I heard Rosita click off the light and gently set my book on the nightstand. She lay down next to me and curled her body into mine, her arm resting on my side, her breath rising and falling on my neck. I didn't wake until I heard hundreds of geese honking in the early dawn.

I WENT OUTSIDE WITH a cup of coffee and stood in the midst of a fog that was so thick I felt as though I were standing inside a cloud. No, the sensation was more compelling than that. I felt as though I were not in Louisiana but on the mythic Celtic island of Avalon, at the beginning of time, when man first looked up through the trees and saw light shining from the heavens and thought that he was standing in a cathedral whose pillars were the tree trunks that surrounded him.

In another hour I would be out on the right-of-way, where the men I had hired would pull the welding hood over their faces and bend to their work, the welding hood shaped exactly like the helmet of a crusader knight, each man thickly gloved to the elbow, one knee anchored on the ground, as though all of them were genuflecting in preparation for battle.

Those were fine thoughts to have. The Arthurian legend and the search for the Grail are always with us and define who we want to be. But the chivalric stories of Arthur and Roland are hard to hold on to, and we're dragged back into the ebb and flow of a world that celebrates mediocrity, wherein the forces governing our lives remain unknown and beyond our ken.

I heard the phone ring inside our room. It was Linda Gail. "Roy

Wiseheart lied to me. He told me he went to our house to check on Hershel but couldn't find him."

"How do you know he lied?" I asked.

"Roy's neighbor told me Roy was playing tennis with him all day. He didn't go anywhere."

"You're calling me in Louisiana to tell me Roy lied to you?"

"Roy's friend said he called a policeman. I thought maybe Roy sent this policeman out to the house because he didn't want to be bothered."

"Maybe he felt uncomfortable," I said. "Maybe he was afraid. I'm not sure what Hershel might do."

"Will you let me finish? I talked to our neighbor across the street. He's a nice man. He asked Hershel to go fishing once. He said the cops asked if he thought Hershel was suicidal."

"That's why we're all concerned, Linda Gail. Maybe the cops are trying to help."

"The neighbor told the cops Hershel likes to drink sometimes at an icehouse on West Alabama, back in our old neighborhood."

"What about it?" I said.

"The owner told me Hershel's truck was there, but a wrecker towed it away. He doesn't know what happened to Hershel; he said he'd been drinking a lot."

I had been standing. I sat down in a chair by the writing table. The receiver felt warm against my ear. I saw Rosita looking at me. "He disappeared?"

"The two cops who came out to the house were plainclothes. One of them left his card with the neighbor. Here, I'm looking at the card now. His name is Hubert T. Slakely. Does that name mean anything?"

IT WAS DARK and cold when Hershel took his bottle of Jax outside the icehouse and sat down at one of the plank tables under the canvas canopy. He was wearing his beat-up leather jacket and a cloth cap, but neither seemed to keep the cold off his skin. He felt as though his metabolism had shut down and his body was no longer capable of producing heat, not even after four shots of whiskey straight up.

Maybe it was just the weather, he told himself. It was too cold for the other patrons, who were inside by the electric heater, playing the shuffleboard machine and talking about Harry Truman integrating the United States Army. Hershel salted his beer and took a sip from the glass and listened to the wind swelling the canopy above his head.

Three blocks away he could see the red and yellow neon on the spire of the Alabama Theatre printed against the sky. This was a fine neighborhood in which to live, he thought. The houses were mostly brick bungalows built in the 1920s, the streets shaded by old trees. The buses to downtown ran every ten minutes and cost a nickel. The local grocery store sold its produce out of crates on the gallery, and the customers signed for their purchases and paid at the end of the month. Why did they have to move to River Oaks, where they didn't belong? Why did Linda Gail have to discover Hollywood? Why did Roy Wiseheart have to come into their lives?

For the most part, he had been able to put aside the war and the things he had done and seen others do. Sometimes in his sleep, he heard the treads of a King Tiger clanking through the forest, the rounds of his Thompson flattening or sparking off its impervious plates, but he always managed to wake himself up before the worst part of the dream, the moment that left him shivering and hardly able to control his sphincter, a moment when seventy tons of steel tried to grind him into pulp inside his cocoon of ice and broken timbers and frozen earth.

A black man was cleaning cigarette butts and food wrappers and pieces of newspaper from under the tables with a push broom. His eyes were elongated, almost slits, and the peaked hat with earflaps that he wore tied under the chin gave his face the appearance of a sad football.

"Where you from?" Hershel asked.

"Mis'sippi, suh," the man said.

"You like it here'bouts?"

"Yes, suh, I like it fine."

Hershel shook a Camel loose from a pack and stuck it in his

mouth. He watched the black man and didn't light the cigarette. "What do you think about the president integrating the armed forces?"

"I don't study on it, suh."

"You don't have an opinion? None? Is that correct? You're a man of color living in a segregated society, but you don't have an opinion about integration?"

"It ain't nothing I have control over."

"You want a smoke?"

"Thank you. I'm not supposed to light up on the job."

"I figure if a man has fought for his country, he should have the same rights as any other man," Hershel said.

The black man raised his eyes long enough to glance at the men inside the icehouse. "Yes, suh, that would make sense."

"What's your name?"

"Lawrence."

"A colored washwoman saved my life. She was a juju woman. I was wrapped up in a rubber sheet. If she hadn't looked through the window and seen me, I wouldn't be here today."

"I got to get on it, suh."

"Can I ask you a personal question?"

"Yes, suh, that would be fine."

"Did your wife ever mess around on you?"

"I ain't ever been married. I thought about it, though. There's a lady at the church I go out wit'."

Hershel lit his cigarette. The smoke rose from his mouth as white as a cotton bole. What had he been talking about? The subject seemed to have dissolved into thin air. His head began to droop, his concentration to fade. "Sorry, I feel like I got malaria. Except I don't. I guess I better go home."

"Suh, there's two men yonder in that car. They been looking at you. Maybe you shouldn't be driving nowhere right now."

"Which men?"

"They got suits and hats on. One of them comes in here. He's a bad white man."

"Say that again."

"I didn't mean nothing by it. I just didn't want to see you have no trouble."

"When a colored person says a white man is bad, he's pretty bad. Have I got it right?"

"I ain't saying no more."

When he stood up, Hershel had to steady himself with the tips of his fingers on the tabletop. "I hope you marry the church lady. I bet she'll do right by you."

"That's your truck on the street?"

"That's it. Give me your arm, will you?"

"Suh, don't do this."

"You know how to count cadence? Tell you what. I'll count it and you march it, and the two of us will get me over to the truck."

Lawrence backed away, shaking his head, his eyes on the ground, his hands clenched on the broom handle. "Suh, I need this job. I cain't be getting in other people's business."

"I cain't blame you," Hershel said. "Take care."

"You, too, suh."

Hershel walked past the soda cooler and the ice chute into the darkness. There seemed to be bottle caps everywhere, crunching like glass under his feet. The sensation reminded him of walking barefoot as a boy on a gravel road in rural Louisiana, when his father worked all day for a dollar-and-a-half WPA grocery order.

The wind was colder, blowing through the trees on the unlit street where his truck was parked in the shadows. Behind him, he heard Lawrence stacking crates and pushing the broom along the concrete walkway by the side of the icehouse. An unmarked prewar Ford was parked by a fire hydrant, its hood pointed toward West Alabama, giving the occupants a clear view of the icehouse, the plank tables under the canopy, and Hershel's truck. When Hershel stepped off the curb, he felt as though he had set his foot down on the deck of a ship just after it had pitched into a trough. He heard both doors of the Ford squeak open and two men get out on the asphalt. He removed his truck keys from the pocket of his leather jacket and opened the truck and dropped the keys on the back floor. When he turned around, he was facing the two men, who wore suits and hats with wilted felt brims.

"I was fixing to take a nap, not drive," he said.

One man was duck-footed and had short, thick legs and a chest like an upended beer keg. The other man was tall and lean all over, his posture as stiff as a coat hanger. "I'm Detective Hubert Slakely, Houston PD," he said. "Are you carrying a firearm?"

"I own one. It's at my house. So I cain't say as I'm carrying it."

"Your name is Hershel Pine?"

"Yes, sir, it is. I'm not aiming to drive this truck anywhere, if that's the issue."

"There's a report you're suicidal."

"I don't figure I'm worth shooting. So why would I want to waste money buying a bullet to shoot a person I consider worthless?"

The detective took off his hat and drew a comb through his hair. The moon was shining through the live oak over the street. Hershel could see a peculiar luminosity in the detective's eyes, one he had seen in the eyes of Klansmen and redneck sheriff's deputies and gunbulls who worked in Angola and cashed their checks at Margaret's whorehouse in Opelousas. All of them sought a badge, a flag, a banner; it didn't matter what kind. Their enemy was the human race.

The detective clipped his comb inside his shirt pocket and replaced his hat on his head. "Would you mind putting your hands on the side of the vehicle?"

"I'm too tired. I think I need my nap now."

"It beats a night in jail."

"I cain't say. I've never been in a jail. I know you, don't I? Or at least your name."

"Lean against the truck and spread your feet."

"I not only know who you are, I know why you're here and who you work for," Hershel said. He could feel a fish bone in his throat. He coughed and started over. "Your name gets around. You're the one who arrested Rosita Holland."

"Now I'm arresting you." Slakely removed a pair of handcuffs from a leather pouch on his belt. "Turn around, please."

"If my father was here, he'd tell y'all to kiss his butt. Or he might give you a whipping. I ain't going to no damn jail. The man who thinks he can put me there had better—"

That was as far as he got. The blackjack had been handmade by a convict and was tapered like a darning sock, the lead ball on the heavy end wrapped in rawhide, the lower end mounted on a spring and wood handle that doubled the velocity of the blow. Hershel bounced off the side of the truck and struck the concrete on his face. Slakely leaned over and beat him in the back and shoulders as though breaking up ice in a washtub. Then he began kicking Hershel with the point of his shoe, holding on to the truck for purchase, kicking every exposed place on his body he could target.

"Captains," said the black man named Lawrence. "He's just drunk. He didn't mean no harm."

Slakely turned around. "You better get out of here, Sambo."

"Yes, suh."

"You tell anybody about what you saw here, we'll be back."

"Yes, suh, I know that."

"Glad we agree."

For seconds or perhaps minutes, the only sound Hershel could hear was the wind in the oak limbs and the easy drift and sweep of leaves across the asphalt. The voices of the two police officers sounded as though they were resonating off the walls of a well that had no bottom.

"Is he—?"

"No, he's all right. When you cain't see the blood is when you got a problem."

"You kind of lost control, Hubert. Jesus Christ."

"He was resisting. He had it coming. There's no problem here."

"Want me to call it in?"

"Maybe he learned his lesson. Can you hear me, Pine? Did you learn something tonight?"

"The guy's a mess, Hubert. I think we've got a problem."

"You got a point. He'p me lift him up."

"What are we doing?"

"Cleaning up the street."

Hershel landed hard in the trunk of the prewar Ford. His head was jammed against the spare tire, his knees against a box of tools, his face half buried by a tarp stiff with paint. For an instant he saw Slakely staring down at him, his hand balanced on the open hatch.

Don't do it, he thought he heard himself say. *Please.*

The hatch slammed down an inch from Hershel's face, the stars in the sky gone in a wink.

Roy Wiseheart called Linda Gail early in the morning, before the sun was up. The receiver felt cold against her ear. She stared through the back window at the blueness of the dawn and the bareness of a tree that was wet and gnarled and looked scraped of leaves. She wanted to be back in California, wrapped inside the fog that rolled off the ocean on mornings like these.

"Jack called late last night. He wants me at a meeting in the morning," Roy said.

"Jack who?"

"Jack Warner. Who else would I be talking about?"

"I don't know. Maybe Jack Valentine. Except he's dead, isn't he? Killed in South Central L.A."

There was a beat. "I'd like to see you before I go."

"You want to see me? After you lied?"

"Lied about what?"

"You said you checked on Hershel. Your friend Mr. Green said you never left his house, that you were playing tennis all day."

"It's fifteen minutes to your house from mine. Green was on a business call for almost an hour. It was about noon. I'd gone over to your house already, but I went a second time. I also called the police. Why do you always think the worst of me, Linda Gail?"

"Because I don't know what to believe. Never. Not on one occasion."

"Believe that I love you. Let's have breakfast and talk. I don't want to fly out of here and leave things in the state they're in. You're going to drive me to the grave. That's not an exaggeration."

"Roy, you have to let me alone. I can't think straight."

"That's why I want to be with you. We'll face these things together."

"You know what bothers me most, Roy? You know what bothers me right now, more than anything else in the world?"

"I have no idea."

"You haven't asked about Hershel," she replied. "Not once. He could be dead or out working on his truck. You didn't ask or show the least curiosity. How do you explain that?"

TWENTY MINUTES LATER, the phone rang again. "Hershel?" she said.

"No, my name is Albert," a man's voice said. "I help out at the relief center here. Who's this?"

"I think you have the wrong number."

"You said Hershel. That's the name of the man I'm calling for. Hershel Pine. I got your number out of his wallet."

"I can't understand what you're saying. Don't hang up. Please. Are you saying you found my husband's wallet?"

"I found *him*. He was inside some cardboard boxes behind the center. He looks like somebody beat him up. I thought maybe he wandered in from the highway."

"How bad is he hurt?"

"The way people get hurt in a fight."

"Can you put him on the phone?"

"He's sleeping now. It got pretty cold last night. His teeth were clicking. I covered him up on a cot."

"What are his injuries? Please tell me. My husband doesn't get in fights. How bad is it?"

"There was a pint of wine in the pocket of his jacket. It was broken. I don't think it cut him. Lady, this neighborhood is mostly colored. Ask yourself why he was down here, because I don't know. He's no stew-bum. That's why I called. I think somebody put the boots to him and dumped him here."

She followed his directions to a rural neighborhood on the two-lane highway to Galveston, a neighborhood with dirt streets and shotgun and paintless frame houses that had peaked tin roofs and neat yards and coffee cans planted with flowers on the galleries. It reminded her of the sugarcane and rice-mill towns of southern

Louisiana, trapped between the softly focused culture of the agrarian South and the petrochemical industries that chained the Gulf Coast. She pulled up to a clapboard church set among cedar and pine trees and parked in back by a rain ditch. The man named Albert helped her put Hershel in her car. Albert was dressed in an off-color, ill-fitting suit and unshined dress shoes with white socks; his hair looked like paint poured on a rock.

"You're a minister?" she asked.

"No, just a drunk trying to get well. Fine car," he said.

"I want to make a donation to your church," she said.

"You can if you want. You don't have to. Can I tell you something, lady?"

"Yes."

"You shouldn't cry. He's gonna be all right."

"No, he's not. But you've been very kind." She opened her purse and took out a fifty-dollar bill. "Take this. Don't argue."

"Ma'am, if you're in some kind of trouble, maybe you should call the police. I don't like to see you drive out of here crying like that. You could have an accident. Let me call the cops for you. They'll know what to do."

Chapter 26

CHRISTMAS MORNING I received a person-to-person call at the motor court outside Morgan City. I heard the operator tell the caller to deposit two dollars in coins. "Weldon?" Linda Gail's voice said.

"What's happened?" I said, fearing the worst.

She told me everything she knew about the beating Hershel had taken, then had to deposit more coins. My stomach felt sick. I looked across the room at Rosita. I knew the target was not Hershel; it was us, and our choices were starting to run out.

"What are you going to do?" I said.

"I don't know. I've put him to bed," Linda Gail said. "Our doctor says he may have had a psychotic break."

"It was Hubert Slakely who beat him?"

"That's the name Hershel gave me. I called the police. Somebody is supposed to call me back."

"Where's Roy?"

"I don't know. I left a message at his office."

"Did you call his house?"

"No."

"I see."

"Don't take that attitude with me, Weldon."

"I didn't mean to. We're heading back to Houston."

"I've closed my eyes to what's going on. Dalton Wiseheart plans to take over y'all's company. That's what all this is about."

"There's a lot more involved than our company."

"Is Roy mixed up in any of it?"

"If you don't know, how would I?"

I didn't intend to hurt her. But when you deal with those who have chosen to inflict great harm on themselves and their loved ones on a daily basis, whatever you say to them about the reality of their lives will either prove inadequate or offend them deeply, and leave you with feelings of guilt and depression. It's not unlike walking through cobweb.

"I sometimes think you hate me," she said. "What bothers me is that I feel I deserve your contempt."

"If I gave you that perception, it was unintentional." I looked through the window. The day was blue and gold, the palm fronds in front of the motor court lifting in the breeze off the Gulf. It was Christmas, a day when the rest of the world seemed at peace. "Where are you calling from?"

"A pay phone," she replied.

"Which pay phone?"

"Outside the drugstore. The one by the River Oaks police station."

"Have you used it often?"

Again, I probably assaulted her sensibilities in asking a question that indicated surreptitiousness was a natural part of her life.

"Several times," she replied.

"I'll call you at your home later and see how Hershel is doing," I said. "In the meantime, I want you to hear me on this: I think you're a good person, Linda Gail. You read me?"

I don't know if she replied. The operator asked for more coins, then the connection was broken.

ROSITA AND I checked out of the motor court and began the long two-lane drive down the Old Spanish Trail through the bayou country to Lake Charles and the Texas border. Back then, Christmas morning in the southern United States seemed to produce a strange environmental and cultural phenomenon that I could never quite explain. The weather was always mild, the sky more like spring than winter, the grass a pale green, sometimes with clover in it. The streets would be almost empty, except for a few children playing on the sidewalk with their new roller skates or Western Flyer wagons. The celebration of Saturnalia on the previous night would fade into the quiet predictability of a sunlit morning and a sense of abeyance that allowed us to step out of time for a short while and be safe from one another.

That was the mood in which we drove over the high bridge that spanned the Calcasieu River west of Lake Charles and dropped down into a complex of chemical plants where a few years ago there had been only gum and cypress and willow trees that used to remain red and gold all the way to the salt until at least mid-November. On this particular stretch of highway, the toxicity in the air was nauseating and so thick and palpable, it was impossible to keep out of the automobile. But the people who lived in the small town by the chemical plants seemed to give little heed to the degradation of their environment and were thankful to have the jobs and the homes they did. I wondered again about the sacrificial nature of life, the collective triage we performed with regularity on our fellow man, and the wars and human attrition we accepted as the cost of our survival.

Would that *The Song of Roland* defined our experience and not this gloomy projection of our future, I told myself. I couldn't afford to lose myself in abstractions. Rosita and I were on our own. Or that's what I thought at the time.

We crossed into Texas and entered a coastal area where hundreds of United States Navy ships had been mothballed after the war. They were anchored in bayous, canals, and brackish bays, their guns plugged, their scuppers bleeding rust, their decks and hulls scrolled with the shadows of giant cypress trees that had lost their leaves. It was a strange sight, as though our greatest creations had become refuse for which there was neither purpose nor means of disposal.

East of Beaumont, I could see traffic slowing down and stopping, as it does where there's an accident. I pulled up to a café next to an outdoor fruit stand that sold pecans and pralines during winter. We sat in a booth close to the counter. Through the front window, I could see several of the mothballed ships inside a black-water swamp, the sunlight dying behind the clouds, the juxtaposed images like a still life of death on a massive scale, but for reasons that made no sense to me.

"This place is great for Mexican food," I said.

Rosita looked at a calendar on the wall. "Merry Christmas," she said. She rested one foot on top of mine under the table.

"You have the most beautiful eyes I've ever seen," I said.

She shaped the words "I love you" with her mouth.

A trucker came in, not happy with the traffic situation. "What's the deal up there?" he asked.

"They put up a barricade," the counterman replied.

"For what?"

The counterman shook his head and didn't answer.

"Well, what the hell is it?" the trucker asked. "I thought your brother-in-law was a deputy sheriff."

The counterman leaned over and lowered his voice. He was a huge man, his hair jet-black, his forehead ridged like a washboard. "They're looking for a couple of Communists that tried to kill a Houston police officer."

"Communists? What the hell are Communists doing around here?" the trucker replied.

I kept my eyes fixed on Rosita's.

"Be with y'all in just a minute," the counterman said.

The directions and the key to Lloyd Fincher's duck-hunting camp were still in my wallet.

"Just coffee," I said.

WE DROVE ONE mile back toward the state line and turned south on a dirt road that followed a bayou through pine woods and gum trees and pastureland dotted with palmettos. I could smell the salt in the air, and through the water oaks and persimmons, I could see the sunlight glittering on the Gulf of Mexico like thousands of bronze razor blades. Something else was occurring in the passage of the sun and the shifting of the light and the way the wind scudded across the algae that resembled green lace around the base of the cypress. The air was colder and damper, the shade alive with the smell of stagnant water and animal dung and carrion, the shadows of the plugged guns on the mothball fleet lengthening across a skeletal woods.

Up ahead was a cattle guard that looked in bad repair, like the one on Grandfather's ranch years ago, the one he had warned Clyde Barrow about.

Then I saw something I tried to dismiss as a hallucination, the release of an image buried in the place where memories lived. It was the 1932 Confederate. It was moving down a dirt road toward the water with four occupants, their silhouettes as stiff as mannequins, dust rising off the wire-spoked wheels.

What did they want? What were they trying to tell me?

"Are you okay, Weldon?" Rosita said.

"The light was in my eyes," I replied. "Will you get out and open the gate? Be careful where you step. There may be a broken spar in the cattle guard."

I waited while she took the chain off the gate and pushed it back. She looked down at her feet and stepped carefully back on solid ground, then leaned in the window. "Stay to the right," she said.

After I drove over the guard, she closed and latched the gate and got back inside the car. "How did you know the cattle guard was broken?"

"I think Fincher told me."

"You *think*?"

I shrugged.

THE PLACE THAT Fincher called a camp looked more like a mid-nineteenth-century planter's home that had gone to seed. The main building was constructed of plaster and old brick, with wood trim and a wide, roofed porch. The house had electricity and running water, but the mortar was crumbling between the bricks, and the sinks were striped with an orange residue as crusty as metal filings, the fireplace and the front of the chimney blackened with soot. There was no telephone or radio.

"After dark, I'll go back to the highway and find a grocery store," I said.

Rosita was standing in the middle of the living room, gazing at its bareness. "There's nothing here that has a name on it. The magazines don't have address labels. All the drawers are empty. Why would Fincher let it get so run-down?"

"Maybe he's fallen on bad days."

We looked at each other. We were thinking the same thing. An impoverished or desperate man is not one you want covering your back.

I cleaned an owl's nest out of the chimney and started a fire. Through the window, I couldn't see any other buildings beyond the railed fences that marked the boundaries of Fincher's property. "Let's do a little recon," I said.

The sky was an ink wash of purple and black, the air thick with a stench that was like offal burning in an incinerator. I had to clear my throat and spit before I spoke. I didn't want to mention the odor or what it reminded me of. "When I was a little boy, my father took me fishing for gafftop catfish west of here, over by Freeport," I said. "They were the biggest catfish I had ever seen."

"Where's that odor coming from?" she asked.

"It's probably a garbage fire. Look, you see those mounds down there, close by the swamp?"

"No," she said, distracted by the smell blowing through the trees and across the water onto the land.

"Those are burial or ceremonial mounds. There were fisher people here before Indians had tribal names. Maybe the fisher people weren't even Indians. Maybe Semitic explorers were here thousands of years ago, men in boats made from papyrus reeds."

She wasn't listening. Sometimes a look came into Rosita's eyes that I could not undo, any more than I could erase the memories that lived in both her conscious and unconscious. Those who had stood in front of the ovens and chimneys and scaffolds were never the same, and no power on earth could change that.

We were almost to the edge of the swamp. I squatted by a mound and picked up a handful of sandy soil and broken seashells and let them slide off my palm. "See? This was probably a hummock, the kind you see in the Florida Everglades today. They were peaceful people who lived in groups of twenty-five or thirty. They lived almost idyllic lives."

"Where did they go?" she asked.

"They were infected with European diseases. Some were enslaved." I stood up, my knees creaking. I looked back at the house. The wind had dropped, and the smoke from the chimney was rising straight into the sky. "I'll go back to the highway and get us some food. We'll be fine."

My words were a vanity. I was looking at the remains of people who probably thought the same way I did, people who one bright morning saw sails on the southern horizon and walked into the water to welcome the strange-looking men who had hair on their faces. Rosita clutched my arm and rested her head on my shoulder. "Oh, Weldon," she said.

That's all she said. Just that. *Oh, Weldon.*

AFTER DARK, I drove back to the two-lane and found a small grocery store and bought milk and coffee and sugar and lunch meat and bread and eggs and two steaks and packets of Kool-Aid and a quart of peach ice cream. I fixed a fine meal for us. In the warmth of the fire, my sense of apprehension began to fade. I had heard and seen nothing out of the ordinary at the grocery. Nor did I see any police presence on the road. It was Christmas night and the stars were bright over the Gulf, the moss in the cypress trees straightening against the moon, the smell of the garbage fire gone. There were no electric lights out in the woods or on any of the land that adjoined Fincher's property. Tomorrow would be a new day, I told myself. We had survived a war that was the worst in human history. One way or another, as we approached the year 1948, we would prevail.

We found blankets and sheets and a quilt in a closet and slept on the floor in front of the fire. I slept without dreaming, with Rosita's body molded into mine. I heard rain tinking on the roof in the middle of the night, and I was sure that when I woke in the morning, the grass would be greener and spangled with dew in front of Fincher's house, the wind blowing fresh and cool off the Gulf, the world filled with promise.

Oh, Wilderness were Paradise enow!

THERE'S A GROUP of men in Texas you have probably never met. I hope you never do. Contrary to the biblical admonition, you will not know them by their deeds but by their western dress and coarse speech, their nativism and misogyny. They often wear long mustaches and do not shave for several days at a time. The decals on their vehicles proclaim their politics and might contain a message of warning to the incautious. They may be as lithe as a buggy whip or as unhealthy in appearance as a washtub of clabber milk. The reality is they're poseurs and thespians. With rare exceptions, they've never busted broncs, ridden drag on a cattle herd, shoved their hand up to the armpit in a cow's uterus, gone eight seconds to the buzzer at a fairground, roofed a house in an electrical storm, been stirrup-drug through a dry riverbed, or huddled in a cellar while a tornado ripped the house off its foundation and funneled livestock into the sky. Their symbols of power are their trucks and their firearms. They shoot deer at salt licks and on game farms and take enormous pride in the trophies they hang on their walls, all of which assure them they are the givers of death and will never be its recipient.

They came at dawn, perhaps twenty of them, armed with shotguns and lever-action Winchesters, fanning out from their vehicles, the ground fog puffing whitely around their knees, some of them with badges of auxiliary lawmen clipped on their hand-tooled belts. I wondered if they had any idea how many tactical errors they committed, slamming truck doors, calling out to one another, approaching an adversary with the sun in their eyes, their chrome-plated belt buckles glinting like the crossed bandoliers on the British Redcoats our ancestors potted from two hundred yards away.

I was barefoot when I went outside, unprepared, stunned, and angry at myself for having trusted Lloyd Fincher. As I stared at the men approaching me, I felt like the Dutch boy who had stood in front of the dike while fissures spread outward from a single hole he tried to plug with his thumb. I could have stuffed the Luger in the back of my belt, but it would have done no good and perhaps would have provided this fraudulent collection of tobacco-chewing nativists with the excuse they needed to kill Rosita and me. I don't remember what I said to them. It was probably not a rational statement. I know I hated them as much as I had hated the Waffen SS or any group who preys upon the weak or the outnumbered. I know that whatever I said was greeted with a rain of blows that knocked me to the ground. I know that for a few seconds I could see only the billowing fog and the dampness of their cowboy boots and tight jeans. I know that when I rose into the sunlight again, I was trying to get my Queen knife free of my pocket. My design was simple. I was going to spill their entrails in the dirt, lay open their unshaved faces, and leave at least one of them with a carotid artery pumping a bright red jet all over his shirt.

That was not what happened. I was shoved facedown in the dirt and handcuffed with my wrists behind me while a stick was tied in my mouth. My Hebrew warrior woman from the House of Jesse was paraded off the porch and locked inside a white restraint jacket, one made out of double-stitched canvas-like cloth that tinkled with straps and buckles, the kind a medieval court jester might wear.

I thought of my mother and the day she was taken away to the psychiatric ward at Jeff Davis Hospital in Houston. I thought about killing people and in large numbers. I saw a filmstrip in my mind that showed me doing things I wouldn't have thought myself capable of.

Chapter 27

LINDA GAIL CALLED Roy Wiseheart at his office and was told he would not be in during the holidays. "Has he left for Los Angeles?" she asked.

"If you'd like to leave a message, I'll make sure he gets it," the receptionist said.

"I've already done that."

"Who's calling, please?"

"That's a good question."

"Pardon?"

"I said I'm not sure who is calling," Linda Gail said, and hung up.

She fixed a sandwich and a glass of milk for Hershel and turned on the radio for him, then put on her sheerest stockings, a black suit, high heels, long white gloves, and a purple pillbox hat with a veil, and drove in her Cadillac to Roy Wiseheart's home. Two automobiles she didn't recognize were parked in front. The columned porch was brightly lit by the carriage lamps. Clara Wiseheart answered the door.

"I need to see Roy, Mrs. Wiseheart," Linda Gail said.

"My impression is you have seen quite a lot of him."

"Great injury has been done to Hershel. I won't take much of Roy's time."

"Hershel? Oh, yes. Sorry, I'm forgetful with names. And what does Roy have to do with Hershel?"

"That's what I'd like to find out."

"You look quite nice. You seem to have taken on a new persona. It's funny how Hollywood can transform an individual."

"I need to talk to your goddamn husband, Mrs. Wiseheart."

"You *are* a little potty mouth, aren't you? Follow me out to the terrace. Jerry is here. So is another gentleman. Let me know what you think of him."

Clara Wiseheart walked ahead of her through the dining room and opened the French doors onto the terrace. It was lit by gas flares and warmed by electric heaters placed on the flagstones. Steaks two inches thick were smoking on a grill. Roy and Jerry Fallon were having drinks at a round redwood table with a third man Linda Gail thought she had seen before. Was it at the Shamrock? Or a party in Beverly Hills?

The third man was half reclining in his chair, his legs extended in front of him, a highball in one hand, his thick lips wrapped around a cigar. His graying hair was cut tight, his eyes as devoid of light as charcoal. "This is Mr. Carbo," Clara said.

"Frankie Carbo?" Linda Gail said.

"That's me. I'm pleased to meet you," he said. He didn't rise from the chair. The accent was adenoidal, Brooklyn or Rhode Island. "We met before?"

"I saw you at a hotel opening."

"At the Shamrock? Yeah, I was there. I bet you know who I was with. I can see it in your face."

"I'm sorry, my memory doesn't serve me well sometimes."

"I was with Benjamin and Virginia. She could have had a Hollywood career, too. I think being with Benjamin hurt her."

"You're talking about Bugsy Siegel and Virginia Hill?" she said.

"I never called him by that name. We grew up together. Virginia and him both looked like stars. The studio gave him a screen test, but they didn't want him around. It's like that out there."

Like what? she thought. She didn't want to ask. She couldn't believe she was having a conversation with a man who had been a suspect in a half dozen murders. Jerry Fallon was smiling at her, his face warm from either alcohol or the red glow of the space heater. Was he telling her something? Not to say any more?

"People out in L.A. are worried about you," Jerry said. "We can't go off schedule, love. There's only one unforgivable sin in the industry. You don't lose other people's money."

"Don't start picking on her," Roy said. His julep glass was wrapped with a cloth napkin, the shaved ice dark with bourbon, a sprig of mint stuck in it. His face was dilated and oily, like that of a heavily medicated man working his way through an illness, his knees close together, pointed away from Carbo.

"I need to get some information from you, Roy," she said.

But he wasn't finished talking with Jerry. As always, his words were necessary to define the discussion, to complete a thought, to close down a particular moment, to leave his signature at the bottom of the last paragraph hanging in the air. "She's a good girl. You all don't deserve her," he said. He stood up from his chair. "Have a seat, Linda Gail. Don't pay attention to these guys."

"Two policemen almost killed Hershel," she said. "They locked him in a car trunk. Hershel can't stand to be trapped in tight spaces. He almost suffocated inside a rubber sheet when he was a baby."

"Which policemen?" Roy said.

"One of them is named Slakely."

"That doesn't ring any bells."

"You know the police. Don't pretend you don't."

"I've never heard of this fellow. We'll straighten him out, though. Please sit down." He glanced once at Clara, then back at Linda Gail.

"I wouldn't talk about a police officer like that," Carbo said. "You say something careless, and a rumor starts. You call a lawyer. That's how you handle it. That's why lawyers were invented."

"Sit down by the heater, Linda Gail," Roy said. "Clara made some eggnog."

"Yeah, sit down," Carbo said. "I hear you're working for Mr. Warner. Benjamin lived right next door to him. He saw an empire in the Nevada desert. There's a word for that. Visionary? I think that's why he was killed. He was shot four times in the face. The bullets blew his eye out on the rug."

Linda Gail's knees felt weak. From the corner of her eye, she could see Clara Wiseheart obviously taking pleasure in her embarrassment and discomfort.

"I had better go now," Linda Gail said. She waited for Roy to speak.

He took a sip from his julep, his eyes on hers. "You still like it pink around the bone?" he said.

"*What?*" she said.

"Your steak," he said. "I'll put another one on."

"I'll walk you to your car," Jerry said.

"Thank you," she said.

She took his arm, her high heels catching on the edges of the flagstones, the heat from a gas torch bright on the side of her face. She looked once more at Roy. He was turning a steak on the grill, watching the grease flare on the coals. His gaze lifted to hers. He pointed a finger at the back of Carbo's neck, grinning, his thumb cocked like a pistol. He jerked his finger as though he had just pulled the trigger.

Jerry opened the driver's door on her car. Clara Wiseheart had gone back inside the dining room. Carbo was talking to Roy, who kept looking through the piked gate at Linda Gail.

"What's that man doing here?" she said.

"He's the laddie you see if you want into the fight game," Jerry said. "You know what the sports wire is?"

"It has to do with Las Vegas?"

"The people who control it control all the gambling in the United States. Some of the money gets laundered in the film industry. The Mafia already controls the projectionists and stagehands. You think that guy in there is bad? You ought to meet Charlie Luciano."

"Hershel might die, and I'm responsible. Did Roy have Jack Valentine killed?"

"He knows the guys who could do it. I doubt Roy would go to the trouble with a guy like Valentine. Frankly, who cares? People live, people die. Carbo was just telling us he was pals with Bugsy Siegel. Some people think he was involved in Siegel's murder. It's not ours to worry about. Move your husband out to Santa Monica and forget all these people in River Oaks. There's nothing that goes on in Roy's house that doesn't go on in the government. At Okinawa I strafed Japanese fishing boats because they had radios on them. There were families on those boats. It's the way of the world. We're wayfaring strangers. We're born alone, we die alone."

"You got that from Roy."

"It's the only thing in life he's been right about, except for his infatuation with you."

"I don't have the power to deal with these people. I don't know what to do."

"You're the one with the talent. They're the ones who want to buy it. What's that tell you? Take their money and treat them with the contempt they deserve."

"I quit."

"Quit what?"

"The picture," she said.

He stepped back from her and turned her shoulders so the carriage lamps shone on her face. "Look at me," he said.

"You heard what I said."

"Don't even think those words." She started to speak, but he pressed one finger to her lips. "No," he said. "You did not say what you think you did. You imagined those words. You did not say them. You do not throw hundreds of thousands of dollars of studio money into the incinerator."

She got into the Cadillac and started the engine. Jerry was trying to hold on to the door handle and walk alongside the Cadillac, talking all the while at the glass. He didn't let go until she smacked into a ceramic urn by the entrance and bounced over the curb into the street, a hubcap rolling down the asphalt.

WHEN I WAS released from jail on the streets of downtown Houston, I knew what a derelict felt like. My coat was gone, my clothes filthy and torn, my face unshaved. There was blood in my hair. One eye was swollen into a slit. My wallet was gone, my car towed to an impoundment somewhere outside Beaumont.

Our enemies, whoever they were, had created a masterpiece of misery. There were no criminal charges against Rosita or me, so we had no way to seek redress. Rosita had been locked up in the psychiatric ward at the county hospital and was now classified as a mental patient and ward of the system. Wasn't it the responsibility of the state to care for the insane? Anyone who doubted she was ill could examine her record of abnormal behavior, her insularity and detachment, her connection with Communists, her scalding of a police officer's face. Hadn't she been in an extermination camp? Perhaps she had been used in experiments that had driven her mad.

I walked to my office and borrowed money from my secretary to take a cab to our house in the Heights. Our maid, Snowball, and her daughter had moved into the back room and taken good care of Grandfather. I showered and shaved and put on fresh clothes and placed an ice bag on my eye before I let him see me. He was in the sunroom, reading the newspaper, his boots on, his trousers stuffed in the tops. "Where's Rosita?" he said.

"They got her."

"Say again?"

I told him.

"That fellow Fincher sold you out?" he said.

"That's what it looks like. I think I'm going down the drain, Grandfather."

"I don't like to hear you talk like that."

"I'm fixing to call up Dalton Wiseheart and tell him he can have our company at market price."

"That's not what they're after, Satch. They want to break your spirit. Spit in their mouths."

"What about Rosita?"

He removed his reading glasses and stared at the lawn. It was bright and sunny outside, as though the weather were mocking our problems. "I made a mess of everything in my life," he said. "I shouldn't be giving you advice."

"What would you do?"

"What I always did. Sling blood on the trees. But look where it got me. None of my children, including your mother, have ever forgiven me for the violent and drunken man I was."

"Will you be all right if I'm gone for a while?"

His pale blue eyes were rheumy and distant. "I wish I was younger," he said.

I HAD NO ACCESSIBLE target for my rage and sense of helplessness. I couldn't prove my suspicions about the treachery of Lloyd Fincher. I shouldn't have been surprised by his behavior. He had been a midlevel functionary all of his life, one of those who liked nothing better than a public admission of wrongdoing so he could quickly move on to the next disaster in the making. Fincher's kind of corruption was endemic to the system he served. He was the gland that prevented the infection from reaching the brain of Dr. Frankenstein's monster.

There was only one face I could put on all our troubles. My lawyer had told me a few things about him, but nothing I wouldn't expect in the file of a bad cop, and nothing that told me of his day-to-day patterns. For that very reason, I had retained a private investigator, a friend, to take a close look at Hubert Timmons Slakely.

I called the PI. His name was Boone Larson. He had worked for the Pinkertons and once told me the agency believed Butch Cassidy had not been killed during a bank robbery in Bolivia but had lived until 1937 in Spokane, Washington. I always liked that story.

I did not tell Boone of the attack on Hershel or the vigilante raid on Fincher's hunting camp. "If a fellow wanted to have a private chat with Slakely, where would he catch up to him?" I asked.

"You might try his apartment."

"Somewhere else."

"What's wrong with his apartment?"

"He might be having friends or relatives over. Why disturb him?"

"Are you sure you want to do this, Weldon?"

"I'm curious about what a guy like that does in his free time."

"He's got a place he goes to on weekends or on his off days. You know he used to work vice in Galveston?"

"Right."

"I think he has yearnings for the old days."

I went upstairs to the attic and opened the army-surplus footlocker where I kept many things from my boyhood: pocketknives, my *Boy Scout Handbook,* my first jitterbug bass lure, my collection of arrowheads, my catcher's glove, three musket balls I had cut out of a dead cottonwood tree, an Indian trade ax that had a small tobacco bowl on one end and an air passage drilled through the handle so it could be smoked.

I waited until dark and drove to the place twenty miles outside of town where Slakely kept a shiny tin trailer on a bayou that dumped into the San Jacinto River. A fine mist was falling when I cut my headlights in a woods and walked toward the trailer, wearing gloves, a bandanna tied across the lower half of my face, a shapeless fedora pulled down on my brow, the trade ax hanging from my right hand. From the edge of the woods, I could see the trailer, a pickup truck, a toolshed in back, trash burning in an oil barrel, sparks twisting into the mist, a light burning on a pole above a boathouse, an old water tower silhouetted against the sky. Through a small pair of binoculars, I could see Slakely drinking a bottle of Pearl at a table in the trailer. He was talking to a young, round-shouldered, thin-hipped girl in a shift printed with pink hearts. Her face had no expression. She blinked when he raised his finger to make a point.

I went to the toolshed and kicked a pile of newspapers across the floor, then poured a can of paint thinner on them and set them alight with a paper match. The flames climbed up the wall and spread around the sides of a broken window, a draft sucking it out of the glass into the cold air. I went back into the darkness of the trees and waited. I told myself I had no plan. I had not taken the Luger with me. If I'd been acting with premeditation, I surely would have carried it on my person, wouldn't I? There was no registration on it, no chain of possession that could link it to me. The lethality of a trade ax was a subjective matter. It could be used as a tool to cut meat or to make pemmican; it could be used as a ceremonial pipe. I had chosen latitude over specificity. When you roll the dice, you roll the dice and let the arithmetic take care of itself.

It all seemed quite reasonable to me.

The fire was not long in gaining Slakely's attention. He came out the side door of his trailer without a hat, pulling on a raincoat. Sparks were fanning from the oil barrel onto the shed, and I'm sure he thought they were the cause of the fire. He turned on a garden hose and extinguished the flames inside the shed first, then flooded the barrel. He turned off the faucet and went into the shed to examine the damage.

He was bent over, trying to determine where the fire had started, and had no awareness that I was standing immediately behind him. He kicked at the can of paint thinner. Then he saw me. Even in the poor light, I saw his mouth open and the blood go out of his face.

"Who are you?" he said.

I stared at him and said nothing, as though he were the aberration and not I. His eyes dropped to the trade ax in my hand. "Maybe you don't know I'm a detective with the Houston Police Department. If this has to do with the girl, she's a runaway. I was trying to he'p her. That's why you're here? The girl?"

His face was glistening with rainwater, his hair splayed on his scalp, which was striped with welts where Rosita had scalded him. I saw him wet his lips and swallow. The holster of a small nickel-plated revolver was clipped on the left side of his belt.

"Let's get the girl down here, if it'll make you feel better. She'll tell you everything is okay. You hearing me? You deaf or something? Maybe you got no voice box? Look, Flora's coming now."

It was a poor ruse, but one he probably used successfully before.

Deceit, manipulation, guile, cruelty, and fear were the sum total of who and what he was. Back then we often sent his kind as our emissaries into black neighborhoods and later wondered why they hated us. I continued to hold my eyes on his, my fingers squeezing the hardwood handle of the ax.

I knew it was coming. What is "it"? "It" is that moment when the coward's fear is so great, he has nowhere to put it except inside eternity, and that's when he steps irrevocably across a line. His right hand reached for the butt of his revolver.

My first blow caught him across the side of the face, laying open a huge flap of skin, one of his eyes bulging like a marble. I hit him again, somewhere in the neck, then in the head. He was bent almost double, like a man with a violent stomachache. I could no longer see his right hand or determine if he had gotten his hand on his revolver. I knew only that I was hitting him, the blade of the ax rising and falling as though it had a will of its own. I knew that with each blow, he descended closer and closer to the floor, taking his evil with him. I knew, as Grandfather had said, that I was slinging his blood over every surface inside the shed. Let no man tell you our simian ancestor is not alive and well and waiting for his moment to come aborning again.

When I stopped, the only sounds I heard were a pinecone tinkling across the tin roof of the shed, a boat horn blowing on the river, an owl screeching in the trees. I backed out of the shed, unable to take my eyes off what I had done, the ax dripping in the dirt. When I turned around, the young girl from the trailer was staring at me, trembling in the cold, too frightened to speak.

"Don't be afraid, Flora," I said.

"How do you know my name?"

"He used it when he tried to trick me into looking behind me. You're in no danger."

"Is he dead?"

"I'm not sure. It doesn't matter. It's over."

She had a pug nose and freckles and chestnut hair that was cut short and curled on the ends; her shoulders and arms were prickled in the wind. The accent was East Texas. "I won't tell. I promise," she said.

"Did he harm you?"

She turned her cheek into the light from the trailer so I could see the bruise on it.

"What else?"

"What else what?"

"What else did he do to you?"

She began to breathe through her nose, her lips pressed tightly together.

I picked up Slakely's revolver from the floor of the shed and threw it out the broken window into the mud. Then I removed his wallet from his back pocket. It held around sixty dollars. I could not tell if Slakely was alive or dead. His eyes were shut, his mouth open. A piece of tooth was on his lip. I took twenty dollars from my own wallet and gave it and Slakely's money to the girl.

"I'm going to take this bandanna off. I'm going to do so because I don't like frightening you. This man did great injury to people I love. One of those people is my wife. Because of this man, I may lose her. He also pulled a weapon on me, and I'm sure if he'd had the chance, he would have killed me. You can stay here or ride with me back to Houston. If you like, I can drop you at the train station or the bus depot."

"You'd do that?"

I flung the trade ax end over end into a bog by the river's edge. "Do you have a coat?"

"He took it from me."

"Put this on," I said. I draped my jacket across her shoulders. "I bet you have a lot of good things waiting for you down the road. I bet you're a fine young woman. The bad things are behind you, the good things are in front of you. It's that simple."

I TRIED FOUR TIMES to see Rosita at the county hospital. I was told she couldn't have visitors. She was "undergoing treatment and resting" and "being reclassified for possible release or transfer." For a moment I felt a surge of hope in my chest, as though a terrible mistake were about to be corrected and I would discover that a conspiracy was not at work in our lives, that in effect the problem lay in my perception. Then the nurse looked again at the clipboard in her hand and knitted her brow. "Excuse me, I was wrong. The diagnosis has been completed, but no determination has been made regarding treatment," she said. "You'll have to come back later. She's in good hands."

"You listen to me—"

"Sir, I think you should go."

I glanced through a glass window down a corridor and thought I saw two men in white uniforms taking Rosita through a set of doors quilted with thick pads. She was wearing a smock tied loosely in back and slippers that looked made of cardboard. I tried to open the door, but it was locked. I beat on it with my fists and was escorted to the front entrance by two uniformed police officers.

I could not stand the thought of what was being done to Rosita. Two days passed and there was nothing in the newspapers about my attack on Hubert Slakely. My lawyer was of no help. I wondered if I was being taught a lesson about the nature of power: You either gave in to it or you were crushed by it. Tearing Slakely apart was poor redress. My attack upon him was similar to the hanging of the misanthropes at Nuremberg. They deserved what they got, but they were the instruments, not the designers. The orchestrators of the Reich skated, sometimes committing suicide, but they never had to look their victims in the eye.

I knew only one person who had the power and money to undo our problems. Unfortunately, I did not know who lived in his skin. I guess I wanted Roy Wiseheart to be more than he was capable of. So maybe the problem was mine and not his.

It was Wednesday morning when I shined my shoes and put on a suit and tie and went to the office he kept by the Rice Hotel. As always, he seemed unbothered by the intrigue and contradictions that seemed to define his life. His face glowed with health; not a hair was out of place on his head; his handshake was firm, his eyes clear. "Did Linda Gail tell you about meeting Frankie Carbo? I think it unnerved her a bit."

"No, she didn't. She doesn't report to me," I said. "What are you doing with a guy like that?"

"You're a funny one to ask. He's your uncle's business partner."

"What?"

"Cody Holland is your uncle, isn't he? The man who lent you the money to start up your pipeline company?"

"Yes," I said, the back of my neck tingling.

"Your uncle is a boxing promoter. Nobody gets into the fight game without dealing with Frankie Carbo. Come on, let's go to the club and play some handball."

"Say that about my uncle again."

"I'm not judging him. He's a smart businessman. Can you name one human being who wouldn't touch money because it had germs on it? Look, maybe you can help me. Linda Gail is talking about quitting the picture. Jack Warner is down with the flu and wants to halt production for a couple of weeks to straighten out some union trouble, so we're temporarily off the hook. Will you talk to her? It'll cost the studio a fortune if she quits."

I sat down in a straight-back leather chair by the window. I looked up at him and wondered why I had come. His concerns were always about himself: In his mind, the world was a tin globe on a stand that he could spin and observe and stop whenever it suited him. I also wondered if Roy Wiseheart could read people's minds. Whenever I was about to write him off, he would say something of a redeeming nature that caught me off guard and made me revise my condemnation. "How's Hershel?" he asked.

"Not good."

"I wish I could change what happened. What you've never understood about me, Weldon, is—"

"I've never understood anything about you. You're Proteus rising from the sea, always changing shape."

"Hardly anything so grand. The truth is, I'd like to be you. You're a self-made man. You've got the guts of a back-alley beer-glass brawl. You'd put your hand in a fire for a friend. You're probably the only honorable man I've ever known."

"I need you to get Rosita out of state custody. Not just out of the psychiatric ward. You know the people who can do it. They can have my pipeline company. They can have whatever they want."

"You overestimate my importance."

"Don't tell me that. You know people who can buy Guatemala with their Diners Club card."

"These are people who listen to my father, not to me. In some ways I'm like you, a man traveling on a tourist visa in his own country. Without my father's name and my wife's money, I'd be nothing."

"Tell it to the chaplain."

"You're always a hard sell," he said. "Did you see the story about that cop Slakely, the fellow who's been causing trouble for everyone?"

"No, I didn't see the story," I said, letting my eyes go flat.

"It's here in the *Post,*" he said, flipping open the morning paper on his desk. "Somebody chopped him up with an ax. Probably couldn't have happened to a more deserving fellow. Here, you want to read it?"

"Not particularly."

"Even though this is the man responsible for the charges against Rosita?"

"I hope he found a shady place."

"I admire your objectivity. Too bad the bugger made it."

"Say that again."

"The bastard lived. The story says it may have been a robbery. No suspects." He perched one thigh on the corner of the desk and gazed down at me. "Still water runs the deepest."

"You're talking about me?"

"I said you were heck on wheels."

"Thanks for your time."

"You know what I dream about every third night? Going down on the deck so I could get my fifth kill."

"Go out to the navy hospital. Talk to the psychiatrist. Join a church or start a new religion. Why do you have to keep telling me about it?"

"Because you're a rich man, Weldon. You're rich because your nightmares are about the deeds of others, not your own. There're no regrets in your life. How many men can say that?"

Chapter 28

OUR LIVES SEEMED to be unraveling, not unlike a spool of movie film across a floor. I went into Grandfather's bedroom and closed the door behind me. I could hear Snowball fixing lunch in the kitchen.

"Home a bit early, aren't you?" Grandfather said. He was in a rocking chair by the window, smoking his pipe, wearing a flannel shirt and his boots and Stetson, the window opened high, even though the weather was cold and the heat was escaping the room. The woman next door, who was young and strong and had large breasts and upper arms the size of hams, was hanging wash.

I pushed the window down. "Have you thought about finding a lady friend your own age?" I said.

"Who wants a ninety-year-old lady friend?" he replied.

I sat on his bed. He made his own bed every morning. The quilt was always pulled tight, the pillow puffed and squared away. Outside, the sun was bright on the trees and lawn and the shoulders and blond hair of the woman shaking out her damp clothes from a basket and fastening them to the clothesline with wooden pins. "I think I went across the wrong Rubicon," I said.

"In what way?"

"I caught up with Hubert Slakely," I said.

"Not in his office or on a street? Caught up with him in a more serious fashion?"

"He was in a trailer out by the San Jacinto River. He had a young girl with him. She was a runaway. He'd left his mark on her."

Grandfather's gaze was focused out the window but not on the woman. "What'd you use?"

"An Indian trade ax."

"That sounds like it'd do the trick."

"It didn't."

"Too bad. Did he draw down on you?"

I nodded. Then I said, "How did you know?"

"You wouldn't have hit him otherwise. It's not in you. You think it is, but it's not. Why aren't the police here now?"

"I had a bandanna over my face. I didn't speak. I took the girl to the bus depot."

"I'd say case closed."

"I flat tore him apart, Grandfather. I tried to kill him."

"If you'd tried to kill him, he'd be dead. You'll never make an assassin, Satch, so stop pretending you are. You need to stop fretting yourself over a waste of oxygen like Slakely. The wrong people always worry. The people who are the real problem never worry about anything."

Grandfather should have been an exorcist.

"There's another matter on my mind," I said.

"The day hasn't come when there wasn't."

"Did you ever see specters or illusions? I mean really see them?"

"Like pools of heat on the horizon?" he said.

"Remember the stolen car Bonnie and Clyde were driving, the one I shot into? It was a 1932 Confederate. I've seen it. Not once but twice."

"There're probably a lot of them around. I think you need to turn off your brain for a while and discontinue this line of thought."

"I saw it in a gas station just before my former commanding officer gave me the key to his hunting camp. I saw it at the camp, too, before the vigilantes took away Rosita. Four people were in it. They looked like cardboard cutouts. They didn't look alive."

He never took his eyes off the yard. "I see spirits with regularity these days. They're on the edge of the shade just yonder. If you turn real quick, you'll see them, too. I don't like to dwell too much upon this sort of thing." He got up stiffly from the rocker and took off his Stetson and sailed it crown-down onto the bed, a lock of his white hair falling across his eye, like a little boy's.

"You see them out there now?" I asked.

"Don't pay me any mind or listen to anything I say. Let's see what Snowball has fixed for lunch."

LINDA GAIL HEARD something drop through the mail slot and hit hard on the floor. It was a cardboard mailer with no return address. Inside was a brown envelope that contained individual head shots of four women. All of the women were Caucasian and wearing smocks; their mouths were open, their hair in disarray, their eyes locked in a private vision of despair they could never share with others, their heads tilted as though there were no reason to hold them erect. A typed note in the envelope read: "Medical science is doing wonders for disturbed people these days. We hope your friend is better."

She drove to Roy's office and went inside. "Tell Mr. Wiseheart that Linda Gail is here, please," she said to the receptionist.

"He's on the phone right now. He might be a while," the receptionist said.

"No, he won't," she replied.

Before the receptionist could reply, Linda Gail brushed past and shut Roy's door behind her. She turned the envelope over and sprinkled the photos and the typed note on his desk. "Check this out," she said.

He was holding the phone receiver to his ear. "I'll call you back, Senator," he said, and replaced the receiver in the cradle. "Where'd you get these?"

"From the mailman. Read the note."

"Who are these women?"

"Would you read the note, please?"

He picked it up from the desk blotter, his eyebrows bronze-tinted in a ray of sunlight shining through the window. There was hardly a line in his skin.

"They were lobotomized," she said. "They're vegetables. I called the reference librarian and got some information about the procedure. A steel probe is shoved under the eyelid into the brain."

"How do you know they were lobotomized?"

"I don't. Maybe they went through electroshock. What difference does it make? This is something that belongs in the Middle Ages."

"Does Weldon know about this?" he asked.

"I'm going to his house now. I'd like you to go with me."

She waited. This was the moment, she thought. All he had to say was *Let me get my coat.*

"No, I don't believe I should do that. Weldon was here earlier. He knows I'm doing everything I can to help Rosita. What neither of you understands is the political position she has put other people in. I was talking to a United States senator when you came in."

She looked at him dumbly. "You won't go with me to Weldon's house? That's going to disrupt your day?"

"Did you hear me?" he said. "We have to deal with reality, not the way things should be. Fairly or not, she's been tagged a Communist. No politician, particularly in the state of Texas, is going to risk his career for someone accused of being a member of the Communist Party."

"Which United States senator were you talking to?"

"It doesn't matter. I don't think anyone can help Rosita."

"You're the bottom of the barrel, Roy."

"You're angry, so say what you wish. But you're wrong."

"I think I've figured you out," she said. "You want to be a hero. But your heroic deeds have to be public. There has to be a trade-off. You won't take risks unless there's personal gain."

Her words seemed to have no effect on him. "These photos and this note are the work of a miserably unhappy human being. The people who want to destroy Weldon are a far more serious group. They have ice water in their veins. When they decide to act, you'll know it. They don't send a warning."

"What's your idea of serious? What do you call locking up an innocent and perfectly sound woman in an asylum?"

"The people I'm referring to are capable of killing the president of the United States. I've heard them talk about it."

"I don't believe anything you say."

"Your innocence is your great virtue, Linda Gail. I knew that when I first met you. I knew it would prevail over your ambition and your temporary lapses into the temptations of celebrity. That's why I fell in love with you. That's what Jack Valentine recognized in you when you walked out on the porch of that country store. Jack was a swine, but he knew a winner when he saw one."

"On a train, two newsmen asked if I knew that Rosita was a Communist. I said I would report her if I thought that. What do you think of me now?"

"You break my heart, that's what I think of you."

He sat down behind his desk and stared at the photographs, breathing audibly through his nose, his thumbs pressed into his temples. Then he gathered the photos and the note and pushed them back into the mailer and handed it to her. "I talked to my father about helping Rosita. He walked out of the room. Do you know whom I actually have influence with? Hollywood people. And that's because most of them aren't that bright. The other bunch are Frankie Carbo's friends. Everybody does business with them, but I'm the only one who'll have dinner with them."

At that moment Linda Gail realized she would probably go through many changes, even dramatic transformations, on her journey toward the grave. The laws of mutability were not unlike the wind blowing on a weather vane, and in all probability they would take their toll on her or reward her in ways she never anticipated. Her career would fail or succeed; age would steal her looks but perhaps give her a degree of wisdom; she might divorce and remarry, or stay with Hershel, or live out her life as a single woman. One day she might enjoy enormous wealth, the kind that was the envy of every person she had grown up with. But there was one thing she was absolutely sure of: She would never be entirely free of Roy Wiseheart or understand how she had slept securely in the arms of a man who was more wraith than flesh and blood. Nor would she get over her lover's greatest tragedy—his total ignorance of how much joy he could have given others. So who had been the greater loser? She didn't want to answer that question.

IT'S FAIR TO say that mortality takes many manifestations, but so does the indomitable nature of the human spirit, and it does so in ways that are sometimes hardly noticeable. Hershel was sitting in the passenger seat of the Cadillac when Linda Gail turned in to our driveway. I went outside to greet them. He rolled down his window. "How you doin', Loot?" he said.

I knew the purpose of their visit would not be a cheerful one. It was hard to put a good hat on our situation. I also knew that the odyssey we had begun in the immediate aftermath of the war was approaching its conclusion. They followed me into the living room and showed me the photographs and the typed note Linda Gail had gotten in the mail. "Who do you think sent these?" I said.

"I showed them to Roy. He said they came from someone who was miserably unhappy," Linda Gail replied.

"Such as his wife?" I said.

Hershel had not taken off his coat and was looking out the front window. It was a grand gold-and-green winter day, the kind that makes you remember the Deep South with fondness. "You didn't gather your pecans this fall," he said.

"Didn't have time," I said.

"Remember in the Ardennes when I was fussing about Steinberg? You know, about him being a Jew and getting the heebie-jeebies on patrol?"

"Vaguely," I said.

"You remember it, Weldon. You told me to knock it off. Then you asked me what my folks did at Christmastime. I told you we picked pecans on the gallery and my mother baked a fruitcake and my daddy made eggnog with red whiskey in it, not moonshine, and we went squirrel hunting with a colored man who worked on shares with us. I remember it just like it happened yesterday."

I smiled but didn't say anything.

"The pecan and oak trees in your yard look just like they do in Louisiana this time of year," he said. "They have a soft quality, like in an old postcard. It's like going back to when we were kids, isn't that right, Linda Gail?"

"Yes, it is," she said.

"Don't be looking at those photographs," he said. "They're meant to hurt us. Don't give these people any more satisfaction."

"I think you're right," I said, and put the photos and note back in the mailer.

"Would you mind if I go out there and gather up some of your pecans?" he said.

"Not at all."

That's what the three of us did. I got a quart of eggnog out of the icebox, and we sat on the porch steps in the sun and cracked the pecans with a pair of pliers and picked the meat out of the shells and ate it, and passed the eggnog back and forth, drinking from the carton, ignoring the fact we were adults and that William Blake's tiger still prowled the earth and that somewhere on the edges of the park or the neighborhood or the city limits or the country's borders, thieves waited to break in and steal.

"What do you want me to do with the photos and the note, Weldon?" Linda Gail said.

"Burn them," I replied.

After they left, I went back to the county psychiatric ward where Rosita was being held and was told she had been transferred to the hospital at Wichita Falls.

When I returned home, I went into Grandfather's bedroom. "I'll have to be gone for a few days," I said.

"Where to?"

I told him.

"They perform lobotomies there?" he said.

"It's the asylum where my mother probably would have undergone electroshock treatment if we hadn't gotten her back." I saw a painful flicker in his eyes.

"What are you doing with that Luger?" he said.

"I haven't thought it through."

"Take me up there with you. Maybe they'll listen to an old man. It's the only advantage that comes with age. You can yell at people and they cain't do anything about it."

We both knew the folly of his words and the level of hopelessness they represented.

I CALLED A RURAL air service in Tomball and hired a pilot to fly me to Wichita Falls. I was almost out the door with my suitcase, one that contained clothes for both me and Rosita, when I saw Roy Wiseheart's metallic gray Packard coming down the street. I set down the suitcase inside the door so he couldn't see it, and waited for him under the porch light. The night was cold and black, the stars a snowy shower across the sky.

I was filled with conflict as I watched Roy turn in to the drive. I would be justified if I rebuffed him. I was tired of his rhetoric and his Byronic affectations and his self-manufactured aura of martyrdom. I wondered if he had any idea of the damage he had done to Hershel; if he had any idea how much Hershel loved Linda Gail. I wondered if he had any idea how courageous and humble and decent a man Hershel Pine was. I wondered if Roy ever thought about anyone except Roy.

I stepped down off the porch and met him in the middle of the yard.

"You headed out somewhere?" he said. He was holding a package the size and shape of a cardboard mailer, wrapped with black satin paper and silver ribbon.

"Rosita has been moved to the asylum at Wichita Falls. I think your friends want to physically destroy her brain."

"These are not my friends, bud."

"You come out of the same background, you belong to the same clubs, you went to the same schools. You make a religion out of denying any connection with the world that has given you everything you have. The reality is, you're one of their acolytes."

"That hurts me deeply."

"I have a feeling you'll survive."

"I came to ask a favor. Please give this to Linda Gail when she's alone. It's my way of saying good-bye. I'm not sure I'll ever get over her."

"What is it?"

"Bunny Berigan's recording of 'I Can't Get Started with You.' She loved this song."

"Your wife told me you gave that record to her."

"I'm surprised she remembered."

"I'll say good night to you now, Roy. I wish you well. I don't think I'll be in contact with you again."

"You're disappointed in me?"

"Who am I to judge?" I replied.

Typical of Roy, he didn't let go easily. He walked to the porch and leaned the gift for Linda Gail against the bottom step. "You're a heck of a guy, Weldon. Make them wince," he said.

"That last part is your father's mantra."

"Sometimes the old man gets it right," he replied. "By the way, in case you didn't read it in the paper, Lloyd Fincher died of carbon monoxide poisoning in his garage. It's a great loss. Half the hookers in San Antonio will be out of work."

LINDA GAIL ALWAYS loved books and did well academically. Even after skipping ninth grade, she was placed in the high school honors program. Her favorite treat during the summer was the visit of the old WPA bread truck/bookmobile to her rural neighborhood, where many of the parents were barely literate and her peers spent their spare time shooting songbirds with air rifles or making what they called "nigger shooters" from willow forks and strips of inner tube. Her favorite books were the Nancy Drew and Hardy Boys series, Richard Halliburton's *Book of Marvels*, Anna Sewell's *Black Beauty*, and *The Yearling* by Marjorie Rawlings. Rarely did she get to read books like those in Honors English. In her sophomore English class, the students memorized and recited long passages from "The Rime of the Ancient Mariner" and "Evangeline." Linda Gail made up for her lack of interest in the material by outdoing everyone in the class. While others barely got through a recitation in front of the class,

Linda Gail memorized twice the number of lines and kept going until the teacher had to stop her, out of fairness to the student who was supposed to follow her, whose recitation Linda Gail was making redundant.

The third time she did it, the teacher had her dropped from Honors English. When the principal told her to report to a class filled with students who could barely stay awake until three P.M., she charged into the office of the teacher after school, crying and in a rage. She called him a snarf and a jerk and a dog turd and said she was going to write the governor about him.

"What's a snarf?" he asked.

"A guy who gets off on sniffing girls' bicycle seats," she replied.

He placed a box of chalk on the desk and told her to write "I will not call Mr. Shepherd a snarf" one hundred times on the blackboard. She picked up the box of chalk and threw it at his head. "You were born for the stage, Linda Gail," he told her. "That's not a compliment."

As she fixed dinner for Hershel and herself, she wondered why, at this time in her life, those memories from her adolescence seemed so important. Unfortunately, she knew the answer. The best moments in her young life had been with the books she discovered on the shelves of the bookmobile. Roy had told her he loved her for her innocence. That was the way she wanted to remember herself, as Judy Garland singing among the Munchkins. She knew the reality was otherwise. Even as a child, she had always been self-centered, never passing a mirror or a store window or the glass trophy case in the school hallway without looking at her reflection. Linda Gail not only stole the lines the other students had stayed up all night memorizing, she committed an act of theft upon herself. She had lied about who she was all these years. The innocent child she wanted to remember had never existed. She was a fraud then and a fraud now.

She wanted to talk honestly with Hershel without hurting him more than she had hurt him already. How do you tell someone you don't love him, that you are not drawn to him physically, that even during your most intimate moments, images of other men have always lived on the edges of your consciousness? Is that person supposed to be consoled because you add that you admire and respect him? There are certain things you never say to another human being. An apology from an adulterer is an apology from an adulterer. Telling the person whom you married and slept with for years that you never loved him was nothing short of calculated cruelty.

Her own thought processes were driving her crazy.

She fixed his favorite dinner—pork chops and sweet potatoes and canned spinach mixed with mashed-up hard-boiled eggs. She set out clean place mats and the good silverware and lit the candles on the candelabra and set it in the middle of the table and sat down across from him. She ate in small bites, her eyes on the plate, wondering what she should say. "Did you know your color has come back?" she asked.

"Think so?" he said.

"I believe it's because of our visit with Weldon. Gathering pecans and sitting on the gallery, like people do in Louisiana."

"Yeah, I'm glad we did that. It was nice, the weather and all."

"He was proud you remembered the time in the Ardennes when he was kind to you. He thinks very highly of you, Hershel."

"You ever notice how your accent comes back all of a sudden?"

"Did you know I have the same speech coach as Audie Murphy?"

"That's something, isn't it?"

"We've gotten ourselves in a mess, haven't we?" she said.

"I want you to go back to Hollywood and finish your picture. I can take care of myself. There's no problem here, Linda Gail."

She touched the tip of her fork to a piece of pork chop but didn't lift it from the plate. Nor did she raise her eyes. "I don't believe I'm cut out for Hollywood. Even if I were, I think they're pretty well done with me."

"No, ma'am, they're not. I always believed your name was going to be up in lights. You were born for the screen."

"My Honors English teacher said something like that years ago."

"He was a smart man."

"He was telling me I was a self-centered brat."

"He was probably jealous, that's all. Sometimes prophecy can come from the mouth of a fool."

"Where'd you get that?"

"I just made it up."

"I'm sorry for all that I've done to you, Hershel," she said.

"When people make mistakes, there's usually a reason for it. These pork chops are something else."

She knew at that moment that Hershel Pine was probably the best human being she'd ever known. She also knew that others aside from her had done terrible damage to her husband and their friends. She determined then that they would pay for it, one way or another, starting with one person in particular.

EARLY THURSDAY MORNING Linda Gail drove downtown to a photography store and had multiple copies made of the typed note and the photos of the four female mental patients. Then she drove to the post office and sent two airmail manila envelopes to Los Angeles.

When she got home, Hershel was working in the yard, repairing the damage he had done to the St. Augustine grass and the flowerbeds. She went into the kitchen, her pillbox hat still on her head, and drank a cup of coffee at the drain board. Then she called Roy Wiseheart's house. A maid answered. "May I speak to Mrs. Wiseheart, please?" Linda Gail asked.

"She's taking a nap, ma'am."

"This is Mrs. Pine. Wake her up, please."

"She don't like to be woke up, ma'am."

"It's in regard to her appearance at the meeting of Daughters of the American Revolution. It's quite important."

"I'll go look in on her and be right back."

Linda Gail waited for two minutes, staring out the window. Hershel saw her and waved. She heard someone pick up a second receiver, scraping it out of the phone cradle. "What do you want, Mrs. Pine?"

"I received the photos and note you or one of your assistants sent me. I wanted to thank you personally for being so concerned about our friend Rosita Holland."

"What photos?"

"Of the lobotomized women. Hershel and I showed them to Weldon and also to Roy, which I'm sure is what you wanted us to do."

"I have no idea what you're talking about."

"You didn't send them?"

"Why would I send you photos of any kind? We share nothing in common. We have no kind of relationship. Because you slept with my husband doesn't give you access to my private life. I think you should talk to a psychiatrist."

"I felt it was only appropriate that I alert you to some phone calls you'll be receiving. You'll be receiving an appreciable degree of media attention, not the kind that impresses members of the DAR. I saw in the newspaper that you'll be their guest of honor at the River Oaks Country Club next week."

"What phone calls?"

"I sent the photos and the note special delivery to Louella Parsons and Hedda Hopper."

"Why should either of them care about photos of mental patients? Mrs. Pine, I'm convinced you're impaired. Why Roy decided upon a dalliance with you is beyond me. He usually likes Hispanic girls he finds in the Islands."

"I attached a statement about my affair with Roy and made it as detailed as possible, including the places where we had our trysts, down in Mexico, at the Shamrock Hotel, wherever or whenever it was convenient," Linda Gail said. "I mentioned as many Hollywood names as I could. I also mentioned that Frankie Carbo was a guest in your home and that Roy was on a first-name basis with Bugsy Siegel. I explained to Louella and Hedda the retaliatory means you've taken to get even for your husband's ongoing infidelity. In short, I wanted them to know what a vicious, hateful, anti-Semitic witch you are, Mrs. Wiseheart. You have every right to despise me, but to do what you've done to Rosita Holland takes a special kind of woman. Good-bye, and I hope you stay germ-free the rest of your life."

Chapter 29

THURSDAY MORNING I woke at sunrise in a room on the fifth floor of a brick hotel in Wichita Falls. From my window I could see a drugstore down below, with a Coca-Cola sign hung like a large red button over the entrance. I could also see a diner and a Western Union office and a five-and-dime store and, down the street, a mechanic's shop with a sign that said WE FIX FLATS. Each of these things was somehow emblematic of both modernity and tradition, or perhaps simply an echo of the 1920s, which was probably the most prototypical decade in our history and the one for which we are forever nostalgic. I was gazing down on the America of Norman Rockwell. It was the America all of us grew up in and believed in and fought for. Now all my thoughts were dedicated to fleeing it, with my wife, in whatever fashion we could. It was a strange way to feel.

I had eight thousand dollars in cash, the clothes in the suitcase, the German Luger and a box of ammunition, and no car. I also had no plan. The pilot who had flown me to Wichita Falls had said his plane would be available in three or four days. He asked if I would be returning to Houston. I told him I didn't think so. I didn't mention that when I left Wichita Falls, I would have someone with me and would probably be in a hurry.

Entering Mexico wouldn't be difficult, I thought. There were still dirt roads that led to wooden bridges over the Rio Grande, with indifferent border security on both sides. The Mexican government never discouraged the presence of gringo dollars in its huge culture of prostitution and narcotics and pornography and police corruption along its northern rim. And the illegals we called wetbacks, who went back and forth across the river with regularity, had been a welcomed source of cheap labor since the Mexican Cession. The challenge was getting out of the state without being arrested.

I looked toward the west. Clouds of orange dust were rising into the sky. They reminded me of the year 1934, when I rope-dragged a bucket of water and a hammer and a nail bag and a box of burlap sacks up on Grandfather's roof and began securing the house against a storm that seemed biblical in proportion. Even though the temperature was close to freezing, I opened the hotel window and unlatched and pushed out the screen and put my head outside. The morning sounds of the city swelled up from the concrete, but it was the wind that defined the moment. It was out of the west, cold and bright and hard-edged and smelling of land that still had the imprints of dinosaurs in its riverbeds. I could feel my face tightening and starting to burn in the cold, my eyes watering. I had a sense of apprehension but also of hope, of new frontiers that awaited us, of finding safe harbor in America's past rather than in the present.

I closed the window and brushed my teeth and shaved. Then I sat down at the small writing desk with my journal and tried to think clearly. There was one issue to concentrate on. I had to get Rosita out of the asylum, away from functionaries who genuinely believed they were helping others by destroying their brain cells. How would I be able to do here what I hadn't in Houston? I'd brought the Luger I had taken off a German officer we'd pulled from the basement of a house hit with a phosphorus shell. His skin had literally boiled on his skeleton, dissolving all of his features. Even his fingers had been burned off. The only remnants of his face were his eyes, staring helplessly out of all that pain. The syrette of morphine our medic tried to inject into his arm was useless. The German officer asked me to shoot him. I wouldn't do it. When we had to move out, he was still alive. Now, with the same Luger I might have used to end a man's suffering, I was broaching the possibility of shooting an orderly, a nurse, a minimum-wage security officer, a janitorial person, a passerby, a sheriff's deputy with peach fuzz on his cheeks.

I wrote in my journal: *Good morning, Lord. We could surely use some help. Please take us safely over Jordan. If you can't do that, at least get us out of Texas.*

I put on a pair of khakis and sunglasses and a tie and my leather jacket and half-topped boots, and with a clipboard in my hand and two fountain pens and a mechanical pencil in my shirt pocket, I took a cab to the asylum. The cabbie said local people called the asylum the White Sanitarium, not because of its off-white color but because White was the name of its first director. The sanitarium was located on a knoll and was two stories high and had a tile roof and a design similar to that of the high schools constructed all over the country during the 1920s. Except it didn't look like a high school. There was nothing ornamental or graceful or redeeming about the building's architecture. It was stark, utilitarian, the fountain in front dry and webbed with heat cracks. Even the solitary tree by one of the walls was as bare as a talon.

"You visiting a family member here?" the cabbie asked.

"I'm trying to track down the survivors of a Nazi death camp. There's a patient here who might know what happened to them."

"You came to the right place."

"How's that?" I asked.

"The personnel here are good folks. This is a right popular place in Wichita Falls."

"Can you drive around back? I'd just like to see the building."

"Sorry, it's restricted back there."

"Why is it restricted?"

He looked at me in the rearview mirror. "I guess they don't want the patients wandering off or getting in people's automobiles. Where you from?"

He dropped me off in front of the building. I was never good at lying. Most Southerners are not. As flawed as Southern culture is, mendacity has always been treated in the South as a despicable characteristic. Notice how often Southerners casually address others as "you son of a bitch" with no insult intended. When the same person calls someone a "*lying* son of a bitch," you know he's serious. I had just lied to the cabbie. And I was about to tell a lot more lies as the day progressed. I didn't know if I would be up to the charge.

There is a trick you learn in the army that you never forget. There will always be a man in your unit named Smith or Jones or Brown. That's why it is so easy to shirk an assignment in the armed forces. All a shirker has to do is scratch his own name off a duty roster and substitute the name Smith or Jones or Brown, and someone else will probably show up on KP or guard or latrine duty in his stead. To my shame, that was the ignoble model I was using.

The receptionist was occupied. I gazed down the corridor and tried to memorize every name I saw painted on the frosted glass of an office door. The light was poor, and I couldn't see the lettering distinctly. Then it was my turn to approach the receptionist's desk. Her name was Leona Penbrook. She was a large, cheerful woman with thick hands and rings of baby fat under her chin. She wore a pink suit and a white rayon blouse with frills flowering out of the lapels. Her bright smile, her perfume, her sanguine nature, her southern Midlands accent, which you begin to hear west of Fort Worth, the aura of goodwill she seemed to exude with no agenda, were as pleasant and unpretentious as we can ask of human beings. The word I'm looking for is "heartening." She was one of those people who remind us that decency and courage and charity are found most often among the humblest members of the human family, and most of them get credit for nothing. This was the lady to whom I was telling the same story I had told the cabbie, and it was creating a sensation behind my eyes like a rubber band about to snap.

"You're a researcher for a refugee group?" she said.

"More or less. Actually, I have a degree in history from A&M," I replied. "I always hoped to become an anthropologist."

"It sounds like you're doing a very good deed for someone. Whom did you say you spoke to?"

"It was the governor's office that called," I said. "I think he talked to someone named Smith and someone named Jones or Johnson."

"We have a Jones here, but he's on leave right now. What did you say your name was?"

"Malory. I just need to talk to Mrs. Holland for a few minutes."

"She's heavily medicated, but I guess you know that."

"Not with any specificity," I replied.

"She's here for a series of procedures. She was in an extermination camp?"

"I think she was in two of them. Terrible things were done to her, Mrs. Penbrook. My outfit liberated one of the camps near Landsberg. After the Ardennes, my sergeant and I went into one of the camps by ourselves. The SS had just pulled out."

I had told the truth about Rosita's history. Mrs. Penbrook knew I was telling the truth, and she knew I had seen the same things a patient in the sanitarium had seen, a woman locked in a room with memories others couldn't imagine, and that somehow I wanted to undo the evil done to that person. For a moment I believed she realized I had lied about my identity and the purpose of my visit and yet was willing to put my deception aside. But in a situation such as mine, one that involved my wife's survival, I knew it was foolish to presume that others will follow their charitable instincts when it comes to their jobs and supporting their families.

"I tell you what," Mrs. Penbrook said. "It's warming up now, and some of the patients are going out on the lawn for a bit. You have a seat, and I'll make sure Mrs. Holland is among them."

Ten minutes later, I walked out on the back lawn, one that sloped through trees to a parking lot enclosed by a cyclone fence. I could see Rosita in a wheelchair, her back to me, a blanket pulled to her chest, a shawl over her head. I knew it was she, my warrior woman from the Book of Kings, the woman who had winked at me from under a pile of corpses, the bravest and most beautiful human being I had ever known. A big-shouldered black woman in a nurse's uniform and a mackinaw attended her. The black woman had dignified features and thick hair with gray swirls in it. She adjusted the blanket to keep the wind off Rosita's neck. The sun was shining in Rosita's eyes, forcing her to squint. I walked between the sun and her chair and looked down at her, waiting for her to recognize me. Her face looked freeze-dried, insentient, her eyes half-lidded, as though she were falling asleep or already inside a dream. "My name is Malory, Mrs. Holland," I said. "I'm here to talk with you about some people you may have known in Germany."

Her eyes looked into mine.

"Tom Malory is my name. I hope you don't mind my pulling up a chair and speaking with you," I said.

"She hears you okay," the black woman said. "She's got an awful lot of medicine in her right now. I'm going over here and let y'all talk. I'll be here if you need anything. My name is Clementine."

I got a folding chair and sat down in front of Rosita, the clipboard on my knees. "I'm going to get you out of here," I said.

I saw a light come into her eyes, the beginnings of a smile. Her lips moved without sound.

"You don't have to say anything," I said. "Nod to show me you understand."

She didn't nod, but she blinked.

"Did they give you shock treatment?" I asked.

She shook her head.

"We're not going to let them," I said.

"Weldon," she whispered down in her throat.

"Yes?"

"Weldon," she repeated.

"Tell me. What is it?"

"I love you," she whispered.

I could hardly restrain myself from reaching out and touching her hand. I knew as soon as I did, someone would realize I was not who I claimed to be.

"Linda Gail and Hershel know where we are," I said. "They'll do everything they can to help us. But you and I will be the ones to get ourselves out of here. That means we have to be good actors. Do you understand? I'm Mr. Malory. That's the only name I have."

Her eyes became sleepy again, her head sinking, although it was obvious she was trying to concentrate. At that moment I wanted to kill the entire Wiseheart family.

Clementine approached us. "She needs to go back to the room," she said.

"Can I see her again this afternoon?"

"Better ask Mrs. Penbrook. I expect she'll say it's okay."

I asked Clementine to step away from the wheelchair with me. "Is Mrs. Holland scheduled for electroshock treatment?" I said.

"I don't have anything to do with that. They got her on the second floor."

"What's that mean?"

"The second floor is for people that's depressed real bad. That might kill themselves. I'll be taking her back now."

I lingered on the lawn in the cold sunshine, the wind like dry ice on my face. I studied the parking lot, the security fence around it, the uniformed guard in the booth by the entrance. How would I get a vehicle inside? How would I get Rosita into the vehicle? The problem seemed insoluble. I glanced up at the second story of the sanitarium and saw Rosita's face in a window. Her breath had crystallized into icy white flowers on the glass. I don't think I will ever forget that image.

I HAD TOLD LINDA Gail and Hershel where I would be. When I returned to the hotel, the clerk took a message out of the key box and handed it to me. Linda Gail wanted me to call her. She didn't say why. If there was a tap on her phone, whoever had installed it would know the city I was calling from and figure out the rest of it. But I couldn't ignore her message. She was an intelligent woman and wouldn't have asked me to call unless something important had happened. I walked down the street and used a pay phone; at least I wouldn't give away the name of the hotel.

She answered on the second ring. "How's our friend doing?" she said.

"About the same," I said. She had not mentioned Rosita's name. I felt better about phoning her.

"Roy would like to talk with you."

"What for?"

"He wouldn't say."

"That's because he wants something. It doesn't matter what the situation is, he always has an agenda. His thinking is no different from a sociopath's."

"He's not one to make frivolous phone calls."

I couldn't believe Linda Gail was still under Roy's influence. "Tell him to put it in a letter."

"Maybe he can do something to help. Give him a chance."

"Dealing with Roy is like picking up broken glass with your bare fingers," I said. "Did he give you the Bunny Berigan record?"

"No."

"He tried to get me to give it to you. He'd wrapped it in satin paper with a ribbon. He believes he's the protagonist in an Elizabethan tragedy, and he wants the rest of us to be his stage props."

There was a pause. I wished I hadn't told her about the record. Maybe Roy had been sincere. Maybe he wanted to do something tender and not embarrass her or hurt Hershel. Maybe he was caught inside the impossibility of correcting the past.

"Can either Hershel or I do anything?" she asked.

"No, I'll be headed back to Louisiana tonight. I'm meeting in Baton Rouge with some geologists from Sinclair."

I had told another lie in case anyone was listening. I felt foolish constructing a conversation to mislead someone who may not exist. That's how the invasion of a person's privacy works. It makes us afraid of shadows and fills us with suspicion about our fellow man, and ultimately, it causes us to degrade and resent ourselves.

"Maybe Roy wants to make amends," she said. "Maybe he can help Rosita."

"Then why hasn't he already done it?"

"Maybe he's tried. He wants your respect. He's like a little boy. He flew his plane upside down on location."

"I don't care about Roy's problems. I don't know how I can get Rosita back. I'm against the wall. They're going to destroy her brain."

I heard her exhale against the receiver, not in exasperation but in surrender. "Can we do something?"

"There's Grandfather to think about. I'll call you all from Baton Rouge," I said, and hung up.

I ate a sandwich at the soda fountain in the drugstore that had a Coca-Cola sign over the doorway. I tried to think through all the events and improbabilities that had occurred in my life since I first saw Rosita. The Greek tragedians viewed irony, not the stars, as the agency that shaped our lives. They were probably right. I was a river-baptized Christian, but I had married a Jew who was a better Christian than I. I wanted to be an anthropologist, but I became a pipeline contractor and a rich man through the use of machines that made the tanks that tried to kill me. Roy Wiseheart was born with everything except the approval of his father and consequently seemed to value nothing. Hershel Pine was a man of humble birth who could have served as a yeoman under Henry V at the Battle of Agincourt, yet he possessed the chivalric virtues of an Arthurian knight. Clara Wiseheart owned unimaginable amounts of money, and seemed governed day to day by the vindictive child living inside her. Linda Gail had stopped for gas at a country store and stepped off the gallery into a camera's lens and a career in Hollywood. And since 1934, the single most influential ongoing event in my life had been my encounter with Bonnie Parker and Clyde Barrow, people who had the cultural dimensions of a hangnail.

Who can make sense of the roles we play? If I could draw any conclusion about the long, depressing slog of human progress, it's the possibility that unseen elements lie just on the other side of the physical universe and that somehow we're actors on the stage of the Globe, right across the Thames from a place called Pissing Alley, whether William Shakespeare or Christopher Marlowe are aware of our presence or not.

More ironic, I was soon to discover that Bonnie and Clyde were not through with me. And I was about to learn that Roy Wiseheart was one of the most determined people on the planet, at least when it came to getting his way. The phone in my hotel room was ringing just as I came through the door. It was 12:55 P.M. I picked up but didn't speak.

"Is that you, Weldon?" the voice said.

"How'd you know where I was?"

"You told me where Rosita had been moved. So I called every hotel in Wichita Falls. By the way, I'm using a phone that nobody has tapped."

"I didn't register under my own name. How would you know to call here?"

"I got the desk clerk to give me the names of the people who had registered in the last twenty-four hours. How many guests named Thomas Malory check in to a run-down dump in a sinkhole like Wichita Falls?"

"You're not a fan of small-town America?"

"Boy, are you a pill."

"Why would the desk clerk give you the names of their hotel guests?"

"I told him I was an FBI agent."

"The only subject I'm interested in discussing is Rosita. If you could help her, you would have already told me. That means I'm going to let you go. I'm asking that you not call me again."

"Give me a chance, pal. We're more alike than you think."

"No, we're not. Stay the hell away from me."

I hung up. It wasn't smart.

I HAD TO GET a car, and I had to get Rosita out of the sanitarium and into the car. Then I would have viable choices, a chance to run for it, to force the other side to come after us if they wanted to try, a chance to make others pay a price for what they had done to us. As long as we had choices, we had opportunities. If you get your ticket ripped in half, you do it in hot blood, and you do not go gently into that good night. Bonnie and Clyde were murderers, but no one can say they didn't have courage when they shot their way into a Texas prison to rescue a friend.

If we had choices, I could drive us across the Red River into Oklahoma and head for the Winding Stair Mountains and on into Arkansas and disappear inside the misty blue vastness of the Ozarks. Or we could go south and catch the Sunset Limited to Los Angeles and buy another car and rent a cottage in the vineyard country and live among Mexicans and southern Europeans who had known Jack London. Or we could drive to a café at a dirt crossroads that served as a bus stop and catch a Greyhound to Nevada and that night find ourselves milling among the crowds on the neon-striped sidewalks of Las Vegas, in high desert country surrounded by purple mountains, under a sky that turned turquoise at sunset and sparkled with stars by eight P.M. Then time would take care of our problems. Others would learn what had been done to my wife, and a degree of sanity would be restored in our lives. That's what I believed. All I needed was a car and a way out of the sanitarium.

My thoughts had run away with me. What would I do about Grandfather and my mother? I had replaced my fear with poetic fantasies. The reality was I felt like a man who had been sucked into a whirlpool and was drowning a few feet away from dry land, while the rest of the world sat by and watched and did nothing.

I WALKED DOWN THE street, past the diner and the drugstore and the mechanic's garage, to an automobile dealership on the corner. Pennants attached to wires flapped in the wind above the rows of new and used cars. Then I saw a vehicle that made my scalp shrink against the bone. It had four doors and a black roof and black fenders and a maroon body and whitewalled wire-spoked wheels. The red leather upholstery was sun-faded but looked like it had been rubbed with mink oil to prevent it from cracking. On the edge of my vision, I saw a man walking toward me, but I couldn't take my eyes off the 1932 Confederate.

"See something you like?" the man said. He had a long pointed beard like a mountain man's and wore an incongruous suit coat and corduroy trousers hitched up on his hips with firehouse suspenders. If he had an expression, I couldn't see it inside his beard.

"Where'd you get that '32 Confederate over there?" I said.

"That belonged to Dr. Jones. He works at the sanitarium. He decided to trade it in on something more sporty. The engine is rebuilt, and the tires are good. Want to take it for a spin?"

"Do you know where Dr. Jones got it?" I asked.

"I think he said he bought it from a banker in San Angelo."

A sunbaked gas ration sticker was still attached to the bottom of the windshield. On the right was a numbered sticker with the name of the sanitarium, the kind issued to employees. I opened the driver's door and ran my hand across the dashboard, then across the edge of the headliner. I touched a spot in the metal molding that had been soldered and sanded smooth and repainted, and I knew this was the spot where the .44-caliber bullet from Grandfather's revolver had lodged.

"Looking for something?" the salesman said.

"I just noticed there was a scratch here. It's not important."

The keys were hanging from the ignition. "Go ahead," the salesman said. "I'll ride with you and have a smoke."

I started the engine, and we bounced out into the street.

"Hums like a sewing machine and turns on a dime," the salesman said. "It'll do sixty on the highway without breaking a sweat. If you happen to be a traveling man, I think this baby has your name on it."

I looked at him, wondering if there was a second meaning in his words. He shook a Lucky Strike out of his pack and lit it. He gazed idly out the window as we drove up the main street and back to the lot.

"I'd like to pay cash. What do you want for it?" I asked.

"You said cash?"

"Yes, sir."

"We're asking nine hundred because it's a collectible. I can give it to you for eight."

"Sold American," I said.

"Let's get the paperwork done. I think it's fixing to cut loose out there. You ever seen such weather? Puts me in mind of the Dust Bowl years. We sure don't need any more of that."

Chapter 30

I CALLED THE HOUSE to check on Grandfather, then drove to a secondhand clothing store and bought a man's overcoat and an old cowboy hat. At three-fifteen P.M. I pulled up to the entrance of the secured parking lot behind the sanitarium. My suitcase and a paper bag from the store were on the floor in back, the Luger under the seat. The security guard wasn't much more than a boy and reading a copy of *Saga* magazine in the booth by a sliding gate. A military-style cap with a lacquered brim was sitting crown-down by his elbow. He had the lean physique and profile I had always associated with the West Texas boys I had known in the army. They were great pals to have, but almost every one of them was an unchurched Calvinist and not given to latitude. He closed his magazine and came outside as I rolled down the window. My heart was thudding so hard in my chest that I had to press my hand against my side. "Good afternoon," I said. "I'm picking up somebody for Dr. Jones."

He nodded politely and glanced at the employee sticker on the windshield. "That's a fine-looking car," he said.

"You bet."

"I'm fixing to get me a convertible. At least when it's a little bit warmer." He placed one hand on the roof and smiled down at me. I didn't know what I was supposed to say. "When I ask my girlfriend on a date, I got to take her on the bus. That don't flush real well."

Before I could reply, he pushed the gate free of the driveway and waved me through.

I parked at the very back of the lot, in a spot where the car couldn't be seen from the security booth. Fourteen or fifteen patients were sitting in the sunshine on the knoll. A sidewalk sloped from the top of the knoll to the curb of the parking lot. I had loaded the Luger that morning. It was hard to believe I had come armed into the midst of people such as the receptionist and the attendant named Clementine and the good-natured kid in the security booth. I felt a terrible sense of shame. I told myself over and over that I had no recourse. My wife's life was at stake. Nonetheless, I knew I was systematically deceiving others and that I might endanger their livelihoods and, if push came to shove, put their lives in jeopardy. I couldn't think my way out of the problem. I had reached the point where I had begun to think in terms of "unavoidable attrition," which was the rhetoric we had used to justify carpet-bombing and dropping incendiaries on civilian populations.

I saw Rosita in a wheelchair and Clementine sitting behind her on a stone bench. I picked up my clipboard and went up the sidewalk. Rosita was wearing a purple kerchief with red flowers instead of the shawl, as though setting aside winter and entering spring, regardless of what the seasons were doing. Her face seemed to have no expression, but when I looked at her eyes, I knew she was smiling inside.

I'd thought I would have a plan by that time. I didn't. At least not one that was rational. I had used subterfuge to gain access to the institution. However, I had reached a juncture where I had to make a choice between more of the same or trusting the potential for charity that secretly we pray is always at work in our fellow man.

I sat down next to Clementine. At that time in our history, it was unusual for a white person to sit next to a person of color. It was acceptable to stand next to one but not to sit. "You know that Mrs. Holland was in a Nazi death camp, don't you, Miss Clementine?" I said.

"Yes, sir, I heard that."

"There are people out yonder who love her and want to take care of her."

"I can understand that."

"There are also people who want to hurt her. That's how she ended up here."

"That'd be a pretty mean thing to do. Hard to imagine."

"It happens, probably more often than people think."

"What are you saying to me, sir?" she said, looking straight ahead.

"I'm not a sir. I gave up being a sir when I was discharged from the army."

"Polite is polite. Bad manners are bad manners."

"Are you a Baptist?" I asked.

"I have been a Baptist all my life."

"I was baptized in the Guadalupe River when I was twelve years old. I think the preacher was drunk. He almost drowned me."

"Better say what you need to say, Mr. Malory."

"I've done many things wrong in my life, but as an adult, I've prided myself on never telling a lie except to avoid injuring someone. I've told quite a few lies in the last couple of days."

Her eyes were on the horizon and the blue sky that was more like summer than winter, and the orange dust clouds that kept rising up like funnels on the plains.

"I saved my wife from the Nazis," I said. "I carried her in my arms through an artillery barrage. I hid with her in a cellar inside Germany until we were rescued by American paratroopers. I searched months for her after the war, and when I found her, I married her in Paris. I'd give my life for her right now, on this spot."

"I believe you, sir."

"Would you like to take a break? I can watch Mrs. Holland. Maybe I'll push her around the yard a little bit."

Her hands were folded together on her knees. "Yes, it's getting mighty cold. We're in the shadow of the building now." She looked at the horizon and at a bird flying out of a bare field. She rose from the bench and buttoned her mackinaw at the throat. "Mrs. Holland would probably like to be in the sun. I'll be back in five minutes with a hot chocolate. Not one second past five minutes. Thank you, sir."

"Thank you, Miss Clementine," I said.

She made no reply, and her eyes never met mine.

I wheeled Rosita slowly down the walk to the edge of the parking lot and paused by the curb, as though we were looking at the dust clouds gathering on the horizon. I helped her from the chair and put her in the front seat of the Confederate and set the chair in the back-seat and closed the doors. I removed the overcoat and the oversize cowboy hat from the paper bag and put them on Rosita and tucked her hair inside the hat. I turned the car around and drove toward the security booth. Then I rolled down the driver's window and leaned my head out as though I wanted to thank the guard. He came out of the booth and waved at me and pushed back the gate, and just that fast, we were out on the street and headed for the highway and the Great American Desert, a ball of tumbleweed smacking the wind-shield.

THIRTY MILES FROM town, a fine mist began blowing out of the south, mixing with the dust, and the sun seemed to dull over and grow cold and smaller inside its own glow. Then a shadow moved across the entirety of the landscape like a shade being pulled down on a window. I turned off on a side road and drove down to a creek bed among a grove of cottonwoods whose limbs glistened with mist and were as pointed and stark as the tips on a deer's antlers. A ribbon of red water wound its way through the bottom of the creek, and I saw raindrops splashing in it like drops of lead. I kept the engine and the heater running. Rosita had fallen asleep with her head on her chest, the brim of the cowboy hat slanted over her eyes. I didn't know how many or what kinds of drugs she had been administered. I suspected the dosage was large. She raised her head, maybe because the car had stopped.

"We need to stay off the road until dark," I said.

She looked into my eyes as though trying to make sense out of my words.

"It's all right to go back to sleep," I said. "We're safe."

"Weldon?"

"I'm right here."

"I was having a dream." She touched my face. Then she touched her own, the way people do when they're looking for the source of a toothache. "Is it morning?"

"No, it's almost nightfall. You've been sleeping. You have your times mixed up."

"I don't know what we're doing."

"We're leaving hospitals and drugs behind us. We have a good car and a lot of money. We'll stay in a nice hotel someplace. We'll eat in a fine restaurant, maybe even tonight. How do you like this car?"

She pushed down on the softness of the leather upholstery. "It's elegant."

"It's funny you choose that word. That's what I thought when I first saw it." I was saying too much, burdening her at a time when her mind was probably on the edge of breaking. "See, the sky is completely dark in the north. In another half hour, we'll be back on the highway."

She pulled her knees up on the seat, canting them sideways, and held on to my arm with both hands and pointed her forehead into my shoulder, mashing the crown of her hat flat.

We drove through the night into Amarillo and ate steak and eggs in a truck stop and saw the sun rise on the badlands. I thought of selling the car and buying another, but any business transaction with an automobile dealer at this point invited a number of risks that could be our undoing. The dust was blowing in serpentine lines on the asphalt. In an army-surplus store, I bought a large piece of canvas with eyelets on the corners, and we parked at a rest stop and I covered the car with the tarp, and we slept for three hours, snug and safe and warm inside our little Bedouin tent on the plains.

When I pulled off the canvas, a sheriff's car and the Texas Highway Patrol passed us without slowing down, although they may not have been able to see the car clearly from the highway.

We changed radio stations constantly but heard nothing on the news about ourselves. By evening we were in New Mexico. Snow was spitting against the windshield, sliding in crystals down the glass, the clouds charged with electricity. The topography had probably changed little since the Ice Age. For miles we could not see a human structure. By sunset, the snow had stopped and columns of smoke or dust seemed to rise of their own accord from atop the mesas and break apart in the wind. Against the horizon, we could see a solitary mountain whose top had caved inward, forming a cone like that of a dead volcano. Along the roadsides were piles of igneous rock that resembled slag scraped from a furnace. Later, I saw the lights of emergency vehicles blinking ahead of us and turned onto a side road and drove fifteen miles before I got back on the asphalt. Rosita watched the country go by as you would on a train.

We spent two days in a motor court downwind from a feeder lot full of Angus that bawled through the night. I could see the influences of the drugs that had been injected into Rosita's body gradually leaving her system. I had turned out the light and gone to bed when she came out of the shower and got under the covers without putting on her nightgown, her hair damp, her body glowing. She made me think of a mermaid rising from dark water. I held her against me and pressed my face in the coolness of her hair and kissed the top of her shoulder.

"Hello, stranger," I said.

"Hello, yourself," she replied.

"Do you know the song 'Hello, Stranger' by A. P. Carter?"

"I don't think so. Is it special for some reason?"

"Once you hear it, you don't forget it. It's like you. A man sees you once, and he never gets you out of his mind."

"If they catch us and take me to another sanitarium, I want you to put me out of your mind forever."

"I'll never do that."

"I'll take my life, Weldon."

"No, you will not. They're never going to beat us, Rosita. We beat them in Germany. We'll beat them here."

She put her arm across my chest and closed her eyes and was soon asleep.

THE NEXT AFTERNOON we checked into a motor court at the bottom of Raton Pass. We had reached a crossroads in our odyssey. Each night a passenger train came down the Pass, actually sliding down the rails, the wheels deliberately locked because of the steepness of the grade, on its way to the coast. We could sell the car and board the train to Albuquerque, Flagstaff, or Los Angeles. Or we could head for the high country in Nevada. Or we could continue north, up Raton Canyon and through Trinidad and into Denver. From there, if we wished, we could take a plane to any city in the United States.

The car was parked under the porte cochere attached to the side of our cottage at the motor court. I walked down the main street to buy a newspaper. The sky was green. A layer of warm air was rising from the desert into the abrupt ascent of the Southern Colorado Plateau. The juxtaposition of miles and miles of flatlands and buttes and mesas, all of it lit by a flaming red sun low on the horizon, and the great, darkening massivity of the Rocky Mountains behind me was head-reeling. I tried to see the tops of the mountains, but they were higher than the clouds, and the clouds were as black and swirling and sublime as smoke from an inferno. I don't believe I ever saw a greater artwork than the one I witnessed that evening. Somehow it seemed an indicator of all the good things that awaited us down the track.

The only newspaper on the drugstore magazine rack was a local one, the kind usually published by a staff of no more than four or five, including the printer. I bought a copy and sat at the soda fountain and ordered a cup of coffee. The biggest local news was about a meeting of the Veterans of Foreign Wars and a grease fire in a café and the theft of a tractor from a barn. Then I turned to a section that was made up of ads and general-interest stories probably pulled randomly off the wire, one just as extraneous to small-town concerns as another. At the top of the page was a follow-up on the reported crash of a flying saucer at Roswell in July of that year. The air force was restating its recantation of the initial claim that it had found the wreckage of a UFO on a local ranch; the salvaged materials were obviously pieces of a weather balloon. Contrary to rumor, no bodies of extraterrestrials had been recovered from the crash site. How strips of wood and rubber and aluminum and tinfoil-like material from a weather balloon could be mistaken for the wreckage of a spaceship was never quite addressed. Regardless, it was good entertainment, no matter which point of view you chose.

I was about to put aside the paper and leave it for someone else when I turned the page. I couldn't believe what I was looking at. The four photographs at the top of the story showed the four brain-destroyed women Linda Gail had shown me. The grainy transfer of the images to newsprint had made them even more macabre. The story had come off the wire in Los Angeles and was written by a gossip columnist who quoted other gossip columnists as the story's source. The details were bizarre and prurient and unbelievable, in the way of stories from *True Detective, Argosy, Saga,* and *Male,* and because they were so unbelievable, the reader concluded they could not have been manufactured.

I saw Roy's name and Linda Gail's and the director Jerry Fallon's and Clara Wiseheart's. The story was basically accurate; the prose was another matter. It was purple, full of erotic suggestion, cutesy about "love nests" and "romance in *Mayheco.*" But as tabloid reporting often does for no purpose other than to satisfy a lascivious readership, the article brought to light an injustice and criminal conspiracy that mainstream newspaper and radio would not have touched.

In other words, the account was less one of fact than a hazy description of infidelity, a movie set that had turned into the Baths of Caracalla, a young starlet seduced by a Texas oilman whose heroic war record and good looks had lured others to his cottage at the Beverly Hills Hotel. Of course, there was the vindictive wife, a human tarantula, who had tried to use her connections with Mafia figures such as Frankie Carbo and Bugsy Siegel to destroy the brain of an innocent woman she had scapegoated for her husband's profligate behavior.

The story could have been borrowed from a history of the Borgias or the manipulations of Nero's mother. The real story, involving greed and the death of my father and the attempted theft of our pipeline company, was not one many people would be interested in. I supposed, however, that iniquity is iniquity, and the story told by Linda Gail and the tabloid writer contained its own kind of truth. Which is the better medium for its portrayal? A grocery list of legalisms or a bloody saga backlit by handheld torches, with the shadows of rogues dancing on the greasy waters of the Tiber? I wanted to send a box of candy to the scandalmonger who wrote the article.

I BELIEVE THE MOST dangerous and vulnerable moments in my early experience as a combat soldier were not what one would think. I was in the second wave at Normandy, and most of the suffering that had taken place along that blood-frothed, ugly strip of coastline was already over. My real initiation would come at Saint-Lô. I wanted to be brave but feared that I was not. My greater fear was that I would prove a coward had lived inside me all my life, and this cowardly presence would come to define who I was.

Before the breakout at Saint-Lô, we laid down one of the heaviest rolling barrages in history. The forward artillery observer was from my platoon, a kid who carried a half dozen good-luck charms in his fatigue jacket and taped his dog tags so they wouldn't tinkle and had no higher ambition than to return to his job as a shoe salesman at a Thom McAn store in New Jersey. A round came in short, right beside his hole, rendering him stone-deaf, cutting his wire, isolating him in the dark. Then the Germans began answering our barrage. Amid the explosions, we could hear him calling for help, his cries becoming weaker and weaker. I went after him, the ground lighting around me as though a downed power line were dancing in a pool of water. I found him spread-eagled on his back in the bottom of his hole, the skin around his mouth webbed with blood. I got him across my shoulders and carried him to a road, where we hid inside a culvert until dawn. He died shortly after sunrise.

In the following days, I began to feel that I was invulnerable. I had been through what, in medieval times, was called "ordeal by fire," and I had proved myself worthy in the eyes of others. I was sure that Providence had intended for me to survive the war. It is impossible for a combat soldier to be more self-deluded or to be possessed of a more reckless attitude.

The article in the Raton newspaper had given me an undue level of confidence. At last Rosita and I had been vindicated by the support of the crowd, I told myself. Unfortunately, I had forgotten that the support of the crowd has a shelf life of about three minutes.

I walked to a phone booth down the street from the motor court and called to check on Grandfather. Through the Plexiglas windows, I could see the highway that led up through Raton Pass and the winding ponderosa-dotted canyon that opened onto the old mining town of Trinidad, where the Earp brothers and Doc Holliday finished paying the debt they owed the Clanton gang.

Snowball answered the phone. She was under five feet tall, weighed over two hundred pounds, and had the blackest skin I had ever seen. She often wore white dresses and blouses, some with eyelets on the shoulders.

"How's Grandfather doing?" I said.

"A little laid up."

"He's sick?"

"More like he fell down. Bruised all over his seat and his back."

"Would you tell me what happened?"

"He made me drive him to the roller-skate rink on South Main."

"I don't believe this."

"You try arguing with him and see what happens."

"He put on roller skates?"

"They didn't want him to do it. He caused a big scene."

"Snowball—"

"It ain't my fault."

"I know it. Can you take the phone to him, please?"

"Yes, suh."

I saw the passenger train that ran from Chicago to Los Angeles coming down the grade inside the canyon, the headlamp on its locomotive wobbling in the dark, the wheels screeching on the rails. If we decided on the train as our way out, we would have to wait until tomorrow evening.

"How's Rosita?" Grandfather asked.

"She's better every day. Are you trying to commit suicide?"

"If I wanted to commit suicide, I wouldn't mess it up."

"Why would you go to a roller rink?"

"I felt like it."

"Is there anything in the papers about Rosita and me or the Wisehearts?"

"Yes, there is. That's not all. That fellow Slakely burned up in his trailer. The paper said an electrical fire."

"Hubert Slakely the cop?"

"Don't get your hopes up. You pulled the tiger's tail. The Wisehearts won't quit. If they let you get away with it, any little pissant in Houston can climb out from under a rock and do it."

"No one knows how to deliver an insult like you, Grandfather." But I wasn't thinking about his ongoing denigration of everything that breathed. I was trying to think through the implications of Slakely's death.

"We need you," Grandfather said.

"Linda Gail and Hershel haven't looked in on you?"

"I didn't rear you up to lose you to a wolf pack, son. Your mother needs you, and so do I. You come back home, you hear me? Just like I told you when you went overseas."

He had never called me "son" before.

Chapter 31

I woke at dawn. The sky was clear and the moon still up, the grass on the foothills of Raton Pass stiff with frost. I placed my hand on the windowpane. It was ice-cold. I let Rosita sleep while I brushed my teeth and shaved and put on a clean corduroy shirt. I had a good feeling about the day. We had managed to get from Wichita Falls to within twenty miles of the Colorado state line without being apprehended or stopped. I told myself that in the greater scheme of things, we were not that important. Also, we had harmed no one and hence were not a threat to others. Bonnie and Clyde, Baby Face Nelson, John Dillinger, and the Barker-Karpis gang had waged war against the banking system of the United States, and it had taken years for our best law enforcement agencies to kill or drive them to ground. We were hardly worth anyone's notice.

I have always believed that the American West, like Hollywood, is a magical place and the biggest stage set on earth. I also believe it's haunted by the spirits of Indians, outlaws, Jesuit missionaries, drovers, gunmen, conquistadores, bindle stiffs, Chinese and Irish gandy dancers, whiskey traders, temperance leaguers, gold panners, buffalo hunters, fur trappers, prostitutes, and insane people of every stripe, maybe all of them living out their lives simultaneously in our midst. The Homeric epic doesn't have to be discovered inside a book; it begins just west of Fort Worth and extends all the way to Santa Monica.

It was out there waiting for us, the Grand Adventure unscrolling beneath our feet. That's what I felt as Rosita and I ate breakfast in a café not far from the train depot built in what was called Mission Revival mode, where we would board the Super Chief that evening.

"What are we going to do with the car?" she asked.

"Rent a garage. We'll return for it later or hire someone to deliver it to Houston."

"Sounds easy."

"Hubert Slakely burned to death in his trailer. Grandfather told me last night."

She was chewing a tiny piece of toast in her cheek, her eyes focused on the red Spanish-tile roof of the depot. She waited until the piece of toast seemed to dissolve in her mouth, her gaze never leaving the train station. "How did the fire start?"

"The paper said an electrical short."

She let her eyes drift onto mine.

"You don't believe that?" I said.

"I think bad people earn their fate. The form it comes in doesn't matter."

"You don't believe it was an accident?" I said.

"Was Lloyd Fincher's death a suicide?" she said. "Was that private detective's death a hit-and-run? I don't care how any of them died. I'm glad they're dead."

"Tomorrow we'll be in Union Station in Los Angeles," I said. "Wait till you see it. It's beautiful. It looks like a Roman villa."

She was smiling.

"What's funny?" I asked.

"Who else would see ancient Rome in the middle of Los Angeles?"

"Any student of history," I replied.

She looked up at me and winked, just as she had the day I found her deep inside Nazi Germany.

Two motorcycle cops came in and removed their caps and sat at the counter. They were wearing leather jackets and knee-high polished boots and jodhpurs with stripes down the legs. Their faces looked tight and blistered, the skin around their eyes leached of color from the goggles they wore on the highway. One of them blew on his hands. Before I could turn away, our eyes met in the mirror.

I looked straight ahead, then out the window, and tried not to scratch my forehead, which is what a person does when he wants to hide his face. I felt I had stepped onto a stage. I cursed myself under my breath for my carelessness in looking at the cops and for my phone call to Grandfather. I started to say something to Rosita. She was eating silently, her face lowered. "I saw them," she whispered.

"We're in no hurry. We have no cares."

"We'll be fine, Weldon," she said, not looking up.

I drank my cup empty and raised it to catch the waitress's attention. I kept my gaze off the cops, but I could feel one of them looking at me in the mirror. I feigned a yawn. "I'm going to the washroom," I said. "Don't ask for the check."

She nodded and smiled as though I had said something pleasant.

I washed my hands and combed my hair, so I would look like I'd taken my time in the men's room. When I came back to the booth, I hoped the cops would be occupied with their breakfast or talking with the waitress. They were waiting on their food; the closest one was still looking at me in the mirror. The waitress put the check on our table.

"Stay here," I said to Rosita. "Don't get up for any reason."

"What are you doing?"

"Paying the check."

I walked toward the cashier, putting on my hat, glancing casually at the check, pausing when I was abreast of the cops. "Excuse me, we're headed east through Clayton and Texline. Do y'all know if there's much black ice up that way?"

"In the shady spots, maybe," said the cop who had been looking at me. "Where you headed?"

"Big D."

"You should have smooth sailing."

"Somebody told me Clayton is where Black Jack Ketchum was hanged."

"If you stop in Clayton, go to the Hotel Eklund. They have pictures of the execution on the wall."

"I don't remember exactly what his crime was."

"You name it, he did it. A general bad guy."

"I hear there's a famous restaurant there."

"It's in the Eklund," he said. "You're from Dallas?"

"No, I grew up in southwest Texas. Thanks for your help."

He said nothing in reply. I paid the check and went back to our booth and placed a tip under my plate. Then Rosita and I walked side by side down the line of counter stools, past the cops. Neither turned around or seemed to take notice of us in the mirror. They were both smoking cigarettes, sipping from their coffee, tipping their ashes in the saucer. The waitress was bending over to get some water glasses from a shelf, her skirt stretched across her shapely rump. The cops looked into space; they did not speak to each other. Nor did they look at the woman.

Rosita and I walked down the street, past the depot, the wind so cold there was no difference between it and a flame.

"What do you think?" Rosita asked.

"We stepped on a land mine."

WE WENT THROUGH the side door of a grocery store and filled a sack with bread and sliced meat and cheese and canned goods and soda pop. From a window, I saw one of the cops come out of the café with his helmet and goggles on. A cruiser pulled into the parking lot. The motorcycle cop talked to the driver, leaning down to the window, the tailpipe of the cruiser puffing smoke. Then the cruiser drove out of view, and the motorcycle cop went back into the café. What did it all mean? I couldn't be sure.

Rosita and I walked as briskly as we could to the motor court. My eyes were watering; my face felt blistered from the wind. The room seemed to crawl with static electricity. If I touched a metal surface, a spark jumped from my fingers. I looked out the side of the curtain. The street and the two-lane highway were empty, newspaper swirling in a vortex next to a knocked-over garbage can.

"What do you want to do?" Rosita said.

"Get out of town."

"Where?"

It was hard to think. If we went south, we would drive into sparsely populated badlands where our level of visibility would be maximized and our ability to change our route reduced to nil. Driving east into the Texas Panhandle would put us in the bull's-eye again. Taos was a viable option, located down a winding road among wooded mountains, but it was full of artists and writers and bohemians, the kind of people who take note of everything they see and hear. The best choice—the only one, in my opinion—was to get out of New Mexico and into Colorado.

"We're a half hour from Trinidad," I said. "We'll be out of sight and out of mind. We can go into the San Juan or Sangre de Cristo Mountains or keep going into Denver. They'll never find us in Denver."

"But they'll find us somewhere," Rosita said.

"Time's on our side."

"I want to talk to Linda Gail. I want to get a message to Roy Wiseheart and his wife," she said.

"I don't think that's a good idea."

"It doesn't matter at this point," she said. "Call them collect. Or would you rather I do it?"

I picked up the phone. "What's the message?"

"Tell Linda Gail that if we live through this, I'm going to kill Roy and Clara Wiseheart."

"That's not like you."

"Look at what they've done to us."

Her attitude was hard to argue with. Clara and her father-in-law, Dalton Wiseheart, seemed to nurse their anti-Semitism like a poisonous orchid, and one or both of them was responsible for the grief we had been through. But prejudice took second place to their lust for money and power. I made the call, although not for the reason Rosita thought.

Linda Gail answered the phone and accepted the charges.

"I'll make this quick," I said. "Our meter may be running out. If something happens to me, the company goes to Hershel. That's in my will. The will also states that my mother and grandfather are to be cared for for the rest of their lives. If you see Roy, tell him I hope he has a good life. If you ever see Dalton Wiseheart, tell him he failed. Tell him that in the House of Jesse, he wouldn't be allowed to clean a chamber pot."

"He failed at what?"

"Destroying me and my wife."

"I don't think you know what's going on here," she said. "Clara Wiseheart came to our house in a rage. Her friends in the DAR won't take her calls. Her picture has been in the newspaper twice, once with her mouth hanging open. Roy went to the airport last night and left town for parts unknown. She thought he went to Los Angeles with me. Spit was flying off her lips while she was yelling at me in the driveway. The neighbors enjoyed the show tremendously."

"I have to go."

"Where do you think Roy went?"

"You and Hershel take care of each other. Take care of Grandfather, too. He's not as tough as he lets on."

"This sounds like a deathbed statement. What's happening? Where are you?"

"We're better than any of them. Remember that, Linda Gail," I said.

When I hung up, Rosita was sitting in a wooden chair by the window. "You don't like to leave threatening messages for people like the Wisehearts?"

"Grandfather faced down Wes Hardin and the Dalton gang. I asked him how he did it. He said, 'You don't say a word. You fill their ears with your silence. The only voice they'll hear will be their own fear.'"

"I meant what I said about not going back."

"I know," I replied.

"There were times in the camp when I wished I had killed myself. If they had put me in the whorehouse, I would have done it. Even after the SS deserted the camp, I didn't want to live anymore. Not with the memories I had. Not until I met you."

"I was a poor catch."

"They're not going to take me alive, Weldon."

As I looked into her eyes, I wondered if Bonnie Parker had thought the same thing on the blacktop parish road outside Arcadia, Louisiana. There was nothing more I could say. Sometimes death is preferable to life. Only a fool, or someone who has never seen suffering on an unimaginable scale, would say otherwise.

"We have to go," Rosita said. "Snow is blowing at the top of the Pass."

It was true. The sun was shining, but high up the grade, one of the steepest in the Rockies, snow crystals were whirling among the rocks and pine boughs like spun glass. Rosita backed out the car while I carried our suitcase and bag of groceries outside. We went through the intersection at the edge of town, and in under thirty seconds, we were climbing the incline toward the heavens, the bottom of the canyon dropping into shadow behind us. I reached under the seat and pulled out the Luger and set it by my thigh.

TOWARD THE TOP of the grade, I saw an old mining town surrounded by piles of rust-colored slag. The streets were made of crushed rock. On one of them was a white stucco church with a small tower that I thought might have been an eighteenth-century Spanish mission. Then I remembered the story. After the Ludlow Massacre in 1914, the Rockefeller family built churches throughout the West to rehabilitate the reputation of their patriarch. The site of the massacre was midway between Trinidad and Pueblo. To me, the white stucco building among the slag heaps told a story that probably few were interested in: an armored personnel carrier firing into striking miners, the burning of their tents, the asphyxiation of eleven children and two women in an earthen pit. Americans did this to other Americans. To me, it seemed a shameful business. But that's not why I mention this instance of egregious cruelty. I felt that somehow Rosita and I were entering the past, stepping into the roles of people who had already lived their lives and were watching us replicate them.

Most of the streets in Trinidad were brick, the buildings constructed of heavy gray stones, the city spread across a broad knoll at the bottom of mountains that soared straight into the sky, more like buttes than mountains. I don't know what I had expected. Perhaps roadblocks or the Colorado state police. I guess everyone believes during a time of duress that the rest of the world is focused on his or her problems. According to Daniel Defoe in his *Journal of the Plague Year,* those afflicted by the Black Death wandered the cobblestone streets of London in 1665 shouting out their sins to anyone who would listen. No one was interested. The shutters of every house and cottage and apartment were slammed shut on their cries.

I pulled into a filling station and asked the attendant to change the oil in our car, primarily to get the Confederate out of view. Rosita and I walked to the public library and talked to the reference lady about the history of the city, all the time glancing out the windows for anything unusual on the streets or the highway. To the north was a huge cattle auction barn and, behind it, pastureland that was still green. The wind had died, and snowflakes were drifting down in the sunshine from a mountain that resembled a vertically serrated steel-blue skyscraper with no windows. I could not have imagined a more peaceful urban setting.

"Are you visiting?" the librarian asked. Her reading glasses hung from a velvet ribbon around her neck.

"We thought we might look around," I replied. "Is it very difficult to drive out in the San Juan Mountains?"

"It can be. Up high, at least," she said. "This time of year you have to be careful. The bad passes are Wolf Creek and Monarch. You're not going there, are you?"

"No, we're casual tourists," I said. "We're not looking for anything very adventurous."

"Nothing exciting happens around here," she said. "Maybe you should spend some time with us. If you like horse racing, summer is a much better time."

"Thank you for the information," I said.

"I hope I haven't misled you."

"Pardon?" I said.

"I said nothing exciting happens around here. Maybe it's better you not pick up any hitchhikers today."

"How's that?" I said.

"A deputy sheriff was in the café earlier. He said something about a kidnapper on the loose."

"Someone who kidnapped a child?" I said.

"I didn't quite get it all." The librarian put her reading glasses back on. "I hope you enjoy your stay."

We went outside. Nothing of substance had changed in the streets. There was no police presence that I could see. But the day was not the same. The air smelled of tar and burned food and dust from a train yard; it had the dry smell of unending winter. The light was harsher, colder. The green pastures were dimmed by snow blowing down from the mountains. I saw cracks in the sidewalk and the asphalt that I hadn't noticed earlier. The nineteenth-century buildings resembled prison houses and asylums rather than Victorian homes. A grayish-green twin-engine plane crossed the sky directly overhead, its color reminiscent of the camouflage paint on a German fighter-bomber. I wondered if doors were slamming all around us, as they had slammed on the afflicted in the time of Defoe.

"Where are we going?" Rosita asked.

"To get the car," I replied, my voice sharper than it should have been.

"I mean after that."

"There's a town up the road called Walsenburg. We can take a train there. We'll leave the car behind."

She put her arm in mine. "Keep looking straight ahead," she said.

"What is it?"

"There's a police car on the corner," she replied.

We waited until the traffic light turned green, then crossed the street and stood in front of a hardware store so we could use the display window as a mirror. The police cruiser went through the intersection and turned at the corner, then drove slowly up a hill toward a stone building that looked like a courthouse or a city hall. The driver seemed to be looking on both sides of the street.

"We're getting on the road," I said.

I paid the filling station attendant for the oil change and for fueling the car. "You headed north?" he said.

"No, we're staying in town. What's up north?"

"A front is moving in. Warm air rises up from the plateau in New Mexico and hits the cold air, and we get dump-truck loads of snow dropped on us. We can have bright, sunny weather, and in ten minutes the sky can turn black as midnight."

"Glad we're staying in town," I said.

We drove out of the business district and onto the highway, past the auction barn, into a buffeting wind, into uncertainty of every kind. I stayed in second gear, the accelerator to the floor, until the transmission was screaming.

It's hard to describe the feeling I had. It was one of those moments when mortality becomes real. It wasn't like the war. War gives you choices, not of the best kind, certainly, but choices just the same, or at least the illusion of them. When mortality steals upon you in an improbable fashion, in a totally innocuous environment, you know it's real because it's not supposed to be there. It's not a crossroads; it's a cul-de-sac.

When I was fifteen, I went to visit my uncle Cody on his ranch in the Gunnison Valley. The train trip was a splendid adventure for a boy my age, particularly during the privation of the Great Depression. My mother fixed me a bag of fried chicken, and my father gave me a dollar watch so I could get myself up before my four A.M. arrival in Walsenburg, where my uncle was meeting me at the station. When my father gave me the watch, he said, "It's probably good for only one trip, but it'll do you."

He was right. The day after I arrived in Colorado, the spring broke. The dollar watch had served its purpose and was no longer of any value. That's how I felt as we sped up the highway into hail clicking on the windshield and glistening like glass on the asphalt. Perhaps our race was almost done, and this was the way our denouement had been written. Perhaps the Fates never intended me to survive Saint-Lô or the Ardennes and I had escaped my destiny by accident. Or maybe Rosita wasn't supposed to leave the camp where I found her; maybe both of us had interfered in a design that was much larger than we were.

I had learned only one lesson in life: History does not correct itself in its own sequence. The moment of correction comes in ways we never anticipate. I believed then and I believe now that we drove into another dimension, one that was not spatial, one that had nothing to do with the banal world of rationality and cause and effect, one that was not imaginary but more real than the one where we measure our lives in teaspoons. In some ways, I had come to feel I was a self-deluded prisoner of *The Song of Roland*. I thought I'd bought into medieval notions of chivalry and cloaks rolled in blood and the clang of swords upon shields because I couldn't deal with the savagery of my fellow man. Now I knew that was not the case. The story of Roncevaux was real, and so were the horns blowing in the canyons high up in the Pyrenees. It was the story that ennobled us and showed us we were more than we thought we could ever be. It was the poem that explained the nature of courage and turned the mystery of death into a heroic couplet. Ultimately, it was the poem that banished fear from the heart and transformed us from actors into participants.

There's another way to put it. Sometimes your luck runs out and you have to accept that the life you planned was a dream written on water. Just south of Ludlow, where the striking miners and their wives and children were murdered by the Colorado state militia and Rockefeller's gunmen, I saw the blue and red lights of several emergency vehicles parked diagonally on the highway, all of them pointed at us, like schooled-up sharks.

I swerved off the highway onto a dirt road, the back end of the Confederate fishtailing in a cloud of dust. I floored the accelerator and followed the road across the hardpan, past the site where the eleven children and two women had died in a pit under a burning tent. I climbed steadily into the high country, out of piñon trees and sage into spruce and grand fir and ponderosa and larch and lodgepole pine. In the rearview mirror, I could see at least three vehicles in pursuit. I worked the Luger from under the seat and set it on the dashboard. Rosita stared at me, her eyes filled with alarm.

The transition from the Southern Plateau into the mountains was dramatic. The road forked three times, and at each juncture I chose one road or the other arbitrarily. The peaks of the mountains were over eleven thousand feet, the fir trees shining with snowmelt in the sun, the boulders in their midst gray and smooth and stained with lichen in the shade. We climbed over a rise and descended an incline that gave us a brief view of a blue mountain higher than all the rest, so high the trees stopped at least two thousand feet below the peak.

Between the mountaintops was a ribbon of blue sky, and beyond it, on both sides of the mountains, rolling black clouds of a kind the filling station attendant had warned us about. The pistons in the Confederate were clattering like bones, the needle on the heat gauge trembling inside the red zone. I had no doubt we would soon blow a rod. Just as we started up the next incline, I saw the same twin-engine plane I had seen in Trinidad. It was making a wide turn, leveling out, coming back toward us for a flyover. I suspected it was a spotter plane working for the state police.

There was another fork ahead. I double-clutched the transmission and shifted into first and gave the engine all the gas it would take. We went around a curve into thicker timber, and I took my eyes off the dirt road to look quickly in the rearview mirror. The police cruisers below had temporarily lost sight of us and probably stopped to see which fork in the road we had taken. I looked back through the windshield and saw immediately in front of us a cliff extending into space with no guardrail. I swerved the car back on the road within two or three seconds of plunging at least a thousand feet to the forest below.

I had to fight to catch my breath. Rosita had not said a word. She had propped one hand against the dashboard, the other on the armrest. Steam was boiling off the hood. The Luger had clattered to the floor. "We should have gone over the edge," she said.

"*What?*"

"I'd rather have it end that way."

"We mustn't think in those terms, Rosita. Please don't say things like that again."

"They're going to get us. You know it. Don't pretend."

"Wrong. These bastards had better not catch up with us. If anyone pays a price, it will be them. We don't punish ourselves for what others have done to us."

"Stop lying. Our car is going to fall apart. Listen to the engine."

"We're never going to give up," I said.

"That's not the point. You're not listening to me."

She was right. I wasn't listening to her, and I didn't plan to, because I knew too well what was on her mind.

Suddenly, we were out of the trees and on a long, windswept, snow-streaked stretch of gray rock that overlooked a valley so far below that the fir trees looked one inch tall.

"Here," she said.

"Here what?"

"We do it. I do it. I don't care which of us does it. Give me the gun."

I stopped the car and got out. I flung the Luger over the cliff. When I got back in the car, her eyes were shiny and wet. She started to open the door. I grabbed her by the arm. "Do you want to give in to these guys?"

"Someone left the door open on the electroshock room. I saw a woman being electrocuted. She had a rubber gag in her mouth. I'll never forget her face."

I popped the clutch and spun gravel off the tires and drove along the edge of the cliff, then turned onto a dirt track through the trees on the west side of the mountain. The descent was the steepest we'd attempted. Even in second gear, the brake bands were squealing, rocks as sharp as knives bouncing under the chassis, banging against the tie rods and oil pan, maybe slicing the tires.

We came out of the woods onto a corrugated road spanning two miles of swampy meadow that offered no cover and exposed us to the twin-engine plane turning out of the sun. The first of three police cruisers emerged from the woods, its red and blue emergency lights housed inside a Plexiglas dome of whirling mirrors on the roof. Two other police cruisers were bringing up the rear.

I can't say I regretted throwing away the Luger. But I felt naked without it, the way you feel powerless in a dream, the way the tankers I saw at the Ardennes probably felt when they were trying to run in knee-deep snow while a German machine gunner locked down on them. There was no doubt in my mind this was it. The Confederate could not outrun the cruisers on a straight road. We would be arrested and separated, and Rosita would be at the mercy of the system.

Earlier I said I believed we had driven into another dimension. The events of the next few minutes would convince me that my perception was correct, but not because of any supernatural factor at work in our lives. I had acted on presumption about Roy Wiseheart, forgetting that presumption and arrogance are one and the same.

"What's that plane doing?" Rosita said.

The twin-engine had made one pass overhead, wagging its wings, then turned and climbed in a maneuver known in the Great War as an Immelmann. The pilot dove toward us, as though his plane were sliding down a ski slope, barrel-rolling, or flying upside down, I wasn't sure which. He zoomed over the treetops behind us and banked up into the ribbon of blue that was rapidly disappearing inside the advancing storm.

Grandfather had said the rich always returned to their own kind. He may have been right about other wealthy people, but he was wrong, as I had been, when it came to Roy Wiseheart.

I had the accelerator on the floor. If we blew the engine, we blew the engine. Maybe the drivers of the police cars were distracted by the plane, or perhaps they had incurred their own mechanical troubles, but for whatever reason, they were dropping farther and farther behind, just as a great shadow began to spread across the valley. Rosita was kneeling on the seat and looking through the back window. For just a second, in my mind's eye, I thought of Bonnie Parker and Clyde Barrow speeding down a Texas road with bullets flying past their heads.

No one shot at us. They never got the chance. I heard Rosita scream. It sounded like the screech I had heard inside the Confederate when I fired Grandfather's revolver through the back window.

"What is it?" I said.

"He's going to kill us!" she said.

He came in low over the road, as though strafing a convoy of Japanese infantry. He roared right over the top of the Confederate, buffeting it the way the slap of a wave would. I thought he would pull up. Maybe that was what he intended to do. But in my relationship with Roy, I never saw him act without forethought, and I never saw him fail when it came to carrying out his intentions. His wheels were up, his speed faster than any safe landing would allow. The plane went over us, blocking out the sky, then belly-landed, sliding like a plow on the road, the propellers locking and then crumpling against the wings.

All the light had gone out of the sky. The meadows were dark and sodden, the water ponds in the grass flanged with ice. The sparks flying from under the plane's fuselage resembled the bright orange drip from a welder's torch. The explosion was not loud, more like a whoosh of heat, like metal rising into the air and collapsing back on itself, like a flash of yellow and red on the snow, like a Christmas log bursting alight.

None of the police cruisers was touched. But they weren't going anywhere. The meadows, frozen or not, were nothing short of a bog. As we drove into the woods on the far side of the valley, I saw the burning plane and the cruisers and the policemen grow smaller and smaller in my rearview mirror, like images frozen in time on an incandescent triptych dissolving inside its own heat.

Epilogue

ROY'S FIERY DEATH was described as a tragedy in newspapers all over the United States. The word was repeated so often that people probably believed it. One of the police officers added to Roy's mystique by stating he could have escaped from the cockpit but had remained in the seat and, in the officer's words, "melted like a candle."

I believe Roy did not consider his life or his death a tragedy. I like to think he had more humility than that. If he had any last thoughts, I suspected they were about his father, a man I considered one of the most worthless human beings on the planet. Roy wanted to be a hero, in the best possible sense. It's not a bad ambition. Regardless, I decided to turn loose of him and not look back on our relationship and not think of it in terms of good or bad. I concluded that he made a conscious choice to rejoin his squadron commander over the South Pacific and undo his mistake in judgment. I prayed that in some fashion, Roy finally found peace, if that was what he ever sought.

I may have been finished with Roy, but Roy was not finished with me. As I had learned from Bonnie and Clyde, the dead lay strong claim on the quick and do not easily take leave of the earth. After the authorities were made to look ridiculous by the press, we returned to Houston and found a package on the dining room table. There was no return address. The postmark was Clayton, New Mexico.

Sorry I couldn't give you this in person. These items came from a storage cabinet at one of my father's warehouses in East Texas. I don't know if he's aware of their existence. I doubt he is. I also doubt he cares. I thought you might like them.

You'll always be an example to me. Give them heck, Weldon.

Your bud,

The Wayfaring Stranger

Inside the box were a wedding ring, my father's wallet, a pencil stub, my dollar watch with the broken spring, a coin purse with two nickels and a dime and one penny in it, and an unstamped postcard addressed to Mrs. Emma Jean Holland. My father was a laconic man and never given to an excess of words or sentiment. The message was not only simple but unsigned. It read: *I've done right well and have saved some money. I'm getting my drag-up check this Friday and I should be home by Sunday. Buy some peach ice cream. We're going to be a family again. And tell that boy of mine I love him.*

Linda Gail and Hershel divorced, and six months later, she married Jerry Fallon. One year later, she divorced Fallon and was nominated for best supporting actress. She remarried two or three times after that. One of her husbands was an aviator; another had been an officer with the French Foreign Legion at Dien Bien Phu; another was a country-club tennis champion and collector of race cars, one of which flipped on a test track and broke his neck.

There were lovers, too, evidently many of them. None of them ever spoke negatively of her to the media or anyone else. If they paid dues for their dalliance, none of them seemed to mind. To my knowledge, she never returned to Texas or Louisiana. She kept her looks and had a stunning career and called Hershel Pine from Mexico City the night before she died in 1968 of an overdose of barbiturates.

Hershel never discussed the content of their conversation other than to say, "She was a good woman."

At the Ardennes, Hershel had told me he sweated uncontrollably, even in freezing weather, when a calamity was about to occur, such as the German breakout at the Bulge. I didn't believe him about the Germans, not until the King Tigers were crashing down on top of us. He also told me he could smell money, particularly untapped oil and natural gas, but he'd struck out when we brought in those two dusters outside New Roads, Louisiana. Even though we held on to the mineral leases, I had given up on them. Hershel never did. We held on to them for over two decades, then went back to Pointe Coupee Parish with new technology and drilled down twenty-one thousand feet. The land was owned by poor black sweet-potato farmers for whom seven to ten acres was a plantation. The reserve we punched into was one of the biggest postwar strikes in the country. Even after years of production, the dome contains an estimated seven billion barrels of oil. The first royalty checks paid to the sweet-potato farmers, checks that would come on a quarterly basis, were in excess of two hundred thousand dollars.

These events all took place in another era. In spite of the war, the country was still innocent about its potential, in the way that a child who does not know his strength can be both innocent and destructive. The dance palladia and the roller rinks like the one where Grandfather fell down were filled with young people for whom the season was eternal. From the Jersey Shore to Pacific Palisades Park, you could hear orchestra music that was always collective in nature, a celebration of ourselves and the victory over nationalistic forces that would have made the world a slave camp. A western sunset that was the color of a flamingo's wings did not signify an ending but a beginning, an invitation to share in the glorious promise that awaited the young and the glad of heart. Highway 66, the Painted Desert, and Hollywood belonged to all of us. If we doubted that paradisiacal vision of ourselves, the radio reassured us nightly that we were part of an extended community where everyone lived next door to movie stars.

I heard Roy's body was burned into a carbon shell and the remnants put into an urn and scattered on the water off Catalina Island by Jerry Fallon. Linda Gail's coffin was misplaced and lost forever in a huge necropolis in the center of Mexico City. On a visit to Santa Monica, Rosita and I bought a dozen red roses, Linda Gail's favorite flower, and walked out on the pier at sunset and threw them into a wave. I always hoped Roy knew who they were from.

ACKNOWLEDGMENTS

I would like to thank my editor, Sarah Knight, and my copy editor, E. Beth Thomas, for their invaluable help on this manuscript. I would also like to thank my publishers, Carolyn Reidy and Jonathan Karp, and my editors at Pocket Books, Louise Burke and Abby Zidle, and all the other fine people in the Simon & Schuster family for the great contribution they have made to my writing career.

ABOUT THE AUTHOR

Born in Houston, Texas, in 1936, James Lee Burke grew up on the Texas-Louisiana Gulf Coast. He attended Southwestern Louisiana Institute and later received a BA and an MA in English from the University of Missouri in 1958 and 1960, respectively. Over the years, he worked as a landman for the Sinclair Oil Company, pipeliner, land surveyor, newspaper reporter, college English professor, social worker on skid row in Los Angeles, clerk for the Louisiana Employment Service, and instructor in the U.S. Job Corps. He and his wife, Pearl, met in graduate school and have been married fifty-four years; they have four children.

Burke is the author of thirty-four novels, including twenty in the Dave Robicheaux series, and two collections of short stories. His work has twice been awarded an Edgar for Best Crime Novel of the Year; in 2009 the Mystery Writers of America named him a Grand Master. He has also been a recipient of Bread Loaf and Guggenheim fellowships and an NEA grant. Three of his novels (*Heaven's Prisoners, Two for Texas,* and *In the Electric Mist with Confederate Dead*) have been made into motion pictures. His short stories have been published in *The Atlantic Monthly, New Stories from the South, Best American Short Stories, Antioch Review, Southern Review,* and *The Kenyon Review.* His novel *The Lost Get-Back Boogie* was rejected 111 times over a period of nine years and, upon its publication by Louisiana State University Press in 1986, was nominated for a Pulitzer Prize.

He and Pearl live in Missoula, Montana.